JEALO

A STRANGE ANG

Lili St. Crow was born in New Mexico and fell in love with writing when she was ten years old. She now lives in Vancouver, Washington, with her husband, three children, and a house full of cats.

Praise for *Strange Angels* and *Betrayals*

'This cracking read is for youngsters and adults alike' *Sun*

'Dru Anderson is the toughest teen gal since Buffy hung up her stake!' *Mizz*

'An elegantly written thriller' *Bliss*

'It actually is a supernatural thriller. A very good one . . . If you prefer supernatural thrillers with a side of romance, as opposed to romance with a side of supernatural thriller, *Strange Angels* is the perfect book for you' Bookbag

'She has managed to craft an excellent story. Her teen characters are well written and believable and she weaves suspense and horror together well' Teen Librarian

'A heart-stopping first book in a thrilling series' Betty Bookmark

'A stellar new series that will spellbind readers and leave them begging for more' Compulsive Reader blog

'*Strange Angels* is *Buffy* and *Supernatural* thrown together . . . St. Crow's writing is sharp and contemporary, with enough sarcasm to make even the snarkiest teen appreciate Dru's voice' Wondrous Reads blog

800 216 95

To Gates. Still holding the line.

First published in 2010 by the Penguin Group
Penguin Young Readers Group
345 Hudson Street, New York, New York 10014, USA

First published in Great Britain in 2010 by

Quercus
21 Bloomsbury Square
London
WC1A 2NS

Copyright © Lili St. Crow, 2010

The moral right of Lili St. Crow to be identified as the author of
this work has been asserted in accordance with the Copyright,
Design and Patents Act, 1988.

All rights reserved. No part of this publication may be reproduced
or transmitted in any form or by any means, electronic or mechanical,
including photocopy, recording, or any information storage and
retrieval system, without permission in writing from the publisher.

A CIP catalogue reference for this book is available
from the British Library

ISBN 978 1 84916 129 9

This book is a work of fiction. Names, characters, businesses,
organizations, places and events are either the product of the
author's imagination or are used fictitiously. Any resemblance
to actual persons, living or dead, events or locales is
entirely coincidental.

10 9 8 7 6 5 4 3 2 1

Printed and bound in Great Britain by Clays Ltd, St Ives plc.

JEALOUSY

A **STRANGE ANGELS** NOVEL

LILI ST. CROW

Quercus

Acknowledgments

Thanks to the usual suspects: Mel Stirling, Christa Hickey, Maddy and Nicky, Miriam Kriss and Jessica Rothenberg. This is getting to be a habit . . .

I am lying in a narrow single bed in a room no bigger than a closet, in a tiny apartment. The pad of paper I've been drawing on this trip is a collection of hard edges against my chest; I hug it harder. Outside the window, Brooklyn rumbles like a big sleeping beast. It's the traffic in the distance, speaking in its own tongueless grumble. They've come back from cleaning out a rat spirit infestation, and they're bushed. Outside the cracked-open door I hear the clink of glasses, liquid being poured, and my father speaks again.

"You have to, August. I can't leave her anywhere else, and I've gotta—"

Augustine interrupts. "Jesus Christ, Dwight, you know how dangerous this is. And she's just a kid. Why leave her with me?"

I snuggle into the pillow. It's Augie's pillow. He had made the bed up fresh for me, in the only bedroom in this crackerbox place. He and Dad thought I was asleep. I took a deep breath. It smelled like a place only a man cleans, frowsty and tainted with a breath of cigarette smoke.

The slam of a shot glass on the kitchen table. Dad was drinking

Jim Beam, and if he was doing it in shots instead of sipping, it was going to be a long night. Augie stuck to vodka. "She's safer here than anywhere else. I've got to do this. For . . . for reasons."

"Elizabeth wouldn't—"

My ears perked up a little, drowsily. Dad never talked about Mom much. And apparently he wasn't going to tonight either.

"Don't." Glass clinked again—a bottle mouth against the shot glass. "Don't you tell me what she would and wouldn't do. She's dead, Dobroslaw. My little girl is all what's left. And she's gonna be here. I think that bastard's up Canada way, and when I come back—"

"What if you don't, Dwight? What if I'm left with all this to deal with?"

"Then," Dad said softly, "she'll be the least of your worries. And you've got friends who know what to do."

"Not any I can trust." August sounded morose. "You have no idea what you're up against. I suppose it would take tying you up and sitting on you to stop you."

"You'd have to kill me, Augie. Let's not push it, not with my little girl in there." Raw bald anger under the edges of the words. If I'd been out there, I would have made myself scarce. When Dad sounded like that, it was best to just leave him alone. He never got violent, but the cold scaly quality of his silence when he was this pissed was never comfortable. "Besides, this could be another wild-goose chase. The bastard's slippery."

"Don't we know it," August muttered. It wasn't a question. "A month. That's as long as I can hold off telling anyone, Anderson. And I'm not doing it for you. That girl deserves to be with her own kind."

Another silence, and I could almost see Dad's eyes turn pale. All the depth would drain out of the blue and he'd look like he'd been bleached. "I'm her own kind. I'm her kin. I know what's best for her."

I wanted to get up, rub my eyes, and walk out into the kitchen. To demand to be told what they were talking around. But I was only a kid. What kid can get up and march out and demand to be told something? Besides, I didn't know half of what I know now.

I still don't know enough.

When I woke up in the morning, August greeted me with almost-burnt scrambled eggs, and by the look on his face I knew Dad was already gone. The kid I was just shrugged, knew he'd be back, and decided that I was going to be doing the cooking from now on. The kid I was then knew everything would be okay.

The kid I am now knows better.

CHAPTER ONE

A **long despairing howl** split the night.

It could have been mistaken for a siren in the distance, I suppose, if you ignored the way it burrowed in past your ears and pulled on the meat inside your head with glass-splinter fingers. The cry was full of blood and hot meat and cold air. I sat bolt-upright, pushing the heavy velvet covers aside. My left wrist ached, but I shook it out and hopped out of bed.

I grabbed my sweater from the floor and yanked it over my head, glad I hadn't worn earrings in a dog's age. The floor was hardwood and *cold* against bare feet; I was across the room and almost ran into the door. Threw the locks with fumbling fingers. A blue-glass night-light gave just enough illumination to allow me to avoid stubbing my toes on unfamiliar furniture. I hadn't been here long enough to memorize anything.

I wasn't sure I would be, either. Not with the way everyone keeps trying to kill me.

Thin blue lines of warding sparked at the corner of my vision.

I'd warded the walls my first night here, and the hair-thin lines of crackling blue light ran together in complex knots, flashing just on the edge of visibility. I woke the rest of the way and cursed roundly at the door, the howl still ringing inside my skull.

Gran would be proud. I was warding without her rowan wand *or* a candle, and it was getting easier. Of course, the practice of doing it over and over again was probably responsible. I wasn't going to sleep *anywhere* without warding now. Hell, I probably wouldn't even sit down without warding a chair, if I could.

I wrenched the door open just as another bloodcurdling howl split the air and shook the hallway outside. Hinges groaned—the door was solid steel, four locks and a chain, two of the locks with no outside keyhole. There was a bar, too, but I hadn't dropped it in its brackets.

I'd kind of guessed I wasn't going to be sleeping through the night without a fuss.

Light seared my eyes. I ran straight into Graves, who was fisting at his eyes as he stood in my door. We almost went down in a tangle of arms and legs. But his fingers closed around my right biceps, and he kept me upright, pointed me the right way down the hall, and gave me a push that got me going. His hair stuck up wildly, dyed-black curls with dark brown roots.

He was supposed to be down in the werwulfen dorms. His eyes flashed green, startling against the even caramel of his skin. He really rocked the ethnic look nowadays. Or maybe I was just seeing what had been there all along under his Goth Boy front.

We ran down the hall in weird tandem. My mother's locket bounced against my breastbone. I hit the fire door at the end. It banged against the wall, and we spilled down the uncarpeted stairs.

That's the thing about the Schola Prima dorms, even the cushy wing where *svetocha* are supposed to sleep. Behind the scenes it's concrete industrial, just like every other school. Just because I had my own room didn't make it any less, well, school-like.

And just because there was a whole wing for *svetocha* didn't mean that there were any more. Just me. And one other, but I hadn't seen her since the other Schola—the reform school someone had stashed me at—went down in flames.

Down two flights, a hard right, my shoulder banged into a door frame, but I just kept going. This hall wasn't even carpeted, so everything echoed, and the doors on either side had barred observation slits.

There wasn't a guard at his door. The whole hall shook as he threw himself against the walls and howled again.

I grabbed the knob; it refused to turn. "*Shit!*" I yelled, and Graves shouldered me aside. He'd thought to grab the key ring from the nail down the hall. The key went in, he twisted, the door opened, and I piled into the room, nearly colliding with almost seven and a half feet of very upset werwulf.

Ash hunched down, long clawed paw-fingers splayed as they touched bare concrete. The howl cut off in midstream, like he was surprised. The white streak on his lean narrow head glowed in the reflected fluorescent glare of the hall.

I sucked in a deep breath. My hair hung in my face, a wild curling mass, and I felt the same leap of irrational fear I did every time I came in this room. Or maybe it was totally *rational* fear. Someone could sweep the door shut and lock it, and then I'd be in here with a werwulf who'd tried to kill me the first time he met me.

And of course, he could always totally lose his shit and go all, well, crazyass werwulf on me again. But after he'd saved my life a few times, I was beginning to think maybe he wouldn't.

"It's okay," I managed, though my lungs were on fire and my

throat threatened to close up. I could still taste the peppermint toothpaste they'd given me. "It's okay, Ash. It's okay."

The werwulf growled. His shoulders came up, corded with muscle, and the shifting textures of his pelt blurred. If I could capture that on paper, maybe with charcoal—but who was I kidding? Like I had time for recreational werwulf portraiture.

His claws made grooves in the concrete, the hard sharp edges screeching as they cut through stone-hard flooring. You could just imagine those claws cutting through flesh, like a hot knife through butter.

Gee, that's great, Dru. Why don't you meditate on that for awhile?

I put my hand down. It looked very small and very pale, and when my fingers touched the thick ruff at the back of his neck, they sank in. Heat poured off him, and the sound of bones crackling filled the room as he tried, again, to change back into human form.

My heart leapt up into my throat and made itself at home. "You can do it," I whispered. Just like I did every time. "Come on."

Shaking filled him in waves. Graves stood in the doorway, outlined in pale fluorescent glare. He tilted back, glanced down the hallway, stiffened like he saw trouble coming.

"You can do it." I tried not to sound like I was pleading. Ash leaned against me, almost knocking me off my feet, the way a dog will lean into its master's legs. He also whined, way back in his throat, and the crackling sound got louder.

Bile crawled up in my throat. My hand turned into a fist in his fur, as if that would help. The marks on my left wrist twinged, sending a bolt of pain up my arm. Two little scabbed-over marks, where the fangs had gone in.

Another great thought. Jesus, Dru. Cut it out.

"It's okay," I coaxed. "It's all right. Sooner or later it'll happen. You can change back."

I heard voices. Male, four or five of them. Boots hitting the ground, the clothwhisper of running. My fingers turned to wood, and Ash growled. The deep thrumming filled up the bare concrete cube, the shelf like bed with its thin mat he never slept on, the low wide toilet bowl, and the metal tray in the corner still sticky with blood—at least he'd been fed. The raw meat was all gone; he wasn't hoarding it like he would if he was sick.

Well, sicker than he was already. There were marks on the walls where he'd flung himself.

A werwulf can dent stone or concrete. If he's going fast enough, if he really wants to. The maybe-not-so-irrational fear returned. I pushed it away.

"Shhh." I tried not to sound just-woke-up and scared. Probably failed miserably. "It's okay. Everything's all right."

It was a lie. He probably knew it, too. His ruined mouth opened as he tilted his head up, inhaled as if he was going to howl again.

I flinched.

Graves half-turned, standing in the door. He drew himself up and dug in his pocket. Why he was wearing his familiar black coat even in the middle of the night was beyond me—he probably even slept in the thing. I was suddenly aware of my naked legs, and my boxers all twisted around. My feet were bare, and the chill from the floor bit them even though Ash pressed against me some more, the vital textures of shaggy pelt rasping against my skin, an unhealthy feverish heat dripping from him.

"She's fine!" Graves's yell cut through the sudden noise. "Calm down. Everything's kosher."

I hoped they'd listen to him. If they piled in here while Ash was still nervous, we'd have another Situation, and I was just too tired. We were at three nights in a row for Ash getting us out of bed, and I was starting to lose hope.

Starting? No, I was already there. It had seemed so simple while I was running for my life. Funny how getting to a safe place always complicates things.

Always assuming that the Schola Prima was a safe place. Safer than the little satellite school I'd been at. The one that had burned to the ground because of me.

If it was safe, Christophe would be here. Wouldn't he?

I flinched again at the thought, and the two healing marks on the inside of my wrist twinged heatlessly. Ash made another whining noise. I tried to dredge up something more, something comforting, something that would help him. I *knew* he understood me talking to him, I just . . . I couldn't find anything to say that seemed to help him.

Ash hunched, his ruined upper lip lifting. His jaw was still man-gled from the silver-grain-loaded bullet I'd shot at him right after he bit Graves. The current theory—Benjamin's theory—was that the silver was at once preventing him from changing and interfering with his master's call.

I didn't know what to think about that.

Here I was in a cell, clutching a werwulf's ruff like he was a naughty cocker spaniel instead of almost eight feet of lethal muscle and bone, not to mention razor teeth and bad attitude.

"Calm down." I didn't have to work to sound weary. "Please, Ash. Come on."

His head dropped. I didn't even know what time it was; my inter-nal clock was all messed up. He leaned against me even harder, his shoulder dropping to rub above my knees. I was jerked forward, my fingers still tangled in his ruff.

"Milady?" Benjamin's voice. "Dru, are you in there? Are you all right?"

Ash growled. The sound rattled my bones.

"Cut it out, you overgrown fur rug." I hauled back on him, achieving exactly nothing—he was way heavier than me—but he did stop making that noise. "That's better. Yes, I'm fine."

"You need to come out of there." Shadows in the door—one of them had to be Benjamin.

The rest were probably his crew. The *djamphir* who'd been stuck with the task of "guarding" me. Great.

Graves leaned back against the doorjamb. His eyes were incandescent. He lifted a cigarette to his lips, flicked the lighter, and inhaled.

Oh, goddammit. I sighed, tried not to roll my eyes.

"That stinks." Benjamin took the bait. "Do you *mind*?"

Graves shrugged. Twin curls of smoke slid free of his nostrils. His silver skull-and-crossbones earring glinted in the dimness. "Nope. I sure don't."

Ash bumped against me. My feet were numb. Now came trying to get him up on the bed and not listening to the whining little noises he made when I closed the door and locked it so he couldn't escape back to his master.

To Sergej. Even thinking the name sent a cold shiver through me. Some of the nightmares I was having lately—when I could sleep, that is—were of a slight teenage boy with coppery skin and honey-dark hair, smiling as something ageless and foul shone out of his black, black eyes.

I'd only seen Sergej once. But that was enough.

Graves exhaled more cigarette smoke. "Thanks for asking, though."

"Can you two have your pissing match some other time?" I kept hold of Ash. It wouldn't do much good if he decided to go seriously buggy, but if I kept my hand on him he kept calm.

I didn't know what to think about that. I was stuck with less speed and strength and stamina because I hadn't "bloomed" yet. I wasn't a serious match for an upset werwulf without a gun and some running room—and even then it was a pretty chancy proposition.

Especially against a werwulf who had killed three or four suckers at a time.

But he never went ballistic as long as I was holding onto him. I still wasn't sure if I was brave or really stupid, getting close enough to him to find out. And I'd escaped him before, hadn't I? Shot him and boogied. Right after I'd killed a burning dog the size of a small pony.

Where had that girl gone—the badass Dru? Right now I was feeling a little less than awesomely tough. And more than a little confused.

"What's he doing, Dru?" Benjamin's tone was taut. I could almost see him outside the door, leaning forward, the spike of an emo-boy haircut swooping over his chiseled face. Some of the *djamphir* are so pretty it almost hurts to look at them. And it was hard to look without feeling rumpled and messy in comparison.

Not that I ever need any help feeling rumpled or ugly. Jeez. At least the plague of zits had passed me by lately.

Go figure. As soon as things most people don't even know *exist* start trying to kill me, I get to stop worrying about pimples. Normally I'd say, okay, sure, as long as I don't go pizza-faced.

But this wasn't a joke. This was my life. And I was kind of wanting the zits back.

"He's leaning up against me and trying to change." It was out of my mouth before I thought about it. My free hand was up, touching my mother's silver locket. The sharp edges of its etching scraped under my fingertips.

"He can't change," someone else said. "He's Broken, right? That's what that *means*."

"Don't tell him that," Graves interjected sardonically. "I don't think he believes it."

"Keep being funny, *loup-garou*." Benjamin was unimpressed. "Dru, you're going to have to come out of there. It's not safe."

Well, it's funny, but this is the place I feel safest. In a cell with a Broken werwulf. I swallowed twice. Let go of the locket and ran my free hand back through my hair. Winced as I hit tangles. "He's not going to hurt me. He only throws himself at the walls when I'm not around."

"Milady. Please." And he had that tone in his voice again, the pleading. Dylan used to sound like that, back at the other Schola.

Nobody had seen Dylan since the fighting broke out. And now that I thought about it, I didn't think we'd ever see him again.

That's what happens when *nosferatu* attack. Final things, things you can't take back. There was a whole mess of things I couldn't take back, starting with the morning I woke up and didn't tell Dad I'd seen my grandmother's owl.

My heart hurt, a sharp piercing pain. If I could just ignore it and deal with what I had in front of me right now, maybe it would go away.

Yeah, good plan, Dru. Stick with it. Maybe it'll get you somewhere.

"I'm not moving." The stubbornness caught me by surprise, set my jaw and made both hands curl into fists. Fur rasped against my fingers, and if I was pulling his hair, Ash didn't make a sign that he noticed. "Dawn's coming. Once the sun's up he'll be better."

"You should—" Benjamin stopped dead. Maybe because Graves had drawn himself up, taking another drag off the cigarette. Maybe because Ash growled again, and I surprised myself by tapping him on the top of his narrow head with my free hand. But gently, as if I was mock-hitting a boy I liked or something.

"Stop that." I took a deep breath. The growl had stopped. *I just bonked a werwulf on the noggin. Jeez.* "You could bring me a blanket or something. This floor's cold."

A beat of silence, then footsteps. Someone padding off to get me a nice little blankie. It wasn't Benjamin because he spoke again. "Very well. But we're staying here, Dru. Just in case."

Like I don't know that. I leave my room for any reason, all of you show up. "You should go back to sleep. Or whatever you were doing."

"We're your Guard. This is what we're doing." Patiently, as if talking to an idiot. Benjamin was almost as good at that tone as Dylan had been.

My heart gave another funny little hurt squeeze. It's been doing that a lot lately, except when I'm busy running for my life. But the pain went away when I swallowed, blinked, and focused on the problem in front of me.

"Jailers, more like." Graves didn't bother to say it softly. He kept leaning through the door, and the cigarette smoke he exhaled smelled like anger. "Leave her alone."

Ash growled again. I dug my fingers in, and the rumbling petered out once more. The marks on my right wrist twinged again, but not painfully. "Stop it, Graves. Jeez. All of you, just *quit* it."

It was looking to be another long wait for dawn.

CHAPTER TWO

As soon as the sun came up, Ash lifted his head from my lap. He flowed away, curled up under the metal shelf, and promptly went to sleep instead of just lying there with his eyes open and nervousness running through him.

My legs were stiff and numb. Graves had smoked his way through half a pack, field-stripping each butt under his boot. The plaid blanket they'd handed in through the door hadn't helped me much. I was so cold my teeth threatened to chatter, but I crawled over and spent a minute or two tucking the Broken werwulf in. He'd rip the blanket to shreds when dusk hit, but it couldn't hurt.

At least, I was hoping it couldn't hurt.

The silvery streak up the side of his head had gotten longer, pale wiry hairs a different texture than the rest of his fur. The messed-up part of his jaw made me wince every time I looked at it. Wulfen are allergic to silver in a big way; the wound was raw but not seeping anymore. It was healing slowly, I guess—and when it did heal over, what would happen? There was still silver lodged in there.

I didn't know nearly enough. Story of my life, I guess. When I was with Dad it hadn't seemed to matter—he was the one who knew what we were dealing with and told me what to do. But since he'd shown up with a serious case of zombie it had been painfully apparent that I didn't know even a quarter of what I needed to, in order to deal with the Real World.

And I was beginning to wonder if he'd really known all I thought he did.

It was an uncomfortable thought. Almost, well, blasphemous. Even if I'm not a big believer in anything other than holy water. I've seen holy water work against roach spirits and some kinds of hexes.

The rest of the God trip I'm not so sure about. There's just too much nastiness happening to people who don't deserve it.

Graves field-stripped the last butt under his boot sole and ground the cherry against the concrete. The ash made a black mark. "Hand up?"

"Nah." I used the shelf-bed to push myself up. Ash made a sleepy sound, chuffing out a breath, and stilled. "Thanks, though." Four numb-drunk steps across the room, then I had to grab for the door-jamb because the muscles in my legs started to wake up, pin-and-needling. "Ouch."

Benjamin leaned forward, peering around the corner. A pair of dark eyes under spike-dagger auburn hair, the bridge of his nose just visible. "You're not dressed." His tone wavered between shock and disapproval, with a healthy dose of primness mixed in. "You've been in there like that the whole time?"

"I'm perfectly dressed." But my jaw kept wanting to clench, muscles locking down with the chill. I shivered, hugged myself. Graves's sweater rucked up against my ribs. "All my bits are covered."

"You'll catch your death of cold," he muttered, and glanced at Graves. "Come, let's get you back to your room. You'll want to change."

"What for?" Even shifting my weight was agonizing. A heavy wer-wulf on your lap makes for some damn painful walking afterward. "It's daytime, right?" Meaning, *We should all get some sleep.*

"A message arrived just after you went to bed. You're due in front of the Council in an hour." Benjamin said it like it pained him. "Alone. To answer questions about Reynard and your escapes from Sergej."

"What?" But I wasn't really surprised. They'd debriefed everyone except me already, including Graves, who refused to talk about the whole thing even with me. Right now he was watching Benjamin closely, long-fingered hands dangling. It occurred to me that Graves had been trying to sleep right outside my door.

The *djamphir* had the rooms all around mine. Just in case. But Graves was *loup-garou*. Not werwulf, not vampire. Something different. And he obviously wasn't going to stay in the dorms like they wanted him to.

I tried catching his eye, but he was still staring at Benjamin like there was something stuck on the *djamphir*'s face. Being surrounded by teenage-looking boys that could be older than your parents gets really weird after a while. You start noticing little things, like how someone moves or goes still, and it shouts their age more effectively than the clues everyone normal wears on their skin.

Benjamin didn't really feel that old. Older, sure, but not as old as Dylan.

God, was I going to have another day of painful thoughts jumping me every time I relaxed? The obvious solution—to just not relax—was kind of sucking.

"The Council," he said patiently. "They run the Prima and every other Schola and, by extension, the Order. They're very interested in you." Behind him, I heard the slight unsound of the rest of them. Three more boys: two blonds, and a mouse-haired thin kid with a weird crooked smile. "We'll wait outside. But you'd better get dressed. They're formal."

I wished Graves would look at me. But he just stood there, glaring out from under his hair. I'm sure he could have painted *fuck off* on his forehead and it would have been more subtle. "Okay. All I've got is jeans." *Like, one pair of jeans. And this sweater and the hoodie, taking turns.*

Benjamin swallowed whatever he was going to say. My legs quit running with iron-tipped needles and steadied. I stepped cautiously out into the hall, between the *loup-garou* and the *djamphir*, and wished I could stay back in the cell.

At least with Ash I knew what was going on. Sort of. Maybe.

Silence stretched between us. They had to move so I could close the door, but nobody seemed much inclined to. The mousy kid with the crooked smile—*Leon*, I remembered with an effort—glanced back over his shoulder, a quick lizardlike flick of his head.

"I guess we'd better close this up, then," I finally said. "You guys'll have to move."

Benjamin stepped forward and I retreated, almost running into Graves. The door was shut and locked in a trice, and Benjamin handed me the key. "You should probably keep this. Since you're down here every night anyway."

He said it like he was disappointed.

I felt my chin rising stubbornly, what Gran called *that's a look like a mule*. "He's better." At least Ash wasn't throwing himself against the walls. As much.

"He's Broken." But Benjamin stepped back, forestalling the same old argument. "To your room, then."

It sounded like an order, but I didn't argue. I didn't have much argue in me.

It was a miracle. But like all miracles, it had a nasty side.

CHAPTER THREE

This is the Schola Prima, the biggest and oldest one in North America: shafts of sunlight falling between velvet curtains to gently brush mellow hardwood floors; priceless antique carpets; more velvet draperies in red, blue, hunter green; marble pedestals holding busts of good-looking teenagers—fighters and diplomats you won't find in any history book because they're *djamphir*. Which meant they fought and made diplomatic agreements with things the rest of the world didn't think existed.

Beeswax, lemon polish, smell of old wood and dry stone. And the exhalation of a school—something halfway between janitorial cleansers and the oily aroma of lots of kids breathing the same air for a long time. There was an uneasy coexistence between the two—the age, and the youth. Any war was over long ago, and the only thing left was a truce where the parties only glared at each other out of habit.

Benjamin paced in front of me, Leon slightly behind and to my left. Graves, his face damp from a splashing of cold water, kept close by my right. It was like being the center of an amoeba. The other two were behind me, and if there's anything guaranteed to unsettle a girl, it's teenage *djamphir* drifting in her wake and staring at her back. Not that I ever caught them staring, but after being the new girl in a million schools across America, you get the sense of being looked at.

I'd call it having eyes in the back of your head. But I've seen that, and it's disgusting. There was this one place in the Oklahoma panhandle—called Wail, if you can believe it—where the guy who ran the general store had an eye in the back of his shaved and tattooed skull. His front eyes were brown, and the behind eye was blue. It wept a thin red trickle on cold days.

He kept his cowboy hat on a lot.

People came from miles around to visit. They brought things to pay for what he could do, like providing hexes or potions. The thing he liked most as payment was the part of the body he had an extra of.

He fried them. Said they were crunchy and salty, good with mustard.

I shivered. I'd drawn eyes for weeks afterward, doodling them on margins and shading in the irises until Dad got that look that said I probably shouldn't.

"You okay?" Graves muttered without his lips moving.

"Just thinking. About eyes."

His shoulders hunched a little under the usual black coat. He wore that thing *everywhere*. It was kind of comforting. "I know what you mean."

The familiar weight settled on me. *I don't think you do.* Opened my mouth to tell him, shut it. He'd already been introduced to more than his fair share of the Real World. When Ash's teeth had punctured his skin, they'd stolen his old life. Never mind that it was a life Graves hadn't wanted. It was still my fault.

"I mean," he continued a little louder, "could it be any *more* obvious that they're watching you? And we can't trust any of them."

Benjamin inhaled sharply.

"The way I figure, about the only ones we can trust are wulfen." Graves stuffed his hands in his pockets, striding alongside me with long grasshopper legs. "Until we know who the traitor is."

Christophe knows. I pressed my lips together over the secret. I used to spend so much time alone while Dad was gone, and I'd wished to have other people around so hard. I'd hardly been alone since I *got* here. The chaos at the front door of the Schola had turned into a face-off between the wulfen boys with me and the *djamphir* boys trying to figure out what to do with me, until finally someone had sent someone somewhere with a message. Orders came back while I stood on the front steps in the weak sunshine, feeling cold, dirty, and very, very exposed.

Two minutes later Benjamin and his crew had shown up to take me to the room and hadn't left me since. I could shut the door and be by myself, kind of, if I didn't have the weird sense that the air itself was listening to me.

"Yap, yap, little dog," someone said behind me, but so low I couldn't tell who it was. And it wasn't like many of them spoke up all that often.

Graves spun, an oddly graceful movement. I grabbed his arm. A pedestal next to him wobbled a little bit, dust puffing off the globe of luminescent stone perched atop it. "Stop it. All of you. Jesus *Christ.*"

They all froze. Even Graves, who gave me a sidelong little look, green eyes glinting.

I decided to try to be tactful for once. "You guys can go on. I'm sure Graves can show me." And if he couldn't, I bet I'd find it anyway. Someone would give me directions, or come to fetch me.

Benjamin inhaled again, like I'd just slapped him. "Milady. We can't."

That word again. *Milady*. What they called Anna. I wasn't sure what to think about that.

"Sure you can." I pulled on Graves's arm, just a little. He visibly subsided. It was amazing. A crazy wulfen and a *loup-garou*, and I hauled them around like they were baggage. They were stronger and faster—at least until I "bloomed"—but they were boys.

I wasn't sure if the word *boys* should mean *dim* or *incomprehensible*. I was hovering between the two, with a healthy dose of *testosterone-poisoned*.

"We *can't*." Benjamin just said it, flatly. Like that was that.

I bristled. "You just toddle off to your rooms, and Graves will take me down to the Council or whatever."

"We're your *Guard*." Benjamin was really getting on the *you are so stupid* tone bandwagon here. I suppose it was only fair since I was snotty myself, but *jeez*.

"So you said a million times, but all you've done so far is—"

"We absolutely cannot do that." Leon was the only one who spoke up. He had an amazingly deep voice for such a mousy, fade-into-the-woodwork kind of kid. Benjamin felt old, but so did he. "If the *nosferat*—or anything else—attack and get near you, we're to fight them off. Or die in the attempt. We're the last line of defense."

"Bodyguards," one of the blonds supplied in a clear tenor. "But why they chose *us*—"

"She doesn't know enough to do the choosing yet, and they haven't held Trials," Benjamin said decisively. "Which leaves it up to us. Enough dawdling. Milady, the Council awaits."

"Call me Dru." I squeezed Graves's arm, hoping he'd get the message. "But I'm not sure I need bodyguards."

As soon as I said it, I knew it was a lie. Maybe it was tact that made Benjamin sigh. He didn't roll his eyes or look pained, which was pretty damn magnanimous of him.

Of course I needed a bodyguard. Now that the suckers knew I was alive, now that we knew there was a traitor in the Order, I needed bodyguards more than ever.

I just wasn't so sure I could trust anyone. Other than Graves, that is.

And Christophe, a little voice inside me whispered. I ignored it.

"Fine." I eased up on Graves's arm, figuring he wasn't going to go postal and coldcock someone. He actually straightened, pulled on his sleeves like stopping had been his idea so he could adjust his coat, and gave me another one of those telling little glances. "Then I suppose we'd better get going. We're probably already late."

"Not late enough," Leon muttered, and gave a queer little laugh. "But they'll wait for a *svetocha*."

I decided I didn't like him much and pulled experimentally on Graves's arm. He took a single step back, and as soon as I let go of him he whirled back to the front as if he was in a military parade. His chin was up, and a muscle in his cheek flickered.

Benjamin led us through more sunlight-striped halls, and it wasn't just the lack of breakfast that was giving me a bad feeling.

* * *

"Through there." Benjamin pointed at the huge double doors. They were massive oak affairs bound with iron, the wood deeply carved with slim lines. It took a moment for me to figure out the carvings formed a heavily stylized face with deep burning eyes. And a mouth open just far enough to show fangs. The tiny space between the doors ran down the bridge of the long hooked nose, and my temples throbbed for a moment. My mother's locket was a warm reassuring weight against my breastbone.

That face looked hungry, and I was suddenly very sure I didn't want to go in there.

But what do you do when there's a bunch of boys looking expectantly at you? You *can't* punk out. Graves had a faint line between his eyebrows, and I wished I had time to talk to him. Alone.

"What are they like?" I tried not to sound like a scaredy-cat and tucked some of my hair nervously behind one ear.

"Assholes," Graves replied promptly. "They interrogated Bobby and Dibs together. Almost made Dibs cry. But they're just assholes."

Benjamin coughed. He'd flushed a little. "They're the *Council*. The heads of the Order, each one a warrior against the darkness. They won't hurt you, Milady. You're the most hopeful thing we've seen in twenty years."

Now *there* was an interesting statement. I opened my mouth, but he stepped back.

"We'll wait here for you." He gave Graves a narrow-eyed, meaningful look. "Him too, if he wants."

"I'm not going anywhere." Graves folded his arms and leaned against the wall between two empty marble pedestals. The velvet hangings framing him just made him look scruffier and more unshaven. He was starting to get a definite bloom of dark stubble on his cheeks now. I didn't think half-Asians ever *got* stubble. It made his cheeks less babyish, and the new faintly mocking expression helped.

Back in the Dakotas, he'd looked eager, or pained. With that edge of desperation that loners have — the black sheep, the ones cut out of the crowd. I think even normal people can smell that powdery bloom of not belonging. It's all over the kids who get tripped, beat up, practical-joked, and just plain savaged all the time.

Now he just looked unpleasantly amused and unsurprised. A big change.

I swallowed hard. Approached the doors, one soft sneaker-clad step at a time.

"Dru." Graves clicked his lighter, and I heard the inhale of another cigarette starting up. Boy was gonna get lung cancer in no time. Did *loup-garou* get cancer?

If I went to classes here, would I be able to ask?

"What?" I stopped, but I didn't turn around, watching the door. I'd heard a little about the Council. Not enough to know anything except Anna was one of them. Would she be in there? Graves hadn't said anything about seeing another *svetocha*. She was supposed to be a secret.

Anna. A shiver touched my back. She'd tried to make me believe Christophe killed my mother. I still couldn't figure out why, unless she just plain hated him.

Christophe had made it sound like it was the Order against the suckers. It looked like it was the Order against itself, too. You'd think people would band together, but if there's one thing I've seen all over America, it's people shooting themselves in the foot like this over and over again.

Graves exhaled, hard. "I'll be right here. You yell; I'll be in there."

"Thanks." I bet he would, too. I tried not to let my face show how much I appreciated the thought. "Don't worry." I managed to sound like I wasn't feeling a little light headed. "Everything's gonna be okay."

I wondered how many times Dad used that phrase when he didn't believe it, either. The thought was a pinch in a numb place under my heart, and when I stepped forward next, the line down the nose of the door-face widened. They swung inward soundlessly, and I saw a short red-carpeted hall with another, smaller door at the end.

I stuck my hands in my jean pockets, touched the switchblade in my right. I'd slid it in while getting dressed in the bathroom and checked to make sure the bulge wouldn't tell under the hem of the long gray hoodie.

You never know. And after everything that had happened, I was damned if I was going *anywhere* unarmed.

CHAPTER FOUR

wasn't sure what I expected. But four teenage-looking guys and two guys apparently in their mid twenties lounging on couches—one of them smoking a cigar thicker than two of his fingers—was so not it.

The room was windowless, and a fire burned in the massive stone fireplace, crackling cheerily. Dark leather, shabby dark-red carpeting that looked Persian, crystal vases on the mantel holding white tulips. One of the *djamphir* looked twenty-five and Middle Eastern. He lowered the newspaper he was hiding behind and gave me a once-over with coal-black eyes. He wore jeans and a crisp blue dress shirt with creases that looked starched in.

I remembered Dad being big on spray starch until I refused to touch the stuff anymore and he had to iron his own jeans. He decided pretty quick that it was more trouble than it was worth. For a moment I was twelve again, ironing and smelling spray starch and fabric softener while Dad played Twenty Real-World Questions with me and loaded up clips of ammo. *How do you disrupt roach spirits?*

What're the five signs of a Real World gathering-place? What are the rules in a good occult shop?

I shoved the memory away with an almost physical shiver. You'd think that if I practiced long enough I could just stop thinking about painful things.

The second door—mahogany, uncarved, and giving the impression of being plenty heavy despite soundless hinges—closed with a whisper behind me.

"Dear God." A redheaded *djamphir* with a flock of freckles that somehow avoided looking baked-on bolted to his feet. "Milady."

There was a rustle, and all of them were standing. I swallowed hard and wished I wasn't in jeans and a gray hoodie that had definitely seen better days. My hair was actually behaving for once, falling in sleek curls. But this was just the sort of situation it would pick to start frizzing out on me. I also felt grainy-eyed and puffy-faced.

"Milady," two others echoed. I almost looked behind me to see who the hell they were talking to.

Another hard swallow. It felt like I had a rock in my throat. "I'm here for debriefing." *Great, Dru. You sound like Minnie Mouse.* "If I'm, uh, late, it's because—"

The one smoking a cigar swept me a bow I'd only seen before in midnight cable historical movies with really good costume budgets. "It is our pleasure to wait on you, not the other way around. Come in. Would you care for coffee? Have you had breakfast?"

Or more like dinner, since the Schola runs at night. What the hell? I blinked. "Um. This is the Council, right? Formal, right?"

"Dear child." This from the Arabic-looking one; he sounded vaguely British. "In here we don't stand on ceremony much. And what *have* you been told of us?"

"I thought . . ." The instinct of secrecy warred with curiosity, and curiosity won out just barely. "I thought the other *svetocha*—Anna— was on the Council?"

Silence filled the room. Even the fire hushed itself. The red-head glanced significantly at a skinny blond in a charcoal-gray suit that looked like it would never even *think* of wrinkling. The one who looked Japanese, not just half-Asian like Graves, smoothed the front of his high-collared shirt gray silk.

"Now, child." The Arabic-looking one raised his eyebrows, and I had a sudden urge to punch him in the face if he called me *child* again. "Where did you hear of that?"

I had to work to unclench my fists and push my shoulders down. Dad said you didn't hunch while you were at attention; that was what attention *meant*. "I saw her. At the other Schola, the reform school. And Dylan . . ." It hit me again, gulleywide sideways. "Dylan's probably dead." I said it like I'd just figured it out. "They attacked the Schola. They had a Burner. That's what everyone called it. A sucker who could set things on fire."

They were still silent, all staring at me. I kept my hands in my pockets, the switchblade's hilt slippery from my sweating fingers. The empty place in the middle of my chest was where a ball of unsteady painful rage had been burning for weeks, ever since Dad hadn't come home that night.

The last night anything was normal for me. Which has never been really what you'd call "normal." But it was good enough for me, and right now I was missing it big-time.

Now that hole in my chest was suddenly just that—a hole. Nothing in it but numb darkness. Which was a relief. "She had red hair," I offered awkwardly. "The sucker, I mean. The Burner. We only *just* got away."

A ripple ran through them. It was the *aspect*, the vampire in them coming out. Fangs peeped out from under top lips, their hair ran with highlights or darkened, and I was suddenly uncomfortably reminded of how strong, fast, and dangerous these guys were.

And here I was with only a silver-loaded switchblade. But I'd come this far; I wasn't about to let a bunch of half-vampires scare me.

Well, not much anyway.

Not so you could see it.

"Let me see if I understand you correctly," the Arab said. His eyes now burned like live coals, and his hair rippled with a slight wave, inky black streaks slipping through the very dark brown. "You have seen the Lady Anna? At a . . . satellite Schola? Where you were until a very few days ago?"

I nodded. "Christophe meant for me to come here. I don't know how I ended up *there*, but they seemed to have been expecting me. But then Dylan found out nobody knew I was there—he said something about a blackout node—and the . . . the . . ." I ran out of words. Regained them. "Haven't you heard all this before?"

"Not precisely. The wulfen knew very little, and the Broken could not be questioned." Arabian Boy glanced at the others. "And Reynard is, as is his custom, nowhere to be found when questions are asked. So. Come and be seated. Would you care for breakfast?"

My stomach growled at the notion. "No thanks. I'll catch something in the caf later." I figured that was polite enough.

"Are you certain?" The *aspect* retreated, turning him into a very handsome guy in his early twenties, but with very old eyes. I was suddenly very sure this guy was even older than Christophe. It shows somewhere back in the pupils, and all of them had that uncanny stillness I'd only seen in older *djamphir*.

And in Christophe. Jesus. I was trying not to think about him because each time I did it either sent a flood of heat or a bucket of ice through me. My internal thermostat was wiggy in a big way. And the marks on my wrist were scabbed over and healing, but they had some funny ideas of their own.

At least when I thought about Christophe, the hole in my chest seemed manageable. Not smaller, but easier to deal with. Like being with Graves made all this seem like something I could possibly handle, as long as he was standing there giving me that *whatcha gonna do, Dru?* look.

I caught the way they were all looking at me, and a childhood spent with Gran's strict rules about "bein' neighborlike" rose up inside me. *When you dirt poor, manners is what you got,* she would always say. *So use 'em.* "If you're all eating, I wouldn't mind a bite." I almost cringed as soon as I said it. I mean, in a room with a bunch of half-vampires and I say *bite*?

But then again, I was part vampire, too, wasn't I? A sixteenth, Christophe said. We were all sixteenths. Something about genetics.

God, Dad, why didn't you tell me? But I could never ask him that even if he was still alive. A splinter of ice lodged itself in my throat. He'd never even said a single word about it. Nothing except warning me about suckers, and I picked up most of that listening around the corners, listening to other hunters. Like his friend Augustine, who'd turned out to be *djamphir* too, and part of the Order.

And who was missing as well. I was thinking an awful lot about Augie lately.

"We would be honored." Arab Boy bowed again, a little less stiffly. "I'm Bruce. Provisional head of the Council."

Bruce? No way. The mad urge to giggle rose up in my throat, met the rock sitting there, and died with a burning, acid like reflux. "Provisional?" It slipped out.

"Provisional, you see, when our head, the Lady Anna, is not with us." He straightened, and the rest of them relaxed a little.

Well. That's good to know. Come to think of it, Anna certainly did have the Head-Bitch-in-Charge vibe.

I didn't let go of the switchblade.

"And especially since," the redhead piped up, "the Lady Anna has been on vacation for two weeks."

* * *

The other room opening off the windowless sort-of-study was a long one, with a mirror-polished table down the middle that would have looked right at home in Camelot, except it was a rectangle. Another table—no more than a shelf—ran along the left-hand side, full of steam dishes exhaling the smell of food. A silver urn and another massive silver thing sat at the end, and three wine bottles stood at attention, one in a silver container of crushed ice. The second massive silver thing on the table was a samovar, I was sure of it.

I wouldn't even know what a samovar was, except for once Dad and I had come across this coven of Russian witches in Louisiana. No, really. They ran a *patisserie* in New Orleans. With a sideline in hexes, cures, potions, and fortune-telling with weird greasy playing cards decorated in gold leaf.

They'd wanted me to stay with them. To learn, they said. But Dad just shook his head, and I held onto his arm the entire time we were in there. I didn't take the *petits fours* they kept offering me. Gran had taught me all about food being a trap sometimes.

It's woman's power, food is. You be sure you know where'n the hook is before swallerin' it, Dru. You mind me, now.

You'd think I'd get used to hearing dead people's voices in my head. Memory is like that sometimes—it takes you by surprise, leaps on you with a roach spirit's scuttling speed, and then you're left shaking your head and trying to figure out where you are here and now.

The chairs were all heavily carved wooden thrones with worn red horsehair cushions. Stone walls, hardwood floor, and a smell like a lot of late nights and cigar smoke fighting with the heavenly aromas of food and coffee. There were no dusty cobwebs in the corners, like at the other Schola. This whole building was spic-and-span in a way that made me a little nervous.

Check that. Everything about this place was hinky as hell. If this was where I was supposed to be sent when that helicopter lifted me out of the snowy hell of the Dakotas, I didn't know if I should feel relieved.

Bruce pointed me toward the head of the table, like I was a visiting dignitary. "Please. Coffee? And what do you prefer for breakfast? Or dinner, given our schedule."

They were all looking at me. New-girl-in-school time again, only I was here with the teachers. "Coffee, yeah. And, um, food. Look, I thought I was going to be—"

"All in good time." Bruce was utterly imperturbable. "We don't believe in hurrying."

"Yeah, I kind of got that. I was stuck for weeks out in the back end of beyond with vampires attacking all the time." I didn't have to work to sound sarcastic. "I'm not so sure I'm safe anywhere, unless it's on my own. So I'm wanting to get this over with." *And get back to Graves.*

Because the emptiness inside me did get smaller when Graves was around. Still, I didn't want to think about how safe I felt with Christophe. It wasn't applicable, was it? Not when he kept disappearing on me.

I was getting to hate people disappearing on me.

The fang marks in my left wrist twinged again, but faintly. I was glad my sleeves were pulled down. The memory rose unbidden, of Christophe's fangs in my flesh. He'd had to do it, to save us—but it hadn't been comfortable. And I was damned if I'd tell any of these blow-dried boys about it.

My voice box had frozen up. Everything about me had frozen. One thought managed to escape the relentless, digging agony.

—please don't please don't not again please don't don't don't—

* * *

But it came one more time, and this time was the worst because the digging, awful fingers weren't pulling at anything physical. Instead they were scraping and burrowing and twisting into me. The part of me that wasn't anything but me, the invisible core of what I was.

I'd call it the soul, but I don't think the word fits. It's as close as I can get.

Digging scraping pulling tearing ripping, invisible things inside me being pulled away, and something left me in a huge gush. My head tipped back, breath locked in my throat. Graves made another small horrified sound and tried to pull me away.

Christophe jerked his head back, fangs sliding free of my flesh, and something wrapped itself tightly around my wrist, below his bruising-hard grip on my forearm. He exhaled, shuddering, and Graves tried to pull me away again. My arm stretched like Silly Putty between them, my shoulder screaming, and I couldn't make a sound.

The silence that fell wasn't comfortable in the slightest. I yanked the chair at the head of the table out, dropped down into it, and glared at them all. The so-called cushion was hard as a rock and the back wasn't much better. And I had to let go of the switchblade in my pocket to sit down.

It was a bad morning and getting worse.

One of the silent *djamphir*, the one with coal-black skin and shockingly white teeth, laughed. His dreadlocks moved as he stalked toward the buffet table. Of all of them, he was the only one in worn-out jeans and a T-shirt. "She's certainly Elizabeth's daughter." He sounded very prep-school, enunciating crisply. But there were odd spaces between his words, just like in Christophe's or Dylan's. Like they were translating from another language inside their heads. It was like the ghost of an accent. I mean, other than the flat nasal Yankee everyone above the Mason-Dixon pretty much speaks.

I don't have an accent. Northerners just talk funny.

"As if there was any doubt." Bruce sounded sour for the first time. "Her face alone is enough to convince one of *that*."

My hands tightened into fists under the table. Dad had never told me I looked like Mom, beyond saying something about my hair once in a while. "Did you all know my mother?"

"I did," the Japanese one said softly. "Bruce did, and Alton too, I believe. Marcus?"

The skinny blond in the gray suit shook his head. "She was before my time in administration."

The other blond spread his hands; he'd left his cigar in the other room. He had thick curly hair, and for a moment I felt lightheaded. Someone had stolen a lock of Christophe's hair from my nightstand — don't even ask how it got there, *a keepsake*, he'd said — and left a single long, curling blond hair behind. It could have been any number of teachers or students at the other Schola. Including shy, gentle Dibs.

I was suspecting everyone now. Except Graves. And Christophe.

"So, some of you knew her. Then you know someone inside the Order betrayed her." My fingernails dug into my palms. "Anna showed me a transcript of the call."

They all went utterly still again. Bruce finally turned away from the buffet table and stared at me, his dark eyes wide. "She *what*?"

The Japanese guy inhaled sharply, like I'd just taken off my clothes or made an embarrassing bodily noise.

I took a deep breath. Jesus, these guys didn't know *anything*. Why had they waited for days before interrogating me? Although this was more like I was questioning them. My stomach rumbled again. "Showed me a transcript. Only Dylan said it wasn't the original but a redacted one. He gave me a copy of the original. Christophe's got it."

Silence. They all kept giving each other little sideways glances. Telling glances, only I had no idea what they were saying. You could cut the silence with a cheap cafeteria spork.

"Reynard." The blond in the gray suit finally spoke, and he said Christophe's name like a curse. "Always thinking he knows best."

"In this case, he very well may." Bruce's expression settled somewhere halfway between amused and worried. "Perhaps we should hear the entire tale. You are a mystery, Milady. Enlighten us."

I struggled with the urge to tell him to call me Dru. On the one hand, this *milady* thing was like being trapped with a bunch of D&D nerds. I mean, they're nice people, but sometimes you just want them to talk like human beings, you know?

On the other hand, these guys were probably old enough to be my father. Or older. It didn't feel right to get all buddy-buddy with them.

A rock made of heavy panic lodged in my throat; I had to work twice to swallow it and winced inwardly. I was beginning to get that *nothing* about this was going to get any easier.

"Okay." I took a deep breath. "You want the whole story? Fine. It started out with me shooting a zombie. But he wasn't just an ordinary zombie. He was my *dad*."

And to make everything even worse, my voice broke on the final word. How could I explain to a bunch of *djamphir* what it meant to shoot a zombie who had been your *father*, for Christ's sake?

"I think this would go easier with some breakfast. By the way, I'm Alton." The coal-skinned kid smiled kindly at me, those white teeth peeping out again. They all looked like a shampoo commercial, healthy and clear-skinned, perfectly proportioned, a group of handsome young men. Their clothes hung on them like they were glad to be gracing such supermodels. And here I was, jeans and a ratty old hoodie and my hair—I could almost feel it start frizzing. This was just the sort of situation where every loose thread and frizz will start poking out.

And every one of these guys could probably kill me without thinking twice about it, unless I had the jump on them and some firepower.

Brains were going to have to be my edge. But I was so, so tired.

"I'm Dru," I said mechanically. Gran would be proud of my manners at least. "Dru Anderson."

"Is that a nickname?" This from the Japanese kid. "I'm Hiro, by the way. It is a pleasure to meet you."

Charmed, I'm sure. "It's going to take me awhile to tell you everything." *And I don't know what I'm going to be leaving out yet.* My palms were damp. I scrubbed them against my jeans and wished the chair wasn't so hard. But if I got up now it would be weird.

Weirder. Maybe. I don't know.

Hiro gave me a look that could only be described as kind. He deliberately pulled out the chair to my left and folded himself down into it. "We are Kouroi. *Djamphir*. We have, my dear, nothing but time."

That brought up another question. "How . . . I mean, you guys are old. Older than a lot of *djamphir* I've seen. And Benjamin, he's older than Christophe. How long do you . . . we?" I decided I couldn't include myself with them. Or could I? Jesus, I had so many questions, it wasn't even funny. "How long do you live?"

Bruce just kind of appeared out of thin air next to me. I strangled the urge to flinch and smelled cologne and fabric softener on a warm draft. None of them smelled like Christophe, either—the spiced-apple aroma that followed him around didn't rub off on other *djamphir*. I wondered about *that*, too. How would I even begin to ask? *Hey, you guys don't smell like bakeries. What gives?*

"We are Kouroi," Bruce repeated and set a plate in front of me. Half a Belgian waffle, scrambled eggs, a small mountain of bacon, and a small glass dish that held melon balls and grapes as well as quartered strawberries like blood clots. "We live until the night hunts us down. Just like *nosferatu*, but without their . . . disabilities."

"Except the hunger." Alton played with the silver thing that wasn't a coffeepot. "Always excepting the hunger."

Hunger. Why don't they call it thirst? The weird place at the back of my palate quivered. The place that liked warm, red, copper-salty fluid. The spot that pushed a button in my head and turned me into a clear-glass girl full of red liquid rage.

And that was another thing, too. Christ, now that I knew what it was like to want to drink someone else's blood, I was having a hell of a time holding on to anything about myself. It was all a whirling mass of things changing before I could get a grip on them.

I stared at the food. Was there a hook hidden in it? I was too hungry to tell. I didn't have Dad's arm to hold onto.

"Try to eat." Bruce laid down a fork and table knife. Unless I missed my guess, they were heavy silver, polished to a sharp gleam I saw through a haze.

My eyes were burning. The food turned into colored gleams.

"Oh, no." The redhead sounded horrified. "Is she—"

"Kir, shut up." Bruce handed me a cloth napkin. "I'll get you some coffee, Milady. There is no hurry at all. You're safe now."

I didn't bother to tell him I didn't believe him. Instead I mopped at my stupid eyes, sniffed back the weight of crying in my nose, and picked up a piece of bacon. I should eat while I could. Even if there was a hook in it.

INTERMEZZO

*T*he hospital corridors *smelled like pain and Lysol. I hunched in the hard plastic seat, arms around my legs. I was still in the jeans I'd been in when I came home from school and found Gran still in bed, the fire almost out and the cold wind whistling in through the cracked-open door.*

She hung on as long as she could for me. I'd bundled her into the ancient Packard—the thing was probably older than Dad—and half-hoped it wouldn't start. But it did, rumbling into life, and Gran had muttered sleepily that she hated going into town, she surely did.

Driving down into the valley took a long time, and I was afraid she'd leave before I could get her to the hospital down the way. I drove half the night, and when I got there the emergency room people took one look at her and whisked her out of my hands. I had to search until I found the room they put her in. Then the questions started.

Who are you? What's her name? Who's next of kin? How old are you?

I just kept saying Dad was on his way and hoped like hell it was true.

But he was gone, like he always was, and not due back for awhile.

I put my head down on my knees for a moment, but there was no resting. It was too dangerous. I pinched the underside of my left arm again, hard. Bruises were already flowering where I'd pinched and pinched all night.

Across the hall was the visiting area. The chairs over there were padded, but this one was too uncomfortable to let me sleep. Besides, if that doctor came back with a cop or a social worker, I could escape at least three ways from here. If I moved across the hall, I'd be trapped.

My fingers made little patterns on the chair arm. They itched with the urge to draw. I wished I had pencil and paper. There was also a window, showing the naked tops of trees. Winter had begun. And on the ledge in front of the glass, Gran's owl crouched. Keeping watch, just like me.

It had been in the room all night, while the machines beeped and Gran's breathing flattened out. Perching on the windowsill, its feathers ruffled and its clear yellow gaze fixed on me. When the lines for her heartbeat finally went flat and the hospital crew crowded around her, frantically trying to tie down a soul that had already slid free of its old exhausted shell, the owl had disappeared between one glance and the next. I'd stepped back and to the side, sliding out the door and into the hall. The less notice the adults took of me the better.

I picked at a scab through the hole on the right knee of my jeans. It was a lulu. I'd fallen down a hillside while out looking for American ginseng. It was called devil's club, for some reason. Good stuff, and Gran always needed more. She'd scolded me when I came home with bloody knees.

The owl ruffled its feathers. I pulled back into myself, all the misery in the air pressing down on me. Gran had taught me how to make myself a fist inside my head, to shut out the confusing babble of other people's feelings. But the touch *hadn't warned me that she was about to leave me.*

Dawn was coming up. Gray light brushed the horizon. I didn't want to leave her here, alone in this bleached place that reeked of despair. But I couldn't hang out much longer—an adult would remember I was here and wouldn't be fobbed off by me saying my dad was on his way. I didn't exactly know what would happen then, but I knew it wouldn't be pleasant.

Oh, Dad. Please hurry. Please be coming here.

The elevator at the end of the hall dinged. My head jerked up, like an old dog's. The elevator had been going off all night, each time making that wheezing little bell sound, like it couldn't possibly open its door after mustering up all its energy to announce it was here.

"There she is," *someone said. I glanced down the hall in the opposite direction without turning my head, using my peripheral vision. It was a heavyset redheaded nurse, her hands on her hips. Behind her was that doctor, quick and ferret-like in his white coat, and a woman in a flowered dress that screamed "social worker."*

I slid off the chair slowly, as if I hadn't heard them. The elevator door was opening. I couldn't make it all the way down there unless I started running now. But I could jag down the stairs and escape that way.

I still had the Packard's keys. They jingled on their wire loop, and I walked, head up, purposefully, toward the elevator.

"Hey! You! Kid!" *It was the doctor. He didn't even remember my name—that was evident.* "Hey!"

The elevator's doors wheezed open. I ran through what I knew of the layout in my head. It was like Gran's game of What's On The Table, where I would have to remember and describe every object with my back turned, or after she'd laid a fresh cloth over everything. Good training, *she'd said.* Use that old meat twixt your ears, Dru. You mind me now.

My heart pounded in my ears. My head was heavy. I heard feathers brush the air as Gran's owl took off from the windowsill, and a moment of glassy, exquisite pain lanced through me. I didn't dare look back to see the owl.

Besides, the normal people here wouldn't see it. That was what "different" meant. It's just another word for lonely.

Get to the stairs. Once in the stairwell you can get to the ground floor and get out. There're fire exits, too. Then you can hole up at Gran's house and—

"Hey! Kid!"

A man stepped out of the elevator. My heart leapt into my throat, started pounding. I didn't realize I was running until my slapping footfalls threatened to jar my head off my shoulders. A short, despairing sound burst out of me as the doctor yelled again.

The man from the elevator opened his arms. Tall, pale blond crew cut, his jeans creased and rumpled, his T-shirt stained with motor oil. He was always so clean and neat, it was a shock to see him like this. I didn't care. There were dark deep bruised circles under his eyes, blue like mine. Like Mom's. His were sharp winter blue, cool and considering, with lavender lines in the irises.

I didn't wonder or care about that either. I ran right into his hug. I realized the motor oil was splashed on his shirt to cover up something else, something reddish, and I could feel a bandage around his ribs. It didn't matter. I hugged him so hard he made a slight whoof! sound, and I didn't let go.

"Dru-girl." One of his callused hands was on my hair, stroking the tangled flyaway curls. I hugged him even harder. "I came as soon as I could. I'm sorry, honey. I'm so sorry. Shhhh, honeychild, angel baby. Everything's all right."

I realized I was making a low hurt sound, and that my nose was full of snot. All during the night I hadn't been able to cry, but now something broke loose in me and I began gushing. I tried to keep it quiet, though. I sobbed into his dirty shirt.

The trio—nurse, doctor, social worker—arrived about ten seconds later and started throwing questions at him. He answered each one in his slow clear drawl, and I knew things were going to be okay. He had all the ID and the papers, though God knew how he'd gotten them. I didn't care. All I knew was that he was there, and that things were going to be all right.

And that I didn't want to let him out of my sight ever again. Not if I could help it.

Not unless he made me.

CHAPTER FIVE

By the time I was finished, I'd taken down enough coffee and orange juice to float a small battleship, and my throat was scraped raw from talking. I wanted a bathroom and a long, long nap.

Of all of them, the redheaded Kir reacted the most. His face went through incredulousness, puzzlement, comprehension, and finally anger. It stayed at "anger" for awhile, a thundercloud over his forehead and his *aspect* on, filling his hair with a wild golden curl and sliding his fangs out from under his upper lip.

I kept half an eye on him.

The blonds—Ezra and Marcus—did most of the questioning, with Bruce interjecting every now and again. Mostly they just let me talk and explain and digress and get nervous, and every once in awhile Hiro would reassure me. "It's all right," he'd say. "We know you're telling the truth."

Which kind of made me wonder. It's not the sort of thing you say to someone you believe. And so I instinctively stuck to my decision to leave out little things—like the flushes and cold spells that went through me when I thought of Christophe. And not so little things, like the fact that he'd bitten me. The marks pulsed erratically on my wrist when I got nervous. I kept my sleeves pulled down as if I was cold.

It was unlike any other visit to the principal's office I'd ever had. I mean, you'd think being called into a room with a bunch of older guys who ran a huge vampire-fighting organization would be like the principal's office, right? But instead it was . . . weird. It was like they just wanted to listen to me.

They looked at me funny, too. As if I was a mythological creature they couldn't quite place. I would glance up from my food, away from Kir or away from whoever had asked me a question, and see one of them frankly staring at me. Which made the food kind of turn to a wad of chewable cardboard in my mouth and made me wonder if I had something on my face. It would be just like me to have a bit of egg stuck on my chin while talking to a bunch of bigwigs.

"Then we got here," I finished lamely. "And after a little bit of confusion, Benjamin and his crew showed up and took me to the room. They say they're my bodyguards."

"Calstead and his protégés," Bruce said. "He's one of our finest youngbloods. Until you know enough to choose your own Guard, it's probably best. And the *loup-garou*, too—Graves?"

"Edgar Hideaki Graves." Hiro set his fork down with a precise little click. "A finer juvenile delinquent I'm sure we cannot find."

I half-choked on a mouthful of very cold orange juice. I almost gave myself a nasal with it, too. *Whoa, wait a sec.* "Edgar?" I all but squeaked.

"So his file says." Bruce nodded. "He was bitten by the Silver-head?"

"Yeah, Ash bit him." They hadn't said anything about Ash. They had to know he was bottled up in the room downstairs. But I wasn't going to bring it up and maybe have them decide he was better off locked up somewhere I couldn't get to him.

I felt . . . responsible.

"The *loup-garou* has a Record." You could just hear the capital letter in Hiro's tone. "Normally he would be at a . . . satellite Schola, even with the happy accident of half-imprinting."

"All the benefits, few of the drawbacks. And less hair." Marcus leaned back in his chair. I didn't see how he could lounge in something so hard and uncomfortable, but he managed it. "He's a fortunate one."

There it is again. Something crystallized inside my head.

There were no wulfen in this room. Here I was full of breakfast, and Graves was waiting outside, probably hungry. These were the heads of the Order, and there wasn't a single wulfen in here. It was always *djamphir* in control and snarky comments about the wulfen. Talking about how lucky Graves was because he didn't get all furry.

Gran raised me in Appalachia, and Dad and I stayed below the Mason-Dixon most of the time. I know the word for behavior like this, and I've seen it all over. It's never pretty. Maybe I'm lucky, since moving around so much showed me people are the same everywhere. Still, there's something ugly down South. When you aren't sure you're at the top of the food chain, it doesn't make sense to make everyone below you on that chain suffer—but people do it anyway, and they do it all the time. Because it makes them feel bigger, more secure.

I was just about to say something—I don't even know what, maybe something like, *He's a person too, you know*—when the mahogany doors swung open. A flash of crimson silk, a long fall of curly reddish hair, and high-heeled boots with buttons marching up their front all came to a halt. Just like a cat will see you looking at it and stop dead, one paw in the air.

Did I just imagine it? I was exhausted and running on nerves, but I swear to God I saw a flash of something nasty far back in the other *svetocha*'s eyes.

Sometimes you meet a girl and it's like matter and antimatter. You just hate each other for no damn reason. I already knew I didn't like her. Besides, she hated Christophe.

Why did I care so much about that?

Anna lifted her pointed chin, and her blue eyes widened just the tiniest bit. She was in a different red silk dress than the one I'd seen last time, something with a full skirt and a bodice that was just short of indecent. A cameo on a thin gold chain rested in the hollow of her slim white throat, and long delicate golden teardrop earrings trembled as she halted. And, God help me, she actually *chirped* at the roomful of boy *djamphir*. "Well! Late again, but I see you've started without me."

"You're safe." Bruce didn't sound surprised. "We worried needlessly."

A taffy-stretching silence ticked by. Kir's chair scraped against the floor as he stood slowly, and the rest of them followed suit. I stayed where I was.

I stayed because my knees had gone mooshy, and the muffled beat of feathered wings filled my ears like a heartbeat. Cold little prickling fingers skittered over my skin, and I was suddenly very sure something was Not Right. A draft of warm perfume dipped in spice marched down the table toward me.

Why did she smell like that? And Christophe, why did he smell like a warm apple pie?

The scalding flush that poured through me at the thought of Christophe being here met the icy consciousness of danger, and they both fought over me. I began to wish I hadn't drunk so much coffee. Why is it that the only thing you can think of when you're terrified is how much you need to pee?

Maybe that's just me, though.

"I was *en vacances*; you know how I lose track of time. Perfectly safe, with my boys watching over me. And it's Dru!" She sounded oh-so-happy to see me, a candy-coated voice and a wide dimpled smile. "When did you come in? I'm glad they didn't keep you at that second-rate Schola for very long."

They? Who was she talking about, *they?* The guys in this room, who didn't seem to have any clue about where I'd been or what I'd been doing?

The standing *djamphir* were completely motionless, but I could feel the tension running through them. Hiro's fingertips rested on the tabletop, half an inch away from his silver fork. I had a sudden Technicolor vision of him picking up the fork and launching himself at Anna. Blood spurting, screaming, the fork making a popping sound as it buried itself in one pretty blue eye.

I sucked in a small breath. Hiro's head moved the slightest fraction, and I was suddenly very sure he was keeping track of me in his peripheral vision.

Maybe it's me he wants to stick a fork in. My mouth started working again. When in doubt, say something flip. "I got in a couple days ago. It was fun."

"Fun?" She raised one exquisitely arched eyebrow, the open door yawning behind her. The fire in the study room popped once. She looked like a storybook illustration, and I wished I could sink back into the chair. My face felt greasy and I could still taste bacon.

It was official. I disliked her. She probably felt the same way. But she was older, right? She wouldn't act like a teenager, would she?

But I couldn't stop myself.

"Yeah, fun. A real blast." My right hand rested on my knee under the table. I stopped it from creeping up to touch the reassuring bulge of the switchblade with an effort of will that threatened to make me sweat. "I almost got burned alive. There was a car chase, too. If it wasn't for Christophe I'd've been dead."

"Christophe? *Reynard*?" Her candy-pink-glossed mouth turned down a little. To give her credit, she didn't look in the least surprised. "Really."

"Really." Flat and unapologetic, as if she'd just insulted me.

"I'll expect your debriefing, then." A sparkle in those narrowed baby blues. Like a cheerleader taunting a nerd.

Even if she was older, she was cut from the same cloth. There's only one reason someone like that is even civil to someone like me.

It's either because they're setting you up for something, or they *want* something.

A nasty supposition rose like bad gas in a mine shaft, up from the very bottom of my mind. I stared at her, wishing I could shut out all the tension and awkwardness in the room and just *think* for a bit.

But one thing was for damn sure—I wasn't going to tell the whole story again. Not to this lacquered, pretty cheerleader. "I've already given it." I made my hands come up and flatten on the table-top. It was hard, with the muffled wingbeats in my ears trying to drown everything out. I hoped Gran's owl wasn't about to make an appearance. That was the *last* thing I needed right now.

Of course, if nobody else could see the owl, I was worrying about nothing. They probably wouldn't think I was crazy. But I wasn't gonna take any chances.

Not anymore. I figured I'd better stop taking chances, starting *yesterday*.

I pushed myself up slowly. My eyes refused to move away from Anna's face. I stared at her liked she was a rattler I wanted to keep in view while I reached for the shovel to behead it. It made me think of Gran, actually. Which was a painful comfort. *Move nice an' slow, and don't you give that snake a reason to strike at you. Just slow an' easy, honey.*

"And very charmingly, too." Marcus glanced significantly at Hiro. "I think we may excuse Milady Anderson; she's very tired."

Bruce stiffened, Kir's eyebrows went up, and Ezra smirked. He smirked so loudly, in fact, that I could almost hear it through the noise in my head.

"Milady." How Hiro managed to make it clear he was talking to me without taking his eyes from Anna I don't know. "I shall escort you to your Guard."

Well, wasn't that nice of him. I got the feeling there were two different groups here. One of them was maybe on my side, but the other was definitely on *hers*. And if it came down to it, she was the queen of the school, right? You bet she'd have her group of adoring boys. Girls who look like that always do.

Anna's face hardened, but her tone didn't change. "I suppose a transcript will be made available to me?"

Good God, if she put any more syrup over that she'd drown in it. I swallowed hard. The stone in my throat had gone away, replaced with a faint tang of waxen, rotting citrus. Gran called it an *arrah* — an aura, like migraine sufferers get right before their heads cave in.

Me, I get it right before someone tries to kill me, when an old friend is going to show up, or when the serious weird is about to happen. If I weren't so busy trying to stand up straight and look a little less scruffy, I might have been laying odds with myself over which one I was looking at now.

"Of course." Bruce said it the way adults do when they really mean, *No, are you stupid?*

Now *that* was interesting. It was tug-of-war in here, and I was the rope. How long had she been here, the only girl in a school full of boys? And looking like that, she probably had a really great time with it. Things were probably so *easy* for her.

It was enough to make you want to hate someone. As if I didn't already feel like she was fingernails on chalkboard.

Hiro's chair scraped against the floor as he pushed it further back. I took that as my cue to get moving, and the taste of wax-rotted oranges flooded my tongue as I stepped away from the chair at the head of the table.

I stopped just once, my gaze still locking with Anna's. Her cheeks had turned pink. A spark of crimson fired in the back of her pupils and snuffed itself out just as quickly.

I got going again.

Walking down the side of the table was uncomfortable, to say the least. I hate being stared at. And by the time I got down to the end, Anna had folded her arms and was standing right in the doorway, framed by the shabby, plush textures of the study.

Which presented an interesting choice. Did I slide right past her, hunching my shoulders and being the good little nerd, or did I say *fuck it* and call her on this cheerleader bullshit? I seriously had to pee, and she was top of the heap here at the Schola.

But Anna hadn't told anyone here about me. What kind of secret was I, for her? Was she "protecting" me? Even though the vampires had found me after all?

She wanted me to hate Christophe, too. Why?

More questions. And I had half a second to decide what I was going to do.

I squared my shoulders, tilted my chin up, suppressed a bacon-smelling burp, and walked straight for her. Hiro made a graceful, blurring movement, and before I knew it he was somehow in front of me. Anna stepped aside, smart as you please, and I sailed past her like I was on a parade float.

"Dru."

I looked over my shoulder. The thought—*I turned my back on her*—made my skin tingle with awareness. Like waiting for the slap of a paper sign taped to the back. Or the prick of a knife blade sliding through cloth.

Anna leaned against the open door, just like an illustration in a fashion magazine. Perfect, poreless, and with a sweetly poisonous smile. Another nasty, tiny little thought struggled in the back of my head, then drowned in the need to find a bathroom really, really quick.

"What?" As in, *What do you want now?*

"Welcome to the Schola Prima, sister." Her glossy mouth quirked up at one corner, a half-smile that held no warmth. "We're going to be great friends."

If she was aiming for sarcasm, she was doing a pisspoor job of it. "Yeah. Great to be here." I didn't have to work to sound snide. "I wonder who's going to try to kill me next."

I followed Hiro's narrow back through the hall, and the uncarved door shut behind us with a dry little click.

"That was unwise." He avoided the chairs with an ease that spoke of long habit and led me through the mahogany door, and I had the sudden sense that I was in an air lock. No windows in here, no sunlight coming in. Just the fire and electric lights, and when the study closed itself up behind me, there was no air moving.

You'd think *djamphir* would want all the daylight they could get.

"What?" I really, really wanted to find a toilet. Next time I drank coffee, it wasn't going to be by the gallon. And good luck getting any sleep for awhile. My heart was pounding, both from caffeine and from the persistent idea that I was somehow in some kind of danger.

It was ridiculous. Here was where I should have been safest, with a bunch of *djamphir* and werwulfen trained or training to fight the suckers off. And the Council were the bosses of the Order, right? And the Order wanted me alive because I was girl *djamphir*. Rare enough that there were only Anna and me, and Christophe telling me I was precious.

"Anna is . . . difficult. She is the head of the Council, head of the Order, the only *svetocha* we've managed to save for years upon years. She's used to a certain amount of deference." One shoulder lifted and dropped, a shrug. "You have friends here. But still . . . be careful."

Be careful about what? "I'm always careful," I mumbled. The soft wingbeats receded, and the taste of breakfast fought with wax oranges over my tongue. "Well, nearly always."

"Be more than careful, then, Milady Anderson." The huge iron-bound door ghosted open as soon as Hiro got near it. "Be *vigilant*."

I could have asked him what he meant, but my bladder was about to explode. And I had a funny feeling I wouldn't get anything but cryptic Christophe-style answers out of him anyway. So I nodded, tried not to notice how relieved Benjamin looked or the thunder-cloud on Graves's face, and got the hell out of there.

* * *

"Standing out in the goddamn hall with half-vampires. Jesus." Graves stalked to my window. It was a bright sunny day, early enough in the morning for birds to be singing, and in the garden my room overlooked, everything was green with springtime. "Supercilious bastards. What took you so long?"

"I had to tell the whole story." I headed straight for the bathroom. Tiled in deep blue with brass fixtures and a tub deep enough to drown a werwulf in, it was acres of uneasy space. I almost wanted to turn on the faucet to drown out the Grand Canyon echo of a severely abused bladder.

A few minutes later and several pounds lighter, I dug in my battered black messenger bag for a comb and came out to find him lying across my bed, fingers laced behind his head and the curtains mostly drawn.

The room was twice as big as the one at the other Schola, and in blue as well. Carpet you could lose quarters in, empty bookshelves with a few antique brass knickknacks—one of them was a small brass tortoise heavy enough to chuck at an intruder if you didn't mind killing someone by tchotchke—but no marble busts, thank God. The bed was king-size, princess-and-pea deep, and in a weird frame swathed with blue gauze. It looked like a fairy was going to choke to death in there at any second.

There was a high-end computer I hadn't bothered to turn on yet and three credit cards lying in paper sleeves on the rosewood desk next to the keyboard, all registered to Sunrise Ltd. A typed sheet with the address and a mail-stop number, as if I was living in an apartment or something. A walk-in closet the size of the *Titanic*, completely empty. All the clothes I'd gotten at the other Schola were gone, and if there hadn't been a small stackable washer and dryer tucked in a separate closet here I don't know what I'd've done. As it was, wearing the same jeans and T-shirt was getting old.

"I think we should get a couple sleeping bags." I dropped down on the bed next to him. "Have you seen Shanks yet?"

"I can find him. If you want him. What do you want sleeping bags for? Got a nice bed right here." He stared up at the ceiling, green eyes half-closed and his expression halfway between angry and constipated. "What happened? Who was that girl?"

Which answered one question. Anna had walked right by him. Where was *her* set of bodyguards? "That's Anna. Another *svetocha*." I almost tacked an *Edgar* onto the end of the sentence, decided at the last second not to. It probably wasn't wise to tease him right now. Though I wouldn't have minded a laugh or two, he didn't look in the mood to chuckle.

He glared at the ceiling, anger winning out. "I thought you were the only one."

What could I say? *So did I, and then I couldn't tell you.* "They kind of keep her a secret so the vampires don't attack, I guess."

Graves snorted. "Yeah, the same way they keep you a secret? Don't tell me you fell for that."

Now that I was lying down, the bed seemed really, really comfortable. My nerves were twitching and jumping from the caffeine. "I think some of them were trying to keep me a secret. But maybe not in a good way."

Because the more I thought about it, the more the Council's reactions didn't make sense. Neither did Anna's. It was like she was trying for damage control. Why? Because here I was at the Schola Prima, her stomping ground, instead of stuck out in the back of beyond at a reform school? She was probably way, way used to being the only girl in town.

I couldn't really think clearly about it, could I? Because she just grated on me. She wasn't just your garden variety teenager, either. If she was old enough to know Christophe she was an *adult*, even if she looked like a cheerleader. And why had she come all the way out to the other Schola? Trying to trap Christophe, for some reason? Did she really think he'd betrayed my mother? It seemed like a lot of people thought so.

Except Dylan, maybe. And me.

Don't hesitate, Christophe had said, holding the knifepoint against his chest. Pulled hard, as if he was going to stab himself. He swore he hadn't betrayed my mother. And he'd been there, in that dark room at the werwulfen compound.

If I need a reason now, Dru, it will have to be you.

I trusted him, didn't I? But he'd left me here. Alone. Again.

Or maybe not alone because Graves was right beside me, thinking. Absorbing what I'd said. That was one thing I liked about him—you didn't have to spell anything out for him. He got there on his own with only a hint or two. But where he ended up this time surprised me. "You don't seem too surprised to see another one of you wandering around."

"She's not like me." It came out all in one breath, immediate and insistent. Thin blades of light slid between the heavy velvet drapes. The windows had steel shutters on the inside, too, just like the ones at the old Schola. Only these looked more durable, and had a pattern of hearts stamped into them—and another iron bar I could brace them with, with its brackets sunk into the stone wall. "Look, Graves . . ." I decided to just keep the Edgar thing to myself for right now. If he'd wanted me to call him Eddie, he would've told me.

"What?" Now he sounded annoyed.

I saw her at the old Schola. She wants me to hate Christophe, and you know . . . I can't even say what I'm thinking to myself. "I don't know what to do." Admitting it out loud was probably the scariest thing I'd done in the last week, and that was saying something.

When Dad was alive, I knew what to do. He *told* me, and he never let me flounder. When he showed up all zombified, things started spinning hard, but Graves had been there. And as long as I was focusing on keeping Goth Boy out of trouble, the not-knowing had seemed more manageable. Plus, I'd been the one with the books and the guns and some knowledge of the Real World. He'd been a civilian. Now we were both in the same leaky boat, and I didn't want him to know I had no idea where we were going.

Graves let out a long breath, closing his eyes. A thin line of dark-brown hair showed at his temples. Roots. The black-dyed bits were growing out. "Right now we catch some sleep. Then I go find Bobby and Dibs and see what they say. Then we find out how to work that computer and those credit cards and get you some clothes." He paused, added an afterthought, glancing at me like he expected me to disagree. "And me, too."

It was a pretty good plan, one I should've come up with. "But what if . . ." I stopped. The vampires probably hadn't found me through the Internet, for Christ's sake. No, they'd been *told* where to find me. Christophe had as much as said so, and so had Dylan. "Then what do we do?"

"Watch and wait." He yawned hugely. I could almost see his tonsils. "Tell Shanks and Dibs the score so they can watch you when I can't. I don't trust those *djamphir*."

"I don't either." *But what choice do we have?* And here he was, thinking he was going to be protecting me now. I wasn't sure I liked that. If I wasn't taking care of him, well, what did he need me for? "Graves?"

"What?" Now he sounded truly aggravated. He flung his arm over his eyes, almost hitting me with his elbow. I didn't even move—he could have cracked me a good one and I'm not sure I would've moved.

"I'm glad you're here." A flush was working its way up my throat, staining my cheeks. I had another thing or two I wanted to talk to him about, but the time never seemed right.

It never does. And how do you tell a half-werwulf Goth Boy that you really like him, especially when he seems pretty determined not to hear? I mean, he knew, right? I'd as much as told him. And here he was.

"Yeah." Another jaw-cracking yawn. "Now be a good girl and don't get into trouble for a bit, okay? I'm bushed."

Irritation flashed through me; I swallowed it. It tasted bitter, and I decided to go brush my teeth. He didn't say anything else when I slid off the bed, and by the time I reached the bathroom door again he was snoring.

I didn't blame him. Sleeping in hallways was probably not good for him.

I stood in the middle of the thin swords of sunlight spearing toward the carpet, my arms loosely crossed like I was hugging myself. Looking at him. With his arm over his face and his mouth agape, all you could see was part of his nose and the stubble. He sprawled across the bed, a black blot on all the blue. Chapped hands and tangled hair, and his jeans were developing holes in the knees. His T-shirt rucked up, showing a slice of belly ridged lightly with muscle, a line of light furring marching down from his belly button and vanishing under the edge of a pair of black boxer-briefs.

I looked away, toward the door. My cheeks burned. All the locks were turned, and I'd dropped the bar into its brackets. I was alone in here with him. The flush spread all over me, from my toes up into my hair. My internal thermostat was shorted out in a big way.

Well, I wasn't going to be sleeping. So I should probably do something useful, like brush my teeth and get some clothes ordered for Graves.

It looked like I was going to be here for awhile.

* * *

I was in the little box of a kitchen when Augustine came back. Two weeks and I'd just gotten him to buy some bread. I once tried for flour so I could make it, but he'd hustled me out of the grocery store like I'd made some sort of strange bodily sound. I was just putting the pan from my dinner—beans and biscuits, since he'd finally brought back some flour last night—in the hot soapy water when I heard the scratching at the door.

I froze and looked at the end of the counter where the snub-nosed .38 sat. If you are in here, sweetheart, and you think it may not be me coming back, you use one of these.

I'd asked him what the hell would happen if I shot him by mistake, and he grinned at me and told me not to be silly. It was kind of like Dad.

Not really.

Brooklyn breathed outside the window. The kitchen looked out onto a blank brick wall. But there was a ledge outside, and August had made me look out at the handholds going up to the roof or down to another window in a hall two floors below. No sunlight ever got in here, but the bedroom window sometimes had some. It was like living in a hole. And he never let me go outside for very long, and never alone.

The touch told me it was August. And that something was wrong.

The door scraped open. He must have been fumbling with his keys. That wasn't like him.

I bolted for the door. There was a gun on the spindly little table right beside it, tucked behind a dusty vase of artificial flowers. He was a hunter, like Dad, so he was always prepared. And he'd taken me through where all the weapons were, just in case.

August spilled through the door, shoving it shut behind him and almost overbalancing. I caught him, and I smelled something coppery.

I knew blood when I smelled it, even at this age. "Jesus Christ." I

*found out I was saying it over and over again, found something differ-
ent to say.* "What *happened?*"

He shook his head, blond hair moving oddly, as if it was wet. Was
it raining out there? I didn't know. August was tall, muscle-heavy, and
almost tipped both of us over as his legs gave out. He was muttering in Polish.
At least, I guessed it was Polish. As if he was drunk. But he wasn't drunk.

He was hurt bad, and there was nobody here to help him except me.

"What?" I had to know if he'd been followed, or what. Dad had never
come home this beat-up. August's familiar white tank top was torn and
dirty, dyed bright red. His jeans were a mess of ribbons, and he held
his blue plaid shirt over his chest with one arm. His boots were soaked
and dark. I started dragging him toward the bathroom. "August, dammit,
what happened?"

He shook free of me and scrambled for the bathroom. I ran through
all the first aid I know—I can handle pretty much anything short of a
gunshot wound, really. First I had to find the damage, then stop the
bleeding, check him for shock—

"It's all right." He made it to the bathroom door, a slice of white tile
behind him. The entire apartment was suddenly too small. I mean, it
was a cracker box anyway: one bedroom, the kitchen and dining room
the size of a postage stamp and papered with movie posters, the tiny
bathroom with its claw-foot tub. "Looks worse than it is. Bring vodka."
His accent—half Brooklyn, half Bronx, all Bugs Bunny—cut every
vowel short. But something else was rubbing through the words, too.
The song of a different tongue.

I made it back into the kitchen on shaking legs. If we had to blow
this place, he wouldn't have asked for vodka. Relief burst through me.

After all, he'd come back. He went out almost every night to hunt.
I guessed New York was pretty dangerous, all those people crammed
together and the things that go bump in the night hiding in all the

corners. I wished I knew a bit more about the things that inhabited here—rat spirits, certainly. Hexes and voodoo, certainly. Sorcery, you bet. Other predators. There were probably werwulfen too, but Dad never messed with those. And August wasn't like Dad; he didn't tell me anything about what he did. I wasn't his helper.

Missing Dad rose like a stone in my throat. I grabbed the Stoli bottle from the freezer, sloshed it, and decided to put a fresh one in. Before I carried it into the bathroom, I uncapped it and took a healthy swallow. It burned the back of my throat, cold fire.

I knocked on the bathroom door. "Augie?"

No sound for a long moment. I had a vivid mental image of him standing in front of the sink, bent over halfway, his lips pulled back from his teeth and a haze of red spreading out from—

He jerked the door open. "Brought the vodka?"

His hair was dry, springing up in soft golden spikes. I didn't think about it. I was more concerned with him bleeding, so I pushed into the tiny bathroom and grabbed the Medikit in its green nylon bag. "Where's the worst of it?"

He screwed the cap off the vodka and took a long pull. If he found out I was sneaking gulps he might have gotten mad. But then, I didn't think he'd notice. Dad never noticed I'd been sneaking Jim Beam. It tasted foul, but it did steady you. Gran always said a bit of hooch was good for the nerves. Her people had been rumrunners back in the day.

I pushed the flannel shirt aside. He winced. There were claw marks, but the blood didn't look to be all his. He was only scratched, the scratches flushed and angry, diagonally across his chest. One of them jagged down like something had tried to eviscerate him, but it petered out. He was lucky.

"Jesus. What did this?" My hands moved all on their own, opening the Medikit and sitting it in the dry sink. I grabbed his shoulder. He *sank down on the toilet. Thank God the lid was down. We had a running battle going on over that. He was male, after all.*

"Nasty things. Nothing a nice girl needs to know about, eh Dru?"

I rolled my eyes, opened up the cabinet, and got the peroxide down. He took another shot of vodka. "Is it raining out there?"

He shook his head, still swallowing. His throat moved. He closed his eyes, but not before I got a flash of color—yellow, like sunshine.

But August's eyes were dark. I didn't know then that he was djamphir. Whenever I thought about it, it made sense. He'd been struggling to keep the aspect down so I wouldn't ask him questions, and I'd been oblivious.

Hey, I was young. And I didn't even know djamphir existed. I'd heard of suckers, of course—everyone who interacts with the Real World knows about them. But Dad never said a word about half-sucker vampire hunters. I never had a clue.

I had the scissors and was cutting his tank top before he realized it. "Settle down," I told him, slapping his left hand away. "Let me look. I patch up Dad all the time." When I glanced up, he was looking at me, and his eyes were dark again.

"It's no problem, Dru. I heal quick."

He did. They were already fading, the claw swipes on his chest. "Jesus." I ripped open a packet of gauze. "I'm going to clean them anyway. You never know."

"If it makes you happy." He shrugged, wincing, and lifted the vodka bottle again.

He stayed long enough to change into fresh clothes and smoke one of his weird foreign cigarettes while I fixed an omelet. He lived on eggs and vodka. Said it kept him young. I mean, he was what, twenty-five? At least, he looked twenty-five. God knows how old he is. If I ever see him again, maybe I'll ask.

Then he told me to stay inside, stocked up on ammo again, and was gone inside twenty minutes. Leaving me staring at a pile of bloody clothes, the ashtray with a still-smoking butt, two spent clips that needed to be refilled, and his plate on the table.

At least he'd promised to bring home some bread. Maybe just to shut me up, I dunno.

I bolted for the window in the bedroom. Sometimes if I was quick enough I could catch a glimpse of him on the street, moving with his head up and a spring in his step. Sometimes he might as well have vanished as soon as the apartment door locked.

Outside, streetlights fought with the darkness. It wasn't raining. It was foggy, a wet cotton-wool fog, and the Hefty bags of trash stacked on the sidewalk were just like they always were. The trucks came around twice a week, but the amount of trash never seemed to go down. It was filthy here, and cold. I wouldn't have minded if I could get out and see some things—I'd've loved to go to the Met, or even just walked around downtown and seen stuff.

But August said no. And he was gone every night.

I sighed, resting my forehead on the cold glass. Every time he left I wasn't sure he'd come back.

Story of my life.

I finally slid off the bed and plodded out into the living room. At least I could clean things up while he was gone. So that if—when—he came back, he'd see I wasn't any trouble. I was pulling my own weight.

Besides, it was something to do until Dad came back.

If . . . when he came back.

CHAPTER SIX

It **was early** afternoon by the time I switched the computer off. I stretched, yawned, padded for the bed and dropped down. That woke Graves up, where my clicking at keys and sometimes swearing under my breath hadn't.

"Huh?" He half-sat up, and I took the chance to rescue one of the pillows from under his head. "Whaaa?"

"Nothing. Go back to sleep." I squiggled around, getting comfortable. "I just finished, that's all."

"Okay." He settled back down again, and I lay there for a few seconds feeling him move around before I opened my eyes and found him almost nose-to-nose with me. His silver skull-and-crossbones earring glinted at me. His irises were oddly luminescent, and a shadow of stubble spread over his jaw.

Weird. He kind of *was* getting hairy, but it was just a five o'clock shadow. I had the sudden urge to touch his jawline, a feeling so intense my fingers itched. The skin underneath, on the curve where his throat made a hollow before his collarbone and shoulder, looked so fragile. His lips were slightly parted, and we looked at each other for a long few seconds before he moved back slightly. "Sorry," he half-whispered. "I haven't brushed my teeth."

"It's okay." I stayed where I was. He was still inside the personal-space boundary, the one that even friends don't cross. "Look . . ." But I ran out of words and courage at the same time.

How did I get to be such a wuss?

"What?" He didn't look irritated, just curious. And was he *blushing*?

He was. High flags of color stood out on his cheeks. The blush spread down his neck, and he went still all at once, like a dog sensing something dangerous or interesting about to happen.

If I could draw him just like this, in charcoal maybe on good paper, catching the way the light slid over his high cheekbones and touched his mouth, I would tear the picture out and keep it in my bag. The one that I keep for emergencies.

I grabbed every last failing scrap of courage I had left and leaned forward. The last time I'd tried to do this, I'd ended up plastering a kiss on his cheek. But since then, he'd admitted to being interested. Sort of.

I was about to find out.

Our mouths met. He was absolutely still, and a flash of hot embarrassment went through me. *Oh, crap. He didn't mean it.*

But then he moved, too. His arms came around me, and we sort of melted together. I'm no prude, really, I've had my share of kissing behind bleachers or awkward snatched moments of makeout in halls or band rooms, so I'm not completely hopeless. It was pretty quickly apparent Graves was a novice.

He learned quick, though. Some people just *get* kissing; others never will. He got it. There was none of the loose-mouth sloppy spit stuff some guys do, none of the mashing that happens when a guy thinks girls like to have their lips crushed against their teeth. Which, you know, jeez. Let a girl *breathe*, huh?

His arms tightened, and I was kind of worrying what to do about *my* arm, the one trapped under my pillow. But then he really got the hang of it and leaned even further in, his tongue doing some really interesting things I'd never even thought of, and I was feeling . . . was I? Yes.

I was feeling *safe*. Not the kind of safe where you know there are still bad things howling outside the door waiting to get in. No, it was the kind of safe where you sink down in your bed at the end of the day and know you can go to sleep and everything is going to be the same tomorrow.

He felt like home. Not like a scary roller-coaster ride, like Christophe.

Don't think about that, Dru. I did my best to shove Christophe out of my head. The thought went quietly.

I got my arm around him and tightened up, but just at that moment he broke away. I ended up with my face in his throat, so close I could smell a healthy boy who needed his daily shower and was just about to get right on that. It was a nice smell, and I filled my lungs with it.

But right under it was another aroma, just as delicious. A copper tang, with a hint of wildness and moonlit nights. It was the fluid in his veins, and my teeth tingled a little. The smell of his blood tickled that place at the back of my throat. The place normal people don't have.

The place where the red thirst lives.

No. Jesus Christ. I didn't want to even think about what would happen if he found out I was growing fangs with my face so near his neck. Was that why he'd all of a sudden gone still again? Could he smell the bloodhunger on me?

Would Christophe smell it?

"Dru," Graves whispered.

I found out I'd snaked my leg between his and curled us up

together like kudzu tangling on a fence. There was definitely something happening below his belt, and confusion swamped me. Did he not like me? Could he help it? What was *with* him, anyway?

I stayed where I was, breathing deep and fast, hoping the tingle in my teeth and the dryness in my throat would go away. It was like that old dream of walking down the school halls and finding out you're naked.

"Dru?" He sounded like he had something caught in his throat. "Look, I'm sorry. I just . . ."

I would wriggle away, I told myself. In just a second. A hot flush suffused me, like the cloudiness in water when you drop the macaroni in. My teeth went back to normal; I swallowed several times.

"I like you too much," Graves said into my hair. He wasn't letting go of me. As a matter of fact, his arms tensed, and I ended up with my face all the way in his throat. Thank God I had a hold of myself now. I could still smell the blood in him, but it wasn't overpowering. "I mean, nobody else's ever been even close to interested in me, all right? I, uh. I just mean I, if you're, you know, not wanting to do this . . ."

The relief crashing through me made me hug him, hard. So hard he lost his breath, so hard my bruises and aches came back. It felt like we were back in Dad's truck in the Dakotas, clinging to each other for dear life. Both of us shipwrecked and holding on to whatever we could.

He was the only thing that hadn't whirled away when everything started spinning. He was the only thing nailed down, and I was not letting go. Not ever, not if I could help it.

"I like you," I muttered against his pulse, moving my lips carefully so my teeth didn't get any funny ideas. "I like you a *lot*, Graves." *You're all I've got, now. When it gets right down to it.* "I, you know, I just really like you."

Then I could have kicked myself. *Way to go, Dru. "I like you" is all you can say?*

"Things are messed up." His breath was a warm spot in my hair. "You know. I don't want to, well, pressure you."

Oh, that is so not even a concern right now. "You shouldn't worry. You're the only decent boyfriend material I've found in, like, sixteen states."

"You're picky." There was the sarcasm. Goth Boy was himself again.

"I have *good taste*, okay? I like you, Graves." I stopped myself from saying Edgar again, with an effort of will.

"I like you too. I just, we should be careful. See what happens. Okay?"

Sure. All right. "Okay." *What does that* mean?

Apparently it meant he was going to untangle himself from me. Which he did. He slid off the bed, not looking at me, and headed for the bathroom. I watched him walk away, in that weird way guys have when they're feeling you watch them. I should have said something, but what? What the hell could I say?

He shut the door, and I lay there for a few seconds breathing, before he turned the water on and I heard him brushing his teeth.

Had he just suddenly figured out he was kissing someone who could get fangs? I mean, werwulfen had big scary teeth too, but . . .

Oh, Lord. I'd just had my first kiss with Goth Boy, and that was good. But I had no idea whether *he* thought it was good, or if I'd just gotten the brush-off. *See what happens?* What did that mean? And he was my best and only friend right now. The only person I was really sure of, here.

I rolled over, stuffed the pillow under my head, and closed my eyes. When he came back from the bathroom, I just lay there breathing like I was asleep. He stood by the side of the bed for a little bit, probably wishing he had somewhere else to roost, then eased himself down and stayed on his side. The space between us had just gotten bigger than it ever was, and in a completely new way.

The more I thought about it, the more it didn't get any easier to figure out.

Great.

CHAPTER SEVEN

I **stared at the** fall of heavy golden late-afternoon sunlight through the window for a little bit, my back against Graves's. Neither of us had climbed under the covers, and I hate the feeling of sleeping in jeans. Everything gets twisted around and pulled up, crawls into cracks it's not supposed to, and you end up feeling like you've been sleeping on nails.

I lay there, breathing softly. The sunlight flickered because a shadow moved across the window. A faint scratching sound, and I tensed, muscle by muscle.

The shadow bobbed again, and I pushed myself up, even my elbows creaking with exhaustion. Graves muttered and moved beside me, and the shape in the window froze. Golden light poured past it, and all I could see reflected on the blue carpet was a distorted blur.

I grabbed for the switchblade on the pretty, postage-stamp-sized blue night table, knocking over the lamp. It fell with a crash, Graves sat up and swore; the shadow disappeared with a final scratching sound. I leapt out of bed, the switchblade snicking free, and was halfway between the bed and the window before I realized yanking it open and sticking my head out might not be a good idea.

"What the *hell*—" Graves said in a slurred, sleepy voice.

I grabbed the sash anyway and tugged the window open, the switchblade almost squirting free of my sweating fingers. A cool spring afternoon drenched in honey light poured in, and the garden a story below was starred and speckled with new growth on old thorny bushes. There would be roses in awhile, and if I was still here it might be nice to open the window on a clear day and smell them.

Instead I inhaled, dragging in the cool breeze. Grass, sunlight, the edge of soft rain last night and more rain on the way, the aroma of the earth waking up after a long nap. I had to snatch my left-hand fingers away from my mother's locket, the chain doing weird things because it had rotated while I half-slept and the catch was stuck in the locket's loop. It was warm, not icy like it would have been if something dangerous was around, and I wondered if it had ever heated up or cooled down for Dad.

I also caught a breath of warm apple spice, and the fang marks on my left wrist gave a throbbing flare of heat.

Oh. "Hello?" I whispered. Tried to look everywhere at once.

"What the fuck are you *doing*?" Graves's voice almost broke. He scrambled off the bed, and I thought I saw something across the square of the garden glinting, a reflection from deep in the shadow of the wall. There were other windows, all of them blank. Of course: no other *svetocha* except Anna and me.

Where did *she* sleep? Did I even want to know?

I stood there in the flood of sunshine and felt cold. The breath of spiced apples was blown away on a brisk, green-smelling wind. Gems of water sparkled on the garden, each one perfectly placed.

I lowered the switchblade. *Christophe?* I opened my mouth to say his name, shut it again.

Because Graves was right next to me, fisting at his eyes. "What's up?"

"I thought I saw something." I swallowed hard, used the windowsill to push the blade back in until it clicked. "In the window."

"Oh." He blinked a couple times, rubbed at his hair. "Anything there?"

"I don't know. Maybe I was asleep." The lie tasted like ashes. I knew I hadn't been.

"What exactly did you think you saw?" He was pale under his coloring. "A dreamstealer? Something else?"

The thought of a dreamstealer and having seizures again after it stole my breath was enough to make all remaining sleepiness jump out the window. My shoulders hunched. "Just a shadow."

He leaned forward, peered out. "A drop straight down. And nothing above to hang onto. But that doesn't mean anything lately, does it?" He sniffed, inhaling deeply, passing the air through his nose the way I've seen people in fancy restaurants smell wine. And gave me an odd, very green sideways look. "Huh."

"What?" The lump in my throat wasn't just my heart.

"I dunno." He pulled the window down. "Think we should lock the shutters?"

I think it was Christophe. The words trembled right on my lips. I shook my head. The air always feels dead when you barricade windows. Like you're under siege. Or buried. "I dunno."

"Okay." He stayed where he was, sunlight edging his threadbare T-shirt and touching his jeans, bringing out the blue in the denim. He leaned forward, like he wanted to get a little closer. "You all right? You look a little . . ."

Stupid? Silly? Sleepy? "Fine." I almost flinched away, stamped back to the bed, tossed the switchblade on the nightstand. The lamp was okay. I picked it back up and settled it where it belonged. Then I dropped down into the bed's softness and wished again that I was wearing boxers. "Sorry to wake you up."

I was also getting to the point of being sorry I'd kissed him. What the hell had he *meant*? But that was useless to think about.

He stood there, irresolute. I got comfortable, putting my arm under the pillow, busying myself with getting settled. My wrist throbbed like a bad tooth.

If I'd known what would happen when Christophe bit me, would I still have done it? He'd needed my blood to save us. Even Shanks agreed about *that*.

But still, I wondered. There were other things I wondered about, too.

Like what he'd said, alone in a wulfen's room with the darkness covering everything and the bloodhunger burning in my throat. *If I need a reason now, Dru, it will have to be you.*

As uncomfortable situations go, thinking about a bossy *djamphir* while a *loup-garou* you've just kissed and been rejected by stands there and stares is pretty high on the scale. Jesus. I *never* used to have problems like this.

Graves slumped near the window. His face was shadowed; I couldn't see his expression.

"You might as well come on back and get some rest." I tried to sound gracious. "I mean, jeez. Unless you want to sleep on the floor."

"Maybe I should go find Shanks."

Hot embarrassment flooded me. Could he make it any more obvious that he didn't want to hang around me? Still, I wasn't giving up without a fight. "Okay. I mean, if you want to. If you do, I'm not gonna sleep though. I'll go with."

He straightened a bit, losing the slouch. "You don't have to."

"You think I want to be alone?" I sounded mad even to myself. "The only time I feel safe is when you're around."

Which was half a lie, too. Because I felt safe when Christophe hugged me, and when he told me he wasn't going to let anything happen to me. It was like being with Dad again and knowing I had a place in the world.

But Graves sounded relieved, and that was worth any kind-of half-assed lie I could dredge up. "Oh." His socks dragged as he shuffled across the carpet. "All right, then." He paused by the foot of the bed. "You okay, Dru?"

I closed my eyes. Put my other arm up so I was hugging the pillow. "Peachy." *As long as you're here, I guess. You're about the only person I'm sure of. I'm just not so sure about some things to do with you.*

"Okay." He settled down on his side stiffly, careful not to touch me. The flaming in my cheeks became hot trickles of water between my eyelids. "Dru?"

"What?" I hated to snap at him, but my throat was full and my eyes were beginning to leak.

A long silence. Then he settled in, moving around a little on the bed the way a cat will turn around before it goes boneless. "Do you mean that?"

What, about liking you, or about feeling safe? "Of course I mean it." I sniffed hard, pulling everything back up into my nose. "You're the only good thing that's happened to me since my dad got zombified, Graves. You want me to put it on a billboard?"

"I just asked. *Jeez.*" But he moved a little closer, tentatively. And when he put his arm around me, I didn't move or protest. I just lay there stiffly until the relaxation started to feel natural. He breathed into my tangled hair, a spot of heat, and all of a sudden I was content just to be still.

It wasn't quite swapping spit, but it was okay. It left me more confused than ever, though.

He fell asleep again after a little while. I could tell by his breathing.

Soon dusk came around, and the Schola woke up again. Nothing else scratched at my window, and I couldn't tell whether I was relieved or unhappy about that.

CHAPTER EIGHT

I brushed my teeth again, tied my hair back, then turned the computer on once more and spent some time poking around. It was your basic intranet with a gateway to the Internet, but the security stuff was way more intense than it had been back at the other Schola. I had to verify three times with the information on the sheet next to the keyboard before it even let me *near* the Web.

I was betting my every keystroke was logged, so I didn't visit anything fun *or* informative. But I was feeling sharper and more myself, so I poked around for more clothes. For me, this time. I'd been so strung-out earlier I'd just gotten Graves some stuff and called it good. Now I looked back at what I'd ordered and about slapped myself on the forehead.

Shopping while sleep-deprived is a Bad Idea.

I sat and compared prices and wondered where the Order's money came from, while I spun the switchblade idly on the desk sometimes and thought about what I was doing.

I'm used to shopping for myself in army surplus stores or Goodwills or something. Getting stuff sent to you over the Net was always a big no-no while I was with Dad. All that stuff leaves a footprint, a happy little trail—and you have to pick it up somewhere; even P.O. boxes and those rent-a-box places need ID of some kind. You have to go back and actually get the stuff you've ordered, and when you do, whammo. There's no better time for someone or something to hit you.

No, the Net's only good for a few things. Research, though you have to apply the bullshit test and cross-check everything. Scams, because you can't spit on the Net without hitting one. And the occasional entertainment. Nothing like people making fools of themselves for the world to see.

Sometimes I wonder what Gran would have thought of the digital age. Of course, it's hard to get broadband down in the hollers and up on the ridges.

She probably would have just sniffed and called it more foolishness than normal. Which is pretty damning, considering what she thought of the whole human race.

I actually had some fun picking out more T-shirts for Graves. I got him a Captain America tee, and one that had a huge dinosaur and lasers screened on it, with the caption *Look out! That velociraptor has a lightsaber!* screaming across it. It made me laugh into my cupped hand, trying to keep it muffled because Graves was muttering a little bit and stirring in the bed. Plus a few plain black ones, large- size athletic fit, not medium, in case he kept bulking up the way he had been. Becoming *loup-garou* had made him way broader in the shoulders.

I knew his sizes from shopping at the other Schola. Before he went out with the wulfen and got kitted out, that was. Maybe they'd do it for him here, but just in case I got him socks and more boxer-briefs, too. He seemed like a tighty-whitey kind of kid when I met him, but I guess that had changed.

I was just sitting there, wondering whether or not to get him an athletic cup—you know, for sparring and stuff, but I had to weigh the embarrassment factor in—when there was a knock at the door. A nice polite three raps, a pause, two more taps.

What now?

My mother's locket cooled abruptly, icy metal against my skin. I pushed myself up from the office chair. It squeaked a little bit, sliding across one of those hard plastic pads they put down to save carpets from the rollers. Then it hit me, and I froze, hunched halfway over.

Oranges and wax. Sliding across my tongue, reaching and touching that place at the back of my throat where the bloodhunger lived, right next to the place ordinary people don't have. The little spot that warns me when danger or weirdness is right around the corner.

I glanced at the bed. Graves lay on his side, curled up as if I was still there, hugging my pillow. I swallowed hard, though I didn't want to with that taste in my mouth. Hooked my fingers around the switchblade and straightened.

I felt ridiculous. It was probably a teacher or something. Or Shanks, or even Benjamin.

You know it's not, Dru. Don't you dare open that door.

The warding's thin blue lines came into view inside my head, seen with the queer non-sight I didn't realize other people didn't have until I was about ten years old. I can remember the moment, too. I'd come home crying from the valley school because the kids had been picking on me, and Gran's mouth had clamped together like a vise. Her disapproval hit me like a wave, and I'd had to admit that if I wanted the kids to tolerate me I shouldn't have been listening to their little secrets with that muscle inside my head even if I thought everyone could do the same thing and just didn't let on.

The problem wasn't actually knowing. It was letting them *know* I knew.

People hate that. They hate it because they fear it. There are places in America where . . . but never mind. That's too awful to think about.

Gran was big on privacy, and she'd had to let me learn the lesson the hard way. Because there just isn't any other way if you're born with the *touch*, she said. And she was right.

I fingered the release on the switchblade and eyed the door nervously. There was the bar on it, even if someone had the keys for the four or five different locks. Two of the locks didn't have an outside keyhole, so that was all right.

But . . . Jesus, someone at my window and someone at my *door*, too? I could tell whoever was at the door meant me no good. The warding said as much, sparking and fizzing as it drew together, blue lines running uneasily under the surface of the visible.

Another scent cut through clotted waxen citrus, filling my nose so my eyes prickled and burned with the overflow.

Warm perfume and spice. A red smell, like silk and high-heeled boots with tiny finicky buttons up their sides. Long hair and a vicious little laugh.

What the hell would she be doing here?

Graves muttered shapelessly, as if he was having a bad dream. The listening silence grew even more intense, and the doorknob jiggled slightly.

Oh, you think I'm too stupid to lock my door? Whatever. But I was shaking badly. She could have a perfectly valid reason for coming here and knocking. She really could.

Christ. I was even doubting the *touch* now, something I'd never done before. Gran would have fetched me one upside the head—figuratively, I mean; she never hit me. Just one glare would've been enough.

Stop dithering about Gran and figure out what you're going to do!

But that was just it. The door was locked and barred, and I didn't *want* to do anything. I just wanted to hunker down and hide. As a long-term strategy it really sucked. But for the short term—like the next few minutes, as the last honeyglow of sunset filled the window and turned the garden into a haze below—it was looking pretty good.

The wards quieted. The thin blue lines went back to their normal patterns, weird circuit-shapes like that old movie about the guy trapped in the computer game, with complex Celtic-looking knots Gran taught me to make holding the doors and windows fast. I stepped sideways in my sock feet, testing the floor for creaks, and was glad about the thick carpet for once.

A few uneasy fizzes. The ward lines dimmed a little but came back, strongly blue. The closer I got to the door, using the weird gliding step Dad taught me to spread my weight out as much as possible over the floorboards, the brighter blue they got. Impatience scraped at the ward, tasting like burnt insulation. I made a face, sticking my tongue out, before I could help it.

The door jumped a little, the warding sparked, and before I knew it there was a high hard *SNAP!* just like a mousetrap going off. I actually *saw* a mousetrap inside my head, leaping up as the spring's energy was released and the mouse skittered away, alive but without its cheese.

Fast light-tapping footsteps in the hall outside. Graves muttered and thrashed uneasily. I found out sweat had sprung up on the curve of my lower back, in my armpits, and along my forehead. A headache threatened, steel bands around my temples.

I blew out a long, soft breath. Lowered the switchblade. As my only weapon, it sucked. As a comfort, it kind of sucked as well.

More footsteps. Heavier, but just as quick. *Djamphir* even sound graceful while they're running. I wondered how they did that and watched the wards.

Not a spark. They just kept humming blue.

"Dru!" It was Benjamin, and he just kept going right on down the hall. "Milady! *Dru!*"

I stuffed the switchblade in my pocket and got the bar unstuck with shaking, sweaty hands. Threw the locks as Graves woke up and cussed again behind me, the window going blind-dark as the sun slipped fully below the edge of the horizon. I tore the door open and jumped out into the hall, narrowly missing a collision with Leon, who stopped on a dime and glared at me through his mousy, tangled hair. He looked like he'd just woke up, but his combat boots were laced up and tied tight, and that takes awhile.

"What the fuck's going on?" he snarled.

"*I* don't know!" I snarled right back. "Benjamin went that way—" I pointed, but the mousy *djamphir* boy was already gone, running with the eerie stuttering speed that verges on disappearing because the eyes can't track it.

"She's here!" Leon yelled. "*Benjamin! Dammit, she's here!*"

The two blonds appeared. They weren't quite twins, but since both of them were wearing black T-shirts and jeans, it was harder to tell them apart. One of them was in sock feet, and the other one carried a Walther PPK, pointing it at the floor as his eyes roved. I grabbed the doorjamb and kept my eyes on him while the one in socks walked past me, turned military-sharp, and leaned against the hall wall on the right side of the door.

Guarding me. It was a nice thought, and I was more comforted than I should have been.

"Are you all right?" the blond with the gun asked me. *Thomas*, I remembered his name with the sort of gut-wrenching mental effort I usually associate only with higher-level math classes. I mean, I can balance a checkbook, calculate a tip from sales tax in sixteen states, and do ammo checks. Calculus? Forget it.

I nodded. Leon appeared at the end of the hall, shaking his head. Right behind him, Benjamin stalked. He looked up, saw me, and stopped dead for a few seconds.

The next thing I knew, he was right in front of the door. "You were here? You've *been* here?"

I *hate* it when they blink in and out of sight like that. I almost flinched. "Uh, yeah." I couldn't even say it like he was an idiot or anything. I was too badly rattled. "Had my door barred and everything. But I . . . heard something."

"Is some sleep too much to ask?" Graves moaned from the bed. "Jesus Christ, what's happening now?"

"This is bad," Leon murmured, finally arriving and casting a mild, raised-eyebrow look down at Blond No.1's sock feet.

Dammit, why couldn't I remember their names? Thomas and something. Something with a G, maybe?

"What did you hear?" Benjamin planted his sneakered feet and leaned forward, like a terrier straining at the leash. "Dru?"

George. I remembered the name and felt immediately, oddly better. Like I'd accomplished something. "Someone knocked. But it didn't feel right. I didn't feel like opening the door." Great. Now he was going to think I was a stubborn brat or something.

So let him. What was Anna doing anyway? Why would the warding react to her and not to the boys?

Because she was up to no good, Dru. Duh. And if you weren't so busy trying to explain it away, you could probably figure out why.

Amazingly, Benjamin looked over his shoulder at Leon. They shared the kind of Significant Glance I was used to seeing between adults. Then the dark-haired *djamphir* shook his emo-boy fringe down and turned his attention to me. "That's good." As if praising me for a test answer. "Don't open your door if you're not sure. You should trust your instincts on this. And we'll post a guard instead of—"

"What did *you* see?" Screw the rest of it. I wanted to know that, first.

"I thought . . ." He shook his head. "I don't know. I thought you were running down the hall to visit the Broken again. I've heard a *svetocha* can do that—make a game out of slipping away sometimes. It must be . . . hard, to have someone with you everywhere you go."

Boy, you don't know the half of it. I shrugged. I'd still prefer it to being killed by a sucker.

Always assuming, of course, that I could trust whoever was guarding me. That was the whole problem, wasn't it?

"What the hell's going on?" Graves wanted to know.

"I don't have a problem with it," I told Benjamin. "I know better." *Unless one of you is a traitor and looking to kill me.* I didn't say it, but I also didn't stop watching the kid with the Walther. He was staring off down the hall the other way, his back to the wall, but it's Rule Numero Uno when there's a gun out—you make sure you know where it's pointed at all times.

"That's good." Benjamin sounded relieved. "That's really good. I thought I saw you running down the hall. But it couldn't have been you, since you were here. Maybe it was a curiosity-seeker or something." He gave *me* a Significant Glance, as if I was supposed to help him out with this.

Yeah, that really makes sense. "I dunno." I closed my mouth after that. Anna was supposed to be a secret, but she sure didn't act like it. And would she be a secret here at the Schola Prima, among all the *djamphir*? She'd walked right past Graves and Benjamin and them to get into the Council room, right?

Still, just because she was all over the place didn't mean I had to hand out information like cupcakes. Besides she predated me here and was the head of the Council.

"Oh, come *on*." Leon actually snorted. "It was the Red Queen."

"Isn't she a myth?" Thomas noticed I was looking at the gun and actually flushed. It went into a holster under his left armpit, and I relaxed a little. "Oh, sorry."

I shrugged. Again. I was getting good with the shrugging. I could practice in front of the mirror and have a different one for each occasion.

Benjamin was watching my face, too. "No, she is not a myth. She's just kept from the *hoi polloi* like us. And very busy with her duties. You saw her this morning."

Thomas absorbed this. "I thought she'd be taller."

Sockfoot George asked the question I wanted answered most. "What was she doing *here*, then? And without bodyguards? Unless they were here in Shadow."

Oh, great. All eyes on you, Dru. "I don't have a clue." And I didn't.

They all stood there for a couple seconds just *looking* at each other. And I jumped—Graves was right behind me. He did something odd, then—he put his arms around my waist and hugged me. We're both tall, but he seemed to have gotten taller. Back in the Dakotas we were almost eye to eye. Or maybe it just seemed that way because he hunched over all the time, his body shutting itself away from a world it wanted no part of.

And the *djamphir* boys stared at me again. I blushed for no discernible reason. I was turning red an embarrassing amount of the time lately.

So first Graves liked me too much, but then he would hug me in front of other boys?

"Yes. Well." Benjamin cleared his throat. "Twenty-four-hour guard. Posted at the door. Someone with her at *all* times."

"It will likely be me, since you don't have waivers yet. Damn paperwork." Leon shrugged. "No worries. This is interesting." As if he was watching a TV show or something, settled on the couch with a beer in hand. Though I couldn't imagine any of them kicking back with a brew. They just seemed too . . . *old*. Or too serious.

Fighting vampires is serious business, yeah. But that seriousness on those unlined faces was oddly, well, obscene. It wasn't what they were *supposed* to look like.

"Terrifying is more like it," Thomas muttered. "The Red Queen."

"Second thoughts, Tommy?" Leon's smile couldn't have been called nice.

The blond *djamphir* grinned back, a wide white showing of teeth. "Not on your life, Fritz." A rumble ran beneath the words, almost like a werwulf's warning growl.

Oh, hold up. "Wait. Wait a second. You guys know about her?"

"The first-years think she's a myth. You don't even learn of her existence until you pass your third-year boards." George looked worried. "Before we got this job a frontline grunt like me would never even *see* a *svetocha*. Now they're coming out of the woodwork. Even mythical ones."

"She's not that old; I remember when she was rescued. She doesn't qualify as a *myth*." Leon sighed. "There's no point in sleeping more. Not with orientation and classes."

"Orientation?" I swear to God my knees almost buckled. I was glad Graves was standing right there. "Classes?"

"Both for you, classes for us. Except Leon." Benjamin effectively shut down further discussion by turning away. "And tomorrow, Dru, I suggest we go clothes shopping."

I already did. But I didn't say it. Because getting out and away from the Schola was seeming like a good idea. A *fabulous* idea. "Okay."

"I'll take you down to the cafeteria first thing." Now Leon's unsettling grin was directed at me. "Food and a bunch of staring eyes. Best just to get it over with, right?"

"Right," I said grimly and shoved Graves back by the simple expedient of stepping back myself. How we did that without getting our legs tangled, I don't know. But we managed it, and I was happy about that. "Sure. Give me fifteen."

"You don't need to hurry. An hour will do."

But I was already closing the door. Graves let go of me, and after I locked everything, I turned halfway and we sized each other up.

He was blushing furiously. So was I. We stood there, crimson-cheeked, and just looked at each other.

"Graves—" I began, but he spoke at the same time.

"Dru—" His eyes were so green; ever since he got bit, they'd been getting lighter and more intense.

We both laughed. It was crazy, hysterical laughter, but that was okay. I leaned against the door, chuckling until tears squirted out my eyes. He bent over and hugged his midriff and made little *ah-ah-ah* sounds because he couldn't get enough air in.

Sometimes you've just *got* to let off a little steam. Especially when you've been running on nerves and adrenaline for weeks.

It was over all too quickly, though. I wiped at my cheeks, he finally got some air in, and we were left where we were before, staring awkwardly at each other.

"What was that?" he finally asked, running his fingers back through his hair. It stood up in black spikes, but the effect was softer now since it was growing out. "I didn't even hear you get up."

"I was on the computer. Getting clothes and stuff." *Do you need a cup, dude?* I swallowed the question and a stray laugh at the same time. "I, um, I guess we should talk."

"After I brush my teeth." But he made no move to step away.

"Jesus, can't get clothes soon enough. I'm getting sick of wearing the same thing all the time."

I hear you. A thin spike of guilt went through me—this was twice that everything he owned got taken away because of me. "I got you some stuff. And it sounds like they're taking us shopping tomorrow."

"They're taking *you* shopping tomorrow." He didn't mean it the way it sounded. Or maybe he did because right after the words left his mouth he looked faintly ashamed of them. His earring swung as he ducked his head, running his fingers through his shaggy hair.

"Us. Or I'm not going." I folded my arms and looked at the blue carpet. "So, can I ask you something? About . . . that."

"About what?"

What the hell did he think I was talking about? But he was a boy, and therefore oblivious. Still, I'd pretty much used up all my brass for today and was going to have to use up tomorrow's in about an hour. So I studied the carpet like it would give me an idea. Said nothing.

He lasted about five seconds, then coughed a little. "I, uh, I mean, jeez. Did I, you know, offend or something?"

"No, no." I shook my head. Goddammit, my cheeks were burning *again*. My mother's locket was warm, and I shot a little glance up at him, just to gauge where we were.

He was looking at me like I had something on my face. I found out I had enough brass left, after all. Or maybe I could borrow some.

"I just, well, wanted to know where we stand. That's all." There. It was out. If I'd been misreading everything, I wanted to know.

"Oh." Then he was quiet for so long I thought I'd scream. "I, uh. Jeez. Well."

Screaming was definitely an option. Okay, so I *had* misjudged. I mean, I didn't think you could misjudge, what with sticking your tongue in a boy's mouth. But I guess I did. He either liked me or he didn't, or maybe he did but I wasn't worth the trouble, or . . .

Jesus. Swearing off guys completely was an option. It wasn't like I'd be having a lot of time for extracurricular stuff, what with vampires trying to kill me and everything else.

But, you know, I would've liked to fit that in. With him. "Okay." I headed past him for the bathroom. "Dibs on the toilet, then. Forget I asked."

"Dru . . ." He said it like he was running out of air.

"No, really. It's cool. I just—"

"I *like* you, okay? I do. It's just . . . you've got all this other stuff going on. And vampires trying to take your head off the hard way."

I swallowed, hard. "Like there's an easy way?" But my heart swelled up like a balloon. It had been a long, long time since I'd felt anything close to this. After a few seconds I decided *happy* was a pale word for it. "Okay. Cool. I like you, too. We've pretty much established it. We're being careful, right?" *Whatever that means.*

"Yeah, uh. Um." Now he had something stuck in his throat. I was grinning like a fool. He hunched up again, like he was expecting a punch or something.

"So, yeah. I guess that's that. Dibs on the toilet." And I bolted for the bathroom like I was running away. I just didn't want to laugh and give him the wrong idea.

I should've been more worried. But there's only so much worry you can stand all the time. And if Graves was with me, well, I didn't have so much to worry about, right? We'd handled everything else the Real World could throw at us. And whatever Anna was doing at my door could wait.

It was the first time in weeks the hole in my chest seemed less angry and empty. And I was really, really happy about that.

CHAPTER NINE

The entire cafeteria, full of fluorescent light and the competing aroma of boys and industrially prepared food, went silent as soon as I showed up. *Djamphir*, wulfen, they all stopped and stared at me. I stood right inside the doors for an uncomfortable ten seconds before Graves pushed me from behind and got me going again.

It was hard to eat with everyone staring. But Graves was there, looking around like he was enjoying himself. He put away a whole plate of pancakes, a mountain of hash browns, and a mound of crispy bacon in the time it took me to pick halfway through my cellophane-wrapped ham sandwich.

Good for him.

Leon led me through a labyrinth of quiet halls away from the sound of slamming lockers and male voices. The flooring changed to hardwood, and the marble busts came back, staring at me like I was an interloper. Long velvet drapes framing the windows were alive with the golden glow of dusk, the kind of light that lasts maybe five minutes before twilight falls and the Real World comes out to play.

I shivered. Pulled my hoodie closer around me, and zipped it up, too.

We ended up at a long dim windowless room with a mirror-polished conference table on the right side — the inner side — of the wall. The other side had windows, but the *djamphir* seemed to hold all their important meetings away from the windows. I'd thought they would want sunshine and fresh air — things suckers seem to hate. But on the other hand, I suddenly thought, it was harder to break into a windowless room. Or pick off someone with a rifle through a wall instead of a window.

I hate thinking things like that.

A slight, short brunet *djamphir* in a red T-shirt stood on one side of the door, his arms crossed. The shoulder holster he wore looked absurdly oversized, and his designer jeans looked painted on. He was pretty even for here, dark curls brushed back, wide liquid eyes in an almost feminine face.

Poor kid. I mean, I *felt* more boy than he looked. He would get a hard time in some of the high schools I've blown through.

If he was human, that is.

Leon glanced in, gave me an unreadable look, and stepped aside. "Safe enough, Milady." He said it a little more loudly than he necessarily had to, and I stepped over the threshold.

And right into Uncomfortable City.

There, at the head of the table, sat Anna. The dimness turned her skin into poreless perfection, not a curly coppery-blonde hair was out of place, and her little red high-heeled boots were on the tabletop. She lounged there like she owned the whole room, a froth of petticoats covering her silk-stockinged legs.

And she *smiled.* "Oh, hello." Bright as a new polished penny. "It's Dru! Did you sleep well, dearie?"

Kir sat at her right, his shoulders hunched. He looked miserable, but he perked up a little when I came in. I wondered briefly if he dyed his hair to match Anna's, but hers was russet gold and he was a carrottop. His was obviously natural, and if hers wasn't, the Order probably had enough money to keep her in salon appointments for a long time.

Next to her, even the prettiest *djamphir* boys looked gawky. I felt myself turn even paler, more greasy-faced, and awkward.

Graves stepped into the room behind me, sniffed audibly, and stopped dead. I could almost *feel* him stiffening, his shoulders hunching.

I understood completely. I just did *not* like her.

I found my voice. "Like a log. How about you?" *Or do you sleep in between knocking on people's doors?*

Her smile widened, pearly perfect teeth. When the *aspect* came over her she would have delicate little fangs. "Like a baby. I was just sitting here with darling Kir, hoping I could see you before you start orientation." That smile was absolutely perfect, and it was kind of like looking at Christophe. I wanted to check for loose threads and stand up straight.

Except Christophe would never look at me like this. Not even the first moment I met him, when he drove Ash away and told me to go home. I'd thought he was a sucker then, and he didn't scare me half as bad as this.

And that's saying something.

How weird was it that this blonde bit of cheerleader was more terrifying than a gruesome death by sucker? It just goes to show my priorities were all whacked-out. It might've been all the excitement lately.

She scared me because I've seen her type all over the country. And if you're not scared when they grin at you, or when they act friendly, you haven't been paying attention and you deserve everything you get. Still, some of them are okay, just thoughtless and irritating without any real malice.

My jury was out on Anna's malice level. But I'm cautious when it comes to things like that. I learned really quick that Dad didn't understand girl cruelty. He understood when I got into fights, but if I came home sobbing after a run-in with a *girl*, where only words were exchanged . . . well, he didn't get it.

Anna's baby-blue gaze swung over, settling above my left shoulder. "And that must be Mr. Graves. My, aren't you the handsome one? If I had a space free on my Guard, I might almost break with tradition and offer you a Trial challenge."

Trial challenge? What? Probably some *djamphir* thing. I could ask Benjamin. Or Leon.

Just as soon as I got out of here.

Kir stiffened. He'd looked handsome in the Council room, but he was pale and his skin gleamed slightly. Was he sweating? That was weird.

I heard cloth moving—Graves was *still* in his long black coat—and the crinkle of paper and cellophane. Then, my God, the click of a lighter and a long inhale.

He was *smoking*. "That's assuming," he said quietly, "that I'd take it."

Kir's hands hit the tabletop, and he made as if to push himself up. The *aspect* folded over him, fangs sliding free and golden streaks spilling through his short hair, and I braced myself. I actually drew myself up as tall as I would go and stared at him.

There was no way I could match a *djamphir* past his drift, let alone one old and powerful enough to be on the Council. Still, I heard Dad's voice, way back from the time before my whole life had turned upside down. *This is where you do the starin' down, before the throwin' down, honey.*

Dogs can smell fear, and people—or things from the Real World—are pretty much the same way. Predators have finely tuned antennae for terror. But ninety-nine times out of a hundred, a dog can also smell when you're the alpha. It takes the same kind of flat look and decision to be fearless as facing down a bunch of jocks bent on harassing someone.

I just hoped I was giving Kir the staredown, and not an exhausted, *oh my God* look.

Anna eyed Kir for a long, taffy-stretching second. She made a soft, sliding motion with one hand, the lacquer on her nails glinting. "Oh, Kir. Relax. Mr. Graves has a sarcastic sense of humor. It's something to appreciate in a man. Boy humor is *so* juvenile."

The redheaded *djamphir*'s face scrunched up like he smelled something *really* bad. I caught Anna's flash of a smirk before she looked directly past me at Graves. I've seen cheerleaders look at boys that way before.

It meant they were marking their next cut of prime rib. My heart gave a sick thump. If Graves wasn't interested in me—or was only kind of interested—maybe he'd be interested in a girl who looked like a fashion model. No matter that she'd chew him up and spit him out. That kind always does.

Gee, Dru, you think you're judging her by what she wears much? I couldn't stop thinking that maybe I was just judging her because I did *not* like her way down in my bones. It wasn't fair.

"It wasn't sarcasm." Graves blew out a cloud of acrid smoke. "It was pointing out a fallacy in your logic, babe."

Anna's jaw actually dropped. For a moment, I wasn't sure if I should laugh or push him out of the room. *Way to go, Graves.*

"I must be late." A pleasant tenor, behind me. Hiro slid into the room, his footfalls eerily silent against the plush carpet. "Kir. Milady."

His lip all but curled, sarcasm dripping from the word. Then he half-turned and looked at me. When he spoke again, it was a respectful murmur. "Milady."

How he could say the same word so differently each time was beyond me. He bent forward slightly, a tiny bow, and I did the same thing before I could help myself. Hey, man, when in Rome, right?

He smiled as he straightened. "Exquisite manners, young one. I regret my lateness. Forgive me."

I was about to say *no problem*, but Kir almost choked. Anna's face was smooth and smiling too, but something glittered far back in the depths of her eyes. Her boots hit the carpet and she rose gracefully from the chair, silk whispering as her dress fell in choreographed folds. The table held her reflection lovingly, but distorted it oddly as she moved. She passed behind Kir's chair, and I could swear the slim redheaded young man flinched as her shadow drifted over him.

She came to a halt at the end of the table, and I squared my shoulders as we sized each other up. The taste of waxen oranges faded, and I smelled her warm spicy perfume.

Her baby blues dropped to my feet, came back up. Measuring me all the while. When she spoke, it was as if we were the only people in the room. "I'd like it if we were friends, Dru."

"Me too," I lied, with feeling. If they think you're stupid enough to be taken in, you can get enough running room for escape.

Always let your enemies underestimate you. Dad taught me that. I wasn't sure if she was an enemy or just one of those antimatter girls. She was another *djamphir* and a *svetocha* to boot. She was in just as much danger from the suckers as I was. We should stick together, at least as far as we could while being on different ends of the social spectrum.

My chest hurt. I realized I was holding my breath, and exhaled.

The *touch* throbbed inside my head, but everything in the room was so tense and mixed-up I couldn't tell where the current of . . . what was it? Fear? Bloodhunger? Rage? But nobody looked even remotely upset in here. Just uncomfortable. Kir's face had gone pasty. His freckles stood out, glaring.

I thought of the flash of red I'd seen down the hall. Benjamin had thought it was a *svetocha*, and I'd been sure it was Anna, but both she and Christophe smelled like spice.

Would Christophe be messing at my door, though? Or maybe it had been the traitor. A *djamphir* I'd never seen, but who smelled like them?

"Good." She held out one slim white hand, her nails perfectly manicured and coated in candy-apple lacquer. It matched her lipstick, and her eyeliner looked professionally done.

I could never in a million years have that high gloss. As soon as I put my hand out and touched hers, bracing myself for whatever the *touch* would tell me, I felt dirty. Like I'd just come in off the playground, covered in muck, and was now standing in the middle of the adults while I hoped they wouldn't notice the smudges and scrapes.

The *touch* rang like a gong inside my head. Whirling images, none of them pausing long enough to be absorbed. She gave my hand one limp shake, then drew back with a patient smile. That smile, by the way, was directed up over my shoulder.

At Graves.

The back of my throat turned rough and dry. I made a sort of *hrmph* noise, clearing it, and Anna glanced at me again, this time amused. *Don't you look at him that way*, I wanted to say—and I probably would have, if I hadn't had to keep my mouth shut.

Because my teeth were tingling. I felt the subtle crackling in my upper jaw as my canines extended.

Call them fangs, Dru. That's what they are.

But I couldn't. I could just stand there, keeping my mouth closed tight so nobody around me would see teeth turning into sharp little points. The warm-oil feeling of the *aspect* didn't slide down my skin, though. I hoped my hair wasn't doing anything weird, decided it didn't matter. Because nobody was looking at me. Every eye in the room, including my own pair, was on Anna.

She swept by, sliding past motionless Hiro with a half-mocking little pirouette, her skirt brushing his knee. I heard her murmur something at the door. Footsteps going away—probably she and the *djamphir* in the shoulder holster and red T-shirt.

Did he put that on to match her? Jeez. And I thought "I'm with Stupid" shirts were pathetic. I breathed deeply, searching for calm.

The crackling in the air went away. Now all the *touch* could bring me was a complex, hot wash of feeling from Kir. I couldn't even name it, it was so messed up. He coughed and pushed himself up from his chair. "So."

"Orientation." Hiro folded his arms. "I think it's best I tag along. You don't have any *objection*, do you, Kir?"

The redheaded *djamphir* smiled. It was an animal's baring of teeth, and I almost took a step back. "Of course not, *brother*."

Whoa, wait a second. "You're related?" I blurted out, and I sounded totally horrified. Graves exhaled another long stream of cigarette smoke. It touched my hair, and I made a face, too.

"No." Kir's face wrinkled up again, like he tasted something sour. "It is the traditional mode of address between Kouroi. To remind us that we are all—"

"—connected," Hiro interrupted smoothly. "And all equally at risk of being murdered by *nosferatu*. Some do tend to forget it."

"No shit," I muttered and stuffed my sweating hands in my pockets.

I suddenly resolved never to be in a room alone with Kir if I could help it. "Can I just go look around on my own?"

"You may if you wish. But the *loup-garou* may not, and before you attend classes you will have to endure orientation in our company." Hiro folded his arms, as if I was Being Difficult. "Milady." This time he said it like the syllables meant *please*.

I wanted to figure out how he did that.

"It was a rhetorical question. So what's first?" I rubbed my palms, trying to get the dampness off, and decided he wasn't so bad. Graves muttered something uncomplimentary, but very softly, and mixed with the smoke besides.

"First, we allow Mr. Graves to extinguish his cigarette." Hiro didn't even blink. "Then we will go over safety rules and take a tour of the school."

"Great." I tried to sound excited, failed miserably. And the whole time, I knew Kir was watching me.

I could *feel* it.

CHAPTER TEN

"**We should go** to Nordstroms," Benjamin muttered for the fiftieth time. Leon's mouth actually twitched, like he was holding back a smile. The two blonds were out in the parking lot on a gorgeous spring afternoon, probably both sleepily leaning against the SUV Benjamin had signed out at the parking garage in the south corner of the Schola's property.

That was eye-opening, the way Benjamin had just casually said, *It's for the* svetocha, and the dark-haired *djamphir* with the sign-out sheet had stared at me like I had something stuck on my face before he fell all over himself pointing out different cars. Being sandwiched in the back of an Escalade full of pretty *djamphir* boys and Graves was a new experience, too.

I rolled my eyes. "There's nothing at a Nordstroms I need or want. Overpriced junk that'll fall apart." I folded up another pair of jeans and stuck them in the red cart. Even under fluorescents the *djamphir* boys looked like models gone slumming. It was hard to pick stuff out with them hanging around looking gorgeous and bored.

When Benjamin said *shopping* he meant Nordstroms at the very *least*. I guess he had some weird idea I wanted couture or something.

When I say *shopping*, especially for clothes, I mean military surplus first, and Target or Dillard's to get soft goods. Like, say, panties and stuff. I'd already made the boys go away while I poked around in the lingerie section. I mean, come *on*. I've been buying my panties alone since I was nine.

I'm used to this. Dad would just give me plenty of cash and a list. I've been doing our shopping, other than ordnance, for as long as I can remember. Dad had enough to do just buying ammo and stuff; I took care of clothes, food, all the little things you need when traveling, or to make a house run. I used to love dawdling in the appliances section at Target no matter where in the country we were. I would make up little stories in my head about how we really needed a bread maker or a Foreman grill. Or an espresso machine. I would compare, contrast, and pretend we weren't moving in a couple of months anyway so why bother with more weight to lug around?

I saw a display of T-shirts that looked okay and headed for them. Graves had taken over pushing the cart, and he was wearing an expression you usually only see when someone in court is sentenced to a long haul. Of course, we'd shopped for him first, and I figured that since he was a guy he wouldn't have as much embarrassment over buying underwear. I'd just told him to go and get a couple packets of whatever he was wearing now. Benjamin looked like he'd swallowed a frog, and I'd given the *djamphir* one of my best glares, an imitation of Gran's *shut-yer-mouth* look. He subsided and muttered something about Macy's. Followed by *Neiman Marcus, please, even that would be better*, under his breath.

I figured if Benjamin wouldn't pay for it with the Order-approved cards, I'd use the roll of emergency cash in my bag to cover it. It wasn't quite an emergency, but Jesus. I wasn't going to have Graves wearing all the same stuff while I was kitted out.

"So where does the money come from, anyway?" I stopped in front of the display and started going through the checklist. V-neck, short sleeves, not bad. I hate fabric crawling up on my neck. All-cotton, good, get them kind of bigger because they'll shrink. A yawn caught me off-guard, I kept it behind a cupped hand. They had four black tees in medium. I grabbed them all and set them in the cart.

"There's plenty." Out of all of them, Leon looked the closest to human under the fluorescents. He was looking at a display of spring dresses, polka-dotted things that would be completely useless if you were running away from something. "Is this what girls wear now?"

"Not this girl," I muttered. "Seriously, where does the money come from? Come on, I want to look at clearance."

"Why?" Benjamin sounded honestly baffled. "A *svetocha* can have anything she wants, Dru; we have plenty of money. The Order invests and has several corporations."

Now that was interesting. Where there was corporation and stock, there were paper trails. At least, you could find out some stuff with public records and other stuff by hack and by crook. I filed that away. "Just because you have money doesn't mean you have to waste it. Target's good enough. And what about a *svetocha* getting what she wants? I thought Anna was supposed to be a big secret." I halted near the clearance racks and started digging. It was a good time to get hoodies because when spring comes they clear out just about everything to make way for the bikini-fest in early summer.

I shuddered at *that* thought.

"She's a secret—from the *nosferatu*. She doesn't mix much with the general population. Busy running the Order and . . . well, it's best to stay out of her way. Out of the way of anyone on the Council, really. They don't get there by being decorative." Benjamin looked even more uncomfortable. "You're actually the first *svetocha* I've personally been in a room with. But it's in all the basic classes—all about *svetocha*, and how they're . . . well, they get everything they want."

"Huh." *Even though there aren't a lot.* I absorbed this. "So I could go shopping anywhere I wanted?" Getting some ammo might actually be a good idea.

"I, um. Yes. You really . . . anywhere, I guess." Benjamin sounded like he was reconsidering telling me about this. Or faintly hopeful that I'd suddenly decide Nordstroms was a good idea.

"Cheer up, old man." Leon actually chuckled and clapped him on the shoulder. "It could be worse. She could be in the dressing room for hours."

With you guys watching everything? No thanks. I know my sizes, that's enough. I decided to test out this *anything* rule. "Okay, so I need a military surplus store, too. Do you guys know what the gun laws are like here?"

"Fingerprinting and licensing. But it boils down to, *Don't get caught if you're in the Order.*" Leon gave me one of his odd little looks. "We can go to the armory, if you like. You can practice."

I shook my head. Found a charcoal hoodie with a zipper and good sleeves, checked it for loose threads. "Just wondering. Hey, Graves, you want to go get shampoo, toothpaste, that sort of thing? And if you need any over-the-counter stuff, you know. Get me some Midol, all right?"

Benjamin all but choked. Leon studied the ceiling with a great deal of interest, a smile twitching at the corners of his thin mouth. While Benjamin looked ready to sink into the floor, Leon looked highly amused.

I decided I liked him.

"I think you should pick your own Midol." Graves even said it with a straight face, but there was a ghost of a grin quirking his lips. He'd found a way to shave, and he looked attractive but normal. Not ultra-gloss like the *djamphir*. "'Cause, you know, there's different types."

"Point." My stomach rumbled. "We should probably go back soon. Is the cafeteria open during the day?"

"Well, yeah. We can get a midnight snack. Midday snack. Same thing." Benjamin's cheeks were scarlet. "Don't you want to do more shopping?"

I surveyed the overloaded cart. Jeans for Graves and me, T-shirts and long-sleeved shirts for him, short-sleeved T-shirts for me, a couple of wool sweaters, sweats for both of us, two or three hoodies apiece, including the clearance-rack one I was holding. Boxers to sleep in. Packets of underwear, four sports bras. A belt for him, a belt for me. Along with everything I'd ordered online, this was really reasonable. The Schola was pretty stocked, but there were things like cotton balls and toner I wanted. And my own brand of shampoo. They had some expensive stuff in the shower. I felt like I was in a fancy-dancy hotel, using it.

Which wasn't bad. I totally love the little samples of stuff they put in the bathrooms at major hotels. Dad sometimes had us in really cushy places with nice high-end samples I stashed in the truck. I rated them according to effectiveness and smell, and I went through a phase when I was about thirteen of saving a bunch of them before I figured out there are always more hotels.

Sometimes I still think about that clutch of little trial bottles in a dark Dumpster somewhere. Like a rock collection or something.

I checked the price and decided what the hell, plopped the hoodie into the cart. "I think that's everything, after we make a run through the pharmacy section. Since Graves thinks I should pick my own Midol. Is there anything you guys need while we're here?"

Leon actually laughed. "They have slushies up at the front."

"Jesus Christ," Benjamin muttered. "Nordstroms. Macy's. We could go to Paris for the spring season. I was expecting transatlantic flights."

I figured ignoring that was best for all concerned. "Is there an Old Navy around here? They've got shorts and stuff." I caught the look Benjamin gave me. "What?"

"Nothing. We just thought a *svetocha* would be more, well, difficult." Leon's mouth twitched. "I *do* seriously want a slushie."

I tried a tentative smile. I definitely liked him now. "I haven't had one in ages. Maybe the guys outside—the double blonds—would want one, too?"

For some reason Leon found that utterly fricking hysterical. He snorted and chuckled all the way through Housewares to the Health and Beauty section, and even Benjamin unbent enough to grin.

* * *

We did stop in the Sports section for a sleeping bag, and I made Graves get a good one, too. Clothes are one thing, but you don't skimp on gear. I also dawdled in the office-supplies section until Graves threw a couple pads of paper and some pencils in the cart, glaring at me like he dared me to take them out.

Benjamin tried to take us to some Italian place for lunch, but Leon asked about Mexican food. And that sounded really good, so we ended up in some hole-in-the-wall place where I hogged a lot of tortilla chips and Benjamin got two margaritas by just smiling at the waitress and asking politely. He looked like he needed them at that point.

CHAPTER ELEVEN

First I was back in Target picking out wedding dresses. Yards of white lace and froth, while invisible people stood around and commented. "No, too small . . . too big . . . will never fit you . . . too classic, too tight . . ."

Until I felt like screaming because all I wanted was a dress that worked. Then I was trying to try them on and there was no dressing room because if I went in there I might disappear, so at the end of a row between clearance racks I was struggling into one dress after another, and they all had holes. Big, wide, moth-eaten holes, my bra and skin peeking through, and someone said, "You'll have to pay for that."

The walls of the store receded, smears of red paint streaking them and turning into long screaming faces. I felt the prickling buzz in my fingers and toes, like when your limbs go so numb you can't even walk.

I know that feeling. It comes with dreams that show me things. "True-seeins," Gran called them.

"Real nightmares" might be a better term.

For a moment I thought hazily that it might be the most horrible dream, the one where my mother picks me up out of my bed and takes me downstairs, tells me I'm her good girl, and tucks me in the hidey-hole in the closet. I struggled toward waking, but the dream had other ideas. It was in the driver's seat, not me. I couldn't fight it.

* * *

I lay on the bed, staring up at the ceiling. It was a regular popcorn ceiling, the kind with gold sparkles. Fluid shadows from the tree outside danced between the sparkles.

The dream-me was a little girl. She was sleepy, drifting in and out of that quiet space where kids suck their thumbs and their eyes stare without seeing from under heavy lids.

Mom had been anxious that day, cleaning everything. Tense, nervous. I was fractious, too, but she had read me stories and rocked me for a long time, then laid me in bed and covered me up. I heard her moving around the house downstairs, the regular noises of her fixing Dad's late-night lunch—because he was working long shifts at the base and sometimes came home for forty-five minutes or so in the middle of the night on his break—somehow missing. I heard a jingle as she dropped one of my toys. She was hurrying, putting them away. I heard her curse softly as she hid my high chair in the pantry.

But I didn't think about it. Instead I sucked my thumb and watched the ceiling.

Tap tap tap. A pause. Tap tap.

Someone at the front door. Not ringing the bell. That was strange.

Silence. The air itself seemed to be listening before I heard Mommy's footsteps, quick and light. She jerked the front door open, and voices drifted up the stairs.

Women's voices.

"What are you doing here?" Mom sounded . . . angry. And a little surprised, like she hadn't expected whoever it was. I could almost see her cocking her head a little, blue eyes turned cool and considering. She sometimes looked at people that way, especially when they wanted something out of her. Grocery store checkers or salesmen paled under that look, especially if they were trying what Dad called "funny business."

Your mom, he sometimes said, when he'd had some Jim Beam and could be coaxed to talk about the past. She didn't stand for no funny business.

"I came to visit. Such a charming little house." Tinkling laughter, and the rustle of silk skirts.

"You're not welcome here." Mommy's voice was sharp and angry, a warning all its own. "I left the Schola Prima, the entire Order, to you. What more do you want?"

The pretense of laughter left the other woman's voice. It dropped away like the mask it was, and when she spoke again her words crawled with nastiness and hurt. "Where is he?"

My mother's tone turned cold and businesslike. "What, my husband? He's human, what is he to you? You even come near him, and I'll—"

"Human? A human husband? You're kidding. Even you wouldn't sink so low."

A charged, crackling silence. I could tell just from the sound that Mom was furious. She was never angry; Dad called her sweet-tempered. He said he'd eat his goddamn hat if she ever said a mean word about anyone.

This was new and strange. I didn't like it. I closed my eyes and turned over, burrowed into my pillow. It was warm and safe up here in my bed, even if the wind fingered the sides of the house with a hungry whispering sound.

"Oh." Sudden comprehension. I heard my mother move, a drawer opening. "He's left, then. He always said he would."

"You know where he is." Sharp and accusing. "You know. He'd run to you."

"He's not here."

"Maybe I should look around and make sure."

The drawer closed with a bang. There was a heavy metallic click. "Anna." The tone of warning was new, too. It prickled through me just like the buzzing static did. Child-me moved restlessly again, kicking at my covers. "Get. Out. Of. My. House. Or I will kill you."

"You're not a good hostess." But was that fear in the other woman's tone? Camouflaged, but still quivering and raw. Of course, if Mommy talked to me like that I'd cry. I was glad she never had. "Swear to me he's not here!"

"I'm not swearing a single goddamn thing to you. Get out of my house. Or I will shoot you and the Order will need a new head bitch."

"If you see him . . ." But the woman stopped, her whine trailing off. I didn't like her voice. It hurt me. My head was full of bad images, mud and blood and sharp teeth, and the only thing that kept me from whimpering was a sudden thickening in the air around me. I was so tired, and if I made a noise, Mommy might come upstairs and talk to me in that cold, angry voice.

And I didn't want that. I would never want that.

"If I see him, I'll tell him you're looking for him. I can't imagine it will make much difference. He does what he wants."

"Oh, I know that." Bitterness now, and I could hear the front door creaking as it ghosted wide open. They hadn't even shut it during this entire conversation. "If I find out you're hiding him here, Elizabeth—"

"I have a life. One that doesn't include him or you and your petty little games. Don't darken my doorstep again."

"Sleep well, then." A smirk even I could hear, upstairs in my room. "Don't let the nosferatu bite." A cruel, chilling little laugh, and the front door slammed.

I heard my mother let out a shaky breath. And the buzzing was back, rattling in my head, running through my bones. I knew what came next.

Next I would fall asleep. And when I woke up in the dark, I knew what would happen. It will be that dream again, the worst of all dreams.

Then the buzzing pours through me, and the prickling like steel needles in my flesh. I struggle against the dream. I don't want to remember this. I never want to remember this, and each time is more painful because I know—

She is leaning over my crib, her face bigger than the moon and more beautiful than sunlight, or maybe it's just that way because I'm so young. Her hair tumbles down in glossy ringlets, smelling of her special shampoo, and the silver locket at her throat glimmers.

But there is a shadow in her pretty eyes; it matches the darkness over the left half of her face. It's like the shadow of rain seen through a window, light broken in rivulets.

"Dru," she says softly but urgently. "Get up."

I rub my eyes and yawn. "Mommy?" My voice is muffled. Sometimes it's the voice of a five-year-old; sometimes it's older. But always, it's wondering and quiet, sleepy.

"Come on, Dru." She puts her hands down and picks me up, with a slight oof! as if she can't believe how much I've grown. I'm a big girl now, and I don't need her to carry me, but I don't protest. I cuddle into her warmth and feel the hummingbird beat of her heart. "I love you, baby," she whispers into my hair. She smells of fresh cookies and warm perfume, and it is here the dream starts to fray. Because I hear something like footsteps, or a pulse. It is quiet at first, but it gets louder and more rapid with each beat. "I love you so much."

"Mommy . . ." I put my head on her shoulder. I know I am heavy, but she is carrying me, and when she sets me down to open a door I protest only a little.

It is the closet downstairs. Just how I know it's downstairs I'm not sure. There is something in the floor she pulls up, and some of my stuffed animals have been jammed into the square hole, along with blankets and a pillow from her and Daddy's bed. She scoops me up again and settles me in the hole, and I begin to feel a faint alarm. "Mommy?"

"We're going to play the game, Dru. You hide here and wait for Daddy to come home from work."

I know what will happen. Daddy will come home and find me, but things will never be the same.

Because that was the night Sergej came, the night he killed her, but he did not find me.

And it is all my fault.

The dream turns to rotting cheesecloth veils, strangling me. Wrapping around wrist and ankle and hip with clammy-cold touch and I struggle up, screaming, desperate for air. I don't want to see, I don't want to see—

"—don't want to see stop it I don't want to see!" I fought, blindly, screaming and sweating and shaking. Struck out with fists and feet, starfishing. Hit nothing but empty air.

"It's just a dream!" Graves said urgently. "Just a dream!"

No, it's not, I wanted to scream. It's real. It happened; it keeps happening.

Someone was pounding at the door. I choked, stared up at Graves. Blinked furiously. I must've been crying in my sleep; my cheeks were wet and my nose was full. The scream died in my throat. I gulped in a breath. My T-shirt was twisted all around, and my new boxers were all bunched up, too. They get that way when you thrash.

Dusk was filling the window with purple. It was my first day of actual classes. And someone was hammering at the door, yelling my name.

"Dru." Graves had my shoulders. "It's just a dream, okay? Okay? You're here, I'm here, everything's okay. You're safe, I promise."

I wiped at my cheeks with shaking hands. It was Benjamin at the door. "Oh," I whispered. "Jesus. I . . . I'm sorry."

"It's okay." Green eyes burning, Graves was almost nose-to-nose with me. I could see the fine golden threads in his irises, and a little crusty from sleep caught in his right eye. It was enough to make me cry with relief, because he was safe and real. His sleeping bag lay wadded up on the floor. "You were moving around a lot, and then you started screaming. Really yelling, like you were . . ."

"Sorry." My heart pounded, I sniffed cry-snot back up. The door was actually shivering against the bar. "That's Benjamin."

"I better let him in. Guess we're going to class." But he still held my shoulders, his long callused fingers gentle. As if he had all the time in the world to half-kneel on my bed and study my face. His T-shirt had a hole in one shoulder, and it made my chest feel kind of weird to see that. "You okay?"

I grabbed myself with both hands, as Gran would say, and nodded. "I think . . . yeah. Sorry. That was . . . pretty intense."

"Okay. I'll deal with Benjamin. You're safe, okay? Nothing's gonna happen." His mouth pulled tight against itself. And now I was having some sort of heart attack. Because when he looked at me like that, my chest started to feel like it was turned inside out. "Promise."

And that—the promise, the way he said it with utter certainty— was enough to make me tear up again. He let go of me and stalked for the door, skinny kid in boxers and a holey T-shirt. His legs had bulked up, too. He wasn't so bird-thin as he was back in the Dakotas. And he was starting to move like the werwulfen, graceful and assured.

I clutched the blankets to my chest and shut my eyes again. Heard him taking the bar off its brackets. "Calm down!" he yelled. "She's okay! Bad dream! It was just a bad dream."

Except they're never *just* bad dreams. But I had other things to occupy my mind. I was grateful, and my eyes snapped open. I fought my way out of the tangled covers and bolted for the bathroom. I didn't want anyone to see me like this, and I wanted to start getting ready to face the day. Night. Whatever.

But most of all, I didn't want to think about what I'd just dreamed. I would do my best to forget it, I decided. It was already fading, retreating quietly into the space where dreams live while you're walking in daylight.

I should have known it wouldn't be that simple.

CHAPTER TWELVE

Two weeks later, dusk fell in purple bands across the city and the Schola Prima woke up. Here there was no bell for wake-up or between class periods. There wasn't even a Restriction bell. I was nervous about what would happen if the suckers attacked, but Benjamin said it didn't happen often.

Not like the reform Schola. And that was just the beginning of the differences. All in all, I liked this place better.

Sort of.

Graves shrugged back into his long black coat, ran his fingers through his hair again. It stood up in wild, vital springing curls, and he grimaced as he ripped through a tangle. He shoved his rolled-up sleeping bag up next to the bed. "Come *on*, you're going to be late."

"Shit." I hurriedly wrote down the last two answers, slammed the book shut, and scooped it into my bag. Grabbed a piece of toast and a new red hoodie and was heading for the door when there was a rattling series of knocks. Graves swept the door open and Shanks poked his head in. He was on duty for the last hour before classes in the morning, and Benjamin seemed okay with a werwulf hanging out at my door so everyone could get ready for the night.

"Jesus," the wulf said, swiping at the emo-swoosh of dark hair across his forehead. It was a popular style this year. "Are you going to be late *every day*?"

"Hey, Bobby. Girl just can't get out the door on time." Graves sounded relieved.

It's not my fault. "Shut up." I hitched the new brown canvas messenger bag up on my shoulder and tried to stuff all the toast in my mouth at once. Graves and I piled out the door, Shanks gracefully avoiding me. He has the longest legs I've ever seen on a boy and moves with a kind of halting lope, waiting for the rest of the world to catch up to him.

Dibs was in the hallway, his golden hair disarranged. He looked like one of those cherubs you see painted on old-lady plates. All cheeks and curls. "Hi, Dru," he mouthed, and immediately blushed and looked down.

Benjamin appeared out of thin air, handing me a sheaf of paper in a plastic report binder. "I got your paper printed. Leon will be with you until lunch; the others and I have a combat practical this morning. Have you eaten?"

I swallowed a huge mass of toast and almost choked, got it all down and nodded. Leon stepped out the room next to mine and swept the door shut. He was carrying—oh, thank God—two paper cups that stood a good chance of being coffee.

"I did." I took the report binder, thought about jamming it in my bag, and decided just to carry it. "Jeez, thanks. You didn't have to do that."

"My pleasure." He grinned, and for a moment he looked very young. His dark eyes sparkled. "I'll bring your Para Bio and chem books to lunch, okay? And George'll get your gym bag before afternoon sparring."

"You're a lifesaver." For once, I didn't think about the irony of saying it to a *djamphir*. "Go on, go. I'll be fine. I'll just make it to class."

"Not if you don't hurry up, you won't." Graves grabbed my arm and pulled. He already had a cigarette lit. "See ya, Benjy."

Oh, for Christ's sake. But Leon was already there, subtracting my hoodie and report, handing over the coffee, and giving my bag a hard look. I hitched it up higher on my shoulder and hurried to keep up with Graves. "Thanks."

"*Nichts zu danken.*" Leon looked about ready to grab at my bag again. But Graves didn't let go of me, and I kept a firm grip on it.

That was one of the weirdest things about the Schola—being expected *not* to carry anything. And another weird thing? Not a single vampire attack since I'd got here. Three whole weeks. I'd gotten so used to one every couple of days, it was like a vacation.

A vacation where I was actually going to classes and learning about the Real World, that is. And getting *some* sleep because Ash was up like clockwork between 4:00 and 5:00 a.m., just the time when everyone was winding down and going to bed. That took up all the time that I'd normally use for homework, which meant a couple hours of slogging after dawn and then falling into bed while Graves half-snored in the sleeping bag on the floor. We went round and round over working out some schedule for sharing the bed or getting a camp cot in here, but he was stubborn. *Like it this way. Good for my back. Go do your chem homework.*

I suspected it was because he thought anything coming in the door would have to walk over him to get to the bed. But how could I ask him about that?

We didn't talk about anything I really wanted to know. He kept his distance, at least an arm's length away at all times. I was beginning to seriously think kissing him was a dream. God knew the Technicolor nightmares were popping up every night, though I'd stopped waking up screaming.

I hadn't seen hide or hair of Anna. The Council "requested" my presence every two or three days, an uncomfortable hour of not-so-small talk where they went over everything about me. Where Dad and I had gone. What I remembered about Mom. Everything Christophe had ever said to me.

Kir stared at me through the whole thing.

They didn't ask me about Anna showing up at the other Schola, and I didn't say anything. I figured it was the safest course. Besides, I was too busy to worry about her right now. She didn't take classes; she was fully trained and fully bloomed. She was occupied with running the Order, and I guess that made for a lot of paperwork. I gathered she was a world traveler, always jetting off somewhere. Paris for the spring season, London when she wanted a change of pace, Fiji when it got too cold, Russia when she wanted something exotic. Plus, I guess, if she moved around a lot the suckers had less chance of finding her.

When and if she showed up again, I'd figure something out.

The windows were full of the syrupy gold of sunset, white marble and greenery both glowing outside. It was actually really pretty, and as soon as we got down the stairs and took a sharp right, we were in a long gallery with windows all along one side. The sun lit up Dibs's hair, gilded Shanks's perfect skin and white teeth, and fired in Graves's eyes. Me, I just blinked and tried not to look half-asleep—and tried as well not to choke on huge gulps of banana latte.

Hey, don't knock it until you've tried it. Banana latte is *awesome*.

The end of the gallery was a big set of double doors, and I inhaled sharply just like I did every evening before Leon swept the door open and glanced out. He nodded, and it was only then that Graves eased up on my arm and we all got through the doors and into a crowded hall full of boys.

Attending a Schola is like walking into a sea of extras from toothpaste commercials and sitcoms. The wulfen are taller and the *djamphir* are built slighter. They're in every conceivable human shade. Wulfen tend to be more brunet, *djamphir* to have more extreme hair colors—not just blond but platinum or gold, not just dark-haired but raven or sandalwood. The skin colors are even and beautiful, not a pimple or discoloration to be found. The eyes are glowing or gemlike, and *djamphir* have sharper facial features. Plus, they move differently. Wulfen move like they're shouldering fluidly through long grass, and boy *djamphir* move with an eerie natural grace. It's not so noticeable if you're just looking at one, but a crowd of them? The wrongness just explodes all over the inside of your brain and tickles that little instinctive spot on the back of your neck. The one that tells you something is dangerous.

Or that could just be me. Because as usual, the moment I stepped out into the hall, they were looking at me.

I guess I'd be curious about the only boy in an all-girls school. It's just, you know, being the only girl in an all-boys school was different. Because it was me being stared at. After practicing invisibility as an art form in school halls all over the U.S., this was new and unwelcome.

Antique metal lockers stood at attention between classroom doors, and the sounds of slamming lockers and drumming feet, as well as the occasional catcall, didn't penetrate the bubble of whispering around me. I put my head down, as usual, and let my shower-damp hair slide forward, curtaining me. Dibs drew closer on my left, and Graves held his chin up, a bounce in his step and his earring swinging. He didn't seem to mind the whispers *or* the looks.

Course, he probably got a fair share of both as a goth boy in a Dakota town. Stands to reason he'd have a good front to show the world. Sometimes he even reached down and took my hand, fingers slipping through mine. It was a touch I was both grateful for and confused by.

But not today. Today I went it alone.

I got another gulp of coffee down, inhaled at the wrong time, and almost sprayed it all over the floor. Being stared at will do that — make you clumsy.

"You okay?" Graves sounded worried.

"I got all my homework done." My nose stung from coffee. I stared at my sneakers on the hardwood. One step, two steps, three steps. Leon cut traffic so I didn't have to worry about running into anyone. "I think . . ."

I really think he's going to change back, I almost said, but shut my mouth. It wasn't the sort of thing to talk about in a hallway. Especially since anything I said would fall into a big rippling pond of quiet.

Each night Ash struggled, bones cracking, to change. And each night I thought he might really do it. Benjamin said he wouldn't. Shanks shrugged. Graves said nothing, and Dibs wouldn't even go near the hall that housed Ash's room. He turned an interesting shade of white every time it was even mentioned.

I almost ran into Leon when he stopped. "Last stop, Grand Central, everyone out," he said with one of his crooked little smiles. Seen in sunlight, his mousy hair took on threads of gold, brown, and ash-blond and was fine instead of lank. He had a sharply handsome face, and I was still trying to figure out how he did the fade-into-the-background thing. It didn't seem natural.

"I'll see you at lunch." Graves took another puff off his cancer-stick. "We'll do Para Bio together. It'll be fun."

I rolled my eyes. "You bet. Bye, guys. Thanks."

"*Ciao*, Dru-girl. Don't forget, Saturday we're doing a run in the park. Graves'll bring you." Shanks waved, slung an arm over Dibs's shoulders. "C'mon, boyo. Race you to Red Wing."

"I won't forget." It was the third time he'd reminded me. But he was already gone. Just like that, heading for the wing where wulfen had their classes. The hall was emptying rapidly, no few of the boys sneaking glances at me. I waited, expectant.

Graves gave me a once-over, green eyes glowing. Apparently satisfied, he leaned in and pressed his lips to my cheek. A quick peck, then he straightened, turned on his heel, and walked off very quickly.

It was the same thing every day. As a public display of affection, it kind of left a little to be desired. Maybe he was taking it slow because of everything going on, or maybe he just . . . I don't know.

Leon made a short, suppressed sound. The door squeaked a little as he leaned back, pulling it open and glancing inside. He waved a slim languid hand at me. "After you, Milady."

God, I wish you wouldn't call me that. But I just hitched my bag higher on my shoulder and stamped past him. It was hard to have a satisfying snit on when you were just wearing sneakers, but I tried.

Since I was a few minutes behind, everyone was already there. Even the teacher, Beaufort, a tall thin late-blooming *djamphir* in a faded blue-velvet jacket and striped hipster trousers.

Late drifters—they call puberty for *djamphir* boys "hitting the drift"—look like they're in their mid twenties instead of solidly teenage. They also have something . . . I can't quite explain it. A shadow around the eyes, or the occasional quick flicking restless movement as if they're in pain. Augustine had done that too. At the time I'd just thought he was weird. A lot of human hunters have tics. Like Juan-Raoul de la Hoya-Smith, another one of Dad's old friends. He hunts chupacabras and other stuff down Tijuana way. He also spits on the floor every time someone says something unlucky, and his idea of luck is . . . weird.

A ring around the moon? Bad luck. Hat on the bed? Major bad luck. Seeing a squirrel first thing in the morning? Good luck. Canadian geese? Good luck. But seagulls? Bad luck. He calls them "rats with wings." But he loves pigeons. Go figure.

Beaufort made an odd movement, as if he wanted to bow and stopped himself just in time, straightening and pulling his cuffs down. Under the blue velvet, the teacher's shirt was frilly and weird. It looked like threadbare silk. "Ah, hello. Hello."

A rustling movement went through the boy *djamphir*. None of them had sat down yet; the sofas and easy chairs arranged in a double circle around the teacher all stood empty. And all of them were looking at me.

This never got any easier.

I picked a sofa in the second row and dropped down. Leon stood behind me, a silent reminder. I knew without looking that his hands were crossed, resting comfortably, and his head dipped forward a bit so his eyes were lost behind a thin screen of fine hair.

He seemed to make just about everyone uncomfortable.

They all sank gracefully down into their chosen seats. The other half of my sofa stayed empty. Just like always.

It was like having the plague.

The teacher cleared his throat. "Pass in your papers, please."

I leaned forward. The kid who usually sat in front of me—hair the color of butterscotch and a fondness for really expensive silk button-downs in jewel tones—glanced back, took the plastic report binder I held out, and blushed bright crimson.

I tried not to sigh. Slid a yellow legal pad and a couple of pencils out of my bag, settled down, and waited. A sketch filled the edges of the piece of paper on top: blocks of masonry, grass shaded in at the bottom, and a huge empty space in the middle.

I could never seem to draw the middle. So all my notes were decorated with this odd churchlike ruin, hovering like a bad dream.

As usual, once he didn't have to look directly at me, Beaufort seemed okay. "Very good, very good. Now, we left off with the first real attempt the *nosferat* made at domination of the civilized world, in 1200 BC. There are garbled legends of this time, mostly concerning the Sea People, though most of the archaeological evidence is spotty at best. So how do we separate fact from fiction?"

"Oral tradition," a blond *djamphir* in the front row said. "Then cross-checking against the archaeological record and extrapolation from what we know of *nosferat* behavior."

The teacher nodded. "Our oral tradition is very precise, specific, and unapologetic on one point. Once, the *wampyr* could move by day. Once, the sun was not a bar to them. They were *weakened*, certainly, by its presence—but it was not the deterrent it is today. So what happened?"

Silence. I glanced back over my notes. Nothing that might answer the question. Of course, I didn't ever raise my hand—but I liked knowing before he called on someone else. Beaufort liked to give everyone time to digest and come up with something, too. He wasn't one of those teachers who delights in catching kids out.

That was one thing I was getting used to here at the Schola. The grading was fierce and the teachers were smart, but they weren't trying to play petty power games. At least not in the classrooms.

The answer surprised all of us. It came from over my right shoulder, and it was a sibilant hiss threading through the quiet of a thinking classroom.

"*Scarabus*." Leon shifted his weight slightly; I almost felt the movement through the couch. "He rose from the sands and walked among them, killing where he chose."

"I see *someone* here has done his required reading. However, Leontus, you are not a first-year student."

Silence again. Leon exhaled, a slight but definite snicker.

I liked him more and more.

"I've heard of that," the blond in the front row finally said. "Scarabus. Thought he was a myth."

The teacher cocked his head. "Oh, he was definitely not a myth. If we Kouroi are said to survive as a species today, it is due to him. His name is lost, but the *wampyr* called him Scarabus. He was *ephialtes*." Beaufort's face puckered up like he'd gotten a mouthful of sour candy against rotting teeth.

I wrote that down, spelling it as best I could. The teacher paused. "Anyone?"

"Greek name," a redheaded *djamphir* off to my left supplied. "Right?"

"It means *traitor*. The term did not originate until hundreds of years after Scarabus, but it is accepted usage now. He was a *djamphir* who specialized in one thing: killing his own kind for his *wampyr* masters. Some few of our kind were allowed to live and hunt their brethren for sport, and also to keep us from banding together and taking on the fiends whose blood we bore."

He's getting really into it. Sometimes this guy got a little too into the history, talking about it as if he was there. I guess you never can tell among a bunch of *djamphir*. And to be honest, this was fascinating.

Beaufort rested a fingertip against his pursed lips. He turned in a complete circle, his blue eyes passing over us all and threads of darkness sliding through his hair. The *aspect* passed through him, his fangs sliding out and dimpling his lower lip. The fangs retreated, his hair returned to normal, and I let out a soft breath, notepaper crumpling under my left hand before I eased my fingers out of the fist.

I didn't think I'd ever get used to the *aspect* passing through a *djamphir*. It's the part we get from the suckers. The part that makes us stronger, faster . . .

. . . and thirsty for the red stuff in the vein.

You don't get used to that. Not easily, and not soon.

"Many *djamphir* have been *ephialtes* in their time," Beaufort said softly. "Even the best of us. Raised to hunt our own kind, we know nothing else. It is the original question of nature versus nurture."

Christophe did that. Hunted other djamphir. A chill moved down my back. After all, he was Sergej's son. They told me Augustine had brought him in, and my mother was the reason he stayed in the Order.

Except Christophe had told me something else.

If I need a reason now, Dru, it will have to be you.

Talk about an uncomfortable thought. The fang marks on my wrist throbbed a little, but I ignored the feeling. I was getting good at ignoring stuff. If there was an Olympics I'd probably qualify. I'd go for the gold.

"After a certain amount of time, every *ephialtes* will question why he is killing his brothers. And what will eventually happen to him once his masters tire of him, no matter how useful he is. Scarabus questioned, and he turned against them. Normally he would have been hunted down by every *ephialtes* and *wampyr* his masters could induce to do such a thing. But Scarabus had an advantage."

Leon stirred restlessly behind me.

Beaufort finished his last slow turn, and his eyes settled on me. "He had a sister."

A ripple went through the room. A few of the boys, unable to help themselves, actually glanced at me and away quickly.

Great. I sank back into the couch, wishing for some of Leon's wallflower juice.

"Scarabus's first act of disobedience was taking his infant sister and hiding her. Their human mother died in childbirth, and Scarabus must have told his master that the child had died as well. Such things being common in antiquity. Nothing more is known until fifteen years later, when the sister was on the verge of *blooming*. He could no longer keep her a secret, so he drank her dry."

My stomach turned over hard. "He *what*?" It burst out of me.

Beaufort actually winced. "He, ahem, killed her. Drank past the point of bonding, past the point of the blood-dark, past the point of crippling. He absorbed his sister. And used the strength in her blood to become something the *wampyr* could not stand against. At least, something the taproot of their species could not stand against. Without that taproot—"

"Whoa. He ate his *sister*?" It was the guy in front of me. I was feeling kind of glad someone else was having the same reaction. Guess chivalry isn't dead.

Beaufort sighed. It was a Dylan-class sigh, but without the shades of patient aggravation Dylan could have put into it. "Essentially, yes. He absorbed her essence and used the resulting aura-dark to strike at the Vampire King. Who was, incidentally, Scarabus's master for most of his life."

"Wait. The aura-dark." I remembered that term faintly. "What is that?"

Nobody breathed or moved for a long few seconds. I was getting used to that, whenever I asked a really basic question. They took all these things for granted, since most of them had been raised *djam-*

phir. It kind of made me wonder what I'd be taking for granted if Mom was still alive.

Now *there* was an uncomfortable thought.

Beaufort looked up over my head, and a faint tinge of pink touched his cheeks. "It is what happens when a *djamphir* drinks blood. After a certain point, the, ah, the *nosferat* part of our heritage rises to the surface. We gain more strength, more speed—and less ability to withstand sunlight. It burns us just as it burns them, when we give in to the craving." His mouth pursed. "We'll cover more of that later, Milady. With your permission?"

So that was why Christophe had hidden from the sun after biting me. I nodded, pulled my jaw back up. Closed my mouth with a snap. Gee, I was just learning new things all over. I wished I had my hoodie on. Gooseflesh crept up my arms, spread down my back.

"Without the King, the Court scattered and gradually lost their ability to walk during the day. Which brings us back to the point of this lecture. Why do you suppose Scarabus had to hide his sister?"

I just knew I was going to say something snide. "For snacking later?"

There were a couple of gasps, one horrified chuckle, and several snorts. A few of the boys looked down at their notepads or books, one or two of them with bright crimson cheeks.

I never used to wise off in class. Things were just changing all over.

If Beaufort's mouth could have turned down any further, he would have looked like a commercial for bitter beerface. "No, Milady. Because the thing that allowed the Vampire King—and therefore the rest of the *wampyr*—to walk during the day was regular ritual infusions of *svetocha* blood. Which is, incidentally, what makes *svetocha* such high-priority targets for both us *and* them." The grimace eased up into a mirthless grin, one that showed his white, white teeth as the *aspect* ran through him again. The fangs look different when they're exposed and lengthening. Thicker, with a distinctive curve. "*Svetocha* have become increasingly rare ever since, for reasons we're still working to understand." He finally turned away from me, his eyes roving the class. "Over the course of four centuries after the killing of the King, the Court scattered. Human populations were also on the move, and a pale copy of the original Court settled in Greece, since Egypt and, by extension, the Hittite empire proved . . . unwholesome. Unfortunately, though, Scarabus and his followers could only train so many *djamphir*; casualties were high, and the *wampyr* had the upper hand until fairly recently, when the Treaty with the wulfen was made." He glanced at the clock over the door. "I think that's enough lecture for today. Open your books to page 285, please, and—"

I dug for my book, but the roaring in my ears drowned out most of what he said next. The marks on my wrist had mostly healed by now. They were just two innocent little bruised-looking divots, right where the radial pulse beat. Marks from Christophe's teeth.

I didn't take. I only borrowed. *Remember that.*

He could have killed me. I remembered the ripping, tearing, *awful* sensation as something more than blood was pulled out of me. And that was only three long, hellish gulps. And after that he'd called up fog to shield us and hunted the vampires chasing us and—

"Milady?" Beauforte's voice. "Be so kind as to read us the first passage on page 285."

"Yeah." I flipped two more pages. "Sure. All right. Two eighty-five."

My eyes wandered and I had something caught in my throat. But I got through three paragraphs on something about the patterns of vampire migration during the Peloponnesian War and wasn't called on for the rest of the class. I made it through by just putting my head down and staring at the pages, my eyes blurring. I'd catch hell for it on quizzes next week, but Jesus. Remembering someone sucking your blood—and soul—out of you isn't comfortable.

What would it be like to have that happen until you *died*?

I shifted uncomfortably every time I thought about it, and by the time class was over I was so ready to get the hell out of there. So it came as a complete surprise when the silk-button-down boy in front of me turned around and leaned over the back of his couch. "Hey."

The book went jammed back into my bag. I grabbed my hoodie, shrugged into it. "Yeah?"

So I didn't sound very welcoming. So what?

"You, um, wanna have some coffee? Sometime?"

What? I stared at him like he was speaking a foreign language, and the shuffling noise in the room as everyone got ready to go crested. Then I realized what he was asking me, for whatever reason.

Words finally occurred to me. "I guess so."

Now why did you say that, Dru? Like you've got time for a coffee klatch. But hell, it was the first time someone had said anything to me that they didn't absolutely *have* to. And yeah, I was the new girl. Always be cautious of the first guy who talks to you—that's the rule for new girls. I could have recited it in my sleep.

But it had worked out fine last time, with Graves. Or not so fine, considering he'd kissed me once and decided he didn't want to go further. And this guy looked so hopeful, and his blue eyes were warm and shy.

"I mean, sure," my mouth replied independently of my brain. "Like when?"

He looked surprised but covered it well. "Um. Huh. Well, when are you free?"

Leon made a stifled noise behind me. I ignored him. "Week-ends, mostly. Except this Saturday, I'm, uh, busy. So, um, Sunday? Like around one or so? We can meet in the caf."

Way to play hard to get, Dru.

He looked like I'd just given him Christmas. "Yeah." He stuck his hand over the back of the couch. "I'm Zeke."

I barely pressed his warm fingers. Some guys go for the squeeze to prove they're manly, but he wasn't one. The *touch* didn't leap to show me anything about him, either. "Dru."

"I know." He gave me a grin, dropped my hand, grabbed his books, and beat it out the door. I would have been insulted, but the way he was blushing was kind of cute.

"The ice," Leon said to thin air over my head, "has now officially broken."

I rolled my eyes, hauled myself to my feet. Said nothing. Sometimes, if you just ignore him when he gets all sarcastic, he shuts up.

Today was not one of those times.

"I suppose you wouldn't care to come out to coffee with any of *us.*" He was still talking to the air above my head, his arms folded.

Oh, Jesus. I kept my hand down with an effort. I was playing with Mom's locket more and more often now. "Nobody ever asks me. I spend every day with you guys. What the hell?"

A single shrug, and he turned on his heel. "You're going to be late. And you should be ready for that sort of reaction, Milady."

"Why? What's so wrong with a cup of coffee? Nobody else bothers to talk to me."

"I really do believe you are a babe in the woods sometimes." He took two gliding strides, cocked his head like he expected me to follow. "You're *svetocha*, Milady. One girl, out of a total of two, in a school full of restless, hungry boys raised and schooled to be Kouroi. And . . ." A quick look around, his fine hair ruffling. The room had emptied. "Wherever you cast your glances, there will be trouble. Some have used that type of trouble to further their own ends."

Did he mean that I'd already made trouble, or something else? Guess which one my money was laid on.

"You mean Anna," I said flatly.

He gave me one of those Significant Glances a guy gives when he thinks you're dumb but you've hit on something anyway. "I mean that your time is more precious than you know. Especially if they hold Trials."

Trials. I'd finally found out what *that* meant, even though Benjamin didn't want to talk about it. Where they slug it out over who gets to be in a particular group—in this case, one of my bodyguards. I didn't like the notion. I mean, I can see the benefit of someone who will successfully beat the shit out of someone else as a bodyguard, but . . . it just didn't seem right.

Besides, someone had tried to kill me in a Schola before. Several times. What's to say that whoever won the Trials wouldn't be someone who would try to put me in front of the suckers again? Or even . . .

Once I started going down that mental road, I started wondering about Benjamin and his entire crew. What if one of them had a reason to hate me? I saw them every day. Their rooms were right next to mine.

I ate *lunch* with them, for Christ's sake.

"I'm not looking to hold Trials." I hitched my bag up on my shoulder and headed for the door, my empty latte cup crumpling in one fist.

He got there first, swept the heavy door open, and glanced out into the hall. "Very wise of you. Or not."

"My thoughts exactly." I pushed past him, out into the hall, and stamped away.

It was going to be one of *those* days.

* * *

Of all my classes, Basic Firearm Safety was probably my favorite. Maybe because the first time I'd shown up, the lean dark unsmiling instructor—Babbage—had asked me what I knew about guns. I played a little dumb, asked him what he meant, and he smirked and showed me a table with a range of handguns, four different rifles, an AK-47, and a crossbow. There was ammo set off to the side, and he asked me if I had any idea what to do with any of it.

In front of the class, I checked, loaded, and laid each handgun; clipped the magazine into the AK-47; and was loading the rifles when the teacher coughed and said, "Well, I guess we know who my assistant *this* semester will be."

Everyone had laughed, and I'd finished loading the rifles too. There was no reason to stop, and it felt good to have my hands performing movements they knew by heart.

I didn't touch the crossbow, though. It looked like a polycarbon recurve, not a compound. The arrows were weird, with a head I'd never seen before. Even the gang down in Carmel who went out to clean sucker holes—the only time I ever heard of humans taking on suckers and winning—used guns, more guns, and flamethrowers. Nothing even close to a crossbow, for Christ's sake.

I couldn't wait for vampire anatomy to be covered in the Paranormal Biology class. Right now we were on basic wulfen anatomy because it was closest to humans. But finding out how to use a crossbow on a sucker—wow. I mean, you never *want* to be face-to-face with a sucker. But still . . . a crossbow.

It really says something about you when that's your idea of fun. Just what it says kind of isn't nice, though.

I loaded the 9mm, checked it, raised it, and squeezed off three rounds.

The echoes died away. I hit the target button to bring it home. Nicely grouped and even, star-shaped holes. I laid the gun down carefully, checked twice, and we all took our ear protection off. The hole-starred target was unclipped and passed around.

Babbage held up the remains of a fired bullet, showing how it had fragged apart on contact. "This is what happens—when it hits tissue, it explodes. Why is this important?"

I could have answered in my sleep, but I didn't. He called on a blue-eyed *djamphir* with a round babyface.

"Bleeding out," Babyface said. I think his name was Bjorn or something, but I wasn't sure. "They heal quick, especially if they've just fed and have a lot of fresh hemo in their systems. So, you gotta cause enough damage to drain 'em. Make 'em weak."

"Even a weak *nosferat* is a dangerous one, though." Babbage laid the bullet down. "So when you go in for the kill, keep your weapon handy. I repeat myself only because so many Kouroi have failed to do so and been uncomfortably surprised."

Nobody laughed at that one. We'd all seen the pictures. Big, glossy 8x10s, bigger versions of the ones you'd see in forensic textbooks. Vampires are only messy sometimes when they feed. But when they kill a *djamphir*, they like to make a statement. There's nothing like hating something that's part of you to make you really savage.

Leon, over near the steel door, had settled back against the wall and half-closed his eyes. He'd probably heard this all a million times before.

"Now let me pose you a question—Matthew, do *not* touch that!" Babbage's tone held a definite warning, and the boy yanked his fingers away from the .22 on the table.

Freaking amateurs. You keep your hands *away* from a gun unless you're paying attention. It just works out better that way.

"Yessir," Matthew mumbled. His spiky inky haircut was fashionable last year, but the sullen-frat-boy look he always wore never goes out of style.

Babbage continued while I toyed with my ear protectors. "You have a wounded vampire down, bleeding out quickly. What is the weapon of choice for dispatching it?"

"Anything that gives you reach," Babyface muttered.

"I second that." This from a tall lanky *djamphir* towhead with thistledown-fine hair. "Headshot, more shots to the torso to bleed, or *malaika*."

Babbage nodded approvingly. I felt like I'd been pinched. Christophe had brought me a set of *malaika*—wooden swords, of all things—and promised to teach me how to use them. They'd probably burned when the redheaded vampire exploded my room at the old Schola.

Someone else asked before I could. "Do they still teach *malaika* anymore? I thought those were—"

"They're still efficient." Babbage glanced at me. A *djamphir* in the first row handed the paper target to me. The shots were nicely grouped, even if I did say so myself. "They are traditionally held to be a *svetocha*'s weapon, since a female's greater reflex speed and coordination gives her an edge. Hawthorn is also deadly to the *nosferat*, for reasons you'll learn in your chemistry and Sympathetic Sorcery classes."

That perked my ears right up. "Sorcery?"

Babbage inclined his head. He leaned a hip against one of the tables, easily and obviously not resting any weight on it. "Surely you've noticed that a *djamphir*'s weapons are not all physical. We are in the process of rediscovering *djamphir* arts and processes that were lost when we were almost extinguished as a species."

I almost hopped from foot to foot. "Are you talking, like, what kind of sorcery? Witchcraft? Ceremonial magic? Hexes, or—"

The interest in his sharp dark eyes mounted a few notches. "*Djamphir* sorceries are largely sympathetic and combat-based. They share some commonalities with standard European witchcraft. Asian and Middle Eastern *djamphir*, few as they are, have inherited some notable sorceries and resistances that we haven't been able to study much, mostly because they are few and secretive. They are also fighting a war on both fronts, with the *nosferatu* and the Maharaj."

I was getting answers, but they were too slow. Babbage was good about answering though. He never looked at me like I was a moron. "What are the Maharaj? I've heard of them, but—"

"You'll hear more about them in the fourth—or is it fifth?— semester of Paranormal Biology. The short answer is, *djamphir* are the products of unions between vampires or *djamphir* and human women. The Maharaj are a clan of descendants of human women and beings referred to as *jinni*."

"I thought everyone knew that," someone said.

I rolled up the target tighter. Didn't look away from Babbage's face. Sometimes a trace of irritation flickered over his chiseled features. Like now.

"If one has been raised *djamphir*, of *course* one knows." He was a master of putting faint but deadly sarcasm into a few little words. "Those who are saved might not, and curiosity is a sign of intelligence."

Saved. As in, snatched from the suckers and brought into the Order. Like me.

The silence was so thick you could cut it with a spoon. I suppressed the urge to cough or smile nervously, looking down at the target as I twisted it tighter and tighter. A paper cone, like the waxed kind you put snow cones in.

I hadn't had a snow cone in *ages*. Dad used to love the raspberry-flavored ones. A bony hand squeezed my heart.

Uncomfortable silence filled the room. I finally looked away, at the chipped concrete floor. Babbage cleared his throat. "Apparently, human women are quite irresistible."

A ripple of male laughter stung the air. The target crumpled in my fist.

"I think that's enough for right now, though," he continued smoothly. "Now it's time for target shooting. Milady, if you'll check everyone into their lanes and disburse the ammo, we'll have practice for the rest of the session."

I swallowed hard and started handing out ammo, going through the checklist with every kid. Leon's eyes were open and dark, and he regarded me as if I'd just done something extraordinary.

CHAPTER THIRTEEN

As soon as I stepped out into the hall, I knew it was going to be something I wouldn't like. Leon stiffened, his head coming up. There was Kir, red hair combed back and That Expression on his sharp face. Even his freckles looked serious. I'd given up wondering how a freckle-faced teenager could look so much like a disapproving granny.

There went my half hour or so to catch up before Aspect Mastery. Great. I was going to be tanking on quizzes next week like mad.

"Come with, okay?" I said as Kir approached. The students separated to give him room— I'd noticed that about the Council members. Everyone seemed to *know* they got space while walking down the hall. "I have Aspect Mastery in a half hour."

"I don't think—" Leon began, but I stepped away from him, walking to meet Kir. The two of them didn't like each other much. I mean, I was totally on Leon's side, but last time they'd almost had a dustup. I didn't want to find out what would happen if Leon could make the redheaded granny lose his temper.

"Milady." Kir, in jeans and a white button-down, looked easy and classic. He didn't glance over my shoulder, but his entire body shouted that he was aware of Leon, glowering from behind me.

That was the Schola Prima. Love and happiness everywhere.

I hitched my bag up on my shoulder. "Let me guess. Council meeting."

Kir shrugged. His eyelashes were coppery. For a moment he looked like he wanted to say something, his mouth opening and the lines of his face softening. Then he shut up, shook his head slightly, turned on his heel, and set off down the hall.

If Bruce came to pick me up I could look forward to some small talk. He was approachable in a way the others weren't. Hiro was generally the nicest and didn't blink no matter how many questions I asked—even if his answers were more like riddles. Kir, though, didn't say a word. He spent the meetings looking at me with a puzzled expression, like I was a dog sitting up and talking instead of barking on the floor where I belonged.

He set a quick pace, too, and I struggled to keep up. Kept my head down and stretched my legs. At least while he was clearing traffic and I was hurrying, I didn't have to really think. It was like tagging along after Dad.

Not really.

Leon brought up the rear, drifting in my wake. He didn't even look out of breath. We arrived at the carved door in a shorter time than I'd thought possible. It opened, and Kir stepped aside. "Milady."

I stepped on through, into the shabby sitting room. It wasn't until the doors had clicked shut behind me that I realized Kir hadn't followed. I stood there for a second, my bag strap sliding down my shoulder, and when the doors on the other side of the room ghosted open I was as ready as I was going to get.

Some part of me was expecting this. I smelled spice and perfume, and the flash of red jerked me up short like a watchdog on a chain.

Anna, framed in the door, stared at me. I stared back.

She looked a bit thinner, but what would make someone else haggard was only glamorous on her. It was the first time I'd seen her in anything other than an old-time dress. She was in fashionably frayed designer jeans and a scrap of red silk that had to be a top more expensive than any sane person would pay for. She was pale, bare arms and cleavage in a peeping-out red lace bra. I'm no bodybuilder, but Dad would have taken one look at Anna's arms and pronounced them "weedy." It wasn't his most damning adjective, but it was close.

She was actually even smiling, heart-shaped face open and bright. "Well, hello there, stranger!"

I swear to God, she *chirped* at me.

A brief uneasiness filled me. I thought of stepping backward, decided it was better to show no fear. It was an article of faith with both Gran and Dad that showing fear was a good way to madden an already unpredictable person or animal.

"Hey. Kir said there was—"

"I asked him to bring you a little early. Girl time, you know." She strolled into the room casually, dropped down on one of the leather couches. It didn't even creak, receiving her the way it would a queen. "It gets so, well, *tedious*. Just boys hanging around."

Something about the way she said it told me she didn't find it boring at all. No, it sounded like she was expected to perfunctorily bemoan it, while looking at her nails and smirking that pleased little half-smile.

I stood there, not wanting to come any further into the room. Had no idea what I was going to say next, but my mouth up and took care of that for me. "Where're your bodyguards? I never see them with you." *And they all wear red shirts, don't they? I'll bet they do. And tight jeans.*

"Oh, them." She waved a hand. "They're around. I don't need them in here with a fellow *svetocha*, of course. They watch from in Shadow when I don't want to be bothered."

"In Shadow?" I repeated stupidly.

She waved one elegant hand. The cameo on a black ribbon at her slim white throat shifted a little. "We *can* go unnoticed, you know. And surely you've noticed that you only have to state a wish before they leap to obey? Such good little boys. I've trained them that way. It was hard work, but I managed."

"Huh." I eased a little farther into the room. Maybe the sense of danger before hadn't been from her specifically.

Well, she hated Christophe. But it was easy to see how someone could. He was just so . . .

. . . what? I tried to come up with a word, but all I could think of was the boathouse at the other Schola. Where he'd held the knife-point against his chest and said, *Don't hesitate.* And where he'd put his arms around me, and I'd felt safe. Not the type of safe I'd felt with Graves, but still.

The fang marks on my wrist burned. I sat down on another couch, one with a straight shot for the door. This was the one Hiro most often perched on, his quick dark eyes taking in everything in the room.

I kind of wished he was here now. I couldn't think of anything else to say.

"That's one thing about a Schola, Dru. Someone's always watching." A bright sunny smile. "*Always.* It's like a big . . . security blanket."

Funny, it didn't sound like a security blanket. It sounded like a threat. Her bright blue eyes were on me, but I didn't sense anything other than lazy contentment swimming through the windowless room. The fire—there was always a fire in here—crackled companionably. The *touch* was quiescent inside my skull, and I relaxed a little bit.

But if it hadn't been Anna giving me the sense of danger before, then *who*? Or what? One of the Council?

The traitor, maybe? Everyone seemed to be so sure it was Christophe. Except me, and maybe the wulfen whose lives he'd saved. I was supposed to find out who wanted me dead here, but I wasn't having any luck.

Jesus, I wish Dad was here. "Anna." I decided a frontal assault would be best, so to speak. "Can I ask you something?"

"You just did." She made another lazy, hand-waving gesture. "But go ahead, dear."

What the hell are you playing at? But I chose something else instead. "Why do you hate Christophe?"

She stiffened a little, eyelids dropping a fraction. The smile fell away, like a china plate dropping from a wall hanging. "I don't exactly *hate* him."

"Then what is it?" I figured out she was keeping one eye on me and one eye on the door. Maybe she was just as nervous about me as I was about her, and the bitch cheerleader vibe was her protective coloration.

It was a sobering thought. Did that mean I'd made a snap judgment about her, the same thing I hated when people did it to me?

"Did he tell you?" One corner of her candy-gloss mouth turned down.

"He was kind of busy keeping us all alive. He didn't mention you." *Beyond*, Oh, Anna, spreading her poison. *Not exactly a ringing endorsement*. And Dylan hadn't seemed too happy to see her either. But I wasn't going to tell her that. It would be a bad idea.

"Would it surprise you to know that Reynard was my first love?" Now her attention was all on me. Weighing, watching, greedy little eyes. I tasted oranges and wax, but faintly. The fang marks in my wrist tingled, itching. The irritation in them was getting more intense. "Yes? I see by your expression that it does surprise you. He's a heartbreaker; it's his one true gift. Along with treachery." She made a slight movement, settling herself more comfortably in the couch. "We were an item for quite some time. A few years."

I *was* surprised. I couldn't even imagine the two of them in the same room together. Not without feeling a little queasy. And why hadn't Christophe told me this? "I don't think—" I began. Was I actually going to defend Christophe to her?

"No, you don't. Let me give you some sisterly advice, Dru. The next time you see Christophe, run. If my experience of him is any indication, he's up to no good. He likes impressionable young girls. A lot of *djamphir* do. Human women, you know. *Svetocha* are supposed to be infinitely more attractive, but there are so few of us." A quiet little laugh. "Just you and me. Don't you feel special?"

Something curdled in my chest. *If I need a reason now, Dru, it will have to be you*. But here she was telling me . . . telling me what?

God, I sure could pick 'em. After a long run of no dating at all, here I was learning all sorts of things about the boys I liked.

Except I didn't like Christophe that way, did I? I'd told Graves flat out that I didn't. That he scared me in some weird deep-down way.

A change of subject would be a great idea, I decided. It was stuffy in here, and I was sweating. My ears were beginning to ring. "Why did you come all the way out to that reform Schola to see me? You could have brought me here." There was a whole Schola burned down, wulfen and *djamphir* dead, and here she was, pretty as a picture and pulling all sorts of strings.

She eyed me like I'd made an embarrassing bodily noise. "I thought the Council *was* going to bring you here." It sounded flat and unconvincing. "We're still trying to find out how you ended up out in the boondocks. "

It had the brassy bitter taste of a lie the liar doesn't really expect you to swallow. Christophe had tried to send me here to the Prima. Dylan himself had tried to get word out that I was upstate and in danger.

I stared at her, she stared at me, and I had just opened my mouth to inform her she was lying, when the outside door flew open hard enough to bang on the walls on either side.

I leapt up, my bag spilling off the couch. Anna laughed. It was a high breathless titter.

Hiro stalked into the room, his *aspect* on and his fangs out. His gaze made one brief pitiless arc over everything in sight—Anna lounging, me with crimson cheeks, breathing hard, and probably looking guilty as hell—and he checked, coming to a complete stop.

Kir trailed behind him. Bruce followed, looking thoughtful. And, once he saw me, palpably relieved.

"Milady." Again, Hiro made it clear—I wasn't sure quite how—that he was talking to me. "Forgive the intrusion."

I swallowed what felt like a good chunk of my heart. The sense of danger returned, the reek of waxed oranges bursting on the back of my palate. "Yeah. I, um. There's a Council meeting?"

"No." Bruce's relief turned to perplexity. "But . . . did you want to call one?"

Call one? What the hell for? I shook my head. "No, I . . . wait, there's no meeting?"

It wasn't until Hiro was already halfway across the room, bearing down on me, that I realized I was scrubbing my left wrist against the hem of my hoodie. Quick as a striking snake, his fingers closed around my wrist, and he dragged it away from my body.

I almost dropped my weight down into my knees, bracing myself to tear my arm away. But he looked down at the marks, pushing my sleeve up. "These are old. Weeks old." He darted a single, malicious glance at Anna. "Let me guess. Reynard."

"What?" Bruce crowded him aside. Inhaled sharply. "Why didn't you tell us you were marked?"

"He . . . uh, well . . . Christophe had to. The suckers were coming to kill us. He asked if he could borrow something from me. I didn't know it was . . . that." Memory swallowed me whole, and I shuddered.

. . . Christophe jerked his head back, fangs sliding free of my flesh, and something wrapped itself tightly around my wrist, below his bruising-hard grip on my forearm. He exhaled, shuddering, and Graves tried to pull me away again. My arm stretched like Silly Putty between them, my shoulder screaming, and I couldn't make a sound.

The winter blue of Christophe's irises clouded, dark striations like food coloring dropped in water threading through the light. They still glowed even more intensely, in a way that shouldn't have made sense. "Sweet," he hissed, and made an odd hitching movement. His chin dipped, and his fingers tightened bruising-hard on my wrist, like he was going to do that again.

I wanted to scream, couldn't. Nothing worked. My body just hung there, frozen and unresponsive.

"Christophe." Shanks sounded nervous. "Um, Christophe?"

The world trembled on a knife edge. Blackness crowded in around the corners. My head tipped further back. Graves held me up, both arms around me now. It was work to breathe. In, out; in, out, my ribs almost refused to rise. There was air outside my face, but it was just so hard to bring it in. Instead, the sea of atmosphere pushed down on me, crushing.

"Jesus," Graves whispered. "What did you do to her?"

"How much did he take?" Hiro asked quietly.

Over his shoulder, Anna's face floated. She was white. Not pale, like she usually was. *White.* As if she'd just seen a ghost. Red pin-pricks flickered in the depths of her pupils, and there was a sudden overwhelming certainty that if Hiro wasn't between us she would want to talk to me. Right up close.

Right up *hard*.

"She's with him," Anna hissed. "A traitor, right under our nose. Just like Eliza—"

Hiro let go of me and turned sharply. He actually bumped me, he turned so fast, and I stumbled back, almost falling on the couch. Bruce's hand closed around my upper arm, bruising-tight, and his other hand shot out, wrapping in the back of Hiro's high-collared gray silk jacket-shirt. The material gave a weird slippery sound, like it was straining.

"You accuse so easily, Anna." Hiro was cold, cutting-calm. Roaring filled my ears. I felt light-headed. "And yet—"

Kir was suddenly there, between the *svetocha* and Hiro. His fangs were out, red hair thickly streaked with pure gold as the *aspect* touched him. A deep thrumming sound tightened all the available air, turned it to soup. Bruce's stance hardened, and he gave me an unreadable glance.

"Let's all be reasonable here," he said quietly. His tone sliced through the growling, and I realized the weird skritching sound was the silk threads in Hiro's jacket stretching and tearing a little at a time. "Dru."

Wait. She was about to say Elizabeth. *Did she know Mom?* My legs had turned to wet noodles. I stood up, though, sweating and shaking. "Yessir?" As if he was Dad, and we were in a bar with a bunch of Real World baddies and someone had just made the mistake of messing with him.

"How much did Reynard take? It hurt, didn't it? How many times?"

"I . . ." I hated thinking about it. The shaking got worse. "Three. Mouthfuls. Gulps, whatever."

Anna let out a hissing sound, like a kettle near full steam. Her face contorted and smoothed, and Hiro leaned forward a little more. Sooner or later that jacket was going to rip, and God alone knew what was going to happen.

"That's all right then." Bruce's grasp on me gentled. "You certainly have led an eventful life, Milady."

"How do we know she's—" Anna began.

"You don't want to finish that sentence." Hiro cut across her words. Some essential tension leaked out of him, though, and Bruce obviously felt it too. Because he let go of Hiro's jacket and braced me. I was going to have a bruise on my arm, though. I could just tell.

"We don't doubt a *svetocha*'s word." Bruce was looking up over my head when he said it, but his jaw was set. A muscle flicked once in his cheek, and his hawklike face had settled into a cruel, beautiful picture, each plane and line pared down. His *aspect* wasn't on, but I sensed it running under the surface, like a current under still black bayou water.

"That's right." Hiro straightened his sleeves. I don't know how he did it, but he seemed a few inches taller. "We don't doubt a *svetocha*'s word."

Anna looked like she'd been slapped. Rosettes of feverish color bloomed high up on her perfect cheeks. Her fangs peeped out, and I swear to God I heard a cat's hiss, too. The prettiness she wore like a shield slipped, and for half a second something ugly showed underneath it.

Then she was gone, moving too quickly to be seen. There was a sound like paper tearing and nasty chittering laughter in its wake as she did the trick I'd first seen after Christophe drove Ash off in the snow, what seemed like a million years ago and miles away.

I swallowed. My throat was burning, a cartload of dry ice. I was cold, even though I was sweating and the fire was putting out a roaring wall of dry heat. The bloodhunger folded back down, leaving just a rasping at the very back of my palate. "What. The hell."

"You shouldn't have done that, Hiro." Kir, shaking his head. His *aspect* was gone now, and he looked oddly sad.

"Little red lapdog." The Japanese *djamphir*'s words could have carried more contempt, I suppose, if they'd rented out a U-Haul. Maybe.

"She is the *head of the Order*," Kir retorted stiffly.

"Gentlemen." Bruce raised his hands. "Let's be civilized. We all know Milady Anna is . . . difficult, and—"

"She drove Elizabeth out, just as—" Hiro began, but Bruce shushed him. Actually *shushed* and looked at me.

I didn't even care. I picked up my bag with shaking hands. When I looked up, all three of them were staring at me.

"I know she doesn't like me." I tried to sound steady. "I can't even figure out *why*."

I was trying to express something about antimatter girls, but I gave it up as hopeless. No matter how adult they were, they were boys. They just wouldn't get it. Why would I explain anyway?

If Anna had a thing for Christophe, and he was hanging around me . . . yeah, I could see where that could make some problems.

Hiro looked about to say something, but I'd had enough. I took two sliding steps to the side. Bruce didn't twitch, but I got the idea he wanted to.

"I'm going to class," I said in a small voice and fled. I ran back up to my room, locked the door, and didn't open it until Leon, Benjamin, and Graves all showed up to pound on it. And I didn't say a word when they asked me what the hell had happened.

I know the rules. You don't squeal, not ever. You take care of things on your own.

And besides, I figured it out while I was hunching in the bathroom, hyperventilating and rocking back and forth. I didn't even want to think about Anna and Christophe, or whatever. He didn't like her, she hated him, and maybe they *had* once dated and she didn't like him hanging around other girls. Who cared? There were bigger problems.

Anna was the head of the Order, and at least one person on the council—Kir—was on her side completely.

Which brought me to the scariest question of all.

Which one—or possibly more—of the *djamphir* guarding me was one of Anna's creatures?

CHAPTER FOURTEEN

The session with Ash was mercifully short that night. He had quieted down long before dawn. I hadn't wanted to leave him, but Graves rolled his eyes and told me *he* needed some sleep. And I was so worn-out and jumpy I just gave in.

I turned over, punched my pillow again. Sighed.

"Want to tell me what's wrong?" Graves's voice, not quite a whisper but not normal volume either. I guess he thought that if he said it that quietly, I had the option of ignoring.

I considered telling him about Anna, but if I did Christophe would come up. That was no good. It was such a tangle I didn't even have it right inside my head yet, and until I did I couldn't hope to explain it to him in a way that wouldn't end up with him thinking something I didn't want him to think. About Christophe, and more importantly, about me.

I decided to test the waters a little bit, so to speak. "Council meeting didn't go well." That was a massive understatement, as well as kind of a lie. There was no meeting.

Just Anna. And Kir. Very chummy, those two. *Little red lapdog,* Hiro had said.

"You don't like those anyway." Sound of shifting material as he moved.

I scooted to the very edge of the bed. Kept my eyes closed, though, and rested my fingertips on the edge of the mattress. "This one was even worse than usual."

As usual, he didn't need any help getting the message. "That girl, huh. The other *svetocha*."

I did *not* jerk as if stung, but it was a close thing. "She doesn't like me."

"Course not. Girl like that." Graves made a dismissive noise, almost a raspberry. "Bet she's been queen bee here a long time. All these boys for her to play with, set 'em against each other. I know the type."

Do you know my type, too? I almost asked him, decided it would sound like I was digging for a compliment or something. "She really seems to hate me, though." Something surfaced briefly—a memory, or a dream.

Don't let the nosferatu bite.

I pushed it away. A shiver raced down my spine.

"Well, duh. You're cuter than she is." He said it like he might say, *Grass is green* or, *Gravity works.*

Something warm opened up inside my chest. It was a nice feeling. I snorted. "I can't even get my hair to lie down."

"Whatever. Anyway, what happened?"

I tried to get it into some kind of reasonable shape inside my head. Silence stretched between us.

"Jesus," he said finally. "I can't help if you don't talk to me."

Dammit, give me a second to think. "I'm trying to figure out how to say it."

More silence. I fidgeted. So did he.

"Dru." Very soft, just a breath of sound. "My mom did that, you know. She'd clam up. Every . . ." A deep gulp of air, like he was swimming and had just reached the top. "Every time one of *them* hit her. Her boyfriends. She would try to act like nothing was happening. But I could see the bruises. I'm not stupid."

It was the most personal thing he'd ever said to me. I got the idea he didn't like talking about how he ended up squatting in a back office at the mall. And, you know, I had my own personal stash of stuff I never wanted to share. Most of it involved Dad and the various jobs we'd done all across the States. Some were from schools a long time ago, when I hadn't been so practiced at sliding by unnoticed.

I pushed my hand off the edge of the bed. It hung in space as I stretched, my fingers touching emptiness.

"She hates me. Because Christophe bit me." I almost whispered the words into the pillow, kept my arm out straight. My cheeks burned. If he could see me, he could probably tell something from the way I was blushing. The fang marks in my left wrist tingled faintly, but the sensation receded.

When his fingers laced through mine, it was both a shock and a relief. Warm skin, a gentle touch. He absorbed this, and then he said the last thing I'd expect.

"Girl like that won't believe you don't like him." He coughed slightly. Guess he was wishing for another cigarette right about now. "Jesus."

"I don't like it here." I sounded way young. And scared. "I've got some money. We can get supplies."

He thought about it. "At least you're not being attacked by vampires anymore. That's something."

"You told me it was us against the world." *You were holding my hand then, too.* "I figure we can get out of here. Run and keep running. I can teach you how to—"

"They know things you don't. And Shanks and Dibs watch out for you when I can't."

He had a point. Still . . . I considered tugging my hand back out of his. "Have you changed your mind?"

I didn't mean to sound like a toddler with a toy taken away. I really didn't. He sighed, heavily.

"No. If you're serious about getting the hell out of here, Dru, I'm going with. But . . . it really does seem safer here. That girl's just a petty bitch. Why let her run you out?"

Someone here wanted me dead. That's why we were stuck at the other Schola. That's why the other Schola burned down. The words stuck in my throat. I'd been counting on him wanting to come with me. "You didn't see her." I couldn't put it any clearer than that. "She really meant it."

His fingers slipped away from mine. I tried not to feel bereft. He moved around, and the next thing I knew, he was pushing me over so he could lie down on the bed. He stretched out, moved around and got comfortable, his hands laced behind his head. His eyes glimmered, little green gleams. I breathed him in—salt and male, the tang of *loup-garou* like silver in the moonlight.

"I think you're safer here. I'm learning all sorts of stuff. Even you said you didn't know enough."

"I know how to run." *How to get cash and how to keep our trail clear—hopefully.* But he was right, sort of. If I could stay here long enough, learn enough, when I bolted I would be better prepared.

Or I just might leave too late and end up dead.

I wish Dad was here. The thought was like probing at a sore tooth. A thin thread of anger worked its way around inside my chest. *Why did he have to go and get himself killed?*

It wasn't really fair, I guess. But why was he going after Sergej anyway?

I could guess. For Mom. He missed her at least as much as I did.

"Don't leave without me. I'm just sayin', Dru. We might stand a better chance if we stick around here for awhile. Get our hands on some more stuff, find out more."

I rolled away, turning my back on him. "Okay."

He waited a little bit. "What?"

Was he deaf? I sighed, half-pushed myself up, turned my pillow over, and dropped back down again. "Okay. You've got a good point. We'll stay here for awhile." *I just hope I live to see us leave.*

Contemplating your own gruesome demise is a sure way to make you definitely un-sleepy. But there hadn't been an attack the entire time we were here. I could just stop going to Council meetings and stay out of Anna's way. Sometimes bullies just got tired of it and left you alone after awhile.

Except I was the only other girl in the whole Schola. It wasn't like I could blend. I wished there were some wulfen girls around, but they don't come to the Prima. They either stay at home to help protect the compounds, or they attend satellite Scholas as day students. Still, it would have been nice.

Though with my luck, they'd probably hate me, too, for some reason. I've never been the girl other girls like.

Graves lay very still. "I think you're the only person who's ever listened to me."

"The other wulfen did." I closed my eyes. Sleep was an impossibility, but my entire body was so heavy.

"You know what I mean." A restless movement went through him. "Ah, Dru?"

Now that I knew what I was going to do, I felt heavy all over. I've always been like that—the thing that bugs me most is not having a plan. "What?"

"Can I . . . I mean, do you mind if I sleep up here? If you don't, I, um, understand. I just—"

"Yes." The word bolted out of me. "Yes, please. Maybe I'll be able to sleep if you're here."

"Okay." Did he sound pleased? Was he just tired of sleeping on the floor? Did he have something, well, a little more active in mind? Like another liplock? Or was he afraid I'd take it the wrong way if he asked to sleep up here and expect a liplock?

Sometimes having a pretty active brain is no picnic. Because it starts serving up fifty different *what-ifs* for the way anyone acts, and having to choose which one to believe revs your mental engine until it wears you completely out.

We lay there. I listened to the sound of him breathing. I think I dozed after awhile, lulled by that steady inhale-exhale. The last thing I remember is his arm creeping around me as gray dawn came up outside the window. He settled against me. I sighed and he froze, but then I relaxed all the way.

I finally felt safe again.

When he spoke again, it was a quiet murmur in the darkness. "Dru? Don't leave without me."

What could I say to that? I said the only thing I could.

"I promise."

Chapter Fifteen

At lunch I scanned the cafeteria for the rest of them. Leon had been awful quiet all morning, including through forty-five minutes of Aspect Mastery, where—thank God—I wasn't the one who had to sit in front of the class and make the fangs pop out and retreat on command while the teacher lectured about the physiological changes. My turn wasn't until later that week, and I hated having people *staring* at me while the place at the back of my throat where the bloodhunger lived woke up and tinted everything with red.

It's damn hard to sit still and just do it when you can smell the fluid in everyone's veins. I guess maybe that was the point, but I still didn't like it. Especially when the ampoules of blood came out and we started having to identify them according to the characteristics on the sheet. The other guys got partners. I did each one alone, and everyone stole little glances at me while I did.

It didn't help that it was laughably easy. Female. Male. Brunette. Blond. Wulf blood. *Djamphir* blood. Each one had its own distinct smell, and the *touch* helped, too, telling me which was which. It would help us track, they told us, and help us identify *nosferatu*.

Sometimes they prefer a particular type of prey.

Lunchtime was always a relief. Getting the first few bites down was hard, though. I was usually so hungry that once I forced myself to start, things went okay, but those first few bites might as well've been sand.

"Jeez, where are they?" I went up on tiptoe as *djamphir* boys stepped around me, their ranks parting like waves.

Leon said nothing, just folded his arms. He was probably hungry, too.

And even though I knew he wouldn't, I made the offer, like I did every time. "Well, go on. Go get something to eat. I'm in front of a million *djamphir*; nothing's going to happen."

"Please." It didn't even merit a shrug from him. "Will you stop saying that?"

Which was kind of nice of him, unless he was on Anna's side. Whatever weird side *that* was. I wondered, each time I saw any of my so-called bodyguards, which one—or ones—it was. All of them? None? Just a few?

I gave an aggrieved sigh, rolled my eyes, and saw Benjamin across the lunchroom. His face was set, mouth pulled down, and Graves was right beside him. Graves actually leaned in, his mouth moving as he said something fierce and low in the *djamphir*'s ear.

Benjamin's mouth twisted wryly. He made some sort of response, and if I was better at lipreading I might have been able to catch it. As it was, I only caught my name and a shrug with hands spreading. Then something about Anna.

I stiffened.

Graves caught Benjamin's shoulder. For a moment I thought Ben was going to round on him. But no, Benjamin just looked down at Graves's coppery fingers, then up into his face. They stared at each other for a long, tense-ticking ten seconds. Then Benjamin shook Graves off and nodded. Said something else, but Graves's gaze had come up and latched onto mine.

I realized I was clutching my mom's locket, warm silver metal under my fingers. My eyebrows went up, and my entire face must have been shouting, *What the hell is going on?*

"They won't agree," Leon said quietly. "It's not in Benjamin to listen to a wulfen, even a prince like the *loup-garou.*"

"What are they arguing about?" I had a right to know, didn't I?

Leon just shook his head. "Let's get something to eat. I'm starved."

And what could I say to that? He could give lessons in polite rudeness, just like Babbage.

I hitched my bag higher up on my shoulder. "Fine." And stamped for the steam tables.

It should have weirded me out, but the Schola Prima was like the other one. The food appeared from behind a fog of something weird, a billowing vapor hiding shadows and suggestions of shapes. Lunch monitors took the pans to the steam tables. Everyone had a turn working during lunch.

Everyone, that is, except me. I didn't kick too hard about *that.*

All the same, I would have liked to see who was cooking my food. I was missing my own kitchen more and more. Industrial food is okay, especially when they spare no expense for the linen napkins and fresh ingredients. But I wanted my mom's cookie jar. I wanted the spatula I always used for grilled cheese.

I wanted my life back. The kitchen implements were just a symbol.

Eating with the Council had been a whole different level of uncomfortable. Mostly because I'd been watching the door, waiting for Anna to come in, and also because they kept looking at me like I was some exotic creature. Good thing I wasn't planning on doing it ever again.

I felt the eyes on me again. Was *everybody* looking?

A flash of red caught my attention. Kir, across the lunchroom at the entrance to the hall leading to the teachers' wing. He inclined his head slightly, drew back into the shadow of the hall's entrance, and vanished. Had he noticed that I'd seen him?

A faint taste of waxed oranges slid across the back of my tongue.

What the . . . I stared at the empty archway, my fingers still glued to the locket's curve. The metal cooled under my fingertips. My thumb rubbed across the spidery symbols etched on the back, their edges suddenly scraping-sharp.

I knew *he* was definitely on Anna's side. What was this, then? A message? Just to throw me off or scare me?

It worked. My heart was pounding, and my palms were slippery.

Leon made a short annoyed sound. "Don't stare. You think we're the only ones watching you?"

"No." I found my voice. "No, really, I don't think that at all." *Chew on that.* I headed for the steam tables again, but the funny thing was, I'd lost my appetite.

Graves and Benjamin appeared as I set my tray on the table that we'd claimed my second day here. I tried asking what the hell that was about, but neither of them answered. Instead, they both tried so hard to amuse me I was able to just make noises and let them circle each other verbally. I shoved my food around with my fork, and afterward I couldn't even remember what I'd been not-eating.

CHAPTER SIXTEEN

A **couple of weeks** went by, and no Anna. I stayed as close to Graves and the wulfen as I could, and I noticed some of them—tall boys with muscled shoulders and a habit of dropping their heads and stepping aside when I glanced at them—showing up in the halls and sticking around. Benjamin said nothing, but I caught him and Leon exchanging glances. The blonds seemed oblivious, but their shoulder holsters were now in plain sight instead of quasi-hidden under jackets.

I kept hoping Graves would decide to come back up on the bed. But no. He went back to sleeping on the floor in his sleeping bag, and he moved the bag a little farther away each night until he ended up almost at the door.

So I just went to class, kept my eyes and ears open, did my homework, and endured Aspect Mastery as well as I could.

It was the only school I'd ever been to where I actually looked forward to gym class. At the other Schola the directive had been to stop me sparring with anyone. All part of the plan to keep me dumb and vulnerable, and poor Dylan hadn't known what to do. I hadn't been there long enough for him to figure out how to go about breaking the rules over me either.

Here, though, things were different.

I hit the mats hard and bounced up, warmth flooding my body as my teeth tingled. "*Very* good!" Arcus yelled, teeth white against the darkness of his face. "Turn, turn turn!"

I did, instinctively throwing an elbow up to catch his strike. My arm went briefly numb; his fist headed for my face. I ducked aside instead of back, grabbed his wrist with clumsy fingers, and *pulled*. My teeth stopped tingling and ached, a bolt of warm sensitivity crackling along my jaw, and the fangs would have dimpled my lower lip if my mouth hadn't been open while I gasped for air. Sweat flew as I helped him fly past me, my knee bolting up. The strike had no weight behind it because I had to fall back and get my balance.

He whirled on the balls of his feet, the *change* rippling under his ebony skin. Wiry dark hair sprang loose, crawling up from his flesh like a fast-forward of plants growing. He was built like a football player, and pretty graceful too. His wide nostrils flared, taking in quick sharp breaths. "No! Press your advantage while you can!"

"Don't have the footing!" I snarled back. "You'd knock me over!"

"Then you shouldn't *lose* your footing, girl!" He spread his arms, the crackling of bone receding as he dropped back into human form, hair retreating along his cheeks.

I skipped back half-nervously, hands up and ready. Watched him.

He feinted; I didn't fall for it. Moved closer, looked like he wanted to close with a jab or two, but I faded to the side. As long as I had plenty of room I wasn't doing too badly. He hadn't pronounced me completely hopeless, at least, which I've heard he sometimes does.

They had me sparring with wulfen teachers here because the

happy stuff in a *svetocha*'s blood—the same stuff that will make me eventually toxic to suckers after I hit the girl version of the drift and bloom—tends to drive *djamphir* a little crazy once it hits oxygen. Wulfen can smell it, sure—but it doesn't drive them nutzoid.

Not any more than just-plain-human blood does. Which is to say, just a little. But I wasn't bleeding yet. And Arcus was careful.

All the same, I wondered why Dylan hadn't just had a wulfen teacher start training me. But he'd been a by-the-book sort and terminally indecisive as well. I couldn't hold it against him, though. Seeing as how he'd done the right thing and given me the unedited transcript.

And seeing as how he was probably . . . dead.

I ignored that thought, too. While I was fighting I didn't have to think about any of that. It was pure action and reaction, and sometimes I even forgot what was going on and thought it was Dad pushing me to work harder, be faster, think better.

And at the end of gym class, I could usually steal ten minutes or so for *t'ai chi* in the locker room's echoing damp-fogged space. The familiar movements soothed me, and after the first half-minute I didn't care so much that I was basically practicing in a bathroom. *Do it where you gotta* was one of Dad's mottos.

Or was it a mantra? That's one of those questions that'll drive you crazy.

Arcus blurred in, with the spooky streak-on-glass speed wulfen use, and I went down hard. But my sneaker came up, socked a good one into his midriff, and he tumbled over me with a short growl of surprise. I rolled, gaining my feet in a graceless lunge, and skipped back some more. A curl had worked loose of my braid and fell in my face, blonde veining along its length as the warm-oil feeling of the *aspect* flooded me in fits and starts.

It was doing that more and more lately. I was closer than ever to "blooming" and having the real fun begin. When I hit my drift, I'd suddenly be faster, stronger, harder to kill. I'd become toxic to suckers. I might even get a bit taller or have my weight distribution change, which I figure was a fancy way of saying *might get more breasticles maybe*. My face might change, too. It would happen over a week or so, and afterward the real fun would start.

Yeah. Couldn't wait. *Not*.

Arcus should have been coming after me like a freight train. Instead he'd frozen, looking up over my shoulder. I didn't snap a glance to see, but the silence filling the long windowless room wasn't normal. Usually, this gym is full of first-year students learning katas or doing light sparring. The mats covering the floor are in good repair, and there are even bleachers pushed up against the walls, ready to be pulled out for basketball games.

I hear wulfen are really big into hoops. Hadn't seen a game yet, though. *Djamphir* are supposed to play polo or lacrosse. I mean, what the hell? I'd rather watch werwulf basketball any day.

Arcus straightened. He cast me an unreadable glance, and I was vaguely gratified to see he was sweating a little too. I must've given him a run for his money.

The head gym teacher, a *djamphir* with short feathery platinum hair, appeared to my left. "Milady. A moment?"

I still didn't look away from Arcus. *Never take your eyes off 'n 'em*, Dad always said, and it was good advice. I swallowed hard against the stone in my throat, pushed the thought of Dad away, and kept my stance loose and easy.

"Milady?" The teacher sounded nervous. I backed up another two steps. Arcus did, too, and I could swear the wulfen looked pleased. He dropped fully into human form, the extra bulk sliding away and a brief flash of orange lighting in the center of his pupils.

"What's up?" I finally swung my gaze around and discovered the teacher was pale.

"I'm to clear the room. You're to wait here." He paused, his blue eyes darting nervously. "*Milady.*" His eyebrows rose significantly.

I wished they wouldn't call me that, but then I cottoned on. My stomach twisted up into a high hard knot. "Oh. I . . . okay, I get it." And I couldn't help myself—I looked around for Benjamin. Didn't see him. I *did* see Shanks across the room, idly leaning against the wall near the double door heading out to the east hall. The emo-boy swoop across his forehead, fringing his dark eyes, was shaken down even more emphatically than usual. "I just wait here?"

The teacher—I remembered his name, Frederick—lifted his eyebrows, and a little of his color came back. "Yes, ma'am." He turned on his heel, and the news had traveled by jungle telegraph. Boys looked curiously or gratefully at me and left, heading for the locker room. When I glanced back, Shanks was gone.

Crap. Here it comes. I should have backed up to the wall. But I just stood there. Whatever happened now I'd ride out; then I'd get Graves somehow, and we'd go.

I couldn't say I was sorry.

The gym emptied out. Dust motes danced in the air under falls of fluorescent light.

I felt curiously naked. It was the first time I'd been really truly alone in forever, and the gym was a huge empty space. The boys' locker rooms were huge as well, with at least twenty communal tubs full of the weird waxy bubbling stuff that soothed hurts and made everything heal up like crazy.

But the girls' locker rooms were tiny in comparison, though big enough to do a complete Yang long form in. None of the three or four gyms I'd gone to sparring practice in had more than a three-tub girls' locker room.

Because *svetocha* were so rare. I shifted my weight nervously and tried to figure out what she would want from me now.

Maybe I'd get a chance to tell her Christophe wasn't my thing.

Yeah. That'd be real fun all the way around. And the more I thought about it the more I knew Graves was right. She wouldn't believe that.

Sweat itched all over me, and I pulled my T-shirt down. There was a scrape of rug burn on my forearm, past my elbow. Or would you call it *mat burn*, since I'd gotten it scrambling to get up while Arcus—

"Hello, Dru."

I half-turned, and there Anna stood in a pair of clinging pink sweats and a red tank top. Slim and pretty, her curling red-tinted hair pulled artlessly back and her fangs dimpling her candy-glossed lower lip as the *aspect* slid over her. The curls lengthened and loosened. She looked like an ad for Victoria's Secret workout gear.

I slouched shapelessly. Sloppy gray T-shirt, green knit shorts I'd borrowed from somewhere, and my socks were probably dirty, too. They even felt gray against my toes, and my sneakers were new but already showing signs of hard use. I don't believe in getting clothes that just look pretty or that'll fall apart—they have to stand up to a lot of abuse.

Dad was real big on dressing for efficiency.

Anna surveyed me from head to foot, and my mother's locket cooled against my chest. I'd tucked it under the T-shirt, but I never took it off. I could replace the chain if it broke during sparring, but I didn't want to lose the locket by setting it down somewhere.

It was all I had left. And I suddenly didn't want her greedy little blue eyes on it.

We were in here with just each other. I couldn't see her bodyguards, and I wished like hell someone had stayed behind to watch this.

It didn't look like it would end well. This sort of thing never does. I know what it feels like right before it starts.

Like thunderstorms threatening, prickling against the skin. Only this one felt like a hurricane just looking for a place to come to shore.

"What the hell do *you* want?" I didn't have to work to sound unwelcoming. The space at the back of my palate that warned me of danger dilated, roughening, and this time the taste of rotting wax oranges was spoiled by a copper tang. The pressure of fangs against my lower lip turned probingly insistent. They were sharp, but I didn't want to open my mouth and show them off.

She stepped forward, and I dropped into stance without thinking about it. Weight balanced, arms loose and ready, and every nerve awake.

"You're bristling," she said finally. A wide, sunny smile stretched her candy-gloss lips, but it didn't reach her eyes. "You look like your mother."

From anyone else, it would have been a compliment. She said it like a curse.

The dream turned over uneasily inside my head. This time I didn't fight remembering it. "That just burns you up, doesn't it?" My mouth bolted, the way it was beginning to do. I was sucking at the keeping-my-head-down thing. But having people try to kill you over and over again kind of robs you of a lot of tact. Not that I ever had much to begin with. I hadn't needed it with Gran, and Dad didn't care what I said as long as I didn't cuss around him. "Why did you hate her so much?"

Anna actually rocked back, her weight on her heels as if I'd pushed her. Her eyes narrowed, her face contorting and smoothing in under a second. The grimace was so quick I almost doubted I'd seen it.

But that flash of hate in the very back of her pupils stayed longer. This time I was sure. And I'd just guessed, yeah. But it didn't take a rocket scientist to figure out that in Anna's personal hate sweepstakes, Christophe and my mother were about neck and neck. Score one for me guessing someone else's dirty little feelings. I didn't even need the *touch* to do it.

So why did I feel guilty?

The *svetocha* took a gliding step to the side and I tracked the movement, the way Dad had taught me to. *When it's just one person you keep your feet down and your eyes on 'em, honey. Don't let 'em move you around much, but don't back down neither.*

God, if I could just stop hearing his voice in my head, maybe it wouldn't hurt so much.

"I didn't hate her." The sound of the lie was a sweet, tinkling bell. She had such a pretty voice. Candy over venom. "I just thought she should leave certain things alone. Certain things she wasn't cut out for."

"What kind of things?" My pulse picked up, running just under the surface of my skin. I've been in enough schoolyard fights to know the difference between them and deadly serious business. This one could go either way, and it all depended on the next few minutes.

Anna kept just out of range. Another few gliding steps and the doors were behind me. At least I had room to back up.

This is crazy. She's another svetocha; *she's supposed to be on your side.*

But I didn't believe it. Not the way she was looking at me.

Over Christophe? Because she hated my mother? What did that have to do with *me*? I wasn't either of them; why couldn't she just leave me alone? I'd always thought antimatter girls grew out of it. That it was just a phase or something.

Guess I was wrong.

"All sorts of things. Things you'd do well to leave alone, too."

Jesus. I've had enough of this. "Oooooh." I mimicked a shiver.

"So scary. Why don't you go play your mind games somewhere else? I'm busy with important stuff." *Like surviving. And trying to figure out who here wants me dead.*

A cold finger touched my spine. *Other than you, that is.* The same nasty thought that had been floating around in the back of my head came back to the front, but I didn't have time to chase it down because Anna's face contorted and smoothed itself out in one swift motion. She bolted forward two steps. I braced myself and felt the warm oil of the *aspect* sliding down my skin.

Anna pulled up short. Her fangs were out, too, and we stared at each other over a field of air gone hard and hurtful, full of sharp edges. I heard soft muffled wingbeats and hoped Gran's owl wasn't about to show up and complicate things.

I ignored little flickers of motion in my peripheral vision. The back of my throat ached, the bloodhunger throbbing restlessly in its special place. I tasted copper, and the scent of warm perfume that followed Anna around turned thick and cloying. It was damn hard to breathe with that reek all around me.

Then, something meowed.

No, seriously. I glanced down and saw a large tortoiseshell cat twined around Anna's ankles. It put its ears back, its head a wedge shape like a snake's, and hissed at me. Blue sparks crackled from its blind-looking eyes, and I exhaled sharply.

It was an *aspect* in animal form. Some powerful *djamphir* have them. It was the first time I'd seen one.

"You're a very impolite little girl," Anna said softly. I think she meant to be terrifying, but I was busy staring at the cat. "You should be taught a lesson."

I looked up just in time to catch her fist with my face.

CHAPTER SEVENTEEN

I 've been socked in the face before. It hurts like hell, but if you're wanting to put someone down, a face-shot isn't the best way. Especially if they're used to it, or if they know not to pay attention to the shock factor of getting a shiner. Most people who haven't been trained flinch and think about saving their good looks.

No, if you want to put someone down, go for a gut-shot. Which is what I did. My head snapped back, I loosened up my knees and dropped down, then nailed her a good one right in the belly. My fist went in, meeting precious little resistance, and the cat hissed again, yowling. She folded over; I brought up my knee, and her nose crunched against the bony part.

Shit. Now it was really on. If I was serious about just staying under the radar, I should have just let her hit me.

I backed up, shuffling and hyperventilating, trying to push the red rage away. The world threatened to turn into the clear plastic goop that hardens over everything when the really weird shit goes down, the thing that slows down the world so I can move faster. It's hard to fight that feeling off, and it's even harder once the goop closes over you and the world tries to drag you into being slow and, well, human again.

But I stopped, panting. I couldn't get enough air in through the crimson wash of fury bubbling and boiling around the empty place in my chest. Every muscle in my body locked as I struggled against pure rage. I'd lost it just once at the other Schola; I could've hurt Shanks pretty bad that time. It scared me so bad I don't want to ever go near that point again.

I should've put her on the floor and kept kicking, if I was serious. But you could kill someone doing that, and she was another *sveto-cha*. And my body froze on that knife edge between rabbit-hunching down in a terrified hole and the cold nasty place that doesn't care who you hurt.

The tortoiseshell cat leapt, yowling, straight at me. I screamed, a short sharp cry, and Gran's owl veered out of nowhere, claws outstretched and yellow eyes glowing. It hit the cat with a crunch like continents colliding. Anna, her face a mask with blazing holes for eyes and a bloody rictus-grin under her gushing nose, screamed and leapt for me.

The smell hit me then. Copper, fresh salt, and an undertone of spice and something nasty.

Blood. *Her* blood.

My fangs stopped aching and turned sensitive, quivering, and I blocked her next strike, slapping her hand down contemptuously and locking her elbow. I twisted and she yelped. I heard the snap of wings as Gran's owl broke away and gained some altitude. I shoved her and she went down hard, smacking the mats a good one before springing right back up like a bad jack-in-the-box.

It was like I was in two places at once. Part of me was on the ground, closing with Anna as she kicked at my left knee. If she'd connected she might've popped it out of the socket or something—it's amazingly easy to take out someone's knee and put them down on the ground. But I avoided it and cracked her a good solid punch to the face while Dad's coaching ricocheted inside my head like a .22 bullet in a concrete room.

The other part of me, calm in a strangely disconnected way, was a sharp beak and feathered wings turning in a tight circle and diving, air flooding past and a fierce hurtful joy spilling through the rage to turn it wine-red instead of crimson. It struck to kill, its target the oddly colored cat crouching on the mats. They crunched together again, in a ball of exploding feathers and multicolored fur.

I got an elbow in the face. She was impossibly fast, but I hadn't been raised to back down and I was moving pretty fast myself. *Too* fast, as if I was like her.

Move it move it move it! Dad yelled inside my head, and for once it didn't hurt to think of his voice. I did what he'd taught me—I moved, fist blurring, and the *aspect* poured through me. I blocked her strike, almost swept her legs out from under her, and drove her back across the mats with a flurry of punches. Hooked my fingers and got my fingernails in her skin, yanked on her hair when she tried to flee. She hit me a good few times, too, but I was past caring.

You can't fight past a certain point if you care about getting hurt, and I've had some practice in running for my life. That will kind of put a different shine on anything, even a girl fight. Only this wasn't just a catfight. This was something else. I didn't even know what word to put on it, unless that word was *serious*.

We broke apart as if we'd both planned it that way, as if we were dancing. And I could not ever remember the world being so vividly bright before, each color painted on with deep acrylics, the texture of the mat surfaces achingly rough, every chip and fleck in the paint on the walls crying out in its own voice. I tasted copper, the smell of her blood in the air mixing with mine, and the fangs in my mouth physically *ached* to get some flesh underneath them.

The way my throat ached for hot blood to stroke the rough spot, to soothe the raging thirst threatening to swallow me whole.

I skipped back, she straightened, and the cat leapt as my owl-part missed it by bare millimeters. Another wing-snap, and it veered away, the gym opening like a flower under its belly.

Anna stared at me. My eye was puffing shut, but I could still see her. And the warm balm of the *aspect* soothed the hurts all over me. I could still feel them, twitching and twinging, but they were strangely unimportant. She snarled, her upper lip wrinkling, and I snarled right back. The dual sounds hit an impossibly deep register, stroking the walls and rattling the wooden bleachers.

The only other time I'd felt the bloodhunger this intensely, I'd wanted to put my face in a wulfen boy's throat and *drink*. The Aspect Mastery practice wasn't doing any good. Because now I just wanted to hurt her, and it scared the hell out of me. The fear spurred the rage, both fueled the hunger, and I almost threw myself at her again. Stopped just in time.

She was looking at me like I'd grown another head. One petite manicured hand came up, lacquered fingernails shaking a little, as if she wanted to touch her nose.

She should get that set, I thought in that weird dispassionate way. *It's broken. Probably hurts like hell, too.*

Good, a deeper voice replied. *I hope it hurts. I hope she chokes on it.*

"Bitch." Her voice was a trembling half-hiss, staggering under a load of pure hatred. "Oh you *bitch*."

"Look who's talking." It was hard not to lisp, because the fangs meant my tongue hit the roof of my mouth weird. "You started this."

"And I'll *finish* it, too." She twitched, as if she wanted to go another round. I stiffened, and the owl's clear *Who? Who?* reverberated through the gym. "You're just like her. *Just* like her. Elizabeth."

It shouldn't have made me feel better, but it did. I got my hair from Mom and my eyes from Dad, and Gran said I got her beaky nose. Maybe she was just being nice. But hearing someone else say I was like Mom, even when their face screwed up like the very thought of it was a bad smell, was good. It shouldn't have warmed me up, but it did. The feeling cut straight through the rage pulsing under my skin, spiking it with gasoline. The fumes filled my head, just waiting for a spark.

I swallowed the rage as best I could. It only made the burning in my throat worse. "Good," I said quietly. "I'm glad."

Anna's hair was pulled half-down; blood smeared her face. She didn't look so glossy now. "You shouldn't be. She was *weak*."

"Braver than you." I don't know what made me say it. It was like someone else's voice in my mouth. The sound of wingbeats echoed in my ears, and the owl called again. The cat was spitting and hissing, but I ignored it. I had all I could deal with right in front of me. "When was the last time *you* really went anywhere without a bunch of bodyguards, huh? Did you bring them when you came creeping around my door? I'll bet they're waiting right outside for you after you finish picking your fight with me. And getting your ass handed to you, *bitch*."

Anna went pale, two splotches of ugly color high up on her flawless cheeks. People hate it when you call them on jackassery. That's a big fact of human nature: Not a lot of people want to be called on being assholes. They prefer to do their assholishness in the dark and cover it up with fancy words. Because they don't mind being evil — they just hate being evil where people might see. People who matter, that is, instead of "victims."

A lot of them won't take on anyone who might bite back. They just like to cull the weak out of the herd. It's Wild Kingdom all over.

Anna straightened. Air snapped and crackled with electricity. The cat's yowl faded away, like it was being carried on a train out of town. She stepped back mincingly, and I found out I was shaking. The urge to go running after her, fists flying, had me in its teeth like a terrier with a toy.

"You're going to regret this." Now she was calm. Or at least, she sounded disdainful, cool as a cucumber. The mask of blood on her face said otherwise, along with the dead paleness and the splotches of feverish ugly red high up, an unhealthy mix. Somehow her sweats had gotten torn and there was a stripe of blood high up on her biceps along with flowering red marks that would certainly turn into bruises; I didn't remember how that happened. I struggled to stay still, to keep my feet in one place.

Because a good bit of me wanted to leap across the room and finish this fight.

"You started it," I reminded her. "You had everyone clear the room twice now because you thought I'd be easy. You came creeping by my door when you thought I was asleep. *Coward.*"

She actually *flinched*, like I'd thrown something at her. "You should have stayed with your stupid human daddy." The ugly red spots became a flush suffusing her entire face, spreading down her neck. "You'll *never* be good enough. They won't love you. Not the way—"

"Nobody loves *you.*" I didn't know it was true before it came out of my mouth. It stung like a bad hex biting before you can unravel it. The owl banked, dove sharply across the space between us, and veered off just at the last second before its talons hit. The wind of its passing ruffled Anna's hair, and she actually ducked, the rest of her not-so-carefully-coiffed-anymore curls falling down. The *aspect* fled her, and she looked like a little girl before she broke and ran for the door with eerie, stuttering speed. It opened, she piled through, and I heard boy voices.

I braced myself, waiting for whatever would happen next.

The owl cruised in another tight circle overhead. I wasn't inside it anymore, just inside my own scraped-raw, throbbing skin. The *aspect* retreated, and I sagged, my knees hitting the mats with a jolt that smacked my teeth together. They were only bluntly human now. I was glad. Sharp fangs might have taken a chunk out of my lip, and that would have been no fun.

What the hell was that?

I bent over. My stomach hurt. Nausea filled it, kicked against its rubbery insides, and I was glad I hadn't eaten lunch.

"That was interesting," someone said from behind the bleachers. They rattled a bit as a shape slid out from behind them.

What? I turned my head gingerly. Blinked a couple of times. The clarity had gone, and the world was getting fuzzy.

Shanks picked his way over the mats, shoulders hunched. "You don't look so good."

"How—" I bent over as a retch came painlessly up from my guts and was kept occupied by the struggle not to paint the mats with anything my stomach could come up with.

"Figured I should stick around. Graves is going to shit a brick over this one."

"Don't . . ." I tried swallowing; it hurt my throat. Smelled the fur and wildness on him, a collage of brunet scent that made up his gangly long legs and quick dark eyes. It was like the pictures the *touch* painted inside my head when the ampoule of blood broke open in Aspect Mastery. "Don't—"

I meant, *Don't come any closer.* The bloodhunger was clear and unavoidable, burning just under my skin. Like the *touch*.

Like the anger. *Rage*. It was just looking for an outlet.

If I got to Graves first and told him about this, maybe I could somehow make him understand that we needed to leave this place before things got any worse.

Shanks squatted, an easy graceful movement. "Don't worry, I can smell the red on you. Not gonna get close until you calm down." A quick flick of a glance up over my head. The owl gave one last soft hoot, and the sound of wingbeats retreated. "Which you'd better do soon, before someone comes in here and finds you like this. You're bleeding."

That, right now, was the least of my worries. I shut my eyes and dragged a deep breath in. Blew it out between pursed lips. "Don't. Tell." I needed to talk to Graves first. To *explain*.

"Hm." He didn't agree or disagree, just made a noncommittal noise. "I never thought I'd see the Red Queen in person. She don't show herself to the peasants much." He glanced up at the door she'd retreated through. "Jesus."

Red Queen? I made a shapeless noise, but it was definitely a question.

"Oh, yeah." A small, humorless laugh. "Wulfen know about her. We're not stupid, Dru. We like to know who's playing the game."

CHAPTER EIGHTEEN

I **was bruised and** scraped all over, both my shoulders ached like they'd been dislocated and put back wrong, and my legs were like wet noodles. The shiner had gone down, though. A bit. Now it looked deep blue, fading into green-yellow instead of fresh and dark red. The baths worked wonders.

I was still standing there, looking at myself in the stripe I'd swiped away from the condensation on the mirror, when someone banged on the locker-room door. "Dru! You in there?"

It was Graves.

Shit. I watched my eyes widen and my mouth pull down and wished for a better poker face. "Yeah," I yelled back. My split lip had closed up, but it was still tender and puffy. I pulled down the neck of my T-shirt, winced at the cuff of bruising crawling up my shoulder. "Go on, I'll catch up." *As soon as I can figure out how to explain this to you.*

"No *way*. I'm on duty right now. Benny and Leon got called away for something." The door opened a bit more, but he didn't stick his head in. Echoes bounced eerily off blue tiles, split themselves on the edges of the shower stalls and choked over the top of the bubbling of the not-water in the sunken tubs. "You're gonna be late! Come on!"

"Just *go!*" My voice broke. I turned the cold tap on as high as it could go. Maybe it would take some of the swelling down, and the sound of it would drown out whatever he wanted to say.

I should've known better. Because he banged the door open and stamped right on in.

"For Christ's sake, can't you be on time even once in your…" His boots squeaked as he stopped. I grabbed both edges of the white porcelain sink and shook my hair down. "Dru?"

My knuckles were white and my legs refused to quite hold me up. So Shanks hadn't said anything. Or if he had, Graves had shrugged it off.

He touched my shoulder. I flinched.

The breath left him in a hard puff, as if he'd been punched too. He was staring at the swipe in the mirror, where he could see my bruised, puffing face. "Jesus *Christ.*"

"It's not bad," I lied and jerked away from him. He grabbed my arm, though, quicker than he should have been able to. I kept forgetting how fast he was with the *loup-garou* burning inside him. His fingers sank in, and I let out a short bark of pain as they ground into a fresh bruise. "Graves—" I searched for the words to make him see. *We have to leave. Please listen to me this time.*

"Who?" He all but shook me, and the deep vibration under the surface of the word was a *loup-garou's* command-voice. The wulfen use the Other inside them to put on fur and strength, but someone half-imprinted and inoculated against wulfbite like Graves uses it another way—for mental dominance. I'd seen him hold a roomful of angry wulfen back with that voice. I'd seen him press a fellow wulf down into a crouch with just the weight of his will alone.

He was full of surprises, my Goth Boy.

The steam in the air shredded away in shapes with sharp teeth and pointed noses. I tore myself away and grabbed at my own arm, a fresh bruise rising under the old one. "Ow!"

He drew himself up, shoulders straining under the black fabric of his coat. "*Who?*"

He sounded just like my grandmother's owl. The thought hit me sideways with unreliable, unsteady, panicked hilarity. I choked down a laugh that felt like a sob. "Graves, we have got to get out of here. Please. Let's just go."

Because I knew something else; I'd known it even when we started whaling on each other. It would be her word against mine, and she wouldn't have come down here without a good story in place to cover her ass. The fact that Shanks had seen the whole thing wouldn't help in front of the Council—he was a wulf.

Not a *djamphir*.

Besides, you don't ever be the first one to tell. It's not Dad's code. It's kids' code, learned every day at lunch and recess. Anna could break it—she was an adult, even though she looked my age.

But me? I couldn't. I didn't want to tell. I wanted to get the hell out of here. Sooner rather than later.

Like *now*.

Graves's eyes glowed, sharp green. He obviously didn't believe me. "*Who?*" The word rattled the mirror against the wall, its plastic brackets chattering. The steam streamed away, surrounded us like the white flying bits inside a snow globe. The kind that you shake while it plays a stupid song from some forgettable saccharine Disney movie.

"Don't worry about it." I shrugged my hoodie further up, zipped it all the way to my chin. "Let's just go. I've got money; we can get off the grounds before they even know we . . ." I ran out of words, staring at him. "Please." I searched for more to say. "*Please*, Graves. I have to get out of here."

He stared at me, deathly pale under his even caramel coloring. When he did that, he looked almost gray. His mouth set itself in a thin line, and his hair all but stood up, snapping with vitality. His earring glittered, a sharp dart of light.

"You've got to calm down." I sounded pale and unhealthy even to myself. "Graves. Please. You have *got* to calm down. I need—"

He lifted one hand, a fist. His index finger popped out accusingly, and he pointed at my face. There was a faint crackling sound as he bulked up. He wouldn't get hairy, but he does definitely sort of swell when the *loup-garou* comes out. "Who. Hit. You?"

That's not fucking important! Why couldn't he just *listen* to me? "I just . . . just . . . I . . . Graves—" Of all the times for my mouth to fail me, this was the worst. But his rage, swimming in the air and rasping against the *touch*, made it hard to think. And worst of all, the bloodhunger came back, circling that special space at the back of my palate with cat-tongue fingers. Rasping. My entire mouth tingled.

If I sprouted fangs now, what would he think of me?

"You had better tell me something," Graves said quietly. "I hate not being told, Dru. You know I hate not being told."

What? He was making no sense. I opened my mouth. Nothing came out, and I shut it again.

Because I could feel the fangs lengthening. They touched my bottom teeth lightly, the entire shape of the jaw changing.

Oh, please, no. No.

"Fine." Graves turned on one heel, so fast his coat flared out and touched my knee. Stamped away, paused right next to the door. His head dropped, shoulders shaking, and one fist pistoned out.

The wall gave a crack. Powder and dust puffed out; tiles shattered and split in zigzags. I flinched again. "*Stop!*" I yelled, and every droplet of fog in the locker room flashed. Tiny little diamonds, all hanging spinning in the air.

"When you feel like telling me," he said very softly, "come and find me."

He shrank a little, the *change* receding through him. Took his fist away from the divot in the wall and shook it briefly, flinging little shards of tile away. Startling red spattered on the wall, and the smell of blood exploded inside my head.

Almost-wulfen. A tang like strawberries mixed with incense. Green eyes and the metallic hint of snow, caramel skin and chapped hands. It was like seeing him in four dimensions, an extra layer added onto the everyday Graves who slept in my room and pecked me on the cheek each evening.

I held onto the sink like it was a raft and I was drowning. "Please. Let's just leave. You and me." A faint, girlish whisper. "Graves. *Please.*"

"Yeah. Run away. Sure. Just like my mom. Run away and go back each time." He waved his lacerated hand. The wounds were already closing—wulfen heal fast, and he'd gotten a full dose of that talent, even if he didn't get hairy. "But I swear to God I will find out who did this to you. Even if you don't think you can trust me."

The thirst roared through me and my fingers sank into the porcelain with little creaking sounds. If he went running off after Anna right now . . .

He yanked the door open so hard it hit the wall and more tiles shattered. The mirror above the sink cracked in gigantic zigzags, a spiderweb of expended force.

He was gone. I stood there, clinging to the stupid sink, every inch of me hurting and hot tears slicking my cheeks. I folded down, rested my hot forehead against the cool smoothness, and that's how Benjamin and Shanks found me ten minutes later.

CHAPTER NINETEEN

Shanks leaned against the door, his arms folded. "I guess Graves wanted to surprise you."

"He didn't go to class." Dibs's fingers were gentle. The blond wulfen smoothed some goop over my bruised cheek. He'd bandaged and gooped up the rest of me and was now working on my face with butterfly-light touches. "Hold still. I wish someone would have come and gotten me sooner. I can't do much once it starts to get this dark."

"Sorry," I mumbled. My split lip hurt. All of me hurt. I seemed to have only gotten to the morning-after part of healing—the part where you're stiff and wish you'd never been born, let alone in a fight. I didn't even have the adrenaline rush or the part where you feel like you've kicked the world's ass.

No, I just felt damaged all over.

"He saw you like that?" Shanks kept repeating it. He pulled the sleeves of his blue cable-knit sweater up, his large bony wrists exposed. "Man, oh man. Oh, *man*."

"I didn't have a chance to even talk. He got too mad." I flinched as Dibs started smearing the stuff on my eyelid. Arnica, he called it. Good for the bruises. I'd've preferred Gran's mugwort and a bunch of aspirin. "I, uh. You know." I couldn't even begin to explain it.

"I don't wanna be the wulf in his way when something happens to you." Dibs's wide blue eyes were dark and worried. His black medical bag lay open on the bed next to me. He kept wiping the arnica stuff on his gray T-shirt absently whenever he needed his fingers cleaned. "He's crazy-mad."

I could even feel Benjamin outside the door, waiting and worrying. It was Shanks who had argued him into getting Dibs out of class, and it was Shanks who had shoved him out the door when I got all girlie and started crying some more. A pile of tissues scattered over the blue carpet, and the particular darkness of 1:00 a.m. filled the window.

I was beginning to wish I'd never gotten out of bed. If I hadn't, Graves would probably still be here. It would've been nice.

Dibs dabbed at my eye. I hissed in a short sharp breath, and he gave me a quick look of apology.

"You did pretty good," Shanks said suddenly. "I mean, she's older. And fully trained. You still kicked her ass."

"She's rusty." *And weedy.* I suppressed the urge to shake Dibs's hands away from my smarting eye. "That was the only reason I had a chance. I don't think she practices."

"The Red Queen's dangerous. Hold still." The stuff he was smearing on me smelled nose-numbing weird. "This will sting if I get it in your eye."

Like it matters—what's one more thing to hurt? I had a better question. "What exactly do you know? Was I, like, the *only* person not to know who she is?"

Shanks shrugged. He tilted his head a little, listening to the hall. "Benjamin's gone back to his room. Thank God, that was starting to bug me." A little bit of the tension in him bled away. "I don't know much, really. Just that the head of the Order's the Red Queen. She's been pressing for renegotiation of some Treaty terms for a long time. She gets a lot of what she wants; the Council just gets worn down. My parents used to talk about it after the cubs went to bed." A shrug. "There're just . . . rumors."

"What kind of rumors?" I shut my eyes when Dibs murmured at me. He was so gentle, and I began to feel a little less battered. At least here with him and Shanks, nobody was messing with me.

"Just rumors. Nothing I can put my finger on, just saying that it's better not to be in her way." He gave me a long, measuring glance. "I can see why."

So could I. "I didn't know she hated my mother."

He let out a laugh that was like a bark. White teeth flashed. "You sounded pretty sure."

"It was a guess." Or it was the *touch* blurring in my head, showing me other people's business. Gran was big on minding your own business, but sometimes you just can't. "A pretty good one, I suppose."

Thinking about Gran made my head hurt. Her owl had pretty much saved my bacon so many times. I'd always thought of it as *her* owl because it showed up the night she died.

Now I wasn't so sure.

"Why would she hate your mother?" Dibs finished smearing goop on my face. "Okay, that's it. Let me take another look at that wrist. You're not healing right."

"I don't *know*." I tried not to sound fretful. "What do you mean, not healing right?"

"Too slow, especially if your *aspect* is rubbing through. Could be because you're not fully bloomed yet. I wish I'd thought to bring that textbook. Maybe we should call Benjamin in—"

"No!" I yanked my hand away. Dibs squeaked a bit. "He's already going to ask me what happened!"

"What would be wrong with that?" Shanks peeled himself away from the wall. "I'm a witness. She hit you first."

I didn't think I'd have to explain it to him of all people. "She's the head of the Order, right? Who's going to believe she jumped me first?"

Besides, I couldn't tell him that I wanted to find Graves and get the hell out of here. The need to get on the road was itching under my skin in a big way.

"It's the truth, though." Dibs gently but firmly grabbed my hand, started manipulating my left wrist. It hurt. "Shanks saw it. Right?"

"You're such an optimist." Shanks sighed, crossed the room to the window. "She's right. Her only witness is a werwulf from a reform Schola. Nobody will believe it. On the other hand, you did give as good as you got, Dru-girl. Maybe she'll be embarrassed."

What a cheerful thought. My wrist sent sharp jolts of pain up my arm as Dibs's long slim fingers probed and poked and pulled.

My T-shirt was filthy with dried blood, sweat, and stuff I couldn't remember getting on it. "You embarrass a bully, they'll just lie in wait for you somewhere. *Ouch!* Stop yanking on it!"

"I think maybe I should splint this." A crease deepened between Dibs's fair eyebrows. He's all business when he's patching someone up. Hard to believe he'd barely even talk to me out in public because he's so shy. "So what do we do, then?"

We? I don't know about you, but I'm finding Graves once he's calmed down and making the case to get the hell out of here. Like, yesterday.

"Leave it alone, I'm fine." It hit me hard. I put my head down, breathed in softly. He'd said *we*. He took it for granted that it was his problem too. *We.* I didn't think I'd be so grateful for one little word.

All at once I felt horrible about leaving him behind.

Dibs shrugged. "Wait and see. All we *can* do. Graves might have a bright idea. And Jesus, Dru. You should at least tell Benjamin. He wouldn't have this job if he didn't know how to play the game."

"You keep saying it's a game." I let Dibs mess with my wrist some more. The blond wulfen produced a brand-new Ace bandage from the depths of his medical kit.

"Hold still." He tore the package open with his white, sharp teeth.

Shanks let out an ironic little half-laugh. "Of course it's a game. *Djamphir* are like suckers, always looking to one-up each other." He gave me a guilty glance, tugged at the window sash. "'Cept you, of course. And then there's Reynard. Wonder what the deal is with him and Red. You said she was trying to get you on her side about him."

"If I find him I could maybe get him to answer some questions. Good luck with that, though." It was weird to have someone else bandaging me up. I usually did the first aid for Dad. I remembered patching up August, too, more than once. My shoulders sagged. "Do you have any aspirin, Dibs?"

"Ibuprofen's probably better. We should ice this." He still looked troubled, beginning to wrap my wrist. "Shanks doesn't mean *djamphir* are bad."

He was always like that, looking to smooth over everyone's feelings. Said it was part of being a "sub"—submissive and born that way. The only time I ever saw him with his back up was when he was bandaging someone.

"She knows what I mean, Dibsie." A cold breeze touched the dark wulf's hair, mouthed at his sweater. "I never thought I'd miss reform school." He played with the curtains, his fingers flicking at the velvet. Took a deep lungful of night air, rolling it around in his mouth like champagne. "Huh."

Dibs glanced up. His hands paused, the Ace bandage half-wrapped. His eyes widened, and he sniffed, too.

Tension threaded through my aching muscles. I couldn't smell anything but my own snot, since I'd been crying so hard. "What?"

Shanks cocked his head. It reminded me of the RCA dog on some of Gran's ancient record sleeves when he did that. "Dunno. Just . . . smells unsettled. Could be you, though. Whenever you get upset, the spice comes out."

"Spice?" This conversation was getting better and better.

"You smell like cinnamon rolls," Dibs volunteered helpfully. "All *svetocha* are supposed to smell different—some flowery, some spicy. It's pretty strong on you. They smell that way whether or not they've fed."

"Whoa. Back up. I *smell*?" Heat rose up from my throat, touched my bruised cheeks. Blushing again. At least I wasn't sobbing like a baby.

All things considered, I was doing pretty well. I might earn my tough-girl card back if this kept up. But *ouch*. I didn't want to earn it this way.

"It's not an insult!" Dibs sounded half-panicked. "He's not saying you're a—"

"Just chill." Shanks stood in the window. "I'm not saying you're a glutter."

"A what? You know about me, Shanks. Give me a vowel or something." I mean, I was learning by leaps and bounds, and I'd known about the Real World pretty much all my life, but what Dad and I had been able to piece together was nothing compared to everything the Order had. Things even a baby werwulf would take for granted were news to me.

The blond werwulf finished wrapping my wrist, with prissy

exactitude. "A glutter's a *djamphir* who drinks like the vampires do. It makes them stronger. But they're not supposed to do it. And we can smell them, glutters."

I was beginning to get a very bad feeling about this. "But I've never—"

"*Svetocha* smell because they're, um, when they get to puberty, they . . . " Dibs looked over his shoulder. Shanks said nothing, but his shoulders quivered slightly.

Was he *laughing*?

Dibs gathered himself. He started cleaning up the detritus of used first-aid supplies on the bed. "When they're, you know, fertile. They start smelling good. Glutters smell, too, like candy. Something about metabolizing the hemo. You can't tell if a girl *djamphir* is a glutter, but you can tell if a boy is."

"Oh." I checked the wrist wrapping. If I blushed any harder, my skin would probably combust. And now I was wondering why Christophe smelled like apple pies baking, but none of the other *djamphir* boys did. Was he . . . did he actually . . . "I didn't know about that."

"I thought Graves'd be back by now. He had a lot of mad to run off, but still." Shanks had apparently decided it was time to move on from Teaching Dru About Stuff She Should Know Anyway. "If he's still off-campus by dawn it'll be bad for him. But, still, he's your problem. Or so they think. They might overlook it."

"He was *really* mad," I offered inadequately. "You said something about ibuprofen, Dibs?"

"Have you eaten anything?" He had a huge double handful of Band-Aid wrappers, cotton balls, and an empty tube of arnica ointment. "Because if you haven't—"

"Give her the goddamn Advil, Dibs. Jesus." Shanks leaned out, testing the wind, and I had a sudden, vivid mental image of him falling. The windowsill hit him right in the middle of his quads, and all it would take was a good shove. There wasn't even any screen to hold him back. "She looks like she needs it."

Dibs shrugged and headed for the bathroom to toss everything. The water turned on in there. He was fanatical about washing his hands after bandaging. I thought about offering him a T-shirt, since his was all smeared with arnica.

I watched Shanks nervously.

A few weeks ago I didn't even know these guys, and now here I was worried one of them would fall out a window and hurt himself. I didn't even know if that drop would injure a wulf. They can do some amazing things. "Be careful there, okay? There's no screen on the window."

"I was just noticing that. Seems weird, though. The other ones all have screens." He bent over, braced his hands on the sill. Even so, he looked poised instead of hunched. "Looks like this one had one until recently. There's scratch marks here, too."

It hasn't had a screen since I moved in. My throat was dry. I hurt all over, and suddenly I just wanted to crawl into bed and pull the covers up over my head. "Do you think he'll come back?" My voice sounded very small. The bed was soft, and to hell with climbing into it—I decided I wouldn't mind climbing *under* it and hiding for awhile.

"Graves? Yeah. He just needs to run off the rage." Shanks shrugged. "He'd come back to a burning house for you. Did it once already." He turned on his sneaker heel and stalked for the bathroom.

"What do you mean, he came back?" I remembered the Schola burning, and I remembered Christophe dragging me out. But Graves—

"He was the one who made us go back to pick you and Christophe up. We would have been hell and gone if not for him." The bathroom door shut, and Shanks said something I couldn't hear over the plashing of water.

Every inch of me ached. My heart hurt worst of all. I was beginning to think it was normal to feel like it was being pulled out of your chest all the time. The toilet flushed after a little while, but at least the wulfen were tactful. Whatever they were arguing about, they were doing it quietly. Dibs sounded worried, Shanks determined.

I pushed myself off the edge of the bed, made my legs straighten. Got my hoodie on, zipped it up. Stood swaying for a few moments. The sleeping bag was neatly rolled up and pushed against the night table on this side, and his pillow was tossed back up on the bed. Graves's T-shirts, including the "velociraptor with a light saber" one—which he'd looked pleased over—were still hanging up in the closet, half of the drawers in the huge antique dresser holding them as well. I'd gotten used to the sound of his breathing in the room with mine. Ever since Dad had shown up dead but still walking, Graves had been the one person I could depend on.

What exactly was I afraid of?

The same thing I was always afraid of, I guess. That I'd be left behind somewhere—like in the hospital corridor after Gran died, just repeating over and over again that Dad was coming, that he would know what to do, that he was on his way, and hoping like hell it was true.

Dad had shown back up and taken care of everything, but I was always afraid one day he wouldn't. And one day . . . he hadn't quite come back. Shambling into your kitchen as a zombie and trying to kill your daughter doesn't really qualify as a grand return.

And Graves . . . he was thinking I was like his mother, or something? Had he just decided I was too much trouble to deal with? Or what? Shanks said he'd come back once he got rid of the anger. That's what wulfen do—they run it off.

JEALOUSY

It's either that or hunt something down and eat it. Everyone should be glad they usually go for the former. Except most normal people will never ever even hear of stuff like this.

The weight in my throat, prickling behind my eyes, was loneliness.

The toilet flushed again. All the starch went out of my legs and I sat down hard. Here I was again, sitting and waiting for someone to come back. But I was hearing wulfen argue in the bathroom, instead of just the creaks and thumps of an empty house while the wind moaned hungrily outside.

It wasn't much of an improvement, but I'd take it.

* * *

Dibs gave me some ibuprofen and told me to ice my wrist. He looked unhappy, but he just gave Shanks a meaningful stare and carried his medical bag out, shaking his golden head. Shanks shut the door, turned around, and eyed me.

I stood in the middle of the big blue room and felt shipwrecked. Stared back at him. Deep dark eyes, the long fringe of dark hair over them turned aggressive instead of angsty, his sleeves pushed up to reveal lean muscular forearms. Silence stretched like a big old rubber band.

I wet my lips with my tongue nervously. "Get to it. I mean, if you're wanting to beat me up, too, you'll have to stand in line. And it would waste all the work Dibs just did."

As a joke, it was in pretty poor taste. It had seemed funnier inside my head.

"Please." He rolled his eyes. "Graves would *kill* me. I'm just wondering if you're, you know, concerned."

Concerned? I'm full-fledged paranoiac at this point. "About Anna? Or about—"

187

"About someone taking the screen off your window. Who's been visiting? Or have they not been visiting because someone else is sleeping in your room?" One dark eyebrow vanished into the fringe above his eyes. "I'd ask you which side of the fence you're playing, but the more I hang around you the more I think you ain't playing at all."

The sigh that came out of me would have made Dylan proud. "I'm *not*—"

He held up both hands. "I got it, I know. You wanna take my advice, then, or are you going to snap my head off for even offering it?"

Choices, choices. "Shoot."

"'Cause you know, you're *svetocha* and I'm a lowly wulf fresh outta reform school. You shouldn't even be talking to us, let alone acting like Dibs and me's your best friends."

"But you *are* my best friends. I can't trust anyone else!" I actually pitched forward, throwing the words at him like a dodgeball.

"Like I said. But anyway . . . I don't trust this. Something's hinky. What with Red getting all aggro on you and someone scratching at your window, not to mention the fact that you shouldn't've been sent to our backwoods Schola in the first place *and* more vampires than I've ever seen in my life chasing you down. And let's not even talk about Reynard, okay?" He stopped, waited for my nod, and continued. "I'm saying it might not be so good an idea for you to sleep up here if someone you trust isn't with you. So. Either we stash you someplace nobody knows about, or . . ." His face worked itself up a little, like he was sucking significantly on a lemon. Like I should know where he was going.

It took my poor busted brain a few seconds to figure out what he was suggesting. "Or you stay here. Um, I guess not, Shanks. I mean, I trust you and all, but I don't think that's such a good idea."

He looked almost green with relief. "Well, cool. Because Graves would have a fit. He'll probably be back anytime now. He knows we can't leave you alone. So—"

A lightbulb turned on inside my head. "I've got an idea," I said, and I told him.

Like I expected, he didn't think much of it. "You'll end up with your guts for garters, Dru."

I shook my head. "He hasn't hurt me. Not yet. And can you think of a better place? Nobody would expect it."

"Bad idea." Shanks shook his head so hard his shoulders moved, too. "Jesus Christ. You're nuts. Completely bazonko."

"All you have to do is act like I'm in here." I sounded perfectly reasonable, even to myself. "And for Christ's sake, it's not like I'm not down there every night *anyway*."

"But . . . " He stopped. "You know, it's actually not such a bad idea. Completely crazy, but not such a bad idea."

"Exactly." I stuffed my hands gingerly in my hoodie pockets. The wrapping on my wrist helped. Once you get all bandaged up, the fight is really over. You can afford to relax a little bit.

Maybe. Until the next crisis comes along. And I was jumpy. Who wouldn't be, after all this?

Shanks thought everything over. "But when Graves comes back . . ."

"He's smart. He'll figure out where I am." He would, and he'd either be angry or . . . what? What would he be like when he came back?

I ran up against the wall of everything I didn't know about him. The Council had never mentioned his file again, and I hadn't even been tempted to ask. I figured he'd tell me what he wanted me to know, and—

Shanks made a restless motion, like a dog shaking away water. "If he can figure it out, someone else can too."

Werwulfen function on consensus among themselves. Getting

them to poop or get off the pot is pretty impossible sometimes. Don't get me wrong—when you've got teeth and claws and superhuman reflexes, it's a good thing to want everyone to agree without violence. I'll be the first to admit that.

But sometimes it just drives me up the fricking wall. "Then they can all come down and we'll have a coffee klatch." I rolled my eyes. "He killed three suckers at the other Schola, Shanks. He's good protection."

"I'm not worried about suckers just yet. I'm worried about him going crazy and opening you up like a can of Pringles."

I was getting to the point where that thought was losing its ability to scare me. "Well, then this will all be academic, won't it? And everyone will be ever so much happier without the problem that is me hanging around." I shuffled over to the side of the bed, picked up the sleeping bag and the pillow. "That's what I'm doing. I'll stash myself someplace nobody except Graves will think of to look for me. You just hang out by the door until Benjamin comes to check in on me, and pretend I'm in the room. And ta-da, tomorrow Graves should be back and calmed down enough to be reasonable and we'll figure out . . . something else."

Like getting the hell out of this place. Hey, you can even come along. The more the merrier. I sounded hopeless even inside my own head.

Shanks was looking at me weird. "He'll be back tonight. I'll stick around and wait for him, I guess. You really want to do this, Dru-girl?"

I'd had about all I could take of boys looking at me funny, but I gave him a smile that hurt my face. My split lip cracked a little, and the bruises all twinged. "Yeah. What's the worst that could happen?"

As soon as I said it I wished I hadn't. But Shanks just shook his dark head, opened the door, and peered outside, sniffing. "It's clear," he finally muttered. "Come on, then."

"Thanks. I mean it. For everything." I shifted the sleeping bag around and winced when my arm almost cramped, the way bruises do when they settle down to the painful business of healing.

As usual when I thanked him, he shook it off and snorted. "Always was too curious for my own good. Be careful, okay?"

"I will be." And I set off down the hall before either of us could get any more embarrassed.

CHAPTER TWENTY

The metal shelf was hard, and I probably should have brought my sneakers down here with me. And an extra blanket. But I just unrolled the sleeping bag and made sure the key was in my pocket for the fiftieth time.

You know that feeling—you've got your bus ticket or something important in your pocket, and you have to keep checking just to make sure it's there? Like that. It's like a nervous tic or something when you're traveling or really, really bushed. Or maybe I'm the only person who does it, I don't know.

Ash's breathing was steady. He lay curled up under the shelf-bed, and there was another sticky tray in the corner. I'd gotten close enough to it to smell the red copper of blood, and the image of a brown Jersey cow popped up big as life inside my head, the *touch* throbbing. I'd retreated to the other side of the room in a hurry. At least he was being fed. I would have a crazy well-fed werwulf to contend with instead of a crazy hungry one.

You take what you can get, I suppose.

I plopped the pillow down, fluffed it up, then stood and stared at the sleeping bag. It smelled like Graves. Healthy teenage boy, his deodorant, and the cold moonlight tang of *loup-garou*.

I eased myself down cautiously, my knees complaining when they hit cold concrete. My wrapped wrist twinged, too. I peeked under the shelf.

There was a faint orange gleam of eyes in the deeper shadow. His breathing hadn't changed, but he was awake. Every inhale ended on a slight bubbling sound through his ruined mouth.

"I'm sorry about shooting you." The words surprised me. Even more than that, I was surprised to find out I really *was* sorry. Even if Benjamin was right and the only thing keeping him from doing what Sergej wanted and killing me was a faceful of silver grain, I still felt bad about shooting him. "It must hurt, huh?"

The shadow didn't move, but I could tell he was paying attention by the way the silence in the room changed. Ordinary people can hear that, too—what happens when someone is suddenly paying attention.

"Go figure." The cold of the floor grabbed the bruises on my legs with bony fingers. "This is about the only place I feel safe. And you could bite my head off without even thinking about it. Do I smell weird to you, too? I guess I must."

No answer. Just the soft burble of his breath. The tiny glimmers of his eyes winked out, and he settled farther back, against the wall.

I didn't zip the sleeping bag up, but I did tuck it all around me. The metal was hard and uncomfortable, but no worse than a motel-room floor. I just couldn't get easy, especially with the bruises and muscle aches playing pinball all through me. Every time I shifted my weight the bag's zipper would rub a little bit against the metal bed, or a bruise would set up a yell of pain, or some damn thing. But I was exhausted, and pretty soon I started to feel drowsy.

I woke with a start, hearing the deathly stillness of everyone in the Schola gone to their early-morning rest. It took me a few sleepy seconds to realize it was before Ash usually began his regular 3:00 a.m. yowling, and he wasn't making a sound. Instead, I blinked fuzzily a few times, and in the faint illumination through the barred aperture in the door I saw a long furred shape with orange eyes.

He lay across the threshold, narrow head on his paws, and watched me.

That should really creep me out. But I fell back asleep again. A long slow velvet time of dreamless darkness enfolded me.

And then . . .

The hall was long and narrow, and the door at the end of it glided open. I remembered this feeling—a buzzing cord tied around my waist, drawing me on. I should have been cold in my sock feet and T-shirt, and for a moment I wondered where my hoodie had gone. Then I realized I was dreaming, and the question fell away.

The buzzing started, vibrating through my fingers and toes. It was like static between channels in the back ends of America, the ancient televisions in fly-spotted, grease-carpeted motel rooms all tuned to blank snow. Some of those places advertise cable, but good luck coaxing the TV to home in on anything resembling a signal.

I remembered this feeling, like pins and needles crawling through numb flesh. I held up a hand and wasn't surprised to see translucent copies of my nail-chewed fingers. They wiggled when I wiggled them, obediently, and I put my hand down. My feet just brushed the floor. I was moving slowly. Like waterskiing but only at about quarter-speed, leaning back against the pull.

Up the stairs, past the hall that held my room, and the pull intensified. The Schola's stone walls wavered like seaweed. A soft thunder of wingbeats surrounded me, insulating me from the prickling buzz.

The Schola flickered, came back with the colors bled out. Everything was shifting, like really old movies where the grainy color has faded. Or like those painted photographs you see in antique stores— black-and-white portraits with weird blushes over the cheeks and eyes, caught in dusty frames and staring out past speckled, dirty glass.

The voices faded in through the static. I recognized one of them, and the walls of the Schola pulled away. I was outside, the trees shimmering—one moment fully-leafed, the next bare grasping branches.

The voices came back as the trees burst into full summer green again, their shadows turning everything around them to liquid even as color flooded my sight. Sound wavered, but then it was like finding the radio station you want, a chance bump in the road moving your finger on the dial just that perfect amount so the song comes in clear and loud.

"Don't worry," he said. "It will get better."

"She hates me." There was a clack of wood hitting wood, and a short sharp sound of frustration. "I want to go home."

"She can't do anything to you. Not with me here. First form, Elizabeth."

A heatless pang went through me.

It was a half-ruined chapel, vines growing up the stone walls. It was vaguely familiar, and I realized why in a dreamy sort of way. I'd been drawing it for weeks now. There was a wide grassy center and a stone altar, and she appeared between the veils of mist. Her achingly beautiful heart-shaped face, a few long ringlets escaping to bob against her cheeks. She wore black capris and a white button-down, her hair parted in the middle and pulled back. The cut of the clothes somehow said "old." You could just tell she wanted to iron her hair flat and do some macramé.

She held *malaika*, the slightly curving wooden swords, with sweet natural grace. One of them made a half-circle, so sharp you could hear the air being cut. Perched atop the altar, her Keds shuffling as she stepped back and the swords made a complicated pattern, she was a deadly beautiful bird mantling its wings.

"Straighten your leg," Christophe said from the shadow under the wall on the right. The sunlight was a physical weight, golden-grainy like old honey. His eyes burned blue, and he watched her critically, his eyebrows pulled together.

Each time I saw him, it was as if I'd forgotten how well his face worked together, every angle and line fitting just so. He was in jeans and a black T-shirt, his hair pure Liverpool mod touched with blond highlights. "Wrist," he said mildly, and my mother stopped. She half-turned and gave him a Look.

Oh but I recognized that; it was the way she'd look at Dad when he was late for dinner, or when he said something joking about her washing dishes. It was the mock-glare of a pretty woman looking at a man she knows very well. Half-teasing, almost angry, and very aware of him looking at her.

The wingbeats of my pulse paused. The pins and needles stabbing static fuzzed through the scene, but I focused, just like holding the pendulum over Gran's kitchen table and searching for the little internal tickle that would make it answer questions.

I couldn't get enough of seeing her again. She was breathing easily, and she pushed away a stray curl with the back of her hand, the malaika held as easily as a butter knife. She was so graceful. I saw, as if I had a pair of binoculars, that her fingernails were bitten down, too.

Just like mine.

She looked so young. In the picture Dad carried in his wallet, the shadows in her eyes were darker, and she seemed older. Right now she looked, well, like a teenager.

Every little girl thinks her mother is the most beautiful woman in the world. But my mother was. She really was.

Her mock-glare turned into a set expression, mouth firm and eyebrows drawn together a little. "I feel like an idiot, stuck up on here. Why can't we practice inside?"

Christophe's face was unreadable, but he was tense. The tightness in his shoulders, the way his feet were placed just so, told me all about it. "The sunshine does you good. First form, again. Concentrate, Elizabeth."

She rolled her eyes and turned away. "Wish you'd just call me Liz."

"Wouldn't dream of it."

He sounded just the same — half-mocking, light and sarcastic. But something in his tone made me look at him, and just for an instant his face was naked. The aspect was on him, fangs touching his lip and his hair dark and slicked-down.

Christophe stared at my mother like he wanted to eat her.

But my mother had looked up at the destroyed roof of the chapel. Her tone had turned soft and distant, like she didn't even remember he was there with her. "I mean it. I want to go home."

"You are home." He dismissed it with three words, and why was he looking at her like that? It was almost indecent.

"She hates me." A quick, sideways grimace. "You don't get it, Chris."

He straightened. Stepped to the very edge of the wall's shadow. Anger crackled around him. But his face didn't change, and his tone was just the same. "Her hatred means less than nothing."

"You train me out here so she won't see it. Because you're her steady."

"I'm not her steady. It's useful for her to think so, though. First form, Elizabeth."

If he wanted her full attention, he'd gotten it. She actually frowned at him, and I remembered how she used to look when something wasn't going right. When she smiled, the world lit up, but when she looked serious, almost grim, her beauty was more severe. She shifted her weight uneasily. "How can you be so cold?"

Christophe folded his arms. "First form, Elizabeth."

"The girl's crazy about you, youngblood."

For once, Christophe actually looked puzzled. "Youngblood?"

"God, you're such a goon. She thinks you're a fox." My mother laughed, and the sunlight got brighter. "But you are, right? Reynard."

A long pause, while he watched her. She swung the malaika, but halfheartedly.

Finally, he stepped back into the shade. "This is serious business. You have a gift for these, and— "

"Forget it." She dropped both of them with a wooden clatter and hopped down off the square block of stone in one coordinated movement. "Every day it's the same thing. Why don't you just go back and play with Anna instead? I'm sick of all these games."

"It's not a game. It's deadly serious, and the sooner you—"

"Bye." She waved her fingers over her shoulder as she stalked away toward me. My heart swelled to the size of a basketball inside my ribs, and a burst of that static went through the entire scene.

NO! I wanted to yell, but couldn't make my lips work. The buzzing roared through me. I forced it away. I want to see!

Static flew like snow. It cleared enough for me to see Christophe, his hand around my mother's wrist as she pulled away from him. She twisted for the thumb to break his grip; he caught her shoulder with his other hand. She tore away again, her hair flying and a pair of dainty fangs visible as her mouth opened, yelling something.

She slapped him. The sound was a rifle crack, buzzing and blurring at the edges. They faced each other, my mother's chest heaving and her eyes full of tears as if he'd hit her.

Christophe smiled. It was a wide bright sunny grin, as if he'd just been kissed. A handprint showed on his pale cheek, vividly flushed. "Do that again," he said quietly. "Go ahead, Beth. I'll let you."

Her lips moved, but I didn't hear what she said. Because the static was worse, pouring down like a river of white feathers, and the buzzing had become a roar rattling through me, the pins and needles now knives and swords. The line holding me taut at the scene snapped, and I—

—fell with a thump as Ash howled and scrabbled at the door. He was making a noise like stones grinding together, the growl rising and falling as his narrow ribs flickered. He backed up, claws clicking, and flung himself at the door again.

I sat up, clipped a bruise on my shoulder on the shelf-bed. Rubbed at it. "Augh. Ow." Blinked furiously.

Ash whirled. The growl spiraled up, and I froze.

He stared at me, his eyes orange lamps. Then he paced back two steps deliberately, crowding the corner behind the door. He lifted one paw.

My mouth was dry, my eyes sandy, and I suddenly wanted to pee like nobody's business. I hadn't thought of *that* when I'd had this bright idea, and peeing in the metal toilet in the corner just was so not going to happen.

Plus I hate sleeping in my clothes. It always pinches everywhere when you wake up.

Ash's arm jabbed forward, and he pointed his claws at me. Then, very slowly, he pointed at the door. Still growling, his lip lifting and the gleam of ivory teeth under his nose.

I half-choked, grabbed the shelf-bed, and levered myself to my feet. I'd stiffened up but good. My internal clock was whacked up, but I thought it was before dawn.

Ash pointed at me, at the door. Under the growl, an inquisitive, pleading sound went up at the end. It was beyond me how he could make two sounds at once.

"Shut *up!*" I said sharply.

He did.

We stared at each other. He hunched down, his head cocked, and I tasted rotten, waxen oranges. They poured over my tongue, tickled the back of my throat, and I knew something bad was happening.

Ash whined softly in the back of his throat. Hunched down even more, the way a dog will when he needs to go out at night but thinks you'll yell at him if he asks too loud. I considered spitting to clear my mouth, but I knew it wouldn't get that taste away.

"Okay," I whispered. "Okay." I dug for the key with clumsy fingers. Froze again when he moved.

The Broken werwulf went utterly silent and crouched, facing the door.

Footsteps I shouldn't have been able to hear, up above in the silent mass of the Schola Prima. The *touch* quivered inside my head, each footfall distinct against the fabric of the night.

They were wrong—landing too heavily, or too lightly. I knew, in that soundless way the *touch* lays information inside my brain, that they were vampires.

And if they were here, they were up to no good.

Chapter Twenty-One

ghosted across the stone floor on numb feet. If they got to the door before I could unlock it, I would be caught in here with no place to run. And Ash . . .

I was sweating so bad the key almost squirted out of my fingers. I slid it into the lock with a rasping metallic sound, and the footsteps stopped. I couldn't tell how far away they were, but the consciousness of danger made my palms wet and my thudding heartbeats blur together like hummingbird wings.

Oh, crap.

Ash slid forward, noiseless and straining. The textures of his fur rasped against my jeans. A completely, totally inappropriate giggle crawled up in my throat, drowned in the horrible citrus tang. *I'm about to let the werwulf out for the night. It's just like letting out the cat, only there's no scratching or spraying.*

I twisted the key just as the footsteps ran forward, tippy-tapping closer. The sounds echoed, and a bright spear of crystalline hate lashed across the inside of my skull. I let out a garbled half-scream and tried to shove the door open with every ounce of strength I could scrape up. My back seized, but Ash was already moving. He hit the door like a freight train, so hard the steel crumpled. It banged into the wall and gave a hollow *gong!* that would have been funny if a high glassy cry hadn't split the air from up above immediately afterward. I stumbled out after him, desperate to be out of that little room.

A headache sank bony claws into my skull. I breathed out, pulling the *touch* up like a clenched fist. It was the only way I could keep myself *separate*, the only way I could tune out the hatred humming all around me.

That's the thing about suckers. They hate so, so much. Sometimes I wonder if they replace their blood with pure liquid revulsion. The footsteps poured through the halls of the Schola Prima, drawing closer and closer. So many of them. Yet there was no warning bell, no alarm like at the other Schola.

Ash made a short chuffing sound, turning in a circle so fast his fur made a whispering noise. He all but pee-danced in place, and I stepped nervously out into the hall.

He lunged toward me, and I flinched back down the hall. He stopped short, considered me, lunged again. I stepped back, and he stopped.

Oh.

I got the idea, but it took all the courage I could scrape together to half-turn and set off, one hand touching the wall because I wasn't too steady on my feet. He padded behind me, occasionally almost dancing in place when I slowed down, impatience in every fluidly moving line of him. Blood roared in my ears, almost drowning out the horrible little tip-tapping footsteps, and the most horrible thought in the world floated through my head.

Is he trying to get me someplace safe or is he driving me toward them?

Hell of a thing to think. I'd just been sleeping in the same room with him, and I'd been trusting him all this time. But oh, God, the nasty little mistrustful idea just wouldn't go away.

The hall ran into a T-junction at this end. I glanced back nervously, my hair getting in my eyes, and I gulped in an unsteady breath. "Ash?" I whispered. "I, I don't know—"

He bumped into me. I jumped and almost ran into the wall. He slid past, his shoulder then his chest and his flank touching my hip in one long stripe. His narrow graceful head looked left and right, and I heard the footsteps again. Like Q-tips tapping a drumhead, each one distinct but fuzzy.

They were even closer. Don't ask me how I knew.

Ash kept his head cocked. Then he looked back at me, and the awful human madness in his glowing eyes dimmed a little. He flowed back and pushed me toward the right.

I didn't know where this hall went. If I went down here, I'd be trusting him completely.

You were just sleepin'n there with him at'n the door, Dru. Too late now. Gran's voice, practical and stinging. My cheeks were wet and hot.

I won't lie. I *did* spit. I couldn't stand the taste in my mouth, but it didn't go away. My head hurt, a vise squeezing my temples. My bladder was incredibly full, and I was cold. My mother's locket, touching my chest, was a chip of ice. My fingers were wooden.

Closer. They were closer. My breath actually fogged, I was so cold.

I slid around the corner to the right. There was a door at the end, a big massive oak-bound thing. The type that, here at the Schola, led *outside*.

I let out a soft sob of relief. But the cold crested, poured over me in a wave of ice like I was back in the snow in the Dakotas. And there was a hiss behind me.

"—Sssssssvetosssssha—"

I almost fell against the wall. Ash's growl rose from the subsonic, rattling everything around us.

And if you've never heard a pissed-off werwulf howling as he takes on four vampires in an echoing stone hall, wow, you've really missed out.

Not really.

Get moving! They catch you in here, you die! Dad's bark, the way it always sounded in my head when something bad was happening. I pushed away from the wall, my knees full of water, and almost fell. It was like being in a really bad dream, one where you can't run because your entire body is too heavy to move, and the things behind you are breathing on your neck. Hot meaty breath, or cold, cold, knife-sharp breath.

I had to look back. I couldn't *not* look back. The noise was incredible.

A thrashing mass of squealing, growling, bones snapping, and crunching writhed in the hall. Eyes like lamps, and there were only three of them now because black vampire blood exploded, painting the walls with its acid stink. I half-screamed again, a throaty whisper because I'd lost all my air.

Ash hunkered down, snarling. The vampire he'd killed flopped bonelessly on the floor, bleeding a wide puddle of brackish black. The bright copper taste of adrenaline cut through wax oranges on my tongue as I backpedaled, stone floor rasping skin off my palm and yanking the bandage around my wrist loose, my sock feet scrabbling. Trying to get *away* because their hate poured through my unprotected head and set all of me on fire. A cold gemlike fire, pure frozen evil burning as it scraped every inch of my shivering skin.

I screamed, Ash making that low freight-train noise, the vampires hissing as they cringed back. And to top it all off, a klaxon split the air with its own wild howl. The Scholá Prima took a deep breath and woke, but it was too late. Because the slim pale vampires, all in black gear with leather loops and professional-looking buckles, surged forward, and I knew Ash couldn't hold them off forever.

CHAPTER TWENTY-TWO

My **back hit** the door. I scrabbled for the knob with clumsy fingers, caught in a nightmare. Ash backed up two swift steps, hunched further, and kept growling. Tension ran through him, but the three remaining vampires—one a slight pale female with long dark hair, the other two a matched set of blonds, all with black, black eyes—stared at me. Their narrow white hands hung at their sides like strangled birds, and for a hellish moment I was back in that empty palatial fake adobe in the Dakotas with a ton of snow outside and fiercer cold inside.

The house where Sergej had tried to kill me. His eyes had been like this, too, sucking holes of black tar starred with speckled dust. None of these three had the sheer weight in their gaze to crush all independent thought, but it was bad enough when they opened their mouths and hissed at me. The female dropped back, moving with oily grace.

The worst thing about them was that they looked about fifteen. Sergej himself had looked no older than Christophe, except for his eyes. And oh, God, but the fangs slid free of their upper lips, curving down to touch their chins. Not like a *djamphir*'s smaller canines that only touch the lower lip—no, a full-blown vampire's teeth mean business. Their jaws distend when they hiss, too. Just like a snake trying to get down a big egg.

The female crouched slowly. Her joints moved in weird, inhuman ways. They just moved wrong, worse than seeing a crowd of *djamphir* or werwulfen at once. Ash's warning growl deepened a notch or two. My sweat-slick fingers found the doorknob, twisted—and slipped.

Shit. Of course. The door was locked. It led outside, of course it was locked. The two male vampires moved forward. The klaxon was still going on, the sound of shouts and running feet almost drowned in it.

Think, goddamn you! Think!

But my thinker was busted. My head gave an amazing flare of pain, and the scene unreeled in front of me. The males were going to swarm Ash, and if they could hold him down the female was crouched, ready to spring right over the top of them and collide with me. I'd seen the pictures, what vampire claws do to flesh. I didn't even have my switchblade—I'd just slid the key in my pocket. Stupid, stupid, *stupid.*

I should have left, with or without Graves. But I promised not to leave him behind.

More cries. A howl of despair—maybe there were more suckers up causing chaos all over the Schola. And here I'd thought it was so safe.

Be honest, Dru. You knew it wasn't safe here. But you're tired, aren't you. Sick of all this.

I swallowed hard. Freed my fingers from the slippery doorknob and shook them out, drew myself up.

If I was going to go down, I was going to go down fighting.

I don't know if Ash figured out their plan, but his hindquarters bunched, fur rippling, and he flung himself forward, colliding with the two males. I raised my hands, both of them fists, and almost choked on the taste of rotten, candied citrus.

And everything . . . stopped.

Roaring filled my ears. My mother's locket flared with molten heat; the fang marks on my left wrist twitched like fishhooks in flesh. I had time to see every stone in the walls, every hairline crack as my pupils dilated and the dim hallway turned scorch-bright. The female vampire hung in the air; she'd cleared the tangled frozen mass of the boys duking it out and was stretched out like Superman, her fingernails turned to ten amber-burnished claws, each about four inches long and pointed at me. Her skin was perfect, matte, and poreless, her hair a floating banner writhing with horrible life.

Everything sparkled, encased in hard clear plastic. There was nowhere to go—if I could have ducked aside, I would have. The *snap* like a rubber band that would bring the world up to its regular speed hovered on the edge of my consciousness, held back by mental muscles hardened by the practice Gran had hammered into me in her own way when I was still a toddler.

Did she have any idea what she was training me for?

Something in me I'd never noticed before dilated. Warmth bloomed at the crown of my head, flowed down my skin to my numb-tingling sock feet. My teeth stung a little, the fangs sliding free, and the comfort of the *aspect* fought with uneasy disgust.

Because they had fangs, too. Bigger ones, sure—but the same *kind*.

My knees hit the stone floor with a jolt and I pitched forward, rolling.

Snap!

A bone-jarring *crunch*, a howl and a fresh splatter of acidic black blood. Wetness splashed me. I let out a short miserable cry of panic and disgust, kept rolling. The smell was every foul rotting thing in the world wrapped up together and powdered with rotten eggs, choking-thick in the confined space. The female hit the door with another massive hollow gonging sound, and Ash was down, scrabbling on the floor with the last surviving male. He wasn't growling anymore. Neither of them made a sound.

The female vampire slid down, landed on her feet, and reversed with unnatural, fluid speed. I hit the wall hard, fetching up half-dazed and shaking the noise out of my head, the comforting warmth of the *aspect* still encasing me. My pulse thundered in my ears like feathered wings.

She saw me again, and the hate dancing in those black eyes was enough to make me sick. I threw out my hands, as if I was tossing a dodgeball, a great painless gout of force leaving me. It was like hexing the American history teacher back in the same classroom where I'd met Graves, the sense of steam bleeding through a valve, a relief like lancing a wound.

Only this time I wouldn't feel guilty and pull the hex back like snapping a towel. No, this time it was for real, and I wanted to kill the thing in a female body that was looking to kill *me*.

The hex flew true and hit her squarely just as she was getting ready to leap. It flung her back against the door again with another crunch, and a high crazed laugh burst out of me. Because the force was building again—

—and Gran's owl streaked down the hall, talons outstretched. There was no missing this time either. The bird claws bit deep, black blood exploded, and the female let out a scream so terrible it shook the hall and blew my hair back on a hot stinking draft. I slid farther along the wall as Ash struggled free of the broken body of the last male. He collapsed, hauled himself up again on slippery paws.

My hands slid in hot, greasy vampire blood. I choked again, crab-pedaling back along the wall, my legs pistoning wildly.

The female sucker lurched forward as Gran's owl flapped its wings, each beat muffled and almost touching her hair. The claws were still tangled in her face, and the force streaming through me crested again as the talons bit deeper.

Light burst down the hall. A red streak arrowed past Ash, who sagged aside onto my feet. I barely saw the small doglike creature with a high-held rufous brush of a black-tipped tail as it leapt on the female, biting and clawing. She screamed again, but it was the miserable sound of an animal in a trap.

I grabbed at Ash's pelt. He was bleeding badly, red fluid staining the lake of rotting black we both sat simmering in. The bandage Dibs had wrapped so carefully around my wrist flopped loose, squelching and steaming.

The light was too bright. Someone had flicked a switch and the incandescents overhead were blazing. I wondered, in one of those split-second thoughts that happen when things go crazy, what they paid each year for lightbulbs in this place.

He hurtled down the hall, deadly silent, and I pulled harder, trying to get Ash closer to me. Christophe, his hair slick and dark and the *aspect* shining on him like a halo, tore the female vampire's throat out. Black blood gushed. Her body slumped aside and he jabbed down, the polished wooden stake in his bleeding hands whistling as it clove the air to bury itself with a sick meaty thump in her chest.

He turned on one booted heel. His thin black V-neck sweater was torn, a stripe of red blood painted one perfect, high-arched cheekbone, and his eyes blazed unholy blue. His fangs were out, his entire face a mask of effort and ferocity. His jeans were ripped all over, and he was splashed up to the thighs with black blood.

I don't think I've ever been so happy and so terrified at the same time. "Ch-Ch-Chr—" I stuttered over his name. Gran's owl had vanished, and the little red animal—it was no bigger than a cat—rubbed against Christophe's shin, its narrow black nose raised inquisitively. I flinched and realized what it was.

A fox. Christophe's *aspect* in animal form.

Ash sagged against my legs. My teeth tingled, the *aspect* enfolding me. Christophe dropped the stake. It clattered on the floor, and he stalked forward. I would have backpedaled, but the wall was behind me and there was nowhere to go, especially with pound upon pound of deadweight wulfen on my lap.

He went to his knees, splashing in the vampire blood. Steam rose as the black ichor ate at fabric. I wanted to haul Ash out of it. I didn't have the strength or the leverage.

Christophe reached over the Broken wulf and grabbed my bruised shoulders, his fingers sinking in. His face contorted, and he yelled something at me. I just stared. Besides, he was speaking in some weird foreign tongue, the same one that tinted his English when he was sleepy or upset.

And they say *I* have an accent just because I grew up with Gran and below the Mason-Dixon. Let me tell you something: People up North bite off every syllable like they want to chew it to death instead of tasting it proper.

Christophe inhaled sharply, throat working as he swallowed. Tried again, and this time the words were recognizable English. "*Are you hurt?*"

I took stock. I ached all over. My teeth felt like lightning was running through them. The warm-oil feeling of the *aspect* bathed the hurt and the bruises, but it couldn't erase them completely.

He shook me. My head bobbled. He kept yelling. "God*damn* you, Dru, are you *hurt*?"

I finally shook my head. Found my voice. "Ash. *Ash*." My hands were full of the Broken's pelt, and I didn't like the way he was just lying there against me. You can tell when someone's hurt bad by the way they slump, not even unconsciously holding themselves together.

"Thank God," Christophe whispered and pulled me away from the wall. He got his arms around me, and I smelled spiced-apple pies. The smell filled my nose. He pressed his lips against my aching temple and was saying something in a ragged, broken tone, but I didn't care. Ash was caught between us, bleeding and unconscious.

I wanted to cry. But my eyes were full of hot graininess, and all I could see, my head tilted at a weird awkward angle, was a high curving arc of vampire blood, splashed smoking against the gray stone wall.

CHAPTER TWENTY-THREE

t took three glowing-eyed *djamphir*, all of them torn-up and bloody, to pick up Ash and start carrying him away. I pulled against Christophe's hands. "No, please—*no*, I've got to go with him, *no*—"

"Stay still." Christophe dabbed at a scratch on my forehead, one I couldn't remember getting. "No broken bones, no bleeding. *Dziękuję Bogu, moj maly ptaszku* . . ." Blue eyes sharp, he glanced at my face. The blond highlights had slid back through his hair as his *aspect* retreated. The fox had vanished, but I wasn't worried about that. "Be *still*."

"I want to go with him." I glared at Christophe, my throat full of dry rocks. "Where were you?"

"Keeping watch on your window. I told you I wouldn't leave you unprotected. I also told the wulfen to take care of you. When I get my hands—"

Which brought up another question. I tried to slide away again. "Shanks. Did you see him? Is he—"

Christophe grabbed my shoulder. "Robert? He's wounded but

otherwise hale. Where is the *loup-garou*? I would have thought he'd be with you. Now please, Dru. Be still, calm down, let me work."

"Work? Jesus Christ, those were *vampires!* Ash—is he—"

"He may live. I would never have believed a werwulf could do this. But he's Broken, and . . . well. In any case, you're safe. Everything else is immaterial."

"Reynard!" A familiar voice. Benjamin rocketed around the corner, his sneakered feet slipping in greasy crud and rotting vampire blood. He took in the scene, dark eyes passing over everything in a brief, contained arc. "What the hell are *you* doing here?" He looked like hell. He was beat up and battered, bruises puffing up along one side of his face, his hair wildly disarranged. His clothes were torn, too, and I saw with no real surprise that he was holding a single *malaika* in a white-knuckle grip. He saw me, too, and almost choked. His eyes blazed.

"There you are!" He took a single step forward. "Where were you? What were you doing? How did you escape? We were about to—"

"Leave her be," Christophe said mildly, and Benjamin turned white and almost swallowed his tongue. "Your cadre?"

"Still efficient. Some slight wounding." But the *djamphir*'s shoulders straightened, and he actually looked proud.

"My faith in you is restored." But Christophe didn't look away from my face. His eyebrows drew together. I swallowed hard and slumped against the wall. "Assess the damage to Milady's chambers, if you please, and send me Leontus. Thank you."

I think it was the first time I ever heard a *djamphir* actually dismissed, though not in so many words. Benjamin made a curious little salute with his free hand, glanced at me. "Milady." And he vanished back down the hall, running flat out.

"Have you been sparring hard?" Christophe's hand came up. I

flinched, but he rested his fingertips against my cheek. I'd almost forgotten the shadows of bruising on my face, thought that maybe the confusion would cover it up. I should have known better; he didn't miss much.

"Anna." The single word blurted out, and I instantly regretted it. Christophe's face hardened, and he let go of me.

A swarm of *djamphir* filled the hall now, mostly older students. They were making certain the vampires were out of commission, and the cracking and tearing sounds made my gorge rise. The hall was full of nose-scorching smoke, too, from vampire blood eating into fabric. Christophe started barking orders, and every single one of the djhampir hopped to obey like he was a teacher or something. They even looked relieved that someone was there to tell them what to do.

I know that feeling. I always felt better when Dad was around to tell me what the hell was going on and what my part in it was. I tried not to look at the mess on the floor. Every bruise and muscle I owned began to shake. My hair hung in my face, blonde streaking through the curls and retreating as the *aspect* boiled through me and receded.

A lean blond *djamphir* arrived at a dead run with, of all things, a can of Coke. Christophe plucked it from his fingers with a nod and turned to me. "Here. You need the sugar."

"Reynard." Leon appeared out of thin air. "The Council's got wind of this. They're en route."

"It doesn't matter. She's safe." Christophe pressed my hand around the cold aluminum, the can already sweating condensation. "And I can afford to be caught now that I've run my course."

"I hope you know what you're doing." Leon gave me a dark look. "She's all but helpless. I can't be everywhere at once. Neither can Calstead. Especially since they didn't give him or the others class waivers."

"They didn't . . ." Christophe took this in, shrugged. "Where's the *loup-garou?*" He said it mildly, like he didn't care.

Leon stiffened. "He's not with her?"

"No. Just the Broken. And why, in the name of everything that is holy, was she left alone with Anna?"

"What?" Leon gave me a good hard look, his gaze passing over the shadows of bruising as well. He cursed, slowly and softly. There was a commotion around the corner, drawing nearer. Shouts, information passed along. "Go," the mousy-haired *djamphir* said in an urgent whisper. "If they catch you—"

Christophe's smile was a marvel of edged sweetness. When he grinned like that he looked handsomer than ever, the hint of danger just about threatening to stop a girl's heart. "Why, Leontus. I didn't know you *cared.*" He looked back at me. "I said drink, little bird. You'll regret it if you don't."

I cracked the tab and took a long cold fizzing mouthful. Carbonation stung my throat. Everything wavered in front of me, the hall seen through a haze.

Where's Graves? He should be here. The reality of what had just happened hit me. I turned my head, rusty iron cords in my neck creaking. "God," I whispered. There was a huge black stain in front of the door, still steaming.

I just really, really wanted to see Graves. I wanted to see his face and hear what he'd make of all this. I wanted to have his arm over my shoulders because when he did that I felt like I could handle anything. Including this.

Instead I sagged against the wall and took another mechanical slurp of Coke.

"I'm serious," Leon said urgently, and the commotion around the corner reached a higher pitch.

"*Svetocha!*" It was Kir; I recognized the voice. "Where is the *svetocha?*"

He skidded around the corner, and the hall was suddenly, magically empty. The older students disappeared, and I didn't blame them. It felt like a thunderstorm approaching, or the weird calm after the sirens but before a tornado.

Hiro was behind him, and Bruce completed the trio. All three of them stopped dead. Kir went red up to the roots of his hair, and Hiro surged forward.

Bruce grabbed the Japanese *djamphir*. "Steady on, man."

"Yes, keep him back." Christophe folded his arms. "I would hate to have his family seek to avenge him."

Hiro hissed something, fangs out and lips twisting. It didn't sound like a polite hello.

I couldn't help myself. All the carbonation rose in my throat. and I belched. It was a nice long loud one. But it did settle my twisting, cramping stomach. The sugar in the soda would help stave off shock. I'd crash later, of course.

Leon actually laughed, a chuckle behind his hand as if he wanted to trap it and keep it for posterity.

Christophe smiled very slightly, but he was tense. And the *aspect* hadn't left him. Hiro's eyes had turned an odd amber color. His short black hair stood up, and his hands curled slowly into fists before they loosened—and curled up again like he was imagining Christophe's throat under them.

I didn't care what they did as long I could go lie down somewhere. I was half-sick with wanting to see Graves again.

I decided I'd better get some answers while I had everyone's attention. "Graves. Where is he?" *Because I'm blowing this town. I just can't take any more of this.*

"*I* don't know." Leon's hand dropped back to his side, but I noticed he was placed very carefully between Christophe and the three from the Council. "I thought he was with you, Milady."

"I haven't seen him since . . . since gym." That about took all the starch out of me. From one nasty fight to another, and Ash . . .

There was nothing I could do. I just ran out of steam and stood there woodenly, the Coke half-lifted.

"Is that where you gained those bruises?" Christophe didn't even look at me. He was too busy staring Hiro down. "Love-taps, no doubt. Where was the Red Bitch during my little bird's sparring practice, Kir? You are the one most likely to know, aren't you? And Bruce. I see you've stopped drinking from the vein."

"The Lady Anna is on her way." Bruce still held Hiro's lapels. His own hair was standing up, the dark curls writhing against each other almost like the female vampire's had, and I felt sick all over again. "When she gets here it will force a decision. I don't want to arrest you, Reynard. You'd best leave."

"And leave *moja księżniczko* here to your tender mercies? When she's already suffered *this*? The flower of the Order here, sworn to defend her, and a Broken werwulf has to do the job." Christophe shook his sleek dark head. "I am sorely disappointed."

Kir turned a deeper shade of crimson, almost matching his hair. Bruce gave Hiro a meaningful, gauging look and released him. Hiro brushed the lapels of his gray suit, his long beautiful fingers moving with spiderlike precision.

Leon finally moved. He slid behind Christophe, stepped in front of me. "You should drink more of that. You used your *aspect*, right? It's getting stronger?"

I nodded. "The . . . there were three of them, and Ash . . ."

"Thank God they didn't catch you in that cell. Even so close to blooming, you'd have been killed." He pitched the words loud enough to make it clear he was trying to smooth the ruffled waters, or something. Nice of him.

I searched for words. "Ash went nuts. I . . . I let him out. He led me this way."

"Away from the fighting." An approving nod. Fine lank hair fell in Leon's eyes. He looked just the same as he did every morning, and I was glad about that. If I just focused on him I could shut out all the rest of it. "More of them broke into your room, Milady. Tore it apart looking for you. These three were probably seeking to euthanize the Broken."

"*Euthanize?* Since when do you engage in euphemisms, Leontus? You mean *murder.*" Christophe hadn't relaxed at all. I got the idea none of them dared to get any closer to him. "I trust I have shamed you all sufficiently for you to remember your duty?"

Leon actually snorted. "I was where I was supposed to be, Reynard. Save your ire for whoever betrayed the exact location of this girl's room to a cadre of *nosferatu* killers."

This girl. Like I wasn't even here. I mean, that would have suited me just fine, not being here. I shut my eyes and leaned my aching head back.

I felt her arrival like a storm front. Warm perfume clashed with the rot of vampires and a stray draft of Christophe's apple-pie scent. The mix made me feel light-headed. It was like gas fumes just waiting for a spark.

Leon steadied me. He didn't grind his fingers into old or new bruises, and I was grateful for that. "She's passing out," he remarked calmly.

"Is there anywhere here that qualifies as safe for Elizabeth's daughter?" Christophe's tone could have cut stone.

"Christophe." Anna, strangely breathless. "What's going on?

What are you doing here? Kir, why hasn't he been arrested? He's a traitor—"

"Watch your mouth," Christophe's voice cut across hers. Leon was strong for someone so wiry, and I was really glad, because my knees buckled. The can of Coke hit the floor with a hollow chipping, sloshing sound. More mess to clean up. "I demand a full Trial, according to the Codes."

"You're outside the Codes." You could just *see* Anna's self-satisfied smirk, the way she said it. It occurred to me that she never really had anyone argue with her. She couldn't have, not when she sounded like that. "You're a traitor, Reynard, and you've overreached yourself."

God. None of them even talk like kids. I kept my eyes shut tight. Material rustled. The temperature dropped, almost as cold as it had been a few minutes ago while the vampires were stalking Ash and me.

Christophe's fury was like a draft of air-conditioning against already-chilled skin. "If they come any closer, *Red Queen*, you will lose your pretty bodyguards."

Silence. Tense, ticking silence. I pried my eyes open and looked over Leon's shoulder.

Anna stood behind three slim dark-haired boy *djamphir*. All three had red T-shirts, and I had the not-so-nice idea she'd chosen them for their looks.

Not twins, but brothers, maybe. And in red shirts? Not a good choice. Hadn't any of them ever watched *Star Trek*?

Two of them had 9mms pointed at Christophe. The one in the middle—I'd seen him before—just stood, hands loose and eyes empty, staring at him. Kir, Bruce, and Hiro stood aside, Hiro shifting his weight just a fraction forward. The idea that he might just throw himself at Anna returned, circled my pain-fogged brain.

Anna's blue gaze locked with Christophe's. Her heart-shaped face was bloodless-pale, and her hair was a perfect mass of clustered red-tinted ringlets. She was in silk again, a tightly laced old-fashioned dress with snow-white lace around the square neckline, more lace fountaining from the cuffs.

I got the idea she'd done her makeup up special for this. Not that she needed much. She was utterly and completely beautiful, except for the hate shining in her eyes.

It was like an old Western showdown. I wouldn't have been surprised if there were tumbleweeds.

Bruce cleared his throat. "Actually, he's not outside the Codes."

Anna darted him a bright, venomous glance. "*I* am head of the Council, and—"

"You're *svetocha*," Hiro said flatly. "The Codes are in the keeping of the *princeps* of the Order. Which is Bruce, as provisional head of the Council." He paused. A ghost of nasty satisfaction tinted his tone. "A full Trial is within his purview to declare."

"Just a goddamn second." Kir shifted his weight as if to step forward, thought better of it when Christophe's cold attention settled on him. "How do we know he won't vanish again?"

"I have no intention of vanishing," Christophe informed him. "If you want to find me, you need look no further than wherever Dru is. Her quarters are not kept secret as Anna's are, her Guard not given class waivers as Anna's are, her person in jeopardy"—here he elegantly tilted his head, and Anna's lip curled for a fraction of a second before her face smoothed—"and while she's *in* class, she's in with the general population rather than being given tutors like Anna was. What, precisely, *is* going on here? Be so kind as to enlighten me, Kir."

"I am the head of the Order!" Anna surged forward, petticoats rustling, and pushed past the matched *djamphir*. "This is *Reynard*! He's a *traitor*! He's *Sergej's son*!"

God, she really hates him. I concentrated on beating back the dizziness threatening to swallow me.

"He's also within the Codes to request a full Trial, Milady." Bruce's tone was deceptively mild.

"Council meeting, then. We'll vote."

Bruce straightened, drawing himself up. His chin lifted a little. "It's not a voting issue. But if you wish to call a meeting, by all means do so. We'll have to wait until Milady Dru is able to attend or designates a proxy, though."

I had the idea I should protest this, but Leon shook his head. Just a little.

I just wanted to see Graves. I got the idea he would help me sort this out. Or at least if he was here I could let go of consciousness and know that things would be okay when I woke up.

If I had to, I would beg him to just lie on the bed next to me and breathe. So I could know things were all right.

The realization hit me then.

He'd probably left, the way I'd been wanting to. He probably got tired of all this, of *me*, and left me behind. I'd promised not to leave without him, but *he* hadn't promised.

"She's not fit to be on the Council." Anna's teeth were clenched so tight the words had a hard time getting out. Red sparks danced in the back of her pupils, spinning. "Bruce, you cannot—"

"I can and I will. She's *svetocha*; she has a right. Remember? Your own words will come back to haunt you, *Milady*. I think you'd best be quiet. Especially since I intend to inquire fully into Christophe's accusations. *I* did not sign a directive to put Milady Anderson into the general population."

"Traitors," she hissed. "All of you. *Traitors.*"

"You bandy that word about so frequently." Christophe leaned forward, all his weight on the balls of his feet. I recognized that stance. Dad looked that way when he was picking out someone for a fight. "Why is that, I wonder?"

"You and your little *bitch*—"

I slid over to the side, losing the battle with the darkness. Leon caught me, and at least he didn't bruise me. "Fight later," he said over his shoulder. "Or at least let me get her out of here. For Christ's sake, she's not even *bloomed* yet."

CHAPTER TWENTY-FOUR

For once, August showed no desire to leave when dusk came around. Instead, he settled down on the ancient flowered couch, smoking, loading clips, and staring at the television. He had it turned all the way down and a black-and-white movie played, the light flickering over every surface. I sat on the other end of the couch, folding laundry. He'd brought two big bags of it back from the laundry room downstairs, and while I was glad I didn't have to trudge out to a Laundromat, I felt kind of weird about someone else washing my panties.

August had gone from once or twice letting me go out with him on sunny days to not letting me out of the house at all. He got takeout, or we ate omelets. I was beginning to get itchy, and if Dad hadn't told me to stay put I would have at least snuck out on the roof at night. Just to get some air. All the movie posters on the walls were watching me with blank eyes.

There wasn't even a plant in here. At least I could have talked to a philodendron or something. And the lack of natural light was really begin-ning to get me down. I'd taken to lying in front of the bedroom window, staring up and aching for some sun. But it was gray, the sky threatening snow. I was beginning to think sunshine was something I'd made up.

I held up one of August's T-shirts. Ragged claw marks sliced the thin fabric. It was a wonder there was any shirt left. "What was this?"

"That? Oh. Just some trouble over in Manhattan." He slid the bullets into the clip, each one going in smoothly. He didn't have to look while he did it. His short Russian cigarette fumed in the ashtray, and I wrinkled my nose. On the screen, a very young Marlon Brando sat on a swing and fitted a girl's white glove on his hand, looking up at a slim pretty blonde. "Got 'em cornered in a stairwell. Dark work." August set the clip down, picked up an empty one. Muscle moved under the skin of his arm, left bare by a Rolling Stones T-shirt.

Dark work. Which meant I didn't need to know any more. I nodded, knowing he'd see the movement in his peripheral vision. Tossed the shirt into my mending pile. He had a truly ancient Singer machine, and I'd started patching any clothes of his I could reasonably expect to. Usually T-shirt material is too thin to really repair, but I'd give it a try. At least I never had to ask twice for any supplies—he brought home exactly what I asked for every time. Except bread. He would never bring back any damn bread.

My hands moved without thought, too. I've folded so much laundry that I barely have to pay attention. August used a strange sort of fabric softener; it smelled lemony. "You gonna turn that up? I can't hear it."

"In a bit. This is not a good part for an impressionable young girl." The last word came out as "goil." His lips stretched in a wide, unsettling grin. If I wasn't so used to him, I might almost have felt a moment of unease. But that was just Augie. He seemed to delight in squinching up his face in the weirdest possible ways. Just to keep things limber.

I folded a pair of his jeans. The blood had washed out just fine after some cold-water soaking. Even the greasy gunk ground into the knees had come out. Of course, it had been fresh when I got to it. "You want some coffee?" What I meant was, Are you going out tonight? But I didn't dare ask, in case he decided to. Then I'd feel like I made him do it, and I'd wander around the tiny apartment cleaning things up or clearing a place to do some short t'ai chi. Wishing I could get out and run. Even just a trip to the corner bodega to get a pack of gum would have been fine. But no. August had stopped taking me anywhere, muttering something about smells. I was pretty sure I didn't offend, what with a shower every day. So I didn't ask any questions, just kept asking him to bring home a loaf of white so I could have a PBJ. I craved a PBJ like you wouldn't believe.

I was so fricking tired of omelets.

"No thanks," he said finally. "Staying in tonight."

"Oh. Okay." I found a pair of my jeans and folded them swiftly. Then one of August's flannel shirts. I'd offered to iron them, but he got a weird look on his face and told me not to. I did some anyway, but when he came home and saw them he took the iron and put it somewhere.

Weird. But then, hunters are weird. Even Dad has his tics.

There. I'd thought about Dad. I'd never asked August when he was coming back. Sometimes a job will take awhile, right? I was sure he'd come back.

Wasn't I?

I tried not to think about it. He'd always come back before. But . . . I was never sure, way down deep, if each time he did would be the last.

I looked at the television. For a guy with such a nice bit of plasma hardware, he didn't watch a lot of it. When he did, it was always black-and-white movies. Why have a great TV if all you can see are shades of gray?

Someone banged on the door. My heart jumped into my throat like a jackrabbit on speed. I would have leapt to my feet, but August was already rising, grabbing his cigarette and taking one last drag before grinding it out. "Steady, princess." He looked amused. "If there was trouble I'd be outside, leading it a chase. This is good news. I can smell it."

Now I was folding a blue sweater. I carefully focused on the sleeves while August got the door. Please let it be him, I prayed. Please.

And then, wonder of wonders, God came through. I heard my father's voice.

"Goddamn you, Dobrowski. Why do you have to live up three flights of stairs?" He stamped, as if his boots were full of snow.

August sounded amused. "It's safe up here. You look like hell. Did you—"

Clipped and final. "I didn't get him. Where's Dru?"

August sighed. "Safe and sound. She's obsessed with toast, of all things. Move, so I can shut the door."

My eyes blurred. I let out a long breath, my shoulders sagging. My heart was thumping, a high hard gallop of happiness. I knew what luggage felt like at the airport the moment it was picked up, the instant familiar fingers closed on its handle.

It was Dad. He'd finally come back. He was here, and we were going to move on. Happiness filled me until I thought I would burst, and I swiped the tears away angrily. If I broke down crying he'd get That Look, like I was a weepy girl and he didn't know what to do. But I couldn't stop leaking. Now I could admit that I'd been afraid I would be stuck here forever.

Now it was safe.

I rolled the sweater up as if I was packing it in a box. He was here. It meant we were leaving.

I couldn't wait.

CHAPTER TWENTY-FIVE

White walls. Sunlight. It smelled of lemons, of furniture polish, of fresh air. My eyes drifted open, took this in. I stayed there, just looking, for a long while. Curiously, comfortably numb.

I heard someone breathing, and hot lightning-streak relief poured through me. *Graves? Oh thank God. Do I ever have a lot to tell you.*

I rolled over slowly. My back had stiffened up; so had my arms and legs. My neck twinged. I felt crusty and sweaty, my skin slipping against clean sheets. I was in my underwear and nothing else. Not even the bandage on my wrist, not even a bra.

How did that happen? The ceiling was white plaster, a repeating pattern of diamonds and roses sharply sculpted on it. The other Schola had been dirtier—grime in the corners, the mats in the sparring chapel used until they fell apart, the girls' locker room musty around the edges. Even chlorine can't kill that sort of funk.

But not here. Here at the Prima it was all bright and clean, and I wondered about that. I never saw anyone dusting. You'd think there would be an army of janitors.

There was a lamp on a white-painted nightstand with spindly legs. It had crystal chandelier-drops instead of a shade, and it was still burning. Little rainbows caught in the drops, light reflecting on the antique brass base. I pushed myself up on my elbow, staring at it like it was a spaceship or something.

Where the hell am I?

I hate waking up with that question. It's cliché, sure, but it's also a deep well of insecurity swallowing whatever rest you might have gotten during the night. My pulse leapt. I sat up slowly, clutching the pale cream top sheet and white down comforter to my chest. Cool air brushed my naked, dry-sweat-crackling back.

The room was small but perfect, one wall lined with stripped-pine bookshelves. The windows were huge, open, and full of afternoon sunlight falling past net curtains and a wide white satin window seat. A small white rolltop desk stood across the room, a clunky antique office chair of pale wood with its back to the window in front of it. A slightly open door showed white tile and what was probably a bathroom. Another door must've led to the hall because it was studded with locks and barred. A mirrored door to a walk-in closet was half-open, too, and I saw familiar clothes hanging in there. Big white dresser with a vanity mirror and a white-cushioned satin seat, the vanity's surface curiously bare in front of the antique brass-curlicued mirror frame.

What the hell?

In the shadowed space between the desk and the bookshelves, Christophe sat on the floor. His head was tipped back, his throat stretched out, hair mussed artistically. His eyes were closed and his lips parted slightly. He was deeply asleep, and a shotgun—probably the one I'd seen him with in the Dakotas—lay across his lap. His hands lay limp and graceful, and he wore yet another thin black V-neck sweater and jeans. With his legs outstretched, the tips of his boot-toes fell apart slightly, the worn soles making a V and sunlight caressing their edges.

I reached up, touched my mother's locket. Kept the covers clutched up to my chest while I looked around for some clothes. If all else failed I'd tear the sheet off the bed, but—

When I snuck another glance at Christophe, his eyes were open, blue fires in the shadow of the bookcase. His breathing hadn't changed. Neither had a single muscle. He looked at me, and Jesus. A hot flush worked its way up from my neck, burned in my cheeks. The healed-up fang marks on my wrist filled with an odd tingling, and I forced my fingers away from the warm metal of the locket.

He was smiling faintly, too. Something about the smile made me vaguely uncomfortable. I swallowed hard.

"You're safe," he said finally. And there it was again—the gentle tone, not his usual faint mockery. He never sounded like that with anyone else around. "North wing. This was your mother's room. I had them bring your clothes up. Your computer and everything else will follow, as soon as they're scanned and pronounced safe."

I just kept clutching the covers stupidly and staring at him.

"At sunset, they'll hold my Trial. You needn't worry, though. Everything's going to be fine." He still didn't move, except for his eyelids, a rapid blink. "And by the way, good morning. Would you like some breakfast? Lunch? I suppose it's lunchtime. For daywalkers, anyway."

I had the unsettling sensation that the world had shifted out from underneath me again. "Graves. Ash. Shanks, Dibs. Are they okay?"

"The Broken is in the infirmary, sedated and restrained. He might even live. Robert and Samuel are both well; Samuel's in the infirmary, too. He has quite a gift for medical work."

Samuel? Oh, yeah. Dibs. "Graves? And Benjamin, Leon, the guys?"

"Benjamin and his cadre are very well, all things considered, and standing guard at both ends of this hall. We'll figure out a tutor schedule as soon as this unpleasantness is over, and—"

I didn't care. "Graves. Where's Graves?" *Tell me you've found him.* But I thought I knew.

I just wanted him to tell me I was wrong.

His mouth pulled down, just slightly, before the smile returned. It was a faint ironclad grimace this time. "Nobody's seen him, Dru."

My chest squeezed down on itself. "But . . ."

"Every teacher and student is on the lookout. Unless the wulfen are hiding him in the dorms somewhere, and Robert swears they're not. We've accounted for everyone, wounded or whole, except him. No severe casualties from this attack, thank God."

"Oh, God." I found a word for what was boiling up in my throat.

It was the same old feeling. *Abandonment.* He'd left me behind, just like Mom and Gran and Dad. Where the hell would he *go*?

I realized with a jolt that it didn't matter. Away from me, he was safe. I just never thought he would leave me behind. I honestly didn't.

Except now I was horribly, awfully afraid that he had.

"Did something happen?" Christophe laid the question quietly in the sunshine-flooded room, and he sounded like he really wanted to know. "Between you two?"

"Yes. No. I don't know. I guess. Look, I just . . . are those my clothes?" *And who took my bra off?* My cheeks were about as red as Kir's hair, if the scorching in them was any indication.

Kir. Jesus. A cold shiver traced down my back. He was on the Council, and he was on Anna's side. What if he'd—

Christophe was on his feet in an instant, the shotgun held loosely and expertly, pointed at the floor. I would have been worried about someone wandering around my room with a gun, but he was a professional. And to tell the truth, I was glad he was here.

He'd come back for me. Again. The intensity of the relief was pretty ridiculous. When you've spent your entire life being a piece of luggage for people to collect, even when you're a *helpful* piece of luggage and you know they love you, you get to feeling like a golden retriever when someone comes home.

He swept the closet door open, laid the shotgun down carefully, and stepped inside. "Anything in particular, or just something to cover up? You had *nosferatu* blood on your clothes; Samuel cut them off so you could sleep a little more comfortably. I didn't think you'd mind much."

Did you look? But it wasn't the sort of question I could ask him. I could have played it as a joke with Graves, but not Christophe. For one thing, he was in my closet. For another, there was that shotgun. And I was still blushing and feeling like I'd done something wrong by passing out. "Oh. Okay. I, uh, wondered about that."

"Here." He emerged with an armful of clothes. "One of these, I think. Is there something specific you'd like to wear? Or will . . . here, look." He slid them off his arm onto the foot of the bed. Six T-shirts, two flannels, a hoodie—Jesus. That was a quarter of my wardrobe right there.

"Christophe . . ."

It was the first time I'd seen him even *close* to flustered. "Don't worry, I won't look. See?" He backed up two steps, turned as if he was on parade, and headed for the closet. Scooped up the shotgun and crossed to the window. Stood in the sunshine, the blond highlights in his shaggily cut hair lighting up.

I'd never seen him in full sun before. The blond streaks turned to gold, and the texture of his skin glowed. The light bounced off the metal of the shotgun's sawed-off barrel. His head was down, like he was looking out the window.

Some of what he'd said sank in. My mother's room. There were books on the stripped-pine bookshelves. Hers?

Do that again. . . . Go ahead, Beth. I'll let you. The dream rose up in my head. Was it what Gran called a true-seeing? Dreams were slippery, best not to put any weight on them. What you wanted could turn into what you saw, not what actually was.

But I'd been dreaming more and more lately, about things I found out were true. Like Dad in a long concrete corridor, walking toward his death. Like my mother hiding me in a closet and going out to fight Sergej.

I grabbed a longer flannel and wrapped it around myself, buttoned up. "Where's all my pants?"

"Check the dresser. Your other room was torn apart. Someone betrayed its location. You should be safer here."

Gooseflesh rose hard and chill on my legs as I slid them gingerly out of bed. I was all over bruises, some yellow-green and some red-blue, and my palms were raw. There were also rough red patches like carpet burn wherever the vampire blood had splashed. It doesn't eat through skin, but it *is* caustic. The muscles alongside my spine twitched and sent little *we're not happy* messages all up and down.

After boys hit the drift, they heal up from just about anything in a matter of hours. I was using the *aspect*, but I wasn't healing like they do. Sucks being a girl sometimes.

I shuffled over to the dresser, found out someone had just tossed my undies and bras in higgledy-piggledy in the top drawer on the left-hand side, and was relieved. Whoever had put them there hadn't, well, lingered over them.

It's the little things you end up being grateful for, Gran had always said.

I found a pair of jeans, too. About half my stuff was here. The other half, who knew? Bled on by vampires? Burned? Just left where it was?

And where were Graves's clothes? I grabbed the edge of the drawer, my knuckles turning white.

My voice surprised me. "I hate this."

Christophe didn't turn around. "What?"

"Vampire attacks. I get used to something, and they come riding in and destroy everything. Then I have to get used to something else all over again. It's . . . Jesus. It's *lame*." I couldn't come up with a better word, for once, and felt completely inadequate, standing there with jeans and a fistful of blue bikini briefs.

"I'm sorry." He *sounded* sorry, too. "It will be better now. I promise."

Graves wouldn't have said that. He'd have made an ironic little comment and I'd've laughed and felt better. My heart dropped another few inches. "There's no making it better, Christophe. This is going to keep going until they kill me, or until—"

"They're not going to kill you." Hard and fast. His shoulders came up as if I'd hit him. "Not while I'm here."

"But that's just the point." It was nasty of me, I know. It was also true. "You're going to disappear again, and I'll be dealing with it all on my own. Again."

Mom putting me in the hidey-hole in the closet, telling me I was her own good girl. Gran in the hospital bed, sliding away hour by hour. Dad walking down that concrete corridor toward the door that would open onto something grinning and hateful—and deadly.

And now, Graves.

Christophe sounded like he had something stuck in his throat. "When do you think I haven't been watching over you? But I'm not going to 'disappear' again, Dru. That's done now." Christophe shifted his weight as if he was going to turn around, and I clutched the clothes to me just in case.

"Yeah. Sure." I headed for the white-tiled glare I was certain was a bathroom. I hoped someone had thought to bring my toothbrush, too. If the vampires hadn't bled on it. "Sure it is."

"Wait and see." The mockery was back. "I'll be hard to get rid of from now on, *moj maly ptaszku.*"

I found out it was indeed a bathroom. White and scrubbed, antique brass fixtures and a skylight letting in a flood of sunshine. Wow. You could get a tan standing around in the shower, for Christ's sake. "It's easy to get rid of people, Christophe. All you have to do is rely on them." I swung the door shut and locked it, feeling like I'd won a small victory.

It was ridiculous. What was there to win? He hadn't been fighting.

I just, God, I wished he would have been Graves. I wanted to see that lopsided half-pained smile and those green eyes more than I could even admit to myself.

When you want to tell me, you come and find me.

Which meant he was coming back, right? Where the hell was he? It wasn't like him. But he'd been pretty mad. Put his fist almost through the wall. Because I hadn't been able to open my mouth fast enough.

Even Shanks said he was coming back. But Shanks didn't know him that well, did he? There hadn't been time for them to get really tight.

Did *I* even know my Goth Boy that well?

It was looking like I didn't.

Graves was the one thing I could depend on in this utterly screwed-up situation, and without him around I was . . .

Way to go tough girl, Dru. Jeez. He's just a boy. Get over it.

But he wasn't *just* a boy. He was the only boy I'd found worth dating in God knows how many schools. I mean, ever since he'd been bitten by a werwulf he'd been rock-steady. The best thing about this totally effed-up situation.

And now he was gone. And I had a funny idea, no matter how I tried to shake it, that he wasn't going to come sauntering back into the room and throwing around ironic one-liners.

So you go find him, just like he said. Right?

Except I didn't have a clue where to begin looking. My thinker was pretty busted.

The bathtub was a big cast-iron thing, and the shower looked older than I was. There was a brand-new plastic shower curtain on a ring bolted to the wall. The water ran rusty-red into the scrubbed white bowl of the sink for a few minutes when I turned it on, then cleared and warmed up.

I tried not to think about it.

I found I was crying silently. I didn't look in the mirror above the sink. There was a cabinet built into the wall with fresh white towels that smelled of fabric softener. I muffled the sobs in one of them while the shower ran, then got in and washed my aching self free of the sweat and the snot and the tears and the stickiness of fear, not to mention the stink of rotting vampire blood. There was shampoo. Conditioner. Soap in a waxed paper wrapping with French stuff written on the outside. Someone *had* remembered a toothbrush and the Crest from my room.

It was like being in a hotel room again. Only this time Dad wasn't outside the door, watching TV while he loaded clips or cleaning his guns or looking through his contacts list. No, outside the door there was a listening silence, as if Christophe knew I was crying.

And I hated it.

CHAPTER TWENTY-SIX

There was a tiny table near the hall door, and when I finally stalked out of the bathroom with a handful of damp towels balled up around my underwear, I found out what it was used for. There was a tray on it, with a paper coffee cup. A covered dish, polished silver so it shone. A stack of buttered wheat toast, visibly steaming, and a small bowl of strawberries and blueberries. A little silver thing of cream.

All in all, it looked like the regular Schola breakfast. Down in the caf you don't get the silver. But everything else, sure, spare no expense and feed the kids good. Even if they aren't kids.

"I wasn't sure what you'd want." Christophe picked up the paper latte cup. He was back to the faint mockery. The shotgun was nowhere in sight. "Leontus insisted about this, though."

It was a banana latte. I took it from him gingerly, not touching his fingers. *I guess some things are reliable.* "I, um. Yeah. Thanks. Christophe—"

"I don't blame you." Quietly. "You've been shuttled from one place to another like a chess piece. A pawn. You must have wondered several times if I was placing you as bait, or if I cared at all."

Wow. Uncomfortable, especially since he was right. And my mouth, so used to coming up with smartass at other times, completely failed me now. "I, well. Um."

"I didn't know you existed until your father called me. Augustine never told anyone either."

August. He'd vanished after verifying Christophe was a part of the Order. It was August vouching for Christophe over the phone that made me trust him the first time around. "Why would he call—"

"He didn't know who to trust. I was under suspicion and . . . well, there are other reasons." Taller than me and looking down, His hands hung empty and graceful at his sides. "Your mother, she always wanted a normal life. She was a . . . gentle soul." He made a slight noise, clearing his throat as if embarrassed. "We are not often gentle souls."

The starch threatened to go out of my legs. I backed up, found the bed by running into it, and sat down so hard my teeth clicked together.

Christophe continued, choosing each word carefully. "I don't know how your father found me. It was a surprise, especially since the last time I spoke with him things did not, um. They did not go well." He touched the silver dome over what was probably a plate of breakfast. "At all."

He found you the way we always found stuff out—in spooky little occult stores and other places I pointed him at. Maybe you're what he was looking for all along. I lifted the paper cup to my mouth. Paused halfway because he seemed to have run out of words. "What happened?"

His head dropped forward, as if he was praying.

Gran had been big on prayers. Only hers were a little off the beaten path. She talked to God like some people talk to a psychologist. When she wasn't telling him how things could've been done a little more efficiently, but then, He was God and she was just an old lady and what did she know, eh?

I'm thinking God was in for a hell of a surprise when Gran showed up at the pearly gates.

"I found her. She left the Schola, left everything. Took one small suitcase. She wouldn't tell me why, and I don't think she really thought she could hide from me. Them, yes. Me? No. Not me." A deep breath, his shoulders coming up as if under a burden. "When I found what she'd settled for . . . I was furious. Threatened him. But I never meant anything by it, Dru, I *swear*. She loved him; I could not hurt her by taking that away. She'd already had so much taken. She saw her parents die. Did you know?"

My mouth was numb, even full of hot coffee. I swallowed hard. It burned all the way down. "N-no. Nobody ever told me."

I mean, Gran talked about relatives—mostly dead ones. Dad talked about Gran sometimes; she'd raised him after *his* father skipped out and left her pregnant. But neither of them ever talked about Mom's side of the tree. Dad never talked much about Mom, either. He would just get that look on his face—the *I miss her but don't you dare mention it* look he was so good at.

I didn't ask many questions. I knew better. Besides, what was there to ask? I never doubted he loved me. I never doubted something had happened to my mother. I never doubted Gran loved me, too, but was too old to stay around for me.

I guess when you're a kid you don't think too much about that sort of stuff. It's just there, like your birthmarks. Those were the rocks the world was built on, and they didn't move. Not when I was little.

Now everything was shifting, and I couldn't find a solid place to jump to.

Christophe's shoulders were stiff-tense. He held himself like he expected a punch or two. "I don't know if she told him. Her father was Kouroi, her mother pure human. But they created a miracle. She was fifteen when they were raided. Murdered. Sergej, again. We barely got there in time; she survived only by accident. She was brought in. It was a shock. Her father . . . he wanted her to know a normal life. I suppose he thought that living in the middle of a clear zone, it was a luxury he could afford." A laugh like a mouthful of bitter ashes. "She wanted to be normal; she wanted to go *home*. Over and over she said as much. I thought she would eventually understand it was impossible."

What could I say to that? I licked my dry lips. "She called you young-blood." I guess I wanted to know. If it was real, or if I'd dreamed it.

He whirled and stared at me. The *aspect* slid over him like a cobra's hood, danger radiating in every direction. His eyes burned, his hair slicking back and turning dark. But I felt a weird, curious comfort. I knew I was right, deep down. There's nothing like feeling a little bit of certainty while the world's jigging and jiving around you.

"Yes," he said, finally. "It is . . . was . . . slang. Back then. She found it amusing."

I took another gulp of banana latte. I so seriously needed caffeine if I was going to deal with this. Every bruise twinged a little, settled back into a low-level ache. "So, um. You really liked her."

A shrug. His *aspect* retreated, the blond highlights slipping their fingers though his hair again. "She made certain I stayed here. In the light."

If I need a reason now, Dru, it will have to be you. I knew I hadn't dreamed *that* bit, especially the pressure of his lips against my own. That was right after he'd covered our escape from the other Schola. The burning one, where he'd dragged me out of the flames.

And Graves had argued the wulfen into coming back to gather both of us up.

I took a deep breath. "Do you have any idea how creepy that is, that you were in love with my mom and you're so . . . all over me?" Maybe I should have put it a little more tactfully. But I was running out of all sorts of things, and tact is usually the first to go.

"I'm also too old for you." His smile was wide, brilliant, and unsettling. And those blue eyes, set just so in his perfectly proportioned face, were hungry. "But give me some credit, little bird. Have I done anything to make you uncomfortable?"

I found out I was rubbing my left wrist against my jeans. I almost spilled the latte, I was shaking so hard. "Other than sucking my blood and being around every time vampires try to kill me? And scaring the royal blue fuck out of me? Other than that, well, I guess we're peachy." It felt like I needed to add more. "I trust you." *I guess. Even if you are moving me around like a chess piece. Funny, it was Graves who suggested that.*

I really, really wanted to see Graves now. But how could I explain any of this? Where would I even *start*? He understood a lot, yeah. He was a really understanding guy. But this . . . it would be like telling Christophe that Graves and I were an item, kind of.

It struck me as a Very Bad Idea.

Christophe nodded slowly. "That's more than I get from many of my so-called friends. Have I let you down so far, Dru?"

I thought about it. The first time I saw him was after I'd shot Ash in the face. Christophe had driven Ash away and told me to go home. Then he showed up at my front door, told me about the Order, brought groceries . . . got up on the hood of Dad's truck and told Graves to drive, busted through a wall, and took on Sergej so I could escape. Not to mention pulled me out of the burning Schola and covered our retreat.

Put his arms around me in the boathouse. And later, in the darkness, kissed me on the lips and told me I was going to have to be his reason.

I flushed hot again at the memory.

And at least when Christophe was around I knew what to do. It was sort of like having Dad again. I mean, not really. Because Christophe wasn't comforting in that way. It was just like, well, I knew my place in the world again. I was waiting for an adult to coach me on what to do up against the Real World.

I sat there thinking about it for a little while, and Christophe just stood there. Waiting. He didn't poke or prod or anything; he was just letting me figure it out. I appreciated that.

But I would've appreciated it more if he was Graves.

"No," I finally decided. "But I'm not believing you're sticking around."

"Do I at least I have a chance to prove it?" Still looking out the window. But his shoulders were still drawn up. Still expecting a punch.

I wondered about that. What must it be like to be him? To have everyone be afraid of you because of things you couldn't change— where you were born, what you were made to do?

It was like the *djamphir* sneering at the wulfen. It wasn't pretty and I hated it. And at least Graves had some sort of bond with the werwulfen to get by—he'd made friends almost right away. Christophe's own kind were scared of him.

The least I could do was give him a chance. Especially since he'd always done what he said he would.

"I guess so." It didn't sound welcoming at all. Or happy. But it was all I had.

He slumped. "Good enough. Will you eat breakfast, then?"

"I suppose." But thinking about how I met him brought up what I really wanted to do. "I want to see Ash. And I want to look for Graves." *Even though he's probably two states away by now. I could have been even farther away, by now.*

And yet. *Come and find me.* Did Graves really think I would?

Christophe nodded. "I expected as much. Will you tell me what happened yesterday?"

Weren't you there? But then I realized what he was talking about.

Anna. Which brought up another thing. "What's going to happen to you? What kind of Trial are we talking about?"

"Don't worry about that." He dismissed it with a wave of one hand, turning finally to look at me. The sunlight dimmed behind a cloud. "Everything is well in hand."

No way. Jeez. "Anna really hates you." *Like she hates me. What did I ever do to her? Jesus.*

"Fickle woman," he muttered. "Look, Dru, this is temporary. Let me handle it, and then we can get down to the real business."

Oh, so you're going to "handle" it? A faraway, cool relief filled my numb chest. *It's about damn time someone handled something. I can't do it all by myself.* "Which is?"

"Training you. Making sure Sergej can't get to you before you bloom, and after."

Well, I was all over that. But still, it wasn't comforting. "What's the point? He's just going to keep trying to kill me."

Dad would have recognized the sarcasm and told me not to be fresh. Graves would have rolled his eyes and snorted.

Christophe's smile wasn't nice at all. He directed it at the floor, not at me. It was still cold enough to chill marrow. "You'll notice he hasn't come again himself. He's frightened of you."

I choked on a slurp of banana latte. "*What?*" *He's the king of the vampires, for God's sake! Why the hell would he be afraid of* me?

"You escaped him, Dru. You held him off until help arrived. You were lucky, true, but *you held him off*. Which was more than your mother or even Anna could do." He was looking at me like I should have figured this out myself. "He's sent Ash, and Ash hasn't returned. He begged, borrowed, or stole a dreamstealer, and you still survived. He sent a Burner and has had the help of a traitor in the Order, and you are *still* alive."

"Because of Graves. And you." My chin lifted stubbornly. "It's not me."

"It *is* you, Dru. You're not like Elizabeth. You're a fighter. You can help us turn the tide even more." His eyes glittered, his face set in hard lines. Even cloudy sunlight was good to him, burnishing his pale skin. "This is why you're so important. He's the closest thing to a king they have anymore. Kill him, and—"

My stomach flipped over. "Whoa, hold on a second. Kill him?"

"That is certainly the only solution I can see." The sunlight dimmed even further, and the shadows under his eyes and cheekbones evened out. "But you have hard training before that's even possible. There are other hurdles to clear, too."

"Yeah. You could say that again. Look, Anna's still alive, right?"

"She's never faced Sergej."

Wow. This was just an eye-opening conversation all the way around. "Never?"

"Not once. She was rescued from an ordinary *nosferatu* attack, brought in, and hasn't stirred outside the Schola's walls without a contingent of bodyguards and security that makes the President look like an easy target."

"But she came to the—"

"She came to the reform Schola where she'd diverted you, yes. Why is that, do you think?"

Wait a second. What?

"She . . ." I absorbed this. The latte began to gurgle in my stomach. Have you ever burped acid, banana syrup, and coffee? It's not fun. My lips were numb. My heart was pounding like a freight train's wheels. "I thought we didn't know how I'd ended up there."

"Now I do. What did you think I was doing, other than watching your window? I've been gathering evidence, Dru. And even though you won't tell me what happened between you and Anna yesterday, I can guess."

No, I didn't think he could guess. Not really. The dream I'd been trying to push away for weeks came back, all ash and smoke and terror.

Don't let the nosferatu *bite.*

I sat there. A horrible shape was rising up out of the bottom of my mind, like a body you know isn't human under a sheet. I pushed it away, but it wouldn't go. There was only one thing that would explain all of this, explain everything I'd seen.

The Schola was silent, but I heard the wind outside. It was a soft spring breeze, and I wanted to yank the window open and leap out. I wanted to run. I hadn't really been outside since I got here, and it bugged me. I needed some fresh air.

Right after I threw up everything I ever thought of eating.

"She wanted me to hate you." I sounded about five years old. "I . . . she looked at me like she wanted to know something."

"She did want to know, Dru. She wanted to know what you remembered. She wanted to know what you saw—"

I didn't see. I heard. I was only five! "Shut up." The latte dropped out of my hand and plopped on the hardwood floor. It sloshed but stayed miraculously upright. "*Shut up.*" I even clapped my hands over my ears. "*Shut up shut up shut up!*"

He grabbed my wrists, and I got a good faceful of that apple-pie smell. For some reason it broke everything inside me, and the world went white-fuzzy for a few seconds. When it came back I'd somehow ended up on the floor, my knees still jolting from landing hard, and I was hitting Christophe wildly. Not even any weight behind the strikes, just flailing.

"*Shut up!*" I screamed. I kept screaming it, even though he wasn't saying anything. He was just letting me hit him, deflecting the blows when they threatened to get near his face. When I paused for breath he didn't try to make me stop. He just kept letting me hit him, and when I stopped and bowed forward under the weight of it, he folded me in his arms and stroked my hair while I sobbed.

It wasn't just the horrible thought in my head. It was everything. It was Gran and my dad and the dreams and the locket, the wulfen and the vampires and Sergej and my mother. It was Graves gone and the attacks and the uncertainty and that horrible hole inside my chest cracking open and bleeding. You can only shove shit under your bed for so long before it starts moving around and wanting to get out.

You can only cope for so long before everything breaks. And if he was going to handle something, if I wasn't alone, it meant I *could* break. It meant I didn't have to keep everything bottled up so tight.

I tried hitting him a few more times, halfhearted swipes, crying so hard I couldn't breathe.

"Let it out," he whispered into my hair. "Let it out, *moj maly ptaszku*."

I guess most of all it was because he'd come back for me again. It was like the relief I used to feel each time I heard Dad's truck door close, each time he stamped into the house or the apartment or hotel room or whatever damn place we were living. Each time my heart would swell up like a balloon because he hadn't forgotten me or left me behind. Every kid's afraid of that, right? That someday you'll be left in a corner, like a toy, staring with button eyes and a broken heart.

Christophe kept coming back for me. He was here now. He'd saved my life again.

But God, how I wished he was Graves.

CHAPTER TWENTY-SEVEN

When you cry that hard, it leaves you washed-out and not quite numb. And embarrassed, especially if you have tears and snot all over you. I sat on the floor with my back against the white bed, staring at the sticky stain of banana-flavored coffee. My brain tuned to that weird hum when you've cried yourself past everything and you don't want to think. Everything retreats to white noise again.

Christophe brought me a cool wet washcloth and a box of tissues. He settled down cross-legged on the floor a few feet away. What do you do when a beautiful *djamphir* watches you so closely? He was staring like he saw something green. Or like I had a bunch of snot on me and he was just too nice to say so.

I blew my nose, mopped myself up. The pile of used tissues got larger, and I finally pressed the washcloth onto my hot, aching face. Smoothed it gingerly over the bruises. A nice cool washcloth is good after you've been sobbing your heart out. Gran used to put a cool rag on the back of my neck when I finished crying over something from the valley school, or anything else. It's good after you have the stomach flu and throw up, too. Soothing.

It got hard to breathe through the thick terrycloth, though. So I had to peel it away and face the world again.

He was still watching me, the faint suggestion of a line between his dark eyebrows. Like he was worried about me or something.

I didn't blame him. I was worried about me, too.

After a little while, he could probably tell I was ready. He was looking at me so intently, maybe he was reading my expression. My poker face was really sucking after all this.

"My Trial begins at sundown." His hands rested on his knees, loose and easy. He always looked so impossibly *finished*, every thread tucked away and every surface carefully buffed. I never saw him taking any time in the bathroom to fix his look or anything. I was beginning to think he'd look like that even if he wasn't *djamphir*. "If all goes well, it should take a little over an hour for all to come to light. Then . . ."

"What are you going to do?" I pressed the washcloth against my forehead again.

"I'm going to make certain Anna can't hurt you. I'm going to make certain she pays for what she's done." His jaw set, and I was suddenly grateful he hadn't ever talked about me in that chill, factual way. "When this all ends you won't have to worry. Not about the Order, at least. Unless Sergej's corruption runs deeper than I've found." A muscle flicked high up on one smooth cheek. "But even then, I won't leave you. I'm not going anywhere, Dru."

"Yeah. Sure." I closed my eyes, laid the cloth over them. It felt good. "Whatever. I want to find Graves."

"Everyone is looking for him. He's picked a good hiding spot. Unless . . ."

"Unless what?" I peeked out from under the washcloth.

"I don't know what happened between you and him. But if something did happen, could he possibly have left the Schola?" Quietly, gently, like he was afraid of me breaking down again.

Hearing him say what I'd been thinking only made it worse. "He wouldn't." I bristled immediately. It was like defending Dad. You do it because you have to, even if you don't believe it. "He wouldn't leave me."

I just couldn't stand Christophe saying it.

It wasn't like Graves to ditch me. It just wasn't. He'd been sticking like glue since the Dakotas. *It's you and me against the world*, he'd said. *Don't you dare leave me behind.*

Come and find me.

I settled on what I hoped, as stupid as that was. "Something must have happened to him." The words stuck in my throat. "God."

"If he's still at the Schola we can find him. It will take time, though. Do you want a search of every room?"

It won't do any good. "They won't do that."

"If you ask, they will." Like, *The sky's blue*, or *Vampires drink blood*. With a healthy helping of *duh, Dru*. "They've been trained to leap when a *svetocha* speaks."

"Anna." Like it was a dirty word. It was getting to be. I almost flinched when I said it, as if she would suddenly pop out of thin air. "Christophe?"

"What?"

I sensed him leaning forward. It's weird to feel someone's attention on you that way, like you're the only thing in the world they're listening to. Most of the time people are distracted, or just thinking about what *they're* going to say next. Not a lot of them actually *listen*, and never to me. Adults figure I don't have anything real to say, boys are too busy with their own stuff, other girls are light-years away at the mall or the classroom or something. None of them gets what it's like to break a hex or clean out a nest of roach spirits.

Or to have every person or thing you ever thought was stable and real taken away, one at a time. While vampires snarl and try to kill you.

I searched for something to say. "Do I smell weird?" I opened one eye a slice, peeked at him.

His eyebrows were all the way up, his cold eyes open for a moment instead of walled off. "What?"

"I, um. Some of the wulfen, they tell me I . . . smell. And you, well." *You smell like a Christmas candle, but in a good way. Only, if it comes from blood I'm not sure I like it so much.*

"You're very curious and perceptive, *moja księżniczko*." He coughed slightly. I know that sound; it's an adult getting ready to talk about Birds and Bees. "You do smell very nice. Spice, and salt. It's very pleasant. It means, well, when a *svetocha* reaches blooming age, which is different than physical maturity—"

If he started talking in euphemisms I was going to scream. "That's good. What about you? None of the other boys smell like you do."

"I should be proud of that." But his face had closed up again, the faint businesslike mockery back in place.

"If you're not going to answer what I'm really asking, Christophe, just say so." Now I regretted bringing the whole thing up. I balled up the washcloth and sighed, levering myself creakily to my feet. Washed out and emptied, everything inside me was shut down. It was a different kind of numbness, and one I liked. Even the thought of Dad didn't hurt so much. Like pinching your leg when it's fallen asleep. "What time is it?"

"Three o'clock. Dru—"

"I want to see Ash. Then I want to look for Graves."

"You should rest. Tonight might be difficult."

My chin lifted. It was the "stubborn mule" look Gran chided me for so often. "I'm not the one on trial."

He nodded as if he'd expected that. "True. But you could be a little kinder to me, little bird."

I'm supposed to be nice to you? Then I felt guilty. He'd saved my life, more than once. I wouldn't even be standing there in a white bedroom full of directionless light—because the sun was hiding behind clouds, and the skylights were full of blind glow—if it wasn't for him. The locket on my chest twitched a little as the old familiar anger tried to rise. It wasn't real anger, it was just comfortable. Right now mad was about all I knew how to do.

Even though I couldn't truly feel anything. The crying had washed it all away. The panic-inducing, really terrible thought was still in the bottom of my head. How do you deal with something like that?

Work, I decided. *There's got to be something I can do until tonight.* "I want to go to the infirmary," I said quietly and clearly and tossed the washcloth down in the middle of the lake of drying coffee. The breakfast tray stood abandoned by the front door. "And I want to look for Graves. If he's here, I can find him." *And if he's not, I want to know. I want to know if he's just kicked me like a bad habit.*

"Very well." He rose gracefully, and I had to look away. The white cloth soaked up coffee, turning a weird stained-brown. I felt bad about it for a second. I mean, I've been raised to clean up my own mess. Dad was big on keeping things neat. and Gran was all about everything in its place.

But they weren't here, and I was a ghost. I almost expected to lift my hand and see the light go right through it. I'd cried everything right out of me.

I looked around for shoes. The closet had one lone pair of sneakers in it. Good luck, I guess. I almost groaned when I bent over to pick them up. If I lived to middle age I'd have so many back problems, *damn*.

But I might not ever look any older. The boy *djamphir* didn't, except for something in their eyes. And how old was Anna?

I didn't want to think about it.

I couldn't even imagine being fifty and trapped inside this skinny teenage body.

The last twelve hours caught up with me with a wallop. I leaned against the closet door's jamb and tried to catch my breath. Warm oil slid down my skin, the *aspect* rising like ribbons of heat through tepid bathwater when you twist the knob again to add more. The hurt all through my muscles retreated, and my teeth tingled.

It was too bad the *aspect* couldn't do anything about the aches inside me. I sniffed a little bit. A crying jag will leave your nose raw and messy, but my nasal passages opened up, and underneath the lemon and fresh air in the room there was the distinct note of dust and spiced apple pie.

"Am I on trial with you, too?" Christophe asked softly.

Yes. No. I don't know. "I trust you," I said again. It felt like a lie. "I just . . . none of this is designed to make me a happy camper, all right?"

"Of course." He sounded like he wanted to say something else, but let it go.

Smart of him. I got myself into my sneakers, took a few deep breaths, and the *aspect* retreated. I couldn't feel the fangs anymore when I turned around and faced him.

"Let's go."

CHAPTER TWENTY-EIGHT

Djamphir **and wulfen** both heal pretty quickly. So the infirmary isn't a place you want to end up. If you're hurt so bad you have to go there, it's probably not going to end well.

Ash wasn't in one of the curtained enclosures in the middle of the big vaulted space. He was in one of the stone-walled rooms along the sides, wrapped in white bandages and strapped down to what looked like an operating table while IVs dripped and beeping machines measured his vital signs. Heartbeat, blood pressure, brainwaves, everything.

Underneath the beeping and booping, a humming crackle ran. His fur was matted with dried blood, and the shape of his face kept changing. The slender snout would retreat, fur sliding away until you could almost, *almost* get a glimpse of what he would look like as a boy.

Except for the ruined jaw. You could see where the silver grains went in, and it was still seeping a weird clear fluid. His eyes were closed, and the crackle would rise in waves.

"He's trying to change back." Dibs had a stethoscope on his neck and the businesslike attitude he always adopted around the wounded. "Getting close to it, too. If we can keep him alive long enough to do it. We're feeding him intravenously with five and hypodermically with fifty percent dextrose to fuel the change—"

"What are his chances?" Christophe didn't sound impressed.

"I'm not a doctor yet, you know. They just have me attending because I'm sub enough not to set him off."

"What are his chances?"

"About twenty percent. Better than nothing, though, right? There's hope." Dibs cocked his head and looked at me as if I'd been the one asking questions. "We're doing everything we can, Dru. He's tied down because otherwise he rips the subclavian catheter out. That's how we're feeding him the five percent stuff, see? And the fifty percent solution with a hypo every hour or so. He's holding steady."

The crackle crested again, fur running off and melting. A patch of bare pale skin showed on his chest. I held my breath. The pale spot retreated, swallowed by dark wiry hair.

Ash surged against the restraints. I found out my hands were fists. *You can do it*. The same thing I'd told him night after night. *Come on. You can do it.*

I reached forward, my fingers unloosening just a little.

"Dru." Christophe, warning me.

I ignored him. Touched the back of Ash's paw. Hand. Whatever. Fur flowed away, another bare patch of white skin showing like the moon behind clouds. Long elegant fingers, ending in claws that spasmodically slid free and retracted, clenched and released. It looked like the white streak at his temple was widening, but I couldn't tell for sure.

The skin was an odd texture. Soft, like a baby's. Like it hadn't been exposed to a lot. It was amazing—such a kickass creature, and underneath it all, so fragile. How many times had he saved my life so far?

It was Friday, I realized. Would the wulfen do their regular weekly run tomorrow? Could I go along with them?

And when Sunday came around, would I be able to go down into the cafeteria and act like a normal girl on a coffee date or something?

Good luck with that, Dru.

"I wonder why he's doing this."

"Broken doesn't mean stupid." Dibs stared at the machines keeping track of the rhythms, his fair blond face creasing. "Maybe he knows you want to help him."

"I shot him in the face. With silver. And then after that he wanted to kill me too, but . . ." I replayed the scene in my head. So much had happened, but I was sure of one thing—Ash had been after me before Christophe drove him away, there in the snow.

Christophe stepped closer warily. "Maybe the silver interferes with Sergej's call. I would give much to know if he went limping back to his master and was given a new directive, or if he went to ground and the silver changed him."

"That's the sixty-four-dollar question, ennit? He can't tell us yet." Dibs eyed the Broken werwulf. It was by far the least afraid I'd ever seen him. I guess with Ash strapped down and technically a patient, Dibs could handle it. "Although I think it's the second."

"Why?" Christophe glanced up, his eyes turned lighter and more thoughtful. They were still cold. Dad's eyes had been that blue, but never so freezing. Christophe's were a winter sky, on a day when the wind knifes right through whatever you're wearing. Eyes that can turn you numb when they're looking at you like a butterfly on a pin.

Christophe's interest made Dibs pull his head down like a turtle. "Just a feeling, that's all."

"Well, your hunches are good, Samuel. If he can be saved, you'll save him."

Dibs didn't believe it. At least, he didn't look like he did, and I didn't blame him. Some of the white bandages began to show spots of crimson. Like angry flowers. And I was too drained and numb to react much, smelling the copper salt of blood.

It was a blessing. My fangs didn't tingle.

Dibs sighed. "What worries me is what'll happen after we've got him recovering, not just stabilized. What are they going to do with him?"

"Same thing they *have* done, I'd bet. Make him Dru's problem." Christophe let out a sharp breath. "Have you seen the *loup-garou*?"

"Graves? No. Nobody has. Shanks saw him yesterday, heading away from a sparring gym looking like hell. But he was on duty for Dru and didn't follow him. Weird, huh? He's never very far away from her." Dibs coughed a little, maybe remembering I was standing right there. "Alphas get mad, though. Maybe he's just off cooling down."

It sounded inadequate, and we all knew it. "He's still bleeding." I couldn't tear my gaze away from the ruin of the Broken's jaw, and the spots on the bandages widened. The patch of skin under my fingers shrank, choked with wiry vital fur.

"Crap. He's about to have one of his swings again. Get out of here, Dru." Dibs turned toward a tray of various implements and bottles and scooped up a package, broke it open with a practiced flick of his fingers, and subtracted a hypodermic needle the size of the Death Star. He looked down at the Broken, and his face changed a little. "Last thing I need is you coding on the table. I'm gonna save your life, wulf, whether you like it or not." He glanced back at me as the beeps and boops picked up their pace. "Didn't I tell you to leave?"

Wow. Where had the Dibs who couldn't even choke out his name in a crowded lunchroom gone?

Christophe's hand curled around my arm and he pulled me away. Dibs cursed as something rattled, and a snarl shook the room. Christophe swung the door shut and didn't slow down until we were all the way down to the other end of the infirmary. "Why that wulf was stuck in a reform Schola is beyond me," he muttered darkly. "The Order used to be a meritocracy. Dear God."

"Is he going to be okay?"

"Which one? Samuel can take care of himself. Unless Ash breaks the restraints, and even then he won't see a submissive as a threat. Unless he's crazed. Which is very likely." He palmed the heavy door at the end of the infirmary open, checked the hall, and had probably forgotten his hand around my arm. At least he wasn't giving me another bruise to add to all the rest.

"What about Ash? Christophe, slow down."

He stopped. The hallway was deserted. Shafts of westering sunlight pierced it at regular intervals, and the velvet drapes were still and silent. The busts studding the hall's length peered at each other, never quite looking anyone in the eye. I was beginning to feel like crawling under a bed and hiding for awhile. The more I thought about it, the more it seemed reasonable.

"It's so quiet." I tried to pull my arm away, but he wasn't having any of it. "If you're on Trial, why are they letting you run around like this? Nobody's watching."

"You only *think* nobody's watching, *skowroneczko moja*. This is the Schola Prima; there are always eyes. Besides, I gave my word." He cocked his head, listening.

"You gave your word." I didn't mean it to sound flat and unhelpful, but it did.

"When I say I will do something, Dru, I *do* it. Where would you like to start looking for the *loup-garou*?"

I shrugged. I didn't have a clue. So much for Graves's faith in me.

"Very well. Come along, we'll start with Robert."

"You're going to have to let go of me." This time I was successful in pulling my arm away. We stood there facing each other, and this time I looked away first. If there were eyes watching, I wasn't so sure what I should be doing.

"As you like." The businesslike mockery was back. "You've had a busy day or two. What happened between you and the *loup-garou*, Dru?"

"None of your business." And I meant it. "What's going on between you and Anna?"

"*Touché.*" He grimaced, half-turned, and set off down the hall. I had to follow.

What else was there to do?

CHAPTER TWENTY-NINE

"**J**esus." **My mouth** hung open; I closed it with a snap. When they'd said the blue room was torn to shreds, they weren't kidding.

Shanks folded his arms. He had an ugly shiner that was healing even as I looked at it, yellow-green instead of red-blue and fresh. He moved a little stiffly, but seemed okay. "I been looking for anything to save, but there's not much. The clothes are all torn up; even the carpet's gonna have to be yanked up and redone. Broke everything in the bathroom. The washer and dryer—I mean, you know. Suckers."

I didn't, but this was . . . God. The bed was reduced to splinters and matchsticks, the mattresses slit and springs dragged out. The carpet was shredded, bits of my and Graves's clothing scattered around and splashed with vampire blood. The shutters were wrenched off the windows, the closet door smashed; the dresser looked like it had been hacked to pieces by an overenthusiastic lumberjack. And it *stank* of rotting vampire blood. Great splashes and gouts of it painted the walls, drying to black crusts. "How long were they in here?"

"I dunno. They can do a lot of damage in a short amount of time, and if you'd been hiding in here . . ." Bobby shrugged. He kept giving Christophe peculiar looks, darting little glances from under his emo fringe. He also kept shrugging off my asking him if he was hurt. "Lucky Graves wasn't in here, too."

"Are we sure he wasn't?" Christophe asked mildly enough.

Shanks gave him another one of those little glances. "No itty little bits of him around."

The thought made my stomach cramp. I pushed the bathroom door open a little. The toilet tank was hanging askew, shivers and shards of cold porcelain everywhere. Even the bathtub was cracked, and there was no mirror to speak of, just shards and slices hanging on the wall. "God."

"The destruction is rather biblical in scope, isn't it? Especially when seen for the first time." Christophe crossed to the window, looked at the shutters. The metal was blackened, hanging by scraps. "Did they enter through the window?"

"Majority of them did." Shanks paused. "Someone kindly marked it for them by ripping the screen off."

I gave a guilty start there in the bathroom doorway. Christophe was very still for a fraction of a second. Then he reached up deliberately and gave the shutter a push. "Marked it, you say?"

"The screen was gone earlier. Stank of *djamphir*." Shanks stared at the air over Christophe's head.

I curled my fingers around the doorjamb. I was clutching so hard my arm hurt, and the pain radiated down my abused back. I felt like I'd been dragged behind a couple of mad horses down miles of bad road, as the saying goes.

I swallowed hard. "Christophe . . ." He'd come in the window of my room in the other Schola. Did Shanks really suspect him?

"You were out in the hall? Pretending Dru was in here?"

I finally found something to say. "That was my idea."

Christophe turned on his heel, leveled a stare across the room. "And a good idea it was, too. We can lose a wulfen more easily than a *svetocha*."

I hadn't quite thought of it that way, and it made me even sicker. "Oh, God."

Shanks shrugged. "Don't worry 'bout it, Dru-girl. Price a wulf pays for being in the Order." But he was glaring right back at Christophe, and I had the uneasy feeling that the two of them were drawing lines in the sand.

I cleared my throat. If I didn't distract them both, something might happen. And I really wasn't looking for any more excitement right now. I was plumb tuckered. "Will both of you quit it? We're supposed to be figuring out where Graves is."

"Last place I saw him was stamping away from the locker room after gym." Shanks had a good poker face; he didn't mention the rest of it. "He looked pretty pissed. He didn't show up in the dorms or Dibs would've known. It's not like him not to come back for you."

Hearing someone else say that made me feel a little better. I blew out a long breath. "So where would you go, if you were so pissed off?"

He shrugged, but at least he was looking at me now. Some of the hurtful tension leaked out of the damaged room. "I'd run for awhile. Get it worked off."

"So, outside?"

"He was heading that way. For the east exit."

"Okay." I gathered myself up. "Let's go."

* * *

The east exit wasn't locked. The door had been thrown open so hard it had dented the concrete wall outside, and the thingie on the top that kept it from slamming shut or opening too quick was busted. I didn't have any difficulty imagining Graves stamping through and breaking it. The gym would have been deserted, too, thanks to Anna. Nobody to see him but Shanks, no reason for him to slow down.

A cool late-afternoon breeze touched my cheeks as I pushed it open. Shanks whistled a little. "Boy don't know his own strength."

"Does anyone, really?" Christophe reached over my shoulder, bracing the door. "But yes, quite impressive. Still don't feel like talking, Dru?"

"It's none of your *business*, Christophe." God, he could irritate me even when I was happy he was here.

"It could be my business. So many things happened yesterday, you see. Only a fool wouldn't believe them connected—"

"*Djamphir* don't take no for an answer," Shanks muttered. He slid past us and stepped out into the westering sunlight. It gilded his dark hair and touched his hollow, shaven cheeks while he grabbed the door and pulled it wide, out of Christophe's grasp.

A concrete path dipped away, down toward a copse of ornamental trees, bisecting strips of manicured lawns. Another path peeled off toward a baseball diamond that looked major-league ready, its chalked lines startlingly white and the dugouts freshly painted. The bleachers even looked clean.

Christophe stiffened, but he shut up. I stepped out onto the path and realized it had been far too long since I'd gone outside. The last time I'd felt the wind all over me was weeks ago, hurried little gulps of air while Benjamin had taken us out clothes shopping.

After a long thirty seconds or so, Christophe spoke up again. "Dru. It's near dusk."

I closed my eyes. A pendulum would only tell me what I wanted to hear, so it was useless. Tarot cards might've been a bit better, but still . . . they wouldn't say anything useful. I was too shook up and wanted too much, too badly.

But there were other ways of finding out what you *needed* to know. If I could just clear my head a little bit.

"Dru—" Christophe again.

"Be quiet." I heard my own voice, a queer faraway murmur. "It's not dusk yet." The whisper of feathered wings filled my ears, brushed my face. It was like a big fluffy powder brush, just touching the skin.

I went to a makeup counter in a high-end department store in Boca Raton once, while Dad was doing an ammo run six blocks away. The lady there had brushed some expensive powder all over my face just like this, her fingertip just lightly under my chin, and she smelled like warm perfume and hairspray. Without the hairspray it was almost like my mother, and after a little bit I'd started fidgeting and in the end made some half-embarrassed excuse and got away while she was trying to sell me eye shadow. This reminded me of that.

Shanks drew in a soft breath. Christophe was utterly silent behind me, but warm tendrils of apple-pie scent curled across the cold rain-washed breeze.

I smelled wet earth waking up after winter, the river sending up a flat tang of oily water, the city all around the Schola Prima's grounds in a tide of concrete and exhaust, the classrooms full of chalk dust and the war of young and old. Sap rising in the trees, the hardy green smell of grass's first spring growth mowed in the morning.

The wingbeats crested, like a little feathered thing in my hand, its heart beating frantically. Gran said it was no trick to charm sparrows out of the sky; you had to charm them and return them safely, *that* was the trick.

No use doing what you dunno to undo—or even if'n you kin undo. You mind me now, Dru.

My hand jabbed out, index finger pointing. I opened my eyes and the world rushed in so hard I had to squint against it. Darts of sun speared my eyes, and I had to blink to focus. Hot tears swelled up, trickling down my cheeks.

The lump in my throat wasn't mine. It was Graves's. I could *see* him, a shadowy ghost in the gathering dusk, like powder on a moth's wings. He left a scorch on the air, like a hot kettle set on a counter. It was helpless anger, a ball of rage I would never have suspected him of feeling. He was always so . . .

You don't know anything about this kid, Dru.

He stamped away toward the baseball diamond, coat flapping silently. Phantom pins and needles slid through my fingers and toes. I leaned forward, saw him veer away from the baseball field. He crouched and sprang, his hands jetting out, grabbed the top railing of the bleachers, and cleared it in a swoop of graceful authority no human body would have been able to pull off.

He'd taken to being *loup-garou* like a duck to water.

He stood up on the bleachers, irresolute, his head tipped back as if he was watching the sky. It would have been dark and cold—the middle of the Schola's "day." Shanks would have been inside, trying to calm me down and get me to my room.

The ghost of Graves hunched down, a supple movement. His attention focused outward now, alert. His hair stood up in long curling spikes, vital and powdery black at this distance. You couldn't see his roots.

He leapt forward. A burst of static boiled inside my head. My face jerked aside as if I'd been slapped. I pitched forward, Christophe grabbed at my arm but I evaded him, and I was halfway down the path before I realized I was moving. The pins and needles should have made me clumsy, but they didn't. I ran past the bleachers, was just in time to see the ghost of Graves streaking toward another small stand of oaks.

He ran like the running was joy to him. Wulfen move fast and fluid, and he did it without getting hairy. His coat snapped behind him, a faraway sound, and he plunged into the stand of trees just seconds before I did.

The trees crowded close around a small clearing, and the grass here wasn't mowed. Shade and light whirled together, there was a *snap!* inside my head, and everything . . . stopped.

Darkness dilated in the evening air. The oaks drew close, whispering with their fresh new green leaves, and I caught a confused jumble of activity before Shanks bolted into the clearing and nearly collided with me.

He yelled something unrepeatable and leapt away, almost hitting a tree. I jolted back into my body and stared at him.

"Don't *do* that!" he yelled. "*Jesus!*"

"I lost it!" I yelled back. "I almost had it!"

"What the—" But he shut up as Christophe stepped past him, appearing out of thin air with a whispering sound.

"This is not a good idea." The *djamphir*'s eyes glowed blue in the shade. Light does funny things this close to dying altogether; the shadows moved like live things over Christophe's pale skin and turned Shanks into an umber statue. "Come back inside, Dru."

I searched for the internal tingle that would tell me the *touch* was willing to show me more.

Nothing. Nada. Zip. Zilch.

Until a soundless flash filled the whole clearing, lighting it up inside my head like kliegs on a football field. I stalked past Shanks and stopped, kneeling in front of a weird thorny bush. It might even have been a rosebush, but it looked blasted and half-crushed.

A tiny strip of material, no bigger than my pinkie finger, clung to it. Heavy black cotton, from a long black coat. I gingerly tweezed it free, held it up. It had dried stiff, probably because it'd gone through dew falling. "He came this way. Can we—"

"I don't smell much." Shanks hunched his shoulders miserably. "They cut the grass earlier today, but I . . ."

I waited, but he just spread his hands. The entire clearing was a thick soup of shadows and a chill that wasn't just evening creeping up. It was cold, and I smelled *intent*, like a hex brewing in a dark corner.

My hand turned into a fist around the scrap of material.

"Maybe he just needed to go out and get his head clear." But Shanks didn't sound like he believed it.

"There's nothing we can do now." Christophe's hands dangled loosely by his side, but his entire body shouted, *Ready to move.* "Please, Dru. Inside is better. Especially this close to dark."

"You can't smell him?" I tried not to sound like I was begging Shanks.

"Enough to know he came this way. That's all. He could have just brushed up against it, but he can see in the dark. Like we can."

I let out a deep, frustrated sigh. Heard footsteps in the distance, and was that Leon calling my name? I guess you really can't go anywhere in the Schola without being watched.

Who had been watching me all this time? What *hadn't* I seen?

"Fine." But I stuffed the strip of material in my pants pocket. When I had some time to think I could probably figure something out.

Come and find me.

It wouldn't be the first time I'd found someone with just a scrap of cloth. Once you have that physical link, it's the easiest type of finding.

I let Christophe lead the way out of the stand of trees. The sun was heading for the horizon, disappearing behind buildings.

Time for a Trial.

CHAPTER THIRTY

n the very center of the Schola Prima's main building, the one all
the wings come off of like they're a spider hugging its web, is a huge
open space with a glass roof. I say *glass roof* when what I really mean
is a dome big enough to host a Deep South gun show underneath,
made of huge glass panels webbed with stone supports. It was probably
a marvel of architecture, but it looked like it might come crashing down
at any moment. The space underneath it was stone-floored, except for
long runners of dusty red rugs. A high dais in the center held seven iron
chairs, three on either side flanking a huge confection of spikes and a
big red cushion, hung with swathes of crimson silk.

Two guesses whose that is, and the first one don't count. Hot bile
crawled up my throat. I shuffled along behind Christophe, Leon right
behind me, and kept my head down, glancing up in quick spurts.

The wide spaces were filling up with *djamphir*, most of them
older. The younger ones trickled in and stood near the back, and I
saw one or two wulfen lingering near the exits. They were gone as
soon as I looked twice, craning my neck.

The chairs faced south, and in front of them, set to the left, was a sort of enclosure. Waist-high railings of dark antique wood, carved with crosses and hearts, marched in a square around hard pew benches. Christophe opened a little gate-thingie and pointed me in with a half-bow. "If you please, *skowroneczko moja*. Stay here."

Leon followed me, and when I settled down in the first row, he chose the seat right behind me and a little to the left. Christophe leaned on the railing in front of me. "Whatever happens, Dru, don't worry. I don't think anyone can harm you with the entire Order in attendance."

I didn't say anything. Who knew how many of them had some grudge against me, for whatever reason? Anna hated me, and seeing Christophe wasn't guaranteed to put her in a good mood either.

I had other things to worry about, too.

If Graves was here we could have a whole conversation in a split second just by giving each other one of those Significant Looks. It's not just anyone you can do that with.

But there was that scrap of material in my pocket. As soon as I was alone, I could clear my head out and see if it could lead me anywhere. It wouldn't be the first time I'd found someone using the *touch*.

It would, however, be the first time I'd found someone without Dad.

"I mean it," Christophe persisted. "You're safe. I promise."

More *djamphir* trickled in. I could feel their eyes on me. New girl again, for the three thousandth time. Christophe watched my face, searching it like he expected to find gold there.

"Don't worry about me," I finally said. "Really. I'm more worried about *you*." *And even more worried about where Graves is.*

"Are you?" A fey smile lit his face, and I caught my breath. It was a shock to see him look so happy. "Well, then."

Leon leaned forward, I felt the movement even though he didn't touch me. "Here comes Benjamin. Don't look surprised."

Benjamin stamped across the stone, his face a thundercloud. He pushed past Christophe, through the little gate, and dropped into the pew on my other side. "Goddamn it." It was a jail-yard whisper; his lips barely moved. "Nobody knows anything. What the hell is going on?"

"Have you found Graves?" I didn't care if everyone heard me. "Please tell me you found him."

I knew he hadn't even before he shook his head, dark eyes moving over the crowd. "His personal effects are still in your chamber, Milady. Torn apart and spattered with *nosferatu* ichor, but still there. Wherever he went, he didn't take his clothes with him. Shanks was the last person to see him. Can't find hide or hair of him anywhere. Thomas and George are still looking, but you won't be lacking protection. I've got two other crews on standby, and I'll vouch for them personally."

My face tightened up on its bones. If they had *what the hell* in the dictionary, my expression right then would be the perfect picture. "I know he left his clothes. There was a place, outside the gym—" The words stumbled over each other, trying to get out in time to tell him that I'd seen where Graves went right after—

"Shh." Benjamin made a quick shushing motion with his left hand. "I think something's . . . no, I guess not. Not yet."

A hush fell over the assembled *djamphir*. The crowd had grown while I wasn't looking. The glass dome above filled with sunset, pink clouds and orange glow like a blind multicolored eye. Just figures that the *ceiling* would be staring at me, too. Jesus.

Every time I looked around there were more *djamphir*. When there's a whole sea of them looking at you, you can get to see some faint similarities in bone structure, no matter the skin color. Bright eyes, and whispering passed through them. The *aspect* went in waves over the crowd, fangs peeping out and hair changing shades.

Have you ever heard a cornfield on a breezy afternoon? Or been out on the Great Plains and seen waist-high grass when the wind moves over it, brushing it like hair? Watching the *aspect* in a crowd is vaguely like both. I hunched my shoulders. But Christophe was right in front of me, leaning on the barrier, and every once in awhile a stray breath of apple-pie scent would brush me.

I won't lie. It was comforting. But my roving gaze kept getting snagged on the chair hung with red fabric.

"Wulfen." Leon was leaning forward, his arms crossed on the back of my pew. "They're watching closely, too. Want to bet why?"

"It's insulting." Benjamin's jaw set like concrete, and the emo-boy swoop over his eyes ran with auburn highlights.

"It's not personal." Leon actually snorted a little, laughing. "They don't trust anyone. I don't blame them."

I saw Zeke in a sapphire silk button-down, his blue eyes dark with worry. I actually lifted a hand and waved at him a little and instantly regretted it. He actually blushed, dropping his eyes, and a couple of his friends elbowed him. Someone laughed, and my cheeks were hot.

There went my Sunday coffee date. It wasn't like I was really counting on it, but damn.

Leon laughed again, a weird choked chuckle, and I considered turning around and punching him in the face.

"Who's that?" Christophe wanted to know, but I just slumped down in the pew and rolled my eyes.

"Nobody. He's from my history class." *I wish Graves was here, dammit.* No matter how this ended up, the first thing I was going to do when I got out of here was go looking for him. I was going to slip out of here somehow, anyhow, and follow the *touch* until it led me to him. I was going to find him and *make* everyone leave us alone long enough for me to tell him . . .

. . . what? What could possibly make this sort of thing better?

I didn't know, but I'd find it. I'd say anything I had to, to make him understand.

The crowd went still again, but differently than before. When I looked up I saw why. The Council had arrived.

From left to right they stood in front of their chairs: Kir with his red hair echoing the flaming sky filling the glass, Marcus in another gray suit, and Bruce placed precisely one step out in front, halfway between his chair and the big red throne. On the other side, Alton looked somber as he folded his arms and looked out across the crowd, Hiro stared steadily down at me with something I think was supposed to be an encouraging expression, and Ezra pulled his sweater sleeves down and settled into watchful immobility.

I'd forgotten to breathe. I inhaled.

Bruce tilted his head a little. He didn't have to yell; the words cut the silence like hot knife through butter. "The Kouroi are assembled. The Trial will begin." His mouth turned down for a moment, like he was tasting something bitter. "Christophe Reynard, you stand accused of treason. Present yourself."

Half of Christophe's mouth quirked up. He stayed where he was for a few moments, looking intently at me, then straightened. Turned on his heel and paced toward the dais, where the crowd had magically melted away.

He moved out into that space like he owned every inch of it. "Isn't the head of the Order supposed to be here?" It could have been possible to put a little more *fuck you* into his tone, but some of it might've slopped out the sides.

Kir stiffened. Hiro looked bored, but his eyes glittered. I knew that look, having seen it in a few bars where Dad took me, looking for information on the Real World while I sipped a Coke and ignored pretty much everything except whomever he was talking to.

"You'd think he'd learn to be tactful." Leon's whisper drifted to my right ear. "Breathe, Milady."

"You will be judged by your peers, Reynard." Hiro's weight was all on the balls of his feet, and the *aspect* actually crackled around him. His hair stood up, short black spikes rubbing against each other.

I began to feel sick. Way deep-down sick.

"And who among you is *my* peer? My ancestry is ancient, and my deeds are taught in your classrooms. I've saved a *svetocha*, which is more than any of you have done in the last sixty years. I've kept one step ahead of the *nosferatu* and those sent to kill me—the Kouroi sent to kill me. I'm here because I *choose* to be, because Milady requests it." He tipped his head slightly toward me, and I wondered how he made it so effing clear just who he was talking about. Of course, I was the only girl in the room. But I was looking around for Anna. She had to be here somewhere.

"No Kouroi have been sent to—" Alton began.

"They have." Kir had turned green under his paleness. "I signed the orders. At the Head's request."

Nobody moved; nobody even blinked. Bruce's fangs slid out from under his top lip. He stood, rigid, and I got a very bad feeling about all this. Nausea and terror all rolled together, roiled in the pit of my stomach.

Christophe stood, very straight and slim, his boots placed military-precise against the stone floor. "Set against each other. Divide and conquer. At least she learned well."

"An extermination order on another Kouroi?" Hiro shook his head. "That is against the Codes."

"Milady . . . " Kir shrank into himself. "The Head said it was a matter of necessity. She . . . she showed me a transcript. Of a call made to betray the position of Elizabeth Lefevre. She died eleven years ago, and the transcript was proof that Reynard had betrayed her to the *nosferat*."

Leon's hand came down on my shoulder. He pushed me back down in the pew. "But—" I began. *Lefevre?* That had to be her maiden name. Funny, I'd never thought about it before. It was like Mom's life had only begun with Dad, and with me.

"Be quiet," he hissed in my ear. "*Please*, Dru!"

I subsided.

"*Lies!*" someone yelled from far back in the crowd. "*Lies*, and I can prove it!"

Wait a second. I *knew* that voice, and if Leon hadn't been holding onto me I would have been up out of that pew like a rocket.

Bruce didn't look surprised, but he did lift his head and stare in the general direction the voice had come from. "Approach," was all he said.

"Oh, Christ," Kir moaned. "What have I done?"

"She promised you the *Princeps*, didn't she?" Christophe's hands curled into fists. "I wondered who'd signed the orders. Did you also sign the directive to send wulfen teams after me in the Dakotas?"

Kir actually stumbled back and collapsed in his chair. "I did. I swear to God, Reynard, she told me we had to protect the—"

"What about Dru?" Christophe was pitiless. "Did you sign the directives to keep her in a reform Schola, unprotected and vulnerable? Did you?"

"No." Marcus stood straight and defiant. "I signed those. The Head told me they were for a troublesome new Kouroi, not a *svetocha*. And when I went back later to check them, after Milady Dru told us her tale, I found they had vanished."

Oh. Well, that answered that question. It wasn't like I was surprised, but I was happy to know. Kind of.

Now if I could just keep my stomach from unloading itself all over the floor, I'd be peachy.

An avenue had opened in the crowd. I let out a breathless little cry. It was a *djamphir* I knew, his blond hair mussed and his eyes blazing. He was crusted with dried blood. His standard uniform of white tank top, red flannel shirt, and jeans was tattered and torn. Bruising marched up his familiar face on one side, and he held—of all things—a red collapsible file folder. "I can prove it!" he yelled again. And he held himself ramrod-straight, the same shoulder holster under his arm and the familiar gun butt peeking out as he moved.

"Augie—" It was barely a whisper. My mouth wouldn't work right. *Oh my God, it's him. It's really him.*

"I barely escaped Sergej himself." The name made everyone wince and sent a glass spike of pain through my head. I finally shook away from Leon's hand and made it to my feet. "It's all here. The original transcript and a recording. Treachery so unspeakably vile it would steal the heart of any who heard it. Copies of the directives, signed by each member of the Council, altered after the signing." August gasped in a breath, and Christophe stepped aside, deftly focusing every eye on him. I saw it, even though I didn't believe it. The relief was . . . Jesus.

Indescribable. That was the only word that applied.

August never once used the *aspect* that month I stayed in his Brooklyn apartment. He went out almost every night, hunting, and came back battered sometimes. I'd cooked him dinners. I'd helped him bandage himself, and I hadn't thought much about how fast he healed. In the Real World, anything goes. I didn't have any gift for healing; that was Gran's thing.

Still, seeing him, even as beat up and bloody as he was, was like Christmas.

"*August!*" I yelled and slipped my arms out of my hoodie as Leon grabbed at its back. I was over the wooden railing in a second, and I hurled myself at him. "*August!*"

"Eh, Dru." Half-Bronx, half-Brooklyn, all Augie. "Never thought I'd see you again."

I shoved past Christophe and threw my arms around August. Hugged, *hard*. He smelled horrible, but I caught the familiar tang of cigarette smoke. August could make a thin yellow flame spring up on his index finger.

He was real, and he was here, and he was a piece of the life I thought was gone for good. I forgot everything else, even the tangle that was Graves missing and Anna lurking somewhere, in the flood of scalding relief.

Hot tears slicked my cheeks. I just kept saying his name over and over. He winced, and I eased up on the hug a little.

"Dru—" Christophe said, trying to pull me away.

But I clung to Augie. I wouldn't let go. He wrapped one arm around me. "Easy there, *księżniczko*. Break my ribs, eh?"

"Augie!" The sickness went away. I hugged him even harder, forgetting again that he was hurt. And the smell of dried blood on him didn't make the *aspect* rise. I was too goddamn happy. "Jesus! Augie!"

"Pick one," he said. "Now be quiet, Dru. Got work to do."

I shut up. But I still kept hugging him.

"I got here in time." He lifted the large red file with his free hand. It was spattered with blood, both black and crusty drying red. "It's in here. Christophe?"

"I did not doubt you, Augustine." Christophe subtracted it from his fingers. Opened the accordion file and pulled out, of all things, a mini tape recorder. The papers inside made a whispering sound as he closed the file with its rubber band, then tossed it. A passionless, accurate throw, flying in a perfect arc to land at Bruce's feet.

"I require the Council to view—and hear—the evidence," Christophe said and held the recorder up.

He pushed the "play" button. It was an old-fashioned model, and the hiss of magnetic tape filled the expectant, watery silence. I might've worried about nobody being able to hear it in this cavernous space, but the *djamphir* were all utterly quiet.

I'd read the transcript when Dylan dug it up. Still, I wasn't prepared for the shock. The first voice was cold and male, with a funny lisping tone because the fangs made it hard to enunciate. It was a sucker's voice, chill and final as the grave, rasping with hate.

"*Do you have it?*"

The other voice . . . God. "*The information's well-guarded.*"

The sucker sounded like he was losing patience. "*That's none of our concern. Where is she? We are prepared to pay for the information.*"

"*Keep your money,*" Anna said. "*I just want the bitch dead.*"

The sucker laughed, a horrible silk-soft, rotting sound. "*I can arrange that.*"

Kir let out a high-pitched moan. Nobody paid any attention.

"*How can we be sure?*" the sucker continued. "*He will need some guarantee.*"

Anna made a short, dismissive sound. You could just see her waving her hand, waving it away like it was no big deal. "*Oh, that's easy. I'll take care of that. A prearranged signal, from the very location. You take care of her and I . . .*"

Static filled the tape then. My mouth was desert-dry.

"*Ephialtes,*" the sucker hissed. I was cold all over, wet with sweat under my T-shirt. Aching as I held onto Augie. He had his arm around me. But Christophe had turned, and he was staring directly at me.

Do you see? his cold eyes asked me. *Do you see now, Dru?*

And I did. But I didn't *understand*. How could you sell someone to the vampires? And if Anna was with the Order, she would know what the suckers could do. How they savaged *djamphir*, not stopping until the body was reduced to rags of flesh and splinters of bone.

And I heard her again, from the vault in my memory where the really bad stuff hid. The stuff I didn't ever want to think of again, the things the *touch* showed me that I didn't want to see.

Don't let the nosferatu *bite. A prearranged signal from the very location.* It meant our house. My mother's house. The house where I lay asleep upstairs until she woke me up. The yellow house with the oak tree in front, its branches twisted and blackened by whatever Sergej had done to my mother's body.

How could Anna betray another *svetocha*, even one she hated? How could anyone do that?

"*Keep your commentary to yourself and pass along the message,*" Anna said calmly. And the sound of a phone being laid down in a cradle clicked through, right before Christophe hit the stop button. He still stared right at me, his mouth a thin line, and I got the feeling he was trying to tell me something.

I didn't know what. I couldn't even begin to guess. But it was like he'd thrown me a line, and the thin cord that stretched between us poured a flood of heat into me. It ran up into my cheeks, and I closed my eyes and leaned against Augie. He swayed a little.

"You should look elsewhere for your traitor, Kouroi. Not at me." Christophe's heel scraped the floor as he turned away.

Murmurs raced through the crowd. I wished I could open up the ground and crawl into it. I felt sick all over. It was Anna. Anna had done it, betrayed my mother to the vampires.

Don't let the nosferatu *bite.*

Why?

But I knew why. The horrible shape under the blanket in my head twitched.

Where is he . . . if you're hiding him . . .

"Dru." Christophe was very close now. "You have something to tell us. Something you remember."

I shook my head. *No. God, no.* I didn't want to remember anything about that night. I didn't want to remember what happened after I went to bed. I didn't want to remember Anna's visit or my mother hiding me before she went out to fight.

The only thing I wanted to remember was Dad's face when he opened up the hidey-hole in the closet and collected me. He'd told me I was safe and taken me out to the car, and we'd driven for days to Gran's house.

There was nothing else I wanted to remember. *Nothing.* Not even my mother's face, or her perfume, or—

But Christophe was pitiless. "That was why Anna came to see you at the reform Schola." Patient and calm, like a teacher with a slow student. "You were so close, Dru. So close to remembering. But you didn't, not yet. It was so long ago, and you were so young."

I did remember, but I wasn't going to tell him. "Shut up," I whispered.

"This isn't necessary," Bruce said. "The evidence—"

"It *is* necessary." Christophe's words cut across his as if he was the one in charge here. For all I knew, he probably was. It certainly looked like he was from here. "You won't believe me. You may even hide the evidence or lie about it. But the word of a *svetocha* . . . who can stand against that?" The words were nasty, each one a ragged bullet of rage. They scraped against the inside of my skull like a *nosferatu*'s glassine hatred.

Did Christophe have any idea how he sounded? He sounded like his father.

I wanted no part of any of this. I just wanted to be left alone, so I could figure out how to escape this place. "Shut up," I whispered again. "Shut up."

"You've made your point, Chris." Augie's arm tightened around me.

Christophe whirled away, the fury around him smelling of burnt insulation, broken glass, pain, and the colorless fume of fury. His boot heel made a black mark against the marble floor. "I don't think I have. How many years has it been since the Order has been able to save a *svetocha*? We find them, certainly. We even find them before they bloom. But the *nosferatu* snatch them, sometimes mere hours, a *half-hour*, before we do. Why? Why is that?"

Kir moaned again. "God in Heaven. I didn't know. I *didn't know*."

I wondered if he was trying to convince them or himself.

"Shut up, Kir," Hiro said quietly. "Or I will kill you myself."

He sounded like he meant it, too.

Sounds of papers being shuffled. "These are legitimate." Alton sounded as sick as I felt. August swayed again.

I opened my eyes and tried to brace him. Under the bruising, blood, and dirt, he looked gray. It wasn't good. "Augie?" I sounded as small as I felt. "You okay?"

"Marvelous." His split lip leered as he tried to give me a smile. "It's been a rough week, Dru. Been chased by every *nosferatu* on the planet, feels like, since my pad was blown. Was a real trick to get to the dropoff and get the information Dylan—"

"Dylan?" The breath left me. "He's alive?"

"I hope so." August's pained expression told me everything I needed to know. "He sent it 'fore the other Schola was broken, Dru. Figured he could trust me, I guess."

"Of course they are legitimate," Christophe snarled. "I ask again, *why* have you been unable to save other *svetocha*?"

"Wh-wh-why? Marcus actually reeled and dropped down into *his* seat. It creaked a little under him. "Dear God. *Why?*"

The assembled *djamphir* whispered to each other.

I had a very bad feeling about this.

"Because," Christophe said finally, as if he was answering a question in class, "the Red Queen thinks we only need one *svetocha*."

Someone laughed. It was a high, feminine titter, bouncing and echoing off all the stone and glass. Every head tipped back, and there, high above everyone, on one of the carved stone railings girdling the bottom of the dome, stood Anna.

"*Why?*" she yelled. "You want to know *why?* Ask Reynard! Ask him what he knows! *He made me do it!*"

The careening echoes made me feel even sicker. Between August and me, we were having a hard time standing up. Either he was swaying drunkenly, or I was, or the world was tilting underfoot like a carnival ride.

"*None* of this would have happened without him!" Anna screamed. Even as far up as she was, the hate contorting her face was visible. Her hair was a wildly curling mass of reddish-dark, and she wore red silk, too. Another one of those old-fashioned dresses, fluttering as she hung over the railing. "She *stole* him from me! He was *mine* and she *stole* him!"

Christophe inhaled sharply. "*I never loved you!*" he yelled, and the force of the cry rocked me back on my heels. The *aspect* burned through him, his hair sleeking back, and he looked pissed enough to try to jump up to the dome.

I was betting he'd make it, too. I wouldn't put anything past him right now.

A hideous, dark, burning laughter boiled up inside me. The butt of August's gun was between us, and it wouldn't take much to jerk it free from the holster. I'd have to pick my shot, and I knew just how fast she was now. My palm itched for the gun, and my fingers curled. "You would have, if not for that *bitch!*" Anna's face contorted again. "*You would have loved me!*" Was she crying? It was hard to tell. The nausea crested, the sound of wings filling my ears, and I gasped.

Anna made a quick movement. The assault rifle jammed solidly against her shoulder, and Christophe let out another yell.

"*DRU!*" he screamed, spinning and tensing, about to leap on me. Anna yelled one more time, a wordless cry of loathing and frustration, and pulled the trigger.

Echoes shattered the air inside the dome. *Djamphir* exploded into motion and a hammer blow smashed into my left shoulder. I lost my balance.

August's knees buckled. He went down hard, and I tried to stop him. But he was heavy, and I didn't have a good grip because my left arm suddenly wouldn't obey. My knees hit hard, and I let out a short bark of surprise, trying to keep his head from bouncing off the stone floor. He ended up half in my lap, and his eyes fluttered closed. He said something very low that I couldn't hear over all the noise. Stone chips flew as bullets dug out little divots.

Something else hit me from the side, and I ended up plastered on the floor. The pain came in a huge tsunami wave, my shoulder grinding and screaming. Hands on me, and a familiar wave of apple-pie scent, drenched with copper wetness.

It hurt. It hurt so much, the spot at the back of my throat where the bloodhunger lives slammed shut, closing the *aspect* away from me.

What? I thrashed, caught between August and Christophe. Augie lay on the floor, head tipped back, throat working as he tried to move. Christophe crouched over me, his arms steel bands. "No!" he yelled, almost in my ear. A long string of vile-sounding syllables I guessed were curses in another language before the pain hit again, swallowing me, and the world went a funny gray color, color bleeding away.

Shouts. Screaming. More gunfire. *Cover. Get under cover.* I tried to move, succeeded only in flailing a little bit. Christophe was still crouched over me, ranting, and I realized he was protecting me. More chips of stone flew, and the gunfire reached a crescendo. Christophe's body jerked, and he hissed.

August suddenly jerked back into motion. He rolled to the side, and my head was tipped the right way to see the *aspect* boil over him. White streaks slid through his dirty hair, his fangs came out, and his eyes suddenly blazed, clear yellow instead of dark. I could see that through the haze coming down over me, though the rest of the world was slowly draining of its color, turning into a charcoal sketch.

He curled himself up like a pill bug, then was somehow kneeling, the gun yanked free of its shoulder holster and pointed up as he took his time with the shot. He exhaled, squeezed the trigger, and the gun spoke, its voice lost inside the cacophony.

Everything stopped. The gray curtain came down, and I heard a thudding.

Boom. Boom.

Feathered wings beat frantically. They brushed me all over, little feather kisses, except for the ball of agony high up in my left shoulder. I couldn't feel my fingers or toes, and when I tried to get up, to scramble somewhere to find cover because, duh, someone was shooting, I *couldn't*. A hot egg of agony broke in my chest again, and I whimpered.

Boom . . . boom . . .

A long silent moment, the gunshots fading. Was it over? I tried moving again and whimpered silently. It *hurt* to even try.

The throbbing in my ears was my heartbeat, I realized. Each thud was a brush of feathered wings, and I heard an owl's soft *who? who?*

The numbness crept up my hands. *What just happened? What was that?*

I was still trying to figure it out when the world went white all over. A sound like the whine of a thousand speakers set on feedback filled my head. My heartbeat stuttered, the spaces between each throb growing wider and wider until my overloaded heart . . .

. . . stopped.

CHAPTER THIRTY-ONE

"**C**lear!" **someone yelled,** *and the white glare slammed through me again. Someone was still cursing raggedly. A babble of voices.* "Get him out of here!"

"Dru? Dru, hold on. Just hold on."

"She's still bleeding. Why isn't she healing?"

"Exhaustion, and she's not fully bloomed. Her blood pressure's dropping. Where's that other sliver? They keep disappearing."

"Fragging ammo. Hate that."

"Let's hope none of them punctured her heart. Pericardium seems intact, but she's fading. We can't get claret in her fast enough—"

"Transfuse me." *Cold and calm, Christophe's voice.*

"We can't. It could kill her, we haven't typed her yet—" *Finally, another voice I recognized. Bruce's English accent.*

"Then get out." *Christophe sounded furious. Funny how he just got quiet and icy, kind of like Dad. Only it hurt, when Christophe spoke like that. Dad's mad voice never hurt me because if he used it I knew he wasn't angry at me. He never was.*

"What are you—"

"You can't—"

"I said get out. I am not losing her."

"She's not even bloomed yet!" Bruce sounded deathly tired. I tried to open my eyes, failed, and heard a whimper. Someone was having a bad day.

Gran's voice, quiet and final, echoed through my cotton-stuffed skull. Dru, honey, that someone is you.

A silent thundercrack, and I saw the room in the lightning flash.

It was another stone-walled infirmary cell. A weird directionless silver light drifted like snow, lying over every surface with a powder bloom like moth wings. I stood there quietly and heard machines booping and beeping. A small shape lay on the bed, djamphir clustered around. Bruce faced Christophe, Arab Boy a little taller but Christophe looking bigger because of the vibrating rage bleeding out from him in every direction.

Metal dropped into a pan. "Saline!" someone snapped. "Wash that clean, dammit! Let's get this closed up; she's still losing blood!"

"Blood pressure still dropping. Take it outside, Kouroi, we're trying to save her."

"I know what will save her." Christophe half-turned and shoved toward the white-draped figure on the table. The thudding vibrating through me paused.

Bruce grabbed his arm, and someone yelled, "She's coding again! Clear!"

A glare filled my vision, but not before I saw the head of the figure on the table, face turned to the side and with plastic tubing in its nose. Dark curly hair lay tangled wildly against the operating table, and I saw my eyes were fluttering as if I dreamed. My skin was chalk-white, and Bruce was on the floor.

"Touch me again," Christophe said quietly, "and it will be your last act in life." He shoved aside two dark-haired, lanky djamphir in white coats who were fiddling with the machines, and I saw a huge flayed mess where my left shoulder should be. The blood was almost black. I wasn't seeing color. Flecks of white bone gleamed as another duo of teenage-looking Kouroi probed in the mess with shiny surgical tools and dropped fragments of something in a metal pan. Another djamphir with curly hair stood by with paddles, and I saw the electricity trembling in them like drops of water spattering on a hot griddle.

I'm in bad shape, I thought. It didn't seem particularly important. I just stood and watched as Bruce wiped at his mouth with the back of his hand. "Don't do it, Reynard. We can't afford to lose—"

"I will not lose her. Get OUT!" The yell shook the walls, but nobody moved.

Christophe lifted his wrist to his mouth. He bit down hard, the aspect flickering over him. A flash of red down near his feet, shocking in the black-and-white movie the world had become, was the fox I'd seen before. It was puffed up, baring its teeth and hunching down, ready to spring.

He lowered his wrist. "This is usually private. But if you insist." Something dark dripped down his hand—he was bleeding now, too.

He pressed the ragged wound in his wrist to the mouth of the body on the table. "You can hear me," he whispered, bending down. "You're in there, skowroneczko moja. You're fighting. Fight just a little harder. Take what you need."

Oh, gross. A shiver went through me. My body twitched. I remembered what it was like, that night in the woods, fire and smoke and Christophe's fangs in my wrist. The awful pulling, tearing, ripping sensation as bits of myself—something I would call my soul—were torn away. I couldn't do that to someone else.

But the body on the table stirred weakly. Lighter highlights slid down the tangled curls, and I saw the fangs in my own mouth grow with an imperceptible crackling. The machines were going crazy.

"She's going to strike," one of the djamphir said breathlessly.

My body twitched.

Don't do it. I struggled to open my mouth, to say something. Don't. Don't do that to someone else.

Because when it got right down to it, sucking someone else's blood made me one of the things Dad would have hunted. Didn't it? Especially when I knew what it felt like. When I knew how it hurt to have something invisible inside you scraped away an inch at a time.

The body on the bed jerked. Fangs drove into Christophe's bleeding wrist as I struggled to scream, to move, to stop myself. But the body didn't listen. It took a long, endless gulping swallow.

Christophe had gone an alarming shade of gray, pale skin ash-colored and sickly. The curly-headed djamphir swore softly. Bruce levered himself up from the floor, dabbing at his mouth with the back of his hand. A thin trickle of blood traced down his chin, black in the weird directionless light, and I saw a shimmer near his right shoulder. A bird-shape hovered just on the edge of visibility, but I was more worried about the body on the bed and what it was doing to Christophe.

Another long gulping swallow. Christophe sagged, catching himself on the operating table with his free hand. The fox twined around his ankles, its brush losing the touch of faint color.

Stop it! I wanted to yell, but I couldn't. I was only observing. There wasn't a damn thing I could do. I couldn't even move.

BOOM . . . BOOM . . . BOOM. The thuds startled me. If I hadn't been nailed in place I would have jumped like a cat finding a snake. The feathered wingbeats came back, brushing all up and down my body—or my unbody, because my real body was lying on the bed.

The mess of my left shoulder was knitting itself back together.

Faint color tinged through the tissues, like the tinting on those antique photographs. A pink bloom spread out from the swiftly healing wound, the splinters of bone easing back together with little whispering sounds and the muscles sliding up, shards of metal oozing free on a slick of clear fluid before the skin wrapped itself up. The wound flushed an angry deep red for a moment. Then my shoulder made a convulsive movement, and there was a meaty thud. The ball of the humerus socketed itself back in, and the sound was a shockwave all through me.

Tingles started at the top of my unhead. Christophe's knees buckled, but he kept himself upright. "Take what you need," he whispered to the blind face on the table, its hair writhing and waving just like a vampire's. "Take everything if you must. Just live, little bird. Live."

The thudding grew closer together, beats blurring like hummingbird wings. The tingling intensified as color ran through the rest of my body. The rags of my T-shirt were dark blue and spattered with drying blood, and one of my breasts peeked out momentarily through a rent in the fabric. Faint faraway embarrassment scorched all through me. My skin began to take on a blush, hideous in the middle of that black-and-white world.

Every part of me that wasn't lying on the table lunged for release, battering against the huge weight pressing down, keeping me immobile. The body on the table inhaled through her nose, a slight wheezing sound because of caked crusted blood.

And it began another long, sucking gulp.

Christophe half-fell against the beeping machines, driving them toward the wall. He braced himself, and his face turned up to the ceiling. His mouth fell open, and his eyes rolled back until all you could see were the whites. His hips jerked forward and he almost fell again, chipping and cracking the heavy plastic case of the machine showing the high hard spikes of my heartbeat. The screen fuzzed out with static as I glanced at it, and sparks flew.

"NO!" Bruce roared, and leapt forward. He grabbed Christophe, wrenching his arm away from the greedy, fanged mouth on the bed. A jolt rammed through me, crown to soles, and for a dizzying moment I was standing up and lying down at the same time, pulled in completely different directions like a piece of Saran Wrap someone's trying to untangle. My teeth clicked together with a heavy billiard-ball noise, echoing inside my skull, and red agony tore through me.

Snarling. Sound of fist hitting flesh, a scream of pain that was mine, rising from my burning throat. The place at the back of my palate where the bloodhunger lived was on fire, a hot sweet kick like the Jim Beam I used to spike my Coke with sometimes when Dad wasn't home. My body was a riptide catching an unwary swimmer, flesh constricting around the core of what I was, the me that had just gotten used to freedom. Muscles screamed and locked and I—

—fell, slithering off the operating table and fetching my head a stunning blow. Landed on something too soft to be the floor, writhing underneath me, and my fingers sank into a head of hair before whoever it was surged upward, rolling me away and shaking free. Plastic tubing yanked free of my nose, the loops of it over my ears tearing loose.

Confusion. Yelling. Noise. I screamed again, thrashing as the bloodhunger ignited. It *hurt.* I hurt all over as if I'd been doused with gasoline and set on fire, and I wanted more of the sweet red stuff. I could taste it on my lips, smoke and spice, a smooth hot redness full of the flavor of a boy's lips and the tang of winter-cold eyes. He tasted like danger and wildness and a hot breeze through a car window at dusk out in the desert when you're going eighty and not going to make the next town anytime soon. Cinnamon and male and goodness, and I wanted *more.*

Christophe grabbed me. He was ashen, his cheeks sunken. But his eyes blazed, and the *aspect* on him was like a drenching perfume. I could *feel* it, waves of invisible power lapping at my skin.

Nobody else felt even remotely like him.

My chin jerked forward, quick as a striking snake, and my teeth champed together again, a bare inch from his throat. This close I smelled the salt of sweat on him, and his body half-under mine was maddeningly far away. I was cold and hot all at once, fierce sensations fighting for control of me.

"*Dru!*" he barked, and I froze.

I knew that voice. It was like Dad's *shut up and hand me that ammo* tone. It meant I needed to stop and pay attention, and I did. My eyelids fluttered, turning everything into shutter clicks.

"How many?" Bruce demanded from across the room. Funny, but he sounded scared. "Reynard? *How many?*"

The shudders had me like an animal shaking something in its teeth. But the bloodhunger retreated, and nausea rose with a fast hard cramp.

"Three." Christophe's reply was a breath of sound. "You're lucky she doesn't need more."

"Goddamn you." Bruce moved. A whisper of cloth, and Christophe tensed. I made a weird whining sound. It felt like I'd been pulled apart and bolted back together with the wrong parts, every bit of me aching.

A bolt of heat hit my stomach and spread out, a haze of warm contentment. It soothed the aches and soaked in, and if it wasn't for the fact that I'd just been bleeding all over the place I thought, maybe, that I could stand up.

But I let my eyes shut. It was a relief to just lie there in Christophe's arms and know he was handling it.

A little voice inside me tried to tell me I should be worried about something, but I shut it off. I had all I could worry about already. There was no more room on my worry plate.

"He already has. Go away." Christophe's voice was a dry husk. He cleared his throat. "All of you. Give her some privacy. If the aura-dark hits her—"

"It won't. She's *svetocha*." It was one of the other *djamphir*, and he sounded awestruck. "Look, she's fine. Blood pressure normal, pulse a little elevated but fine—she's going to make it. Look at her shoulder."

I didn't want to look at my shoulder. I curled more tightly against Christophe and thought of my torn T-shirt. Heat stained my cheeks, a different heat than the goodness swirling down my skin. "Christophe," I murmured and felt vaguely ashamed.

"All's well, *skowroneczko moja*." A light touch—his lips against my tangled hair. "Everything is well in hand."

That was what I wanted to hear. I kept my eyes tightly shut.

"You take unacceptable risks." Bruce had to force the words out between clenched teeth. "Do you hear me, Reynard?"

"Yap at someone else, ibn Allas. I've done what I set out to do." Was Christophe actually sneering? It was hard to tell with my face buried in his chest. He took deep heaving breaths. "I'm here, and if Kouroi will stop trying to kill me I'll be the best ally you have. As long as you keep her safe."

"Anna will be caught. She'll pay for what she's done."

"What are you going to do? She's *svetocha*, and her Guard is fanatically loyal." Christophe moved. He surged up from the floor, faltered, and righted himself. "You helped with that. Every one of you on the Council turned a blind eye or actively encouraged it. She's a monster. God willing, the *nosferatu* will find and kill her if she doesn't make devil's bargains with them first."

"She's spoiled and manipulative, but not a—"

"She opened fire on a mass of Kouroi and another *svetocha*, Bruce!" The machines let out sparking, staticky, unhappy sounds. "She betrayed one of our own—*more* than one—to Sergej! When will you see?"

"This will not bring Elizabeth back!"

Silence. And with the silence, a gathering, rising growl. I shrank further against Christophe until I realized the sound was coming from him. My mother's locket was warm and quiescent against my chest.

Footsteps, and the door closing. The sense of presence leached out of the room, and Christophe made a short violent movement, carrying me with him, gaining his feet and making a harsh sound of effort. My nose bumped his collarbone, and one of the machines gave a strangled squeal, stopped its beeping. The one keeping track of my heartbeat kept going, though. My pulse raced, high and fast and hard. It felt like I was on jet fuel, or maybe too much caffeine.

Christophe wrapped his arms around me and put his face in my hair. We stood like that, my shaky legs gradually gaining strength. I swallowed several times, the bloodhunger prickling at that spot on the back of my palate. He still smelled like apples and cinnamon and heat. Each time I inhaled, the scent would stroke across that sensitive spot, and a shudder would go down me. The machine keeping track of my pulse would send out another cascade of beeps.

"What happened?" I finally whispered.

"You should have stayed with Leontus," he whispered back. "The seats would have given you cover."

I didn't know why I was surprised. "You *knew* she'd do something like this?"

"No. I thought it was likely. She's deconstructing."

Is that what you call it? I tried, gently at first, to push myself away from him. He didn't let go. We struggled like that for a little while, me halfhearted, Christophe finally sounding amused.

"You can't stand up on your own. Stop pushing me." But he set me down on the operating table. It moved a little, like it didn't want to support me, but he held me there until I could balance myself. When I braced my unwilling legs against the floor it even felt kind of stable.

I clutched the torn T-shirt together over my chest and blinked. All of me was rubbery and aching despite the heat in my core, the feeling of well-being spreading out in waves.

I didn't want to think about what was in my stomach, providing those waves.

"Here." Christophe made a sudden movement. It took me a second before I realized he was pulling his sweater off over his head. "It's dirty, but . . ."

And then he offered it to me.

I wasn't sure where all the blood I used to blush came from, especially now. But I flushed a deep, deep red and started stammering something.

He pushed the sweater into my hands and turned away, looking at the wall across the room as if it held the secrets of life.

It wasn't so much the sweater or the way half of me was hanging out of my now-only-fit-for-the-rag-pile shirt. It wasn't so much the pale matte of his skin, striped with drying blood.

It was the three angry pucker-shaped holes in his back, looking curiously bloodless as they closed, slowly but visibly healing. Bullet holes, healing before my eyes.

And the scars.

He looked like he'd been rolled in broken glass. The scar tissue crawled up and down his back, pale shiny ropes against the otherwise perfection of his skin, reaching nasty-looking fingers up around his ribs. They moved as he breathed, and I sat there and stared for a bit while my heart thudded and blood soughed in my veins and I found out I was still alive.

"Dru," he said finally, "do you have it on yet?"

"Oh. I, um. Just a sec." It took me two tries to get the rags of my T-shirt off, and my arms shook when I pulled the sweater over my head. It even smelled like him, and there were three holes in the back. But the front was pretty much okay, even if the V-neck was a bit deep on me. He looked deceptively skinny, but I saw the muscle moving as he shifted his weight a little bit, then hardening like a marble statue when he went still in that way older *djamphir* do.

Those were bullet holes. Bullets he'd stopped while he was crouched over me. But the other scars . . . Jesus.

"What are those from?" I whispered.

For just a split second, his shoulders hunched as if he was embarrassed. "We can scar, you know." Flat, quiet. Informing me, nothing more. "Before we hit the drift. And after, if the wound is severe enough. Life-threatening."

I didn't want to point out that he'd avoided the question. Again. My teeth tingled, especially my upper canines.

They're fangs, Dru. Call them what they are.

"What happened?" It seemed like I couldn't make my voice work like usual. The pretty-much-healed fang marks on my wrist twinged once, and I rubbed them against my blood-sodden jeans. The whole room was drenched with the coppery smell, taunting the bloodhunger.

He stiffened. "I was disobedient. Are you done?"

I nodded, realized he couldn't see me. "Yeah. Um. Thanks. Christophe—"

He rounded on me, eyes blazing, crossed the distance between us with two quick steps. I was suddenly nose-to-nose with him, so close the heat coming off him in waves caressed my cheeks like sunlight on already burned skin.

"I *told* you to stay there. There was cover there, and Leontus would have made sure you were safe." The words were raw, like they were sandpaper-scraping his throat to get out. "I could have *lost* you."

My mouth was dry. I said the first thing that came into my head, and it was a harsh husky whisper just like his. "Chris . . . I'm not *her*."

I meant, *I'm not my mother.* He looked startled just for a second, but his eyes never wavered. They were direct and unblinking, and how could I ever have thought they were cold? Because now they were blowtorch-blue. Eyes like that could burn wherever they touched you, and my heart crawled up and lodged in my throat.

"No," he agreed. "You're not. She never caused me this agony."

What could I say to that? The way he was looking at me was making my head feel funny. Was making all of me feel funny, and not just in that *oh God I just almost died way.*

Christophe leaned in. His mouth was mere centimeters from mine. "She never made me think I would die of heart failure. She never, *never* made me fear for her this way."

I swallowed audibly. My throat clicked. If I leaned back to get away from him, I might just topple over on the operating table.

But I didn't want to lean away. "Christophe . . ." His name died on my lips. All of me was suddenly exquisitely sensitive, all my hairs standing up, and I was halfway to forgetting that I was covered in sweat and dried blood.

His lips touched mine. I almost flinched, the shock was so intense. Then lightning hit me.

I mean, I've gotten carried away a couple times, usually with moderately cute city boys when I knew I wasn't going to be around for more than a week or two. This was nothing like sloppy open-mouth puppy kisses in the library stacks, or a stolen half-hour of necking in the secluded part every playground has for games. His tongue slid in, and it wasn't like he was trying to stuff my mouth with it. It was like he was inviting me.

It wasn't like Graves, either, the comfort and the safety. This was . . .

Tingles ran through all of me, not just my teeth. I forgot the usual things that go through your head when this happens—things like *Oh God did I brush my teeth enough* or *I wish he wouldn't breathe like that* or *Someone might be coming*. I forgot about being scared I might do it wrong.

I forgot about everything except the heat and light running through me. One of his fangs brushed mine, a jolt scorched through us both, and I sank into him for a long long moment before breaking away to get in a breath and discovering that, yeah, there was an outside world and it was hard and cold and bright and smelled like blood and metal and pain.

Christophe kissed my cheek. He murmured something I didn't quite hear. Every inch of me ran with multicolored electricity.

Wow.

"Never," he said softly in my ear. His breath touched my skin, and I had the sudden desire to squirm just because I *had* to move, and my clothes were hot and confining. "Do you understand?"

"Um," was my totally profound response.

He reached up, his hands cupping my face, and leaned into me, bumping my knees aside. Stared down at me, and his expression wasn't the hungry-wolf look he'd worn while staring at my mother. It was something else.

Just what I didn't know. It was just . . . something else. Something more vulnerable. Like he was afraid at any second I'd flinch back or tell him not to, or something.

I couldn't stand to see him look that way. So I closed my eyes and tipped my chin up a little, and he kissed me again. It wasn't the same this time.

No, this time it was better. And again I forgot about everything else, including Graves. For a few seconds I was just me again.

And it was *great*.

Then the real world came crashing back in. I stiffened, and he drew back. He still held my face gently, his skin very warm against mine, and I found out I was touching his ribs, running my palms up and down like I was playing with Gran's washboard.

I pulled my hands away. "Um," I said again. "Christophe."

"Dru." Slightly amused. I kept forgetting how well his face worked together.

"I think . . ." I couldn't even say what I was thinking. Except Wow. And more *wow*, and a side helping of *um*.

Yeah. Embarrassing. And Graves . . .

Graves had left me behind. There it was. He'd left me, and Christophe had come back. Was that how it was?

"You're right," he said, as if I'd said something profound. "There are still things to do. And we should clean up. Both of us."

I nodded. He leaned in again, and I was a little disappointed when he only kissed my cheek, a chaste pressure of lips.

"Do you trust me now?" he asked, and I could only nod. And wonder why he asked me *that*, of all things.

CHAPTER THIRTY-TWO

After you have a bad case of stomach flu or something, when you've thrown up everything you've ever even *thought* of eating, there comes a point when you actually feel pretty good. It's usually after you finish a long session of heaving, when you flush, wipe your mouth, maybe brush your teeth gingerly for the tenth time, and find out you can walk. Shakily, like a newborn colt.

The world looks clearer and sharper, and you think you might have the flu beat—but the trembling in your arms and legs tells you you're lying to yourself.

That was how I felt. Bruised and shaky, but pretty good, at least for a little while. I figured if I could get to a bed before the exhaustion hit, I'd be doing pretty good.

But first, I had to see Augustine.

He was in a private room in the infirmary's calm cloister, but this one was different than the one Ash had been strapped down in, or even the one they'd been trying to save me in. His was on an outer wall, a bed and a window, and it looked like a high-end hospital suite. It was even done in peach and cream, and for a second I was so lightheaded I was afraid I would fall down right there and then.

Because it still *smelled* like a hospital. Like disinfectant, medicine, pain. And grief. The *touch* throbbed inside my aching head like a sore tooth.

Augie's apartment in Brooklyn was pretty neat and clean, considering a single guy lived there. I made it shipshape in the month I spent there.

He and Dad worked on clearing out a demonic rat infestation. And then Dad was up near the Canadian border doing something, and I hung with August. Who never, I realized now, let me very far out of his sight even in the apartment. A month in one of the biggest, coolest cities in the world, and all I'd known was that one street in Brooklyn.

Now that I knew Augie was *djamphir*, I wondered if he could teach me to light someone's cigarette that way. I was hoping to get the chance to ask him.

He and Dad had argued all the time about the Real World, whether the authorities knew and were deliberately keeping the knowledge down, or whether people didn't *want* to know and so ignored it. Now the faint smile on August's face during all those arguments made sense.

Other things I remembered made sense, too. Like August's voice while I lay in bed and tried to sleep, listening to him and Dad. *That girl deserves to be with her own kind.* And how beat-up he'd been coming back a few times, and how he'd healed so fast. How many times while I was there had he been killing suckers?

Had any of the suckers he'd killed been after me? Had they even suspected I existed? I could have been in danger and not even known it.

Jesus.

August lay on the bed, swathed in white bandages. His dark eyes were sleepy, blond hair mussed like he'd just spent a hard night tossing around. The bruises were fading, but he had the faraway look of someone on some really good tranquilizers. His right hand lay, curiously pale and unbandaged, against the peach coverlet.

"He's sedated," Christophe said quietly. "Enough to give his psyche and body some room to repair themselves. Shock can kill, more than the actual injuries."

I made it to the side of the bed, Christophe hovering right behind me. "Augie?" I sounded about five years old.

He blinked. His right shoulder was a huge mass of bandaging. "Eh, Dru." The "New Yahk" wheeze cut every vowel short like it personally offended him. "Good to see you, sweetheart."

I grabbed at his hand. I couldn't talk. Everything I wanted to say crowded up in my throat, got jammed, and I let out a sound like a sob.

"Oh, don't do that." For a moment he was the old August, a crooked smile that said he was laughing at the world, his eyebrows lifted just a little. You could see a flash of what he was when he laughed, through his swollen face and the fog of sedation. "What do I got to do to get you to bring me a bottle of vodka, girl?"

A half-sob, half-laugh jolted out of me. I was so relieved I swayed next to the bed. "I can't *buy* vodka, Augie. I'm *sixteen*."

"That never stopped you." He grinned, but his eyes were drifting closed. One leg was bigger than the other under the covers— probably bandaged, too. "Make me an omelet, sweetheart. I'm beat. Been a long night."

"Sure I will." I'd make him *fifty* omelets, by God. "What happened to you, Augie?"

"Soon's you called me I started thinking." His eyes closed, then snapped open as he struggled to stay awake. "Then, nobody knew about you. Couldn't find you for weeks. But Dylan called, and that's when things got *inneresting*."

"He'll be debriefed once he's well enough," Christophe murmured. "Dru—"

"Met him in Pomona. He had a copy of the transcript, told me where to find the rest of it. Whole place was jumping with *nosferat*. We got taken."

"That's enough." Christophe said, more firmly. "I should get her into bed, Augustine. We'll talk later."

"Sergej," Augustine whispered, and I went cold. My teeth threatened to chatter, and a shard of pain lodged itself inside my skull. "Sergej had some of the pieces. Got us both. Dylan . . . we got separated. Poor kid."

I all but choked. So Dylan *had* been alive after the other Schola burned down. Relief warred with fresh worry, fought over me like two dogs with a bone. I was shaking and sweating, and suddenly aware that I couldn't smell too good.

"I found the other stuff, and then . . . but I was being watched. Everyone I visited had a piece, but they got swarmed after I left. *Nosferatu* didn't want us to know, and we were burned. Every one of us, burned *bad*."

I held my breath. "Burned" isn't good. It's what you say when one of your own betrays you.

When you're given to the enemy.

Don't let the nosferatu *bite. . . . Oh, that's easy. I'll take care of that. A prearranged signal, from the very location.*

The shaking got worse. If August hadn't been drugged to the gills he might have noticed me trembling. I heard feathered wings and tasted a ghost of wax oranges.

Anna had come to my house expecting to betray my mother

and looking for Christophe. She'd made sure I was sent to the other Schola and visited it herself to see what I remembered.

To see if I'd told anyone about something I couldn't remember without the help of the *touch*, something I'd had no idea I remembered. She'd betrayed a whole Schola full of kids to Sergej.

But *why*? I was still no closer to understanding that. When you knew what the *nosferatu* did to *djamphir*, when you'd seen what they did to the bodies, how could you *do* that? That was the part I didn't get.

August said something, slurred and full of consonants. And to my surprise, Christophe leaned in from behind me. He freed my limp sweating fingers and squeezed August's hand himself. He also answered in the same language.

The wounded *djamphir*'s eyes closed fully. He sighed and murmured something else. Then he was asleep.

"God." My voice wouldn't work right, but I was going to whisper anyway. You always want to do that when someone's in the hospital. Whisper like a creeping mouse. I'd whispered to Gran as she lay dying, holding on as long as she could for me.

Don't leave me, I'd begged in that same creeping-mouse voice because my throat wouldn't work right. *Gran, I love you, please don't leave me.*

But she couldn't stay. I was always holding onto people, and they were always leaving.

I couldn't help myself. I touched August's limp fingers again. "Don't leave me, Augie." I knew he couldn't hear me, but still. "Okay? Don't go."

"He'll be fine." Christophe put his arm over my shoulders. "I promise he will live, *moj maly ptaszku*."

I almost broke down again right there. My arm stole around Christophe's waist as I straightened. I leaned into him, and he didn't move. It was like leaning against a statue. He held himself absolutely still, the creepy-still of an older *djamphir*. He barely even breathed.

My knees were pretty rubbery. "You mean it?" I tried not to sound like I was begging. Jeez, my tough-girl image was never going to recover from all this.

I wasn't sure I cared at this point.

"I do." Christophe pulled me away from the bedside. "He's survived worse, and he's bandaged and medicated. Now all he needs is rest."

I went reluctantly, glad I was holding onto him. The all-right-but-shaky part of the feeling was going away, and I was beginning to crash big-time. My head felt like a pumpkin balanced on the too-thin stem of my neck, my arms and legs kept doing weird little shaking-away things, and dark little speckles started dancing around the edges of my vision.

"Christophe?"

He got me out through the door, closed it quietly. Braced me, and started heading across the infirmary, my feet dragging against the stone floor. "What?"

I wanted to tell him I needed to see Ash, too. I wanted to tell him I was going to start looking for Graves, since we had time now, right? I also wanted to ask him to sit down and explain Anna from the beginning. I wanted—no, I *needed* to know how she ended up like this.

But the warm spot in the middle of my stomach was shrinking steadily. The hurts had mostly gone away, but I was weak as a newborn kitten. I *felt* like one, too—blind and making little noises. I was still trying to ask him all the questions I so desperately needed answers to when he shushed me gently and half-carried me away.

CHAPTER THIRTY-THREE

White light, smell of lemon polish, dust, fresh air. And baking apple pie. Little slivers of sunlight peeked under my eyelids.

But I couldn't just lie there. I had things to do. So when I turned over and groaned, opening my eyes slightly for the umpteenth time, I found myself staring at the plaster ceiling. Diamonds and roses stood out in sharp relief. My eyes were grainy, so I blinked and rubbed at them. My arms didn't hurt, and neither did my face.

I felt muzzy-headed, sure, but still pretty good. I yawned and sat up, found out I was in Christophe's sweater and my panties, and made a mental note to stop waking up minus some of my clothes. My jeans, crusted with blood and other stuff, lay on the floor next to the bed with my socks.

The room was still the same. Sunlight flooding in through skylights and the window, the vanity dresser glowing, every inch of it spic-and-span. The books on the stripped-pine shelves regarded me, their spines blank closed faces. Had my mother ever sat here, clutching the covers and rubbing at her eyes, and wondered what the hell to do next?

I could smell Christophe, but he was nowhere in sight. The sweater covered most everything, so I gingerly slid my bare legs out of bed. It was neither too warm nor too cold, the air just perfect for rolling out of bed on a lazy Saturday morning before you stumble down to the caf and get something to eat. Then it would be time to attend a couple of classes, but when you were free, you could meet the wulfen in the park and run with them. Like you belonged.

Good luck with that, though. Instead, I pushed myself upright, ready to drop back down on the bed if my legs got squidgy on me.

They didn't. They held me up like they always did.

I bounced a little bit on my toes, testing them even more. I felt . . . strangely good.

Except for everything that was looming over me. Graves disappeared. Ash and Augustine lying in the infirmary. And Anna . . .

I shook my head, my hair slithering against Christophe's sweater. I didn't want to think about that.

I made it over to the dresser, found a fresh pair of jeans and underthings. Made it to the closet and picked a black T-shirt and a charcoal hoodie. Stood there for a few seconds. There was one red T-shirt I'd grabbed on clearance at Target, a splash of color against the dark fabrics I preferred.

I carried it into the bathroom, stuffed it into the trash basket. Eased myself under some hot water, the cast-iron bathtub a little slippery and the curtain on its hoop bolted to the wall rustling every time I moved under the water. Had my mother stood here? Soaped herself and marveled at vanished bruises? My skin was pretty perfect, only a ghostly shadow remaining where the worst had been, if you knew where to look.

Had she been raised *djamphir*, or had her dad kept it a secret? I touched the locket's warm curve, rinsed myself off. She wanted a "normal" life. What would she have taught me to do if she hadn't been murdered?

It kept ending up with Anna. How could you hate someone so much? It didn't even seem human.

Yeah. I liked sucking blood. How human was *that*?

I still felt okay when I got out of the shower and dried off, treating my body like it was a wild horse that might throw me at any moment. I felt morning-hungry, and I wanted coffee, but maybe not a banana latte. Most of all I wanted to make sure Ash and August were okay and get started on finding Graves. I didn't know what I'd say to him because . . .

Christophe.

The memory of lightning went through me again. The healed-up fang marks on my wrist gave another heatless twinge. How would I explain that to Graves?

Did I even *need* to? Would he care? Would he be relieved?

If I left here, what would Christophe do?

I braided my hair. It felt like my hands were shaking, but they weren't. My canvas bag was still sitting on the counter next to the pretty leaf-bowl of the sink. I scrounged a ponytail holder and thought about the roll of cash hidden in there. It was no big trick to get more. Dad taught me how.

I'd never done it alone before. But if I'd survived all this, maybe it would be no big deal.

I held onto the counter and breathed. In, out, steady. Careful. Until the weird nauseating pain in my middle went away. The skylight let in blind sunshine, touching my hair and face. It didn't burn me or hurt my eyes. Sunlight was deadly to *nosferatu*. At least, nowadays.

I'd sucked blood, and the sun didn't hurt me.

When I opened up the bathroom door, ducking through the strap of my bag and settling it against my hip, Christophe looked up from the window seat. The light fell over him again, making him into another kind of statue. He had one of the books in his hands, and his blue eyes took me in and warmed.

But he didn't smile.

"Good morning." He closed the book, laid it carefully aside. "The Council's called a meeting. As soon as you're ready, they want to see you."

I swallowed hard. "What if I don't want to? I want to see Ash and August and . . ." *And I'm leaving.*

I couldn't say it to him.

"I checked the Broken and Augustine not half an hour ago. Augustine is awake and eating breakfast; the Broken is on the mend. Samuel says he'll make it."

I grabbed at the doorjamb. Searched Christophe's face for any sign of a comfortable lie, found none. "Really? He's sure?"

He nodded. Eased off the window seat and took a few steps toward me. "One hundred percent certain, he says. Benjamin and his crew are fine, too; you'll see them at sundown."

It was hard to tell if the weakness had come back, or if it was just relief so deep and wide I could drown in it. It took work to open my mouth and ask the more important question.

"Graves?" I croaked. *Please. Please tell me he's come back.*

Christophe's expression didn't change. "The entire Schola Prima has been searched. He's not here, and nobody saw him leave the grounds. I'm . . . sorry, Dru." He even sounded sorry, though a flicker of something passed through his blue gaze. It was there and gone before I could figure out what it was.

Disappointment crashed through me. "What does the Council want?"

"I don't know. Only that it's important. And I can guess they are eager to make amends to you."

Oh, yeah, I'll bet. "What about *you*? You're the one they put on Trial!"

"Some of them probably already suspected, though they could not move without proof. It's of little account, Dru. You're safe. Anna is on the run. Sergej's bid to divide and conquer has failed."

"Sergej." I didn't flinch when I said his name, though it did make my head hurt. "He . . . But Anna . . ."

"I suspect she thought she could control and manipulate him, too. They are both very, very good at that." A shadow crossed his perfectly proportioned face. "Though he has somewhat more practice. Please, Dru. Come see the Council. Soothe their fears."

Just who the hell is going to soothe mine? But I shrugged. "Okay."

After all, he was the one I was trusting now. Right?

But I didn't take my bag off, and he didn't ask even though I saw him looking at it. I wasn't sure how this thing with the Council was going to go. But I knew I wanted my cash and my emergency stuff with me.

Really, if no place was safe and I wanted to find Graves, why stay here? Why stay anywhere?

The only answer I could come up with to that question was heading across the room. He checked the hall, then nodded. I followed him.

* * *

The Schola Prima felt empty, but I knew better. I couldn't tell who was watching as I followed Christophe through the halls.

He paused in front of the door with the carving of a leering face. "Dru . . ."

"What?" I put my hand down, away from my mother's locket, with an effort.

"I just want you to know something." He indicated the door with a brief sketch of a movement, but said nothing else.

"What?" I repeated nervously. The hall looked just the same as it always did. Velvet, old wood, marble busts. It really wasn't the kind of place I belonged. I shifted my weight, and the funny idea that the bruises might change their mind and come back floated through my head for the twentieth time.

"Whatever happens in here, whatever they offer me, my loyalty is to you. Don't doubt that." His chin tipped down slightly, the *aspect* brushing over him, slicking his hair down and making his eyes glow.

I swallowed hard again. "That loyalty thing . . . isn't that Anna's thing?"

He cocked his head. "Loyalty's all we have. The *nosferatu* have used us against each other many times. Anna isn't the first to turn traitor. She won't be the last, either."

"That's really comforting, Christophe." I didn't mean to sound snide. "Let's get this over with. I want to look for Graves."

He looked about to say something else, but visibly decided not to bother and pushed the door open. I wiped my sweating hands on my hoodie surreptitiously and hoped this wouldn't take too long.

CHAPTER THIRTY-FOUR

Four old *djamphir* standing to attention. The chair at the head of the table was empty. Alton, Ezra, Bruce, Hiro, all stood ranged in front of the table like a firing squad. There was no breakfast laid out this time.

Christophe closed the door. I folded my arms self-consciously, trying not to wonder if any of them had stolen a peek while my T-shirt was torn. My hair was behaving for once, but I was still glad I'd braided it back tightly and drenched it with conditioner to keep the frizzles down. Not that it was frizzing much lately, but habits die hard.

Bruce clasped his hands together. His face was set and white under his coloring, and it didn't do him a lot of good. His eyes were burning coals. "Milady."

Outside the sun was shining, and the birds were chirping. But in here there was no daylight. I shifted my weight uncomfortably. Kept my hands in fists so I wasn't tempted to touch my mother's locket. "What? I mean, what do you want?"

"I think this would go better if you sat down," Hiro said gently.

But I looked past him, and there was a dent of darkness on the table's mellow polished shine.

My heart crawled up in my throat. "God." I sounded half-strangled. "No. Oh, no."

I shoved between Hiro and Alton and grabbed the black thing. It was a long black canvas trench coat. It would go all the way to my ankles, but it would hit him at midcalf. It smelled like cigarette smoke and healthy young male *loup-garou*.

It was torn all to pieces. Another piece of it was in my bag right now. I'd fished it out of my other jeans and stowed it carefully.

There was an envelope, too, heavy cream linen paper with a wax seal on it. The seal had already been broken. "We wanted to make sure—" Hiro began.

I dropped the coat and snatched the envelope. Ripped it apart.

"When?" Christophe was right behind me. "Exactly when? After he disappeared? And where?"

Alton's face was set and ashen. "We don't know. A box was delivered a half-hour ago, containing the coat and the envelope."

One piece of that heavy expensive paper. Spidery but firm antique handwriting, good enough to be called calligraphy. You could almost see a fountain pen scratching at the paper, its nib scraping along like a busy little insect.

Since you have taken my Broken, I will break another.

"No." My mouth kept saying it. "No. No."

Christophe subtracted the letter from my nerveless fingers. Scanned it briefly. "Dear God." He didn't sound horrified. Only . . . thoughtful.

I was horrified enough for both of us.

I picked up the coat again. It was torn, one sleeve almost severed, and there was drying mud splashed all over it. Mud, and another darker fluid that had dried to a crust.

I didn't want to think about it.

A scream was rising in my chest. I shoved it down as hard as I could. It didn't want to go. *Think, Dru. Think.*

I looked up, my fingers turned into claws in the ruin of the coat. Met Christophe's steady, icy gaze. "What are you going to do?"

Even though I already suspected the answer. He was just *loup-garou*. They wouldn't care.

Not the way I did.

Come find me. Oh, God.

"There's precious little we *can* do." Bruce picked up the ripped envelope. A silent snarl drifted over his handsome face, his proud nose wrinkling. "The boy might have left school grounds; nobody saw them take him. It's been long enough—he could be anywhere by now. Sergej hopes we will be drawn into a rescue attempt because of your attachment to—"

"Anna," Christophe said flatly.

Hiro gave him a dark, eloquent glance. "We cannot lay every misfortune at her door."

"Dru 'stole' me; Anna said as much. Why not 'steal' the one person Dru trusts absolutely? It has a certain symmetry, and it's how the Red Queen operates. She knows no other way. We find Anna; she will help us find the *loup-garou*. And answer every question we have about her activities, from eleven years ago to today." Christophe's shoulder lifted, dropped. "Simple."

"Now hold on," Ezra piped up.

"We can't risk—" Hiro, again.

"This is madness," Alton weighed in.

"There's no guarantee—" Bruce began, but I tipped my head back and let out a sound halfway between a strangled scream and a growl, and everyone shut up.

"You *assholes*." This time the *aspect* didn't feel like warm oil. It felt like a crackling cloak of lightning settling over me, and I had to work to pronounce the words the way I wanted them. "I'm out of here."

I spun on my heel, my bag bumping my hip, and pushed past Christophe. Or tried to.

"Dru!" He grabbed my arm, and I seriously had to work to throttle the instinct to punch him. "Don't. Please."

"It's *Graves*!" Tears blurred my eyes. "He's got Graves! I have to *find* him!"

"We will. But you cannot help the *loup-garou* by running out of here without a clear idea of what to achieve. Sergej won't kill him. Not yet."

"Let *go* of me!" My voice broke like a little boy's. "It's Graves! He's *got Graves*!"

It was like a nightmare. Something else kept happening. And I suppose that ever since I'd picked that piece of fabric off the thorns, this was what I'd been dreading. I just hadn't said as much to myself.

Because I was turning out to be a coward. I'd rather accuse Graves of leaving me behind, even if it was inside my own head, than face the fact that I'd gotten him into this. And that he was probably paying for it right now.

I knew what they did to break werwulfen. I'd learned as much at the other Schola.

Sergej was going to do that to Graves.

Oh, God. I struggled against Christophe's hands.

"He will have you too if you run out of here screaming." His fingers bit in. "*Listen* to me, Dru. We'll get your *loup-garou* back. I swear it on my blades and my bloodline. But there's nothing you can do *right this moment*."

I knew he was right, but it didn't help. The numbness was over, and my entire chest was cracking open. Hot water slicked my cheeks. Was I ever going to stop crying? Jesus.

"I swear it." Christophe stared me down like we were the only two people in the room. "The rest of the Council will swear, too. Won't you?"

A long, tense-ticking quiet moment went by. I couldn't look away from Christophe. He stared like he had X-ray vision and was checking out my brain folds.

"Because," he continued inexorably, "they are offering me a seat on the Council, since two of their members are, to put it kindly, unfit. And they were about to tell you that *you*, dearest one, are the head of the Order now."

"Screw their Order." And I meant it. "They can put their Order where the sun doesn't—"

He lifted his hand, and I subsided. It was just like having Dad give me the Meaningful Look. *Bite your tongue, Dru.*

"The Order is a massive organization, well-funded and—once we finish rooting out Anna's holdouts—well-trained and loyal. You stand a much better chance of finding your friend and surviving with them on your side." He paused, and the next thing he said held no shade of businesslike mockery. It was the gentle tone he'd never used around anyone but me before. "And if you do not trust them, *skowroneczko moja*, try to trust me."

"I—" But the protest stopped before I could even find words. His blood was still tingling through my veins, whispering to me. I knew what it was like to have fangs in my wrist and to feel the awful, horrible, draining and ripping sensation. He'd done that for me while I lay dying on an operating table. Anna had been shooting with an *assault rifle*, for God's sake, and Christophe had hunched over me. Protecting me with his own body.

He'd been there at every turn, watching out for me. And coming back for me, time and again.

There was just one question I could ask right now.

"If I stamped out of here right now, Christophe, what would you do?" For once, I didn't care that everyone was watching.

"You wouldn't be so foolish." Amazingly he smiled. It was a slow, very private expression, and it lit up his eyes for a bare moment before it vanished. "If you did, *skowroneczko moja, moja księżniczko*, you would not go alone."

"Now hold on just one moment—" Bruce began.

"Shut up." There was no joy in snapping that and having someone shut his mouth so fast he almost lost part of his tongue. "Are you serious?"

As if I could even ask Christophe that with his blood burning in me and my mouth still tingling, not just from the *aspect* running through my teeth but also from the taste of him.

One corner of his mouth lifted fractionally. Then his entire face turned solemn. "Completely. Trust me, Dru. First we find Anna. Then we hunt Sergej down. With you fully trained and bloomed, the Order has a chance. You do not have to be helpless anymore."

What do you do when someone says something like that? Something that jolts through you like a train skidding to an emergency stop. Something that turns everything upside down because it's so true.

I clutched the coat to my chest. Managed to tear my eyes away from Christophe and look at the rest of them. Bruce looked worried, Ezra somber. Alton had folded his arms and was watching Christophe closely, a line between his eyebrows, his dark eyes snapping and intent.

Hiro looked steadily back at me, his mouth set and his hair stirring slightly as the *aspect* touched him. As if he was urging me to make the right decision.

I didn't know if there *was* a right decision. But I had to make one. It counted, right now. I had to choose the right thing to do, because Graves was . . .

Oh, God. I didn't even want to think about it. But I had to. Because I'd gotten him into this. It was my fault. All of it was my fault, and once I started laying blame I just would not stop. All of it, the whole huge mess, was my goddamn fault.

Time to start doing the right thing, Dru.

With Christophe to help, it might even be possible. It was all I *could* do.

I hugged the coat as I half-turned. I walked down to the end of the table, each step taking a lifetime.

I pulled the heavy carved chair at the head of the polished table out and dropped down into it.

The sighs of relief—Bruce and Hiro, at the same time, with Alton's a fraction of a second behind—were audible. I tried to ignore it. Ezra folded his arms. Christophe stood still, but his eyes were burning. And fixed on me.

"All right," I said, hugging Graves's coat so hard my arms ached. "Where do we start?"

OLIVER HARRIS

Oliver Harris was born in north London in 1978.
His previous Nick Belsey novel, *The Hollow Man*,
is available in Vintage paperback.

C333764649

ALSO BY OLIVER HARRIS

The Hollow Man